**Praise for *New York Times* bestselling author
Lynsay Sands and the Argeneau Vampire series!**

'Sands writes books that keep readers coming back for more . . .
clever, steamy, with a deliciously wicked sense of humour
that readers will gobble up'
Katie MacAlister

'Inventive, sexy, and fun'
Angela Knight

'Delightful and full of interesting characters and romance'
Romantic Times

'Vampire lovers will find themselves laughing throughout.
Sands' trademark humour and genuine characters keep her
series fresh and her readers hooked'
Publishers Weekly

Also by Lynsay Sands from Gollancz:

The Immortal who Loved Me

LYNSAY SANDS

The right of Lynsay Sands to be identified as the author of this
work has been asserted by her in accordance with the
Copyright, Designs and Patents Act 1988.

First published in Great Britain in 2015 by
Gollancz
An imprint of the Orion Publishing Group
Orion House, 5 Upper St Martin's Lane, London WC2H 9EA
An Hachette UK Company

1 3 5 7 9 10 8 6 4 2

A CIP catalogue record for this book is available
from the British Library

ISBN 978 1 473 20500 0

Printed in Great Britain by Clays Ltd, plc

The Orion Publishing Group's policy is to use papers that are
natural, renewable and recyclable products and made from wood
grown in sustainable forests. The logging and manufacturing
processes are expected to conform to the environmental regulations
of the country of origin.

www.lynsaysands.net
www.orionbooks.co.uk
www.gollancz.co.uk

One

Sherry was muttering to herself as she worked. She hated doing taxes. She hated paying them even more.

Snorting with disgust as she calculated the amount of money she'd have to pay this quarter, she saved the program and was about to shut off the computer when her office door burst open. Grumpy after her task, Sherry raised her head, ready to rip into the employee who had barged in without knocking. But, instead, the words caught in her throat and her eyes widened with surprise as she stared at the petite blond teenager who rushed in and slammed the door closed.

The kid didn't give her more than a passing glance as her gaze slid around the room to find the window overlooking the store. The office was eight steps up from the main floor, so it allowed for an eagle's view of everything. On spotting the window, the kid immediately dropped into a crouch, and then moved to it to poke her head up and peer anxiously out over the store floor.

Sherry's eyebrows rose at the action, and she announced, "It's a one-way mirror. No one in the store can see you."

The girl glanced around and frowned at her. "Shhh."

"*Excuse* me?" Sherry said with a half laugh of disbelief at the sheer gall of the girl. Expression turning serious, she said grimly, "This is my office, kiddo. I suggest you explain your reason for being here, or get out."

Rather than put the kid in her place, the words merely drew a full-on scowl from her as she turned and then concentrated a pair of the most amazing eyes on Sherry. They were a strange silver-green and seemed almost to glow with intensity.

Caught by those beautiful and unusual eyes, Sherry allowed her to stare briefly, mostly because she was staring back, but then she arched her eyebrows. "Well? Are you just going to crouch there and gawk at me or explain yourself?"

Instead of answering, the girl frowned and asked, "Why can't I read you?"

A short disbelieving laugh slipped from Sherry, but when the girl simply stared at her with bewilderment, she said reasonably, "Maybe because I'm not a book."

That got no reaction from the girl. She still continued to stare at her, looking almost vexed. Tired of thinking of her as "the girl," Sherry asked abruptly, "What's your name?"

"Stephanie," the girl replied almost absently, eyeing

her now as if she were a bug under a microscope. That examination ended abruptly when a chime sounded from the speaker in the corner of Sherry's office. It announced that the front door of the store had been opened. Seeming to realize that, Stephanie whirled to peer out at the store again, and quickly dropped back to her haunches so that only the top of her head poked up over the bottom of the window ledge.

"I told you it's one-way," Sherry said with exasperation. "They can't see—"

"Shhh," Stephanie hissed without glancing around, simply raising a hand in her direction, palm up, demanding silence.

Despite herself, Sherry obeyed the silent order. There was just something about the girl, a sudden stillness and tension that had been present before, but now intensified. It made Sherry frown and glance past her to the store beyond the one-way mirror as four men walked into the shop.

Using the word "walked" was somewhat misleading. It was too normal, and had they just walked in she would have simply taken note of their entrance and then turned her attention back to the teenager in her office. But there was nothing normal about these men.

All four of the newcomers looked to be in their mid-twenties. They also all had longish, dirty blond hair. One wore it in a ponytail, another actually had it up in a bun, and a third man had gelled it into long pointy spokes that poked out of his head like a hedgehog. But the leader, or at least the man in the lead, had a full, matted mane that made her think of a lion.

Sensing trouble, Sherry watched the men. They each wore jeans that could have used a run through a washing machine. Their T-shirts weren't much better, and they didn't walk in so much as stalk in. There was just something predatory about them, an air that made her feel like a gazelle on the planes of the Serengeti and grateful they were on the other side of the mirror.

Unaware that she had stood and was slowly moving to the girl's side, Sherry watched with trepidation as the lead man raised his head and took a long, deep sniff of the air, scenting it like the predator he made her think of. He then nodded, lowered his head and glanced around to ask, "Where is the girl?"

Not surprisingly, the half a dozen customers in the store continued perusing the kitchenware they'd come in for, probably not even aware that he was addressing them or to what girl he was referring. Sherry doubted anyone but her employees had even noted the girl's entrance, and busy with customers as they were, even they may not have.

When nobody paid him any attention, the lead man scowled and cast a glance back toward his men. The last man, the one that resembled a hedgehog, still stood in the open store door. Now he entered fully and slammed it, sending the bells ringing madly. When the chimes fell silent, so was the shop. Every eye in the place was now on the foursome, and the air seemed charged with a sudden wariness that Sherry was not only aware of, but was experiencing herself.

"Thank you for your attention," the leader said pleasantly, moving forward again. After half a dozen steps, he paused again, this time in front of one of her employees who had been helping a young woman who had a little girl clutching at her skirt.

Sherry sucked in a breath when the man's hand suddenly shot out to the side and snatched the mother by the front of her sweater. He wasn't even looking at her as he grabbed and jerked her forward. Only then did he turn his head toward her, his nose almost brushing hers as he demanded, "Where is the—"

Sherry found herself tensing further when he paused suddenly mid-question. She bit her lip, the hairs on the back of her neck standing on end as he inhaled again, more deeply this time. Sherry didn't know why, but the action made her anxious for the woman, especially when he gave a pleasant little shiver as he released his breath at the end.

"You're pregnant," he announced, a smile growing on his lips. Dipping his head, he ran his nose along the woman's throat, inhaling deeply again. He then released a happy sounding little sigh and announced, "I love pregnant women almost as much as untreated diabetics. All those hormones pumping through the blood . . ." He pulled back to look her in the face as he said, "It's a powerful cocktail."

"Damn."

Sherry blinked and tore her gaze from the tableau below to glance to Stephanie, surprised to find she'd briefly forgotten about the girl.

"What?" Sherry asked, instinctively whispering this time. She didn't know who these people were, or what was going on, but all her inner alarm bells were ringing in warning now. Something very bad was happening and she knew instinctively that it was only going to get worse.

Stephanie bit her lip and then glanced around. "Is there a back exit in this place?"

"That door leads to the alley behind the shops," Sherry admitted quietly, gesturing to a door down another eight steps at the back of her office.

Sherry didn't blame the kid for wanting to run. She wanted to herself, but couldn't, not with her employees and customers out there at the mercy of the men presently filling her small shop. It was like four lions set among a pen full of lambs. Although she supposed that was the wrong analogy. Everyone knew the lioness did the hunting, not the lion. Wolves were probably a better descriptor for these men.

"You don't happen to have a car parked out in the alley, do you?" Stephanie asked hopefully.

Sherry merely stared for a moment. She had heard the question but hadn't seen the girl's lips move. What—?

"Do you?" the teenager hissed, her lips moving this time.

"No. I take the subway," Sherry admitted quietly. Most people did in the city, rather than pay exorbitant parking fees.

The girl sighed unhappily and then peered back to the drama taking place on the other side of the mirror.

Sherry followed her gaze. The leader now had the young mother pressed up against the checkout counter, her body bent back over it, but all he was doing at the moment was sniffing her neck like a dog. It was weird, and might even have been funny if Sherry hadn't noted the knife he now retrieved from his pocket and flicked open at his side.

"Oh crap," she breathed.

"Yeah," Stephanie muttered. "A car would have made this so much easier."

"Made what easier?" Sherry asked in a distracted voice as she watched the man run the side of the blade lightly up the apparently pregnant woman's stomach toward her throat. The woman wasn't reacting at all. Her expression was blank, as were the expressions on the faces of the others in the store. Even her child simply stood there, blank-faced and unconcerned. The only people in the store with any expression at all were the leader and his men. The leader was smiling a soft almost sweet smile, while the three men who could have been his brothers were all grinning widely with what she would have said was anticipation.

"You better start running," Stephanie said grimly, moving to lock the door leading into the store.

"I'm not running anywhere," Sherry said, her words sharp despite her effort to keep her tone soft. "I'm calling the police."

"The police can't help them," the girl said grimly, striding over to pick up the heavy filing cabinet in the corner and carry it down the stairs to set in front of the door that opened to the store floor.

Sherry was so startled by the action that she just stared. The filing cabinet was a tall, four-drawer legal cabinet stuffed full of paperwork and receipts. It weighed a ton. She doubted she could have pushed or dragged it across the floor, let alone lift it like it was an empty laundry basket as the girl had just done. She was trying to work out in her head how Stephanie had done that when movement below drew her attention back to the store floor. The leader had suddenly released the pregnant woman and stepped back.

Maybe he was going to leave. The vague hope had barely formed in her mind when he grabbed one of the mixing bowls off a nearby display and handed that and the knife to the pregnant woman and said pleasantly, "It's such a messy business and this is my favorite T-shirt. Why don't you do it? Bend forward over the counter, put the bowl on that stool there so it's under your throat, and slice your neck open so the blood flows into it."

"The crazy son of a—" Sherry began and then nearly bit her tongue off when the young mother, still with no expression on her face, did exactly as he'd suggested. She turned to bend over the counter, set the bowl on the clerk's stool behind it, positioned herself so her neck was over the bowl and slit her own throat.

"Damn," Sherry breathed with dismay, hardly able to believe the woman had just done that. "I'm calling the police."

"There's no time," Stephanie growled, catching her arm. "He's controlling those people. Can't you see that? Do you think that woman really wanted to slit her own throat?"

"But the police—"

"Even if they got here before Leonius is done, they'd just become part of the slaughter. The only way to save these people is to lead Leo and his boys away from here . . . and to do that I need to get their attention and then run like hell."

"Then *we'll* get their attention and *we'll* run like hell," Sherry said firmly as she hurried down the steps to unlock and open the back door. There was no way in hell she was letting the teenager handle the matter alone. She was just a kid, for heaven's sake. Sherry had just spotted the door stopper to keep the door open when a loud crash made her turn sharply around. She was just in time to see her desk chair sail through the one-way mirror and out of sight. Stephanie had pitched it through.

Sherry hurried back to the top of the steps to look out onto the store floor. The chair hadn't hit anyone, but the noise had definitely caught the attention of the men in the other room. No one else even glanced around, but all four men were now staring through the opening toward them.

Stephanie promptly flipped them the bird, then raced toward Sherry, shrieking, "Run!"

The shout had barely hit her ears when Stephanie was streaking past her, catching her arm in passing and nearly jerking her off her feet as she swung her around. In the next moment, she'd been dragged down the stairs and out the door. Stephanie must have kicked the stopper out of the way as they passed, because the door slammed closed behind them.

The girl was fast. Inhumanly fast. Sherry was moving

like she'd never moved before in her life. Adrenaline gave her a boost and her feet barely seemed to touch the ground, but the teenager was still nearly dragging her off her feet with her own speed. It was a short alley, yet they'd barely traveled up half of it when a loud crash drew her gaze over her shoulder to see the men charging out after them.

Sherry's heart leapt at the sight. Like the girl, they were also fast. Too fast. She would never outrun them. And she was just holding Stephanie back.

"Go!" she shouted, shaking her arm in an effort to break the girl's hold. "I'm just slowing you down. Leave me and run!"

Stephanie glanced toward the men gaining on them, looked forward again, and then did just that. She released her hold on Sherry and charged for the mouth of the alley.

Sherry was glad she had. It was what she'd told her to do, and at the same time being suddenly on her own with those hyenas nipping at her heels was heart-stoppingly terrifying. Despite her fear, or more likely because of it, Sherry managed to put on a little more speed herself, but it was like trying to outrun a sports car. Impossible. Sherry's only hope was that they'd bypass her to chase after the girl.

The moment she had the thought, Sherry began to worry that they would do just that. She couldn't leave the girl to their less than tender mercies without at least trying to slow them down or stop them. That thought in mind, she glanced around for something to help with the effort. The only thing ahead of her in the narrow alley was a pair of garbage Dumpsters.

"Work with what you have," she breathed, and changed direction, angling toward the large blue metal bins. Would she have time to grab one to push toward the men? Would she be strong enough? Did garbage Dumpsters have locks on their wheels, and if they did, were the wheels locked on these Dumpsters?

Sherry never got the answer to those questions because that's when the gunshot rang out. She was sure she felt the bullet whiz past her ear, it was so close. At first she thought her pursuers were shooting either at her or the girl. It made her squint at the mouth of the alley some twenty feet ahead as she sought out the girl to see if she was all right. Her eyes widened incredulously when she spotted Stephanie in a shooter's stance, gun pointed her way while a police officer stood beside her seeming oblivious to what was happening.

Even as she saw that, several more gunshots sounded. This time, though, Sherry heard a grunt from close behind her. She glanced over her shoulder, shocked to see the leader only three or four steps away, his arm extended, hand reaching for her. His fingers actually brushed the cloth of her blouse even as he began to tumble toward the ground.

There were three holes in his chest, Sherry saw as he fell, and his followers were skidding to a halt to help him. With the hope that she might get out of this after all, Sherry turned and ran like crazy. All she was thinking was that if she got to Stephanie and the officer before one of the men gave chase again, she would be all right.

When Sherry reached Stephanie, the girl had lowered the weapon and was putting it back in the officer's holster, saying, "This never happened. You never saw us and you really should patrol farther up the road and stay away from here until the alley is empty."

Stephanie snapped the officer's holster closed on the gun as she finished speaking, and then the officer immediately turned and started up the road.

"What—?" Sherry began with amazement and then snapped her mouth closed as Stephanie grabbed her hand and began to run again, dragging her away from the alley mouth. Since Sherry was more than happy to get away from their pursuers, she went willingly, doing her best to keep up. But as soon as they reached the end of the street and had rounded the corner, she tugged at Stephanie's hand and gasped, "Wait . . . Stop . . . I can't . . . run any . . . more."

"We can't stop," Stephanie said firmly, dragging her up the road, though slowing to a jog at least. "Leo will be after us as soon as he recovers."

"That guy . . . you shot?" she gasped with amazement, still tugging on Stephanie's hand. Even a jog was too much for her labored lungs at the moment, and her words were breathless and choppy as she said, "He isn't . . . recovering . . . anytime soon. He has . . . three bullets . . . in his chest. His next stop . . . is the . . . hospital."

"He won't need a hospital," Stephanie assured her, not the least winded. She glanced around grimly as they reached the end of the short street, and then suddenly pulled Sherry across the road toward a small pizza place on the opposite corner.

"Kid . . . he'll need a . . . hospital," Sherry assured her wearily, but allowed Stephanie to usher her into the restaurant. She even followed docilely as the girl dragged her to the tables along the side between the counter and the windowless wall until they reached the last table, one not likely to be seen from the street.

"Can I use your iPhone?" Stephanie asked as Sherry dropped to sit in a booth with her back to the front of the shop.

Sherry grimaced and wheezed, "I don't have it. Or my purse either," she added with a frown.

"Just catch your breath. I'll get you a drink," Stephanie said, and as quickly as that was gone.

Sherry pushed her hair back from her sweaty face, then closed her eyes on a sigh. The last few moments played through her head like cut scenes from a film; that poor woman slitting her own throat, the chair crashing through the window, the leader of the small gang of hoodlums reaching for her even as he fell from his wounds . . . his eyes, glowing and alien.

Sherry shook her head and covered her own eyes briefly, pressing on them in an effort to blot out the images. She wondered where her nice boring safe life had gone . . . and why she was sitting in a pizzeria like a well-behaved child when she should be calling the police, going back to check on her people and customers, and—

"Here."

Sherry raised her head and sat back abruptly as Stephanie set a soda and a slice of pizza on the table in front of her. Sherry's gaze slid from the two items to the identical items in front of Stephanie as the girl slid into the booth across from her.

"I didn't know what you like so I got you a deluxe slice and Coke," Stephanie explained, picking up her slice of pizza to chomp into the end of it.

Sherry gaped as she watched the girl chew and swallow with relish, and then asked with amazement, "How can you eat?"

"I'm hungry," the girl said simply. "You should eat too."

"I don't eat carbs . . . or drink them. Coke is nothing but syrupy water," Sherry said automatically, and then realizing how stupid those words were under the circumstances, she shook her head. "I don't understand how you can act like this is all just—"

"Sugar is energy," Stephanie interrupted. "And you need to keep up your energy in case we have to run again. So eat," she ordered, sounding remarkably like the adult here.

That fact made Sherry scowl. "We should be calling the police."

"Yeah, 'cause that cop at the mouth of the alley was so useful," Stephanie said with dry disinterest before taking another bite of her pizza.

Unable to argue with that, Sherry frowned and then asked, "Speaking of that, what happened there?"

Stephanie arched an eyebrow, but was silent for a

moment as she finished chewing and swallowing. Then she sighed and said, "You obviously couldn't outrun them, and I couldn't leave you behind for them to catch, torture, and kill, so when I spotted the cop at the mouth of the alley, I ran ahead to grab his gun and shoot Leo to buy us some time. Fortunately, it worked."

Sherry didn't point out that she had been there and seen all that, instead she simply asked, "And the co— police officer, just let you take his gun?"

Stephanie shrugged. "I controlled him. He won't re- member any of it."

"Which will really confuse him when he realizes his gun has been fired," Sherry muttered, but her mind was on the girl's claim that she'd controlled the cop. She wanted to laugh off the suggestion, but the man had looked as blank-faced as the woman who'd slit her own throat in the store. Stephanie had claimed Leo was controlling that woman too. So Leonius had controlled the woman, Stephanie had controlled the cop . . . How? That particular skill set was just not something Sherry knew humans to have.

"There they are."

Sherry glanced around sharply and spotted the four men moving swiftly past the restaurant's front window. She shrank down in her seat when one of them glanced through the window, but they didn't slow or stop, so she guessed she hadn't been seen. That wasn't a surprise to her, considering they were in the dark back corner. What was surprising was the fact that the leader, Leo, as Stephanie called him, was up and walking around as if nothing had happened.

"Damn," she breathed, staring at the man until the group moved out of sight.

"I told you being shot wouldn't stop him," Stephanie said solemnly.

"I know but . . . . how?" she asked with bewilderment.

Stephanie was silent for a moment as she continued to eat her pizza, but after a couple of bites she set it down with resignation and reached for her pop. She took a pull on the drink, and then set that down too, to eye Sherry thoughtfully. After a moment she sighed. "I suppose I'm going to have to explain."

"That would be nice," Sherry said dryly.

Stephanie nodded. "Vampires exist. Although Leonius and his men are no-fangers, they still survive on blood so I suppose they're still vampires. As am I, though I'm an Edentate."

Sherry blinked as the words raced through her mind. No-fangers? Edentate? She had no idea what either of those were, so focused on the word she did recognize.

"Vampires?" she asked, not bothering to hide her disbelief. "Sweetie, I hate to tell you this, but vampires *do not* exist. Besides, vampires bite people, they don't have them slit their own throats open and bleed into a bowl."

"Uh-huh," Stephanie didn't look upset by her words. "So how do you explain his controlling that woman to make her slit her own throat? Or my controlling the cop?"

Sherry considered the question briefly and then suggested, "Hypnosis?"

Stephanie rolled her eyes. "Come on, you don't seem

like a stupid woman. Leo didn't have time to hypnotize her, and I certainly didn't have time to hypnotize the cop." She scowled and then asked, "What's your name?"

"Sherry Carne," she answered. "And fine, maybe this Leo didn't hypnotize the woman in my store, but he did something and it wasn't because he's a vampire. Vampires have fangs and bite people."

"A minute ago you said there were no such things as vampires, now you're saying there are, but they have to have fangs?" Stephanie asked with amusement.

"Well . . ." Sherry frowned. "If you're going with the whole vampire thing to cover the real story, then at least be consistent. Vampires are dead, soulless creatures who crawl out of their coffins and bite people."

"Yeah, that's what I thought too," Stephanie said, sounding weary and much older than her years. Shrugging, she straightened her shoulders and added, "Turns out we're both wrong. Vampires aren't dead and soulless, and while most do have fangs, Leo and his little Leos are an aberrant strain. Like I said, they're called no-fangers. They don't age and they do need blood to survive, but they don't have the fangs to get it, so they cut their victims. They're also usually crazy. But not normal crazy, nutso crazy."

Sherry tilted her head slightly and eyed the girl. There was something about the way she'd passed on the information . . . It had been a lecturing tone, but there was something under the words, some emotion almost like shame, that she didn't understand.

"You don't believe me," Stephanie said with a shrug.

"That's okay, but just let me tell you what's going on. You can believe it or not as you like, but just remember it. It might save your life before we get out of this."

Sherry was silent for a minute, considering the girl, but then decided there was no harm in listening. Besides, it gave her a good excuse to just sit there while she tried to find her second wind, so she leaned back in her seat with a nod. "Go ahead."

Stephanie relaxed a little and even managed a small smile. "Right, just so we're clear, I *am* claiming that vampires exist. There are some with fangs, some without, but both can read and control mortals. Leo and his little Leos—Two, Three, and Four—are one of the variety without fangs."

"Two, Three, and Four?" Sherry asked.

Stephanie shrugged. "They probably aren't Leo Two, Leo Three, and Leo Four, but he names all his sons after himself so they're all Leos number something-or-other, so they just go by their number."

"His sons?" Sherry asked with disbelief. "There is no way those men are his children. They all looked to be the same age."

"Vampire, remember?" Stephanie said pointedly. "Vampires stop aging physically at around twenty-five."

Sherry let her breath out on an exasperated sigh, finding it hard to swallow all of this, but she'd agreed to listen, so waved for her to continue.

"I grew up as normal and ignorant of what's out there as you did, but Leo and some of his other sons kidnapped my sister and me from a grocery store parking lot when I was fourteen," Stephanie announced. Her mouth tightened and then she added, "We were eventually rescued, and Leo's sons were caught and executed by the Rogue Hunters but—"

"Rogue Hunters?" Sherry interrupted.

"Cops for immortals, or vampires, as you would call them. They keep the other immortals in line," she explained. "Anyway, I don't know if it's because of his sons getting killed or what, but for some reason, Leo became sort of obsessed with my sister and me. He wants to add us to his breeding stock."

Sherry stared at her, silently processing, and then she cleared her throat and asked, "What do you mean he wants to add you to his breeding stock? Not . . . ?"

Stephanie nodded. "It's how he got all the junior Leos. I doubt many of the mothers were willing."

Sherry shook her head slightly. "You make it sound like he has a lot of them."

"One of the sons who helped him kidnap my sister and I was Leo the 21st. According to him, he was one of the older sons," Stephanie said with a shrug. "He claimed there were fifty or sixty of them, that there have been hundreds over the centuries, but some killed themselves, some were killed, and Leo killed several others when they refused to do what he wanted, or when they otherwise pissed him off."

Sherry didn't say anything. It was crazy, like a vampire soap opera or something. It couldn't be true . . . could it?

"Anyway," Stephanie continued, "like I say, Leo senior took a shine to my sister and me and said he'd come after us, so Dani—my sister," she added, "Dani and I have been hiding out and protected since."

"Until today," Sherry said.

Stephanie grimaced. "I was protected. I was with Drina and Katricia. They're Rogue Hunters."

"Vampire cops," Sherry muttered.

"Immortal cops really, or Enforcers, but vampire cop will do. Just don't use the term vampire in front of the other immortals. They can get testy about that," Stephanie informed her, and then continued. "Drina and Katricia are both getting married so we went wedding dress shopping. I . . ." She sighed and grimaced. "I forgot something in the car and just nipped out quickly to get it, but . . ." Stephanie shook her head. "It was just my luck to pick a moment when Leo and his boys decided to walk down that street."

She paused briefly and frowned before saying, "There haven't been any reported sightings of Leo and his boys in Toronto since Dani and I were rescued. They cleared out and have been hanging south of the border for a long time. They were last spotted somewhere in the southern states. I never would've gone out to the car if I'd known they were in the area. I just . . ." She heaved out a deep sigh and then said, "Anyway, I spotted them before they saw me. I nipped into your store hoping they wouldn't see me, but I guess they did."

When Stephanie took another bite of pizza and began to chew, Sherry was left to wonder if she believed anything the girl had just said. Oddly enough, while Sherry had started out not believing, she found she now did. She had no idea why. It was crazy. Vampires, mind control, reading thoughts, breeding stock . . .

Sherry pushed those thoughts away for now to switch to a subject that had been worrying her since leaving the store. "How long does the control last?"

Stephanie paused to peer at her briefly, and then understanding crossed her face and she assured her, "Not long. I mean, it can continue for a little bit after the vampire leaves their presence if they put a suggestion in their thoughts, but I'm sure Leo and the boys didn't get a chance to do that before chasing after us. The moment they left the building, your employees and customers probably snapped out of it and helped the woman who cut herself."

"*If* they could help her," Sherry said unhappily, picking up her slice of pizza and shifting it in her hands briefly before taking a bite. It was surprisingly good. Surprising because she wouldn't have expected anything to taste good at that point. She guessed the scare she'd just had, and surviving it, had awakened her taste buds or something. Whatever. It tasted good. Carbs or not.

"They could help her," Stephanie assured her. "She didn't cut deeply enough to hit the jugular. She's probably fine."

Sherry raised her eyebrows. "How do you know she didn't hit the jugular?"

"I gave her a mental nudge to stop her cutting too deep," Stephanie explained, and then grimaced and added, "Which Leo would have recognized right away. That's why we had to make our move when we did.

He would have used the people in the store against us, tortured them to make me come out. So I had to make sure he saw me leave and knew I wasn't there. It was the only way to be certain he'd leave them alone."

Sherry wasn't surprised at the claim that she'd given the woman a mental nudge not to cut too deep. After all, the girl had said she'd controlled the cop too. What *did* surprise her was that the girl had thought of the people in the store at all. Stephanie was a nice kid. There was still a possibility that she was crazy as a loon. Sherry was finding herself almost believing her tale, but it was a lot to swallow. So either Stephanie was a brave, thoughtful kid who had risked getting caught to save the pregnant mother, or she was a nutcase. A nutcase who was a damned good shot, Sherry thought. Stephanie had hit a moving target around her. Nice.

"So where did you learn to shoot like that?" Sherry asked quietly.

"Victor and D.J. take me to a shooting range every other day," she said. The names meant nothing to Sherry, so she was glad when the girl added, "Victor is . . . well he's sort of my adopted dad I guess." She said it quietly, her voice thickening, and then she rushed on, saying, "And D.J. is like the young, pain in the butt uncle who ruffles your hair and embarrasses you in public."

Sherry smiled faintly at the description. "And your real dad?"

"Alive, well, and mortal," Stephanie said casually, too casually, and she was avoiding her gaze. Picking at what was left of her pizza, she added, "He and Mom think I'm dead." Before Sherry could respond, she added, "But Victor and Elvi took me in and look after me. Elvi lost her daughter so I'm a gift, she says, and they're great."

Great, but not her real parents, Sherry translated as the girl turned her head away and dashed quickly at her eyes. Deciding a change of topic might be good, she said, "So, the police can't help us here . . . but what about those Rogue Hunters of yours? We should find a phone and call them so they can hunt down this Leo and his men."

Sherry just couldn't call the man's followers his sons. It seemed impossible that they were his children. They all looked around the same age. Brothers would have been more believable. Realizing that Stephanie wasn't responding to the suggestion of calling in her Rogue Hunters, Sherry raised her eyebrows. "Don't you think?"

"What?" Stephanie asked. Her blank expression as she turned back to face her made it obvious she hadn't been listening.

Knowing the girl's thoughts had probably been with her birth parents, Sherry asked patiently, "Don't you think that we should call your Rogue Hunters?"

Stephanie shook her head and stared down at the pizza crust she'd been unconsciously tearing apart. The slump to her shoulders and defeated air about the girl were a bit alarming. Sherry had no idea what was going on exactly, but she did know this was no time for the girl to fall apart. Sitting back, she deliberately took on an annoyingly knowing air and said, "Oh, I get it."

Stephanie finally really looked at her, her attention caught. Eyebrows rising, she asked with interest, "What do you get?"

"You," Sherry said with a shrug. "I was a teenager once too."

Stephanie snorted. "Please. I don't know how many times I've heard that tired old line. Like you crusty old farts all think just because you were young back in ancient times that you know what life is like for me. You don't. You were young in . . . what? The sixties?"

"I wasn't even born in the sixties, thank you," Sherry said with amusement. "I'm only thirty-two."

"Whatever . . ." Stephanie waved that away. "You haven't got a clue about me."

"Hmmm. How about I tell you what I think and then you can tell me I'm wrong? If I am," Sherry added tauntingly.

Stephanie shrugged. "Whatever."

Sherry tilted her head and eyed her for a moment, and then said, "So, you were wedding dress shopping with this Drina and her friend?"

"Katricia," Stephanie supplied. "She's Drina's cousin, but also a Rogue Hunter. She's getting married too, to Teddy, who is the police chief in Port Henry where I live. We came to Toronto for a girls' weekend and dress shopping."

"Hmmm." Sherry considered that and then said, "And you say they let you go out to get something?"

Stephanie nodded, her gaze sliding away toward the front of the store and a frown flickering over her face.

Sherry suspected the girl was wondering where the

two women were. She was too. Surely they'd noticed Stephanie was missing by now? And if they were in the area, the gunshots should have drawn them. She let that go for now, though, and simply said, "Well, I'm sure the bit about their letting you go out to get something is a lie."

Stephanie glanced back to her sharply. "What makes you think that?"

"Kiddo, if these girls are Rogue Hunters, or vampire cops, and this Leo is after you, like you say, I'd guess they keep a short leash on you to keep you safe. They would not have let you wander off on your own. So, Drina was probably in a dressing room trying on a wedding dress, and Katricia was in there helping her with all the convoluted nonsense involved in putting one of those things on, or trying on one herself. You were probably sitting in the waiting area outside the dressing room feeling bored and neglected. No doubt you reached for your iPhone to either listen to music or watch a movie while you waited, and realized you'd left it in the car." Tilting her head, she added, "It's probably hooked up to the sound system in the car, which is why you forgot to grab it, so you thought you'd just slip out, get it and be back before they noticed.

"Unfortunately," she added, "you didn't get to the car before you spotted Leonius and his buddies and had to duck into my store for cover."

Stephanie didn't hide her surprise. "How did you know all of that?"

Sherry shrugged and reminded her, "You asked to use my iPhone earlier."

"So?" Stephanie asked.

"So, you don't have yours on you, so couldn't have made it to the car."

"Maybe I don't have one and was getting something else," Stephanie suggested.

Sherry shook her head firmly. "There are few teenagers around who don't have cell phones nowadays. Besides, you specified iPhone rather than just saying cell phone, which suggests that's what you have."

"Okay, so how did you know I left my phone in the car, jacked into the USB?" she asked with interest.

"Because I'm always forgetting mine in the car for that reason," Sherry admitted wryly. "I plug it into the USB so I can listen to music I like and then forget it when I get out."

"Hmmm," Stephanie murmured, but she was looking at her with interest now. "Or maybe you have some psychic abilities and that's why I can't read or control you."

Sherry didn't comment. Her mind wanted to rebel at the possibility of anyone controlling her actions or thoughts, but she'd watched the pregnant mother slit her own throat. No one would do that under their own impetus. She *did* believe the customer must have been controlled . . . and if *she* could be controlled . . .

Pushing these disturbing thoughts away, Sherry said, "So, all of this being true, you don't want to call your Rogue Hunters because you're going to get hell for slipping away from your protectors and putting yourself at risk in the first place."

"Nah-ah," Stephanie said with a slow smile.

Sherry raised her eyebrows doubtfully. "You won't get in trouble?"

"Oh, yeah," Stephanie said dryly. "Once Drina, Katricia, Harper, Elvi, and Victor are done raking me over the coals, Lucian himself will probably show up to completely demoralize me," she admitted with unhappy resignation. "But that's not why I'm not calling."

"Okay," Sherry said slowly. "So why don't you want to call?"

"It's not that I don't *want* to call . . . I don't *have* to," she explained. "I already did. They're sending Bricker even as we speak." She tilted her head and then grinned and added, "And he's bringing you a surprise."

Two

"He's here."

Basileios was already on his way up the hall when Marguerite made that announcement. Reaching her side, he glanced out at the SUV now parked in the driveway as the sound of a honking horn reached his ears. He glanced to Marguerite, his eyebrows rising at her concerned expression. "Problem?"

"It isn't like Bricker to be so rude. He should have come to the door to get you," she said with a frown.

Basileios smiled faintly as he gave her a quick hug. "He's not picking me up for a date, Marguerite. He's probably just in a hurry to collect Stephanie and her friend before Leo and his progeny find them."

"Yes, I suppose," she murmured, but he could tell from her expression that she was concerned about the young immortal and what this "rudeness" might mean.

Shaking his head, Basil gave her hand a squeeze and

then turned to slip out of the house, assuring her, "It's fine. I'll call when we get them to the Enforcer house."

Moving quickly, he made his way to the front passenger door of the SUV and slid in.

"I don't know why I'm the one they're sending to pick up Steph," Bricker complained the moment the door opened. "Drina and Katricia should be doing it. They're the ones who are supposed to be guarding her . . . and they're right there in the area."

As greetings went, that was pretty lame, Basileios decided, swallowing his own hello as he pulled the SUV's door closed and grabbed the seat belt.

"And why the heck would they make me take *you*?" Justin continued with irritation. "You're a lawyer for God's sake, not a hunter. What good are you going to be if things get dicey?"

Basileios glanced up from fastening his seat belt, one eyebrow cocked. He didn't know if Marguerite's concern was warranted, but Justin Bricker was definitely in a mood. He didn't know what had caused the man's ire, but didn't let it get to him. Voice mild, he said, "I was not always a lawyer, Justin. I was a warrior for more than a millennia. I've only been a lawyer the last twenty years. If the situation gets dicey—" He shrugged. "We'll handle it."

When Bricker merely scowled at the road ahead, Basileios added, "As for why we're collecting the ladies, I gather Drina and my daughter were sent to clean up the situation at the store. It needed prompt attention to avoid exposure and they were the closest available team. Besides, there's not much chance of things getting dicey.

Apparently the danger has already passed. We're just picking up the girls and taking them to the Enforcer house until Lucian decides how to handle the situation."

"Yeah, babysitting duty once again," Justin groused, and then glanced to him. "So, let me guess, Marguerite wanted you to come because Stephanie is your life mate?"

Basileios shook his head. "No, but she thinks that the mortal, Sherry may be."

Justin's eyebrows flew up. "That can't be. Marguerite hasn't met her," he said, and then frowned and asked, "Has she?"

"Who can say with Marguerite?" Basileios asked with amusement. "She's been doing a lot of shopping for her kitchen now that she enjoys food again, and I gather the woman in question owns a kitchenware store." He smiled faintly and then added, "However, I was told that Stephanie has some skill in the life mate area as well, and she seems to think this mortal is mine."

Bricker glanced around with surprise as he drove. "You've met Stephanie?"

"Yes," Basileios answered, and then frowned and admitted, "Well, I did not actually meet her. We were not introduced, but I visited Katricia at the Enforcer house when the girls first arrived and we saw each other in passing. I presume someone told her who I was just as Katricia told me who she was." Giving a helpless shrug, he admitted, "I am not sure how this identifying a life mate business works, but I presume that brief encounter was enough for her to read whatever it is she reads and decide that this Sherry woman would be a suitable life mate for me."

"Well, hell," Bricker muttered with disgust, hitting the brakes a little harder than necessary as they reached the corner.

The action sent Basil jerking forward until the seat belt caught him. He glanced at the younger man with a touch of exasperation. "Well hell, what?"

"Do you know how many life mates I've watched pair up the last couple of years?" Bricker asked grimly. "I don't even know. There must be at least twenty, although I didn't witness them all from the start. Christian and Caro hooked up in St. Lucia, but they're here now, blissfully happy in their life mate relationship." He grimaced. "I just wish Marguerite or Stephanie would take a minute and find me a life mate."

Basileios relaxed and smiled with mild amusement. "You sound like a mortal child."

"What?" he asked indignantly.

"Mortal children can't wait until they're old enough to drive, then to finish school, then to drink, etcetera," he explained and then added gently, "You're only just over a century old, Justin."

"Yeah, yeah, and some of you guys have waited millennia so I should just be patient. It will happen when the time is right," he mumbled with disgust, obviously having heard the lecture before.

Basileios didn't comment. The man was impatient and bitter and nothing he said would change that. It was better just to let it go. He'd find his way . . . or not.

"How old are you anyway?" Justin asked suddenly. "You're one of the older Argeneaus, aren't you?"

"I was born in 1529 BC," Basileios acknowledged quietly, and wasn't surprised when Justin glanced at him sharply.

"But Lucian and Jean Claude were born in 1534 BC," he said. "That means you're only five years younger than them."

Basileios nodded, unperturbed by the accusation in his voice.

"Hmmph," Justin grunted, and then said bitterly, "I guess the hundred year rule doesn't apply to you Argeneaus."

"I was born in Atlantis, Bricker," Basileios said patiently. "The hundred year rule wasn't in place yet at that time. It was only created after the fall, after Leonius Livius's efforts to make an army of his progeny."

"Right," Justin growled. He was silent for a moment and then said, "So, Katricia is your daughter? You've been mated before?"

"I was mated briefly in Atlantis. However, she wasn't Katricia's mother. We had no children and she didn't survive the fall."

"So, you've been mated twice," he commented. "Nice."

"Actually, no I haven't. Mary Delacort, the mother of my children, is an immortal who is a good friend and nothing more."

Bricker glanced at him sharply. "You had kids outside of a life mate relationship?"

"You make it sound so naughty," Basileios said with

amusement, and then pointed out quietly, "I lost my life mate in the fall, Bricker. I have been alone a very long time. Lucian had his guardianship of the family and immortals and mortals in general to help keep his sanity and humanity. I did not have that. I needed an anchor, someone to care for, a reason to get up in the evening. If I could not have a life mate, then children to care about and look out for was the next best thing."

He glanced out the window and added quietly, "My children are probably the only reason I didn't go rogue like my brother Jean Claude."

Justin glanced at him again, and then asked curiously, "And this Mary? She didn't mind?"

"Fortunately, Mary was in much the same situation. Well, not really fortunately for her, I suppose," he added with a frown. "But you know what I mean."

"Hmmm," Justin released a deep sigh, and asked, "So what is your fantasy life mate like?"

Basileios glanced at him in question. "I'm not sure I understand what you mean?"

"Well, you must have pictured her in your mind over the millennia. What did you imagine your life mate would look like? Tall, short? Thin, curvy? Blond or dark-haired?" he explained, and then added, "And what kind of personality did you imagine? Funny, smart, feisty, sweet . . . ?" He glanced at him curiously. "What did you dream about?"

Basileios considered the question solemnly. Of course he had imagined someday having a life mate and what she might be like. He had never really imagined the whole package, but he supposed he had some ideas. "I prefer blondes to dark-haired women, and I prefer smaller women, short and petite with an agreeable personality, sweet and biddable."

"Biddable?" Justin snorted. "Man, someone's stuck in fifteenth century BC. Women nowadays are *not* biddable." He paused briefly and then added, "Well, maybe if you found yourself a mail order bride from somewhere women are expected to do as they're told you might. But I hear once they're in Canada or the U.S. for any length of time, they get infected with our women's attitude and sass."

Basileios shrugged. He suspected he'd be happy with his life mate despite what she looked like or her personality type. That was what life mates were all about, after all. The nanos selected the one you could be happy with.

"Now me," Justin said suddenly, "I don't care if she's smart or funny as long as she's a tall, curvy, dark-haired gal with sass and a nice ass."

"Ah," Basileios said quietly. It was the only thing he could think to say. After all, no matter what a life mate looked like prior to the turn, they would be at least somewhat altered after it, and whether that alteration included a "nice ass" depended on their genetics. It was also a petty thing to be concerned about when it came to a life mate. Which just showed him how young and immature the boy was. He'd grow up, though, and time would teach him what was important in life and what wasn't.

Sherry stared at the girl across from her with amazement. "You already called? When? How?"

"I used the phone in the office here while I was waiting for the pizza and pops," Stephanie explained. "I had to get help to the people in the store, and make sure a clean-up crew was sent to wipe memories and handle the mess." She tilted her head, smiled and added, "And I wanted to talk to Marguerite and have her send something for you."

"What?" Sherry asked suspiciously.

Stephanie grinned and then said, "Basil."

"Basil?" Sherry asked incredulously. "Your surprise for me is basil?"

Stephanie nodded her head.

"What am I supposed to do with it? Put it on my pizza?" she asked with bewilderment, and then tilted her head. "Or does basil work like garlic to keep vampires away?"

Stephanie laughed and then explained, "Basil the person, not the spice." herb

"Oh," Sherry said, and then, "Oh!" Frowning, she shook her head quickly in denial. "No, no, no, I don't want a man. Why is it everyone wants to set me up with someone?" she asked plaintively, and then mimicked a much higher voice and said, "'Oh Sherry, my cousin is in town and he'd be perfect for you.' 'Oh Sherry, my son is single. I think you'd like him.' 'Oh Sherry, you're such a sweetheart, you should be with a man. I have a neighbor who's single. Why don't I just arrange a dinner and . . .'" She grimaced and shook her head. "I am so not interested.

"Besides," she added quietly, "this is no time to be setting me up on a date. For heaven's sake, my store is a shambles, a woman may or may not be dead or at least badly injured, and we're hiding in a pizzeria from a pack of two-legged wild dogs. Could you pick a worse time to decide you're cupid? This is a serious business, Stephanie."

"So are life mates," Stephanie countered at once.

Sherry pinched the bridge of her nose between thumb and forefinger and murmured, "Right, of course they are. What are life mates?"

"Among our kind—"

" 'Our' kind?" Sherry interrupted sharply.

"Vampires," Stephanie said pointedly.

"Oh, right." Sherry forced a smile. For a moment there she'd forgotten the kid thought she was a blood-sucking fiend. Hell, she might even really be one for all she knew. When had her life turned into a takeoff of *Fright Night*? Shaking that thought away, she said, "Your parents aren't vampires, so you weren't born one."

"No," Stephanie admitted quietly, and then sighed and said, "When Leo kidnapped us, he also turned us both. Dani and I are vampires too."

Sherry's eyebrows rose at this admission, but that was all. She'd guessed that by the way the girl spoke. The truth was, she'd protested at the term "our kind" not because Stephanie was claiming to be one, but because the term made it sound like there were a lot of "her kind," which was disturbing. Sherry didn't get the chance to say as much, though, because Stephanie was now hurrying to explain.

"Anyway, so with immortals, or vampires, there are

certain people who are life mates for us. They're the perfect mate for the immortal. They bring back his or her passions, make food taste good again, make sex mind-blowing, and can live contentedly together for eons."

"Make food taste good again?" Sherry murmured, and then glanced at what was left of the large slice of pizza the girl had nearly demolished. "Food doesn't taste good to you?"

"Oh, I like food still," Stephanie assured her. "But I'm young. I guess after you've been around for a couple of centuries, food sort of gets old and sex gets boring."

"I see," Sherry said slowly, and she kind of did see. Or at least she could see how that would be the case. She was only thirty-two, but many was the night when she considered what to have for supper and nothing sounded appealing. At least, not appealing enough to go to the trouble of making it for just herself.

"Anyway," Stephanie continued, "a life mate changes all that. They're also a very rare find. Many immortals have lived centuries or even millennia waiting to find theirs. Some never do. Others go rogue from the lack of one. So you see, it *is* a very serious business."

"Hmm," Sherry said, and then asked dubiously, "And you think I am a life mate for this guy named after a spice?"

"Basil." Stephanie nodded.

"Why?" Sherry asked.

"Because I've noticed that life mates always give off the same . . ." She paused briefly, and then said, "Well, I guess the best way to describe it is energy signal or frequency. And you have the same type of energy signal or frequency as Basil."

She reached across the table suddenly and clasped Sherry's hand to get her attention. Once she was looking her in the eyes, she added, "This is big, Sherry. This is a once in a lifetime thing. I mean, I know you're upset about the whole Leo thing, and I am too. But rogues like him pop up all the time. That's why we need hunters. A life mate, though? That's like . . . epic."

"Epic, huh?" she asked with amusement.

Stephanie nodded, her expression serious. "Yes, epic. Elvi says the happiness and contentment she's found since hooking up with Victor is like nothing she's ever experienced in her life. She says it's worth waiting for."

Releasing her hand, the girl sat back and tilted her head before saying, "Mind you, Elvi said that after giving me the sex lecture, and I think she's trying to convince me not to sleep around and be a ho 'cause it could never compare anyway, but she doesn't lie to me either, so it's probably true. Besides, I've seen life mates together and been inside their thoughts and—" She grimaced and shook her head. "It's kind of sick how drenched they are in each other. Gross, really. It's like they're in heat or something."

Sherry had to bite her lip to keep from laughing.

"Anyway," she added, shaking off her disgust, "this isn't me playing cupid, or setting you up on a date. This is . . . bigger than winning the biggest lottery. A life mate is precious and . . . and there's a bunch of other stuff too," she finished with a shrug.

"Other stuff?" Sherry asked curiously.

"Yeah, like I guess life mates never cheat on each other, 'cause . . . well, no one else can compare. And the guy would cherish you to the point he'd give his life for you if he had to."

"Just the guy?" Sherry asked with amusement. "The female life mate wouldn't give her life for him?"

"Yeah, she would." The girl shrugged as if that wasn't important. "But the big deal is that the two become one. They work together like . . ." She frowned, obviously searching for a way to explain it, and then she glanced to the crusts on the paper plate and said triumphantly, "Like pizza."

Sherry peered at the remains and asked uncertainly, "Like pizza?"

"Yeah. Cheese is nice on its own, and so is pepperoni, but put them together on dough, and it's perfect pizza. Like it was created to be that way."

"Hmmm." Sherry peered down at her own slice and wondered wryly if she was the cheese or pepperoni—soft, white, and boring, or more colorful and a little spicy? She was probably the cheese, she acknowledged. She was definitely soft in places she'd rather be firm, and she'd been working long hours and barely seen the sun last summer and so was as white as could be. Yeah, she was the cheese . . . which meant this Basil guy was the spicy pepperoni. She supposed that was only fair since he'd been named after a spice.

Sherry shook her head at her own thoughts. In the midst of the chaos that had exploded into her life in the form of one Stephanie the vampire, not only was she making jokes—if only in her head—but was actually now considering this life mate business. She hated being set up on dates, and this was the ultimate setup. This guy named after a ~~spice~~ was apparently being brought to size her up as a prospective life mate. The thought made her squirm and sweat, but it also made her wonder. What would it be like to be a life mate? To have someone meant for you? Someone who fit you like pepperoni and cheese mixed on pizza? To enjoy a happiness and contentment never before experienced?

Frowning, she glanced to Stephanie. "You're sure I'm a life mate for this ~~spice~~ guy?"

"Basil," Stephanie said, and then nodded solemnly. "I'm positive."

"Hmmph," Sherry said dubiously, and then glanced to the girl again with a start when Stephanie suddenly reached out and caught her hand again.

Eyebrows rising, Sherry leaned across the table when the girl tugged, turning her head when Stephanie leaned forward to whisper, "And he's here."

Sherry stiffened, eyes going wide, and then sat back abruptly as panic rushed in to fill every crevice of her body. He was here. Crap. What if he didn't like her? What if he didn't want her for his life mate? What if he preferred redheads, or skinny chicks, or—good God, what was she even doing here? She should be back at her store checking on people and taking care of that situation, not—

Her eyes shot back to Stephanie and she asked in a hiss, "Does he know you think I'm his life mate?"

"Yes."

"Crap," Sherry muttered as the girl glanced past her

and smiled in greeting at someone obviously approaching the table.

Sherry forced herself not to look back like some spotty, eager teenager and simply sat there fighting the panic trying to overwhelm her. It was pretty strong, and for a minute she was torn between jumping up and making a run for it and ducking under the table to hide like a child . . . which was just madness. But really, the whole day had been mad so far. However, while she'd managed to remain relatively calm through the invasion of her store and the chase that had followed, Sherry feared she might actually hyperventilate over being examined as a prospective life mate. Seriously, the timing was just ridiculous, and——

Cutting off her thoughts, Sherry lowered her head, closed her eyes, and forced herself to take deep breaths. She was just starting to feel a little calmer when she sensed a presence standing at her side.

Raising her head, she automatically slid along the booth seat to make way even as Stephanie slid along the opposite booth seat. Sherry's gaze slid from the girl to the dark-haired young man now settling next to the teenager, wondering if he was this Basil person. If so, he wasn't her type. Dressed in black jeans and T-shirt with a leather jacket on, the guy looked like the stereotypical bad boy. Not her scene at all, she thought with something like relief. Stephanie was wrong, she was not a life mate to this man. But even as she began to relax, Stephanie gestured and said, "Sherry, this is Justin Bricker."

Sherry swallowed and nodded in greeting, her entire focus shifting to the heat emanating from the man now settling into the seat beside her. "And that's Basil Argeneau," Stephanie added.

Taking a deep breath, Sherry forced a smile and turned to peer at the man who was supposedly her life mate. She stared at him silently for a long moment, drinking him in.

Basil had blond hair, but golden blond, not the dirty blond of Leo and his boys. It was also cut short. The man had full lips, chiseled cheeks and chin, and the most incredible silver blue eyes she'd ever seen.

Her gaze dropped to what she could see of his body where he sat beside her, and she noted the wide shoulders under the dark, designer business suit, and that his stomach appeared super flat. But that was all she could tell with him sitting so close. It was enough. The guy was . . . well . . . jeez, he was a hotty.

"Definitely the pepperoni," she murmured.

"Excuse me?" Basil Argeneau said uncertainly.

Realizing what she'd said, Sherry flushed and shook her head. She had no intention of explaining that he was hot and spicy like Stephanie's pizza pepperoni. And he was. Certainly he was hotter than any guy she'd ever dated. This guy, though, looked younger than her thirty-two. Maybe twenty-five, she thought with concern, and then recalled Stephanie's claim that these vampires or immortals stopped aging at about twenty-five. Before she considered how rude the question might be, she blurted, "How old are you?"

His eyes widened slightly and then he simply said, "Old."

Sherry frowned at the vague answer and pressed, "Older than thirty-two?"

For some reason that made Justin Bricker snort with amusement.

When she glanced his way, he slid a cell phone out of his pocket, set it on the table and grinned at her as he suggested, "Try adding a couple of zeroes behind the thirty-two and you'll still be three hundred and forty-some years off."

Sherry frowned at the suggestion, not sure she believed him, but before she could question him on the matter, the brush of fingers along her arm made her glance quickly to Basil. His touch had sent a shiver of sensation down her arm, leaving goose bumps in its trail. Sherry unconsciously rubbed her arm in reaction and stared at him wide-eyed.

"Are you thirty-two, then?" Basil asked.

Sherry nodded.

"And you own your own store?" he asked. "A kitchenware store, I understand."

"Yes." Sherry sat a little straighter, reminding herself that she wasn't a breathless teenager, but a grown-up, successful businesswoman who had worked hard and was now reaping the rewards . . . which she got to pay half of to the government. The thought made her scowl again, which made Basil sit back slightly. Noting that, she smiled wryly and said, "Sorry. I was just thinking about my taxes."

If she had thought that would reassure him, she'd thought wrong. If anything it made him frown, and that was when Sherry realized it probably wasn't flattering to be talking to him and thinking of her taxes.

"Are you single?" she asked, to distract him from her momentary faux pas.

"Yes. You?" he asked politely.

"Mostly," she answered at once.

"Mostly?" he echoed, frowning even harder.

"Well, it's . . . I've been dating a guy, but it's just casual; dinner, a movie, the occasional business function. We aren't exclusive or anything," she assured him.

Basil nodded solemnly. "I am."

"You are what?" she asked uncertainly.

"Exclusive."

It was a simple word, but somehow carried the finality of a judge's gavel. Sherry was trying to sort out what it meant exactly, and how she should respond, when a chime sounded from the phone Justin had set on the table. She glanced his way as he picked it up.

He thumbed the screen, and then stood, saying, "Well, kids. You'll have to finish this 'get to know you' thing in the SUV. Nicholas says the street is clear at the moment and we have to get you out of here before Leo and his boys come back around."

Sherry glanced to Stephanie and then to Basil as he stood, noting the hand he was holding out to help her up. So gentlemanly, Sherry thought. She took the offered hand, startled by the tingle it sent through her fingers and up her arm. The man seemed to be full of static electricity. Probably didn't use Bounce in the dryer, she thought absently as he released her hand to take her elbow and usher her toward the front door of the pizza joint.

Sherry glanced over her shoulder as they went, relieved to see that Stephanie was right behind them with Justin on her heels. Sherry had started out trying to keep the girl safe, but suddenly felt like she was in over her head and Stephanie was the only lifeline she had. Weird.

"Here we are."

Sherry turned forward again as Basil urged her out of the pizzeria and to the back door of an SUV illegally parked in front of it. She allowed him to usher her inside, and busied herself doing up her seat belt before she risked looking at him again. He'd settled next to her and was buckling up as well, so she glanced to the front of the vehicle where Stephanie was doing the same in the passenger seat.

"Do we know if everyone was okay at the store?" she asked no one in particular as Justin Bricker got into the driver's seat.

"My daughter and Drina were headed there to take care of matters," Basil announced quietly. "They'll report when they are done, but I'm sure everyone is fine."

Sherry stared at him blankly. "Your daughter?"

"Katricia," he explained.

"Katricia who's getting married?" Sherry asked slowly.

He nodded and smiled faintly. "She met her life mate at Christmas."

"Teddy, the police chief where Stephanie lives," Sherry said, recalling the girl's earlier words.

"Yes." He smiled. "She's settled in Port Henry with him and helping him police the town."

"Right," Sherry murmured, but she was trying to wrap her mind around the fact that this man—who looked no more than twenty-five—had a daughter old enough to marry anyone. She didn't care what Justin had said about adding two zeroes and so on, this man *looked* twenty-five. Clearing her throat, she asked, "And how old is your daughter?"

He paused and squinted toward the roof of the SUV briefly. "Well, let's see. She was born in 411 AD, so that makes her—"

"What?" Sherry squawked with amazement.

Basil blinked and glanced to her with surprise.

Forcing herself back to calm, she asked uncertainly, "You're kidding, right?"

"No," he said apologetically.

"Right." Sherry peered out the window. 411 AD. So if she got together with Basil, she'd have a stepdaughter who was . . . what? Sixteen hundred and some years old? Cripes. This was crazy.

"Do you have any children?"

"Good God, no!" Sherry blurted, jerking around in her seat to look at him with horror at the very suggestion. She wasn't married, for heaven's sake. Although, she supposed that wasn't necessary for having a child nowadays, but the very idea of having children was terrifying to her. She spent most of her time at the store, working ridiculously long hours. She couldn't imagine trying to raise a child, let alone more than one, with the schedule she kept. Maybe someday . . . when things were more settled . . .

Sighing, she shook her head and decided a change of

subject was in order. "So how did you get named after a spice?"

Basil's lips quirked with amusement. "Stephanie mispronounced it. My name is Basil," he said, pronouncing it Baw-zil.

"Sorry," Steph said from the front seat. "Katricia always just refers to you as Father. It was Cheetah who told me your name. I guess he mispronounced it."

"Cheetah?" Sherry peered at her curiously.

"An American Enforcer who was delivering something or other to Mortimer," Stephanie explained, and then glanced to Basil and added, "I don't think he mispronounced your name on purpose. He's from Cleveland. All of his *a*'s are pretty nasal."

When Basil merely nodded and then turned his attention back to her, Sherry forced a smile and said, "So it's Baw-zil, not Bay-sil?"

Basil nodded. "It's short for Basileios."

A car horn honked as he spoke, and she wasn't sure she'd heard right. Tilting her head, she asked, "Bellicose?"

"No, not 'bellicose,'" he said with a chuckle. "That is a temperament not a name. My name is Basileios." He spoke slowly and loudly this time to be sure she heard.

"Basileios," Sherry murmured, and then pursed her lips briefly as the name tickled her memory. "So you weren't named after a spice, but some big snake from Harry Potter? Nice."

He blinked. "A snake? What the devil are you talking about?"

"I think she's getting *Basileios* mixed up with *basi-*

lisk," Stephanie said helpfully, turning in the front seat to grin at them.

"Basilisk, right," Sherry said with a smile, and then shrugged. "They sound very similar."

"They are *not* similar," he said grimly. "My name is 'Baw-sill-ee-os.'"

"Well, you said it fast the first time and it sounded kind of like 'basilisk,'" she said apologetically.

"It did kind of, didn't it?" Stephanie agreed.

"It did not," Basileios said indignantly.

Feeling herself relax a bit, Sherry teased, "Well, if you're going to go and get all bellicose about it, maybe we should just go with the spice and call you 'Bay-sil' after all," she said, pronouncing it like the spice. And then she whispered, "Or Pep."

Apparently, he had excellent hearing. Expression blank, he asked, "Pep?"

"Short for *pepperoni*," she explained with embarrassment.

"As in you're the pepperoni in her pizza," Stephanie said, and burst out laughing.

Basileios stared from one to the other blankly, and then asked Stephanie, "You're quite sure this woman is my match? There is no mistake?"

Stephanie laughed even harder at the question, but Sherry wrinkled her nose at the man. "Be nice, spice boy. I woke up this morning on earth. Five hours later I've stepped into the twilight zone. Cut me some slack here. I was just teasing you to let off a little steam."

"Hmmm," he murmured, and then allowed his eyes

to rake down over her figure as he offered, "There are many much more pleasant ways to let off steam."

Sherry went completely still as images of some of those more pleasant ways suddenly flashed through her mind. They were hot and sweaty flashes of them naked, her head thrown back, neck exposed as his mouth and hands traveled over her naked body.

Cripes, the flashes were so real it was like they were doing it right then. Sherry's body actually responded as such, her breathing becoming low and shallow. Much to her dismay, her nipples even hardened and liquid pooled low in her belly and then rushed down to dampen her panties.

Flushing bright red, she shifted uncomfortably in her seat and then turned to peer steadfastly out the window as she tried to banish the images and her body's reaction to them.

Jeez, she'd never experienced anything like that before. She just wasn't the sort to have sexual fantasies about a virtual stranger. Heck, she'd never even had such powerful imaginings about anyone she ever dated. Truth be told, she hadn't known it was possible to turn yourself on with just a thought. And having them now, in the backseat of an SUV, with Stephanie, Justin, and Basil there . . . well. it was just embarrassing as all hell. It made her glad Stephanie couldn't read her thoughts. She hoped Basil and Justin couldn't either.

Sherry didn't get to worry over that long. Her eye was caught by a mane of dirty blond hair amid the pedestrians they were passing. Focusing, she recognized the man Stephanie had called Leonius. Surrounded by his boys, he was moving through a crowd just starting to cross the street, walking in the same direction they were driving. Even as she recognized him and thought his name, the man turned his head in their direction as if she'd called out to him. His eye caught Sherry's, and her heart stopped as recognition flared in his expression. Then the SUV turned right, away from him, and he was out of her line of vision.

Her breath suddenly caught in her chest, Sherry craned around in her seat as much as her seat belt allowed and sought out the man again, this time through the back window of the SUV. She immediately wished she hadn't when she saw him move to the first car stopped at the light behind them. Pulling the front door open, he dragged the driver out. His men were right there with him, opening the other doors and pulling out the passengers, in order to get in themselves. All but one passenger, she saw, as a woman tried to follow the others out of the vehicle's backseat but was forced back inside by the man with the ponytail, who slid in beside her. Then another of the men got in on the other side, trapping the woman.

"We have company," Basil said quietly beside her.

"I see him," Justin responded grimly, his eyes on the rearview mirror.

"That poor woman," Stephanie said unhappily, and Sherry glanced around to see that, like her, the girl was also staring out the back window of the SUV.

"Nicholas is behind them," Justin said as a dark SUV like the one they were in turned onto their street from the road they had come from. She guessed Nicholas had been watching and following for just this reason.

"Will he be able to save the woman in the car?" Sherry asked with concern even as she noted that there were two people in the SUV. The person in the passenger seat of Nicholas's SUV was a woman who appeared to have a phone in her hand. Justin's phone began to chime as Sherry saw the woman raise the phone to her ear.

"Jo?" Justin said, and Sherry glanced over her shoulder as he added, "Hang on. You're on speaker. Let me turn that off."

He picked up his phone, which he'd apparently set on the console between the front seats, hit a button, and then placed the phone to his ear. "Go ahead."

Sherry's mouth tightened. She wasn't stupid, and doubted it was Stephanie or Basil he was concerned about overhearing both sides of the conversation. *She* was the reason he was taking the call off speakerphone. That could only mean he didn't think she'd like what was said.

"Yeah. I see them," Justin said. "No. I know we can't lead them back to the house."

Sherry turned again, to peer back at the vehicles behind them as she listened to the one-sided conversation. But she returned her gaze to Justin when he said with interest, "A trap? Yeah, that could work. Call Mortimer and have any of our people in the area head this way. He— Shit."

Sherry turned back to the road behind them in time to see the car Leo had hijacked suddenly veer off down a side street. The second SUV, with Nicholas driving, immediately followed, as their own SUV slowed. For a moment Sherry thought Justin was going to turn around and follow the hijacked car too, but then he grunted something into the phone and picked up speed again, the SUV continuing in the direction they'd been headed.

"They're going to follow him and see if they can corner the bastard," Justin announced, tossing the phone onto the console again.

No one commented, and Sherry settled back in her seat and simply glanced from person to person in the SUV. They were all silent, seeming lost in their thoughts. They were also all grim-faced, and Sherry suspected she was as well. This Leonius person was a scary dude. She was glad he'd turned off, away from them, but was now worried about the poor unknown woman who had been trapped in the other car. She hoped Nicholas and Jo could help her.

Three

"Ah crap."

Sherry glanced curiously to Stephanie at those muttered words. They had driven through gates with armed guards just moments ago, wended their way up a long snaking driveway, and were now pulling up in front of a large house. Sherry had been gaping over the size of the building, but now noted Stephanie's pained expression and followed her gaze to the front door and the man who had just stepped outside. He was blond like Basil, but his hair was more platinum than golden. He was also tall, and well built in the tight jeans and T-shirt he wore. His features were similar to Basil's, and like him, he was attractive, or could have been if his expression hadn't been so grim. He looked mean.

"Who's that?" she asked curiously.

"My brother, Lucian," Basil said quietly.

"Oh," Sherry murmured, understanding Stephanie's

reaction to seeing the man. She'd said Lucian would rake her over the coals once Drina and Katricia got done giving her hell, and she supposed this meant Lucian's raking her over the coals would come first. But it made her wonder what his relationship was to Stephanie. Victor was her adopted father, but she hadn't stated who Lucian was.

Sherry was still trying to work out the relationship when Justin drew to a halt and they all unbuckled to get out. Stephanie dragged her feet somewhat, obviously not eager to face the man. Sherry was following Basil out of the back before the girl even managed to open her door. The same protective instinct that had claimed her back at her store made Sherry move up beside the teenager now as she got out, offering her silent support.

Stephanie gave her a weak smile of gratitude and then faced Lucian and blurted, "I know. I messed up. But I just nipped out to the car to grab my phone while Drina and Katricia were in the changing room. And I had no idea Leo was in town. I thought he was down south and it would be okay. If I'd known, I never would have left the shop, even for a minute. I swear. I don't want to land in Leo's clutches again. Ever."

Sherry bit her lip and peered from Stephanie's anxious face to the man named Lucian as silence dropped around them. Her gaze then slid to Justin and Basil. Both men stood silent and still, watching Lucian. In fact, no one was moving, herself included. It was as if the man had pinned them all to the spot with some secret super power. Certainly, she didn't have any desire to move and draw his attention. So they waited what seemed an interminable amount of time and then the front door opened and a petite brunette stepped out of the house and slid her hand through one of Lucian's crossed arms.

"Aren't you going to introduce me to Basil's life mate?" the newcomer asked, and it was the most amazing thing . . . Lucian relaxed so abruptly it was like a marionette's strings being snipped. His shoulders dropped, his arms uncrossed so that he could slip one around the woman, and he turned his head and bent to press a kiss to her forehead. He seemed almost like a different man when he turned back to the four waiting people.

"Inside," he said quietly to Stephanie.

The girl nodded, relief oozing off of her in waves as she leapt past the couple with a grateful glance at the brunette and hurried inside.

Sherry watched her go, feeling abandoned . . . and how pathetic was that? Stephanie was a teenager. She was the adult. Sherry had been very conscious of that on first meeting the kid, and had to wonder how the tables had turned and she'd begun to depend on the girl. Well, that would end now. She was a grown-up successful businesswoman. There was nothing she couldn't handle, she told herself, and then jumped when Lucian barked her name.

"Sherrilyn Harlow Carne?"

Turning sharply to the couple on the steps, Sherry met his gaze as he announced, "This is my wife, Leigh Argeneau."

She offered her hand to the other woman. "Call me

Sherry. I've only ever been called Sherrilyn Harlow Carne by my mother and that was when I was in trouble."

Leigh chuckled and took her hand in a warm grasp. "Sherry it is."

"Yes. You aren't the one in trouble," Lucian announced dryly as the two women shook.

Leigh rolled her eyes at the words and smiled wryly. "Ignore him. We're new parents, so we aren't getting a lot of sleep at the moment. It makes him cranky."

"Yeah, that's what it is. Lack of sleep due to the babies," Justin said with a snort as he moved past them. "'Cause Lucian was just a big huggie bear before that."

When Sherry glanced curiously to the man disappearing into the house, Basil said helpfully, "Lucian is always cranky."

Much to her surprise, when Sherry then glanced worriedly to Lucian to see how he was taking the announcement, he was nodding with agreement and apparent satisfaction. She gathered he was proud of his crankiness.

"Don't mind Lucian," Leigh said lightly. "He just acts all growly and mean around the boys to keep them in line. He's really a marshmallow."

Now it was Basil who snorted.

Leigh wrinkled her nose at the man, and then took Sherry's arm to urge her into the house, saying, "Come, I'll make some tea and we'll get to know each other. We're going to be sisters-in-law."

"Oh, that's not—I mean, I—We—" Sherry stammered helplessly as Leigh led her inside. She fell silent when Leigh patted her hand sympathetically.

"It's a lot to take in, I know. But it's best not to fight it. The nanos are never wrong."

Sherry had no idea what she was talking about when she said nanos, but merely released a sound that was embarrassingly reminiscent of a whimper and fell silent.

"Well?"

Basil tore his eyes from Sherry's disappearing derriere to glance at his brother and raised an eyebrow in question. "Well what?"

"Is she or is she not your life mate?" Lucian asked at once.

Basileios grimaced. "How the hell should I know? I just met the woman."

Lucian scowled. "Did you try to read her?"

"Of course," he said irritably, moving forward to enter the house.

"And?" Lucian asked, following and pulling the door closed.

"I cannot read her," Basil admitted, but added quickly, "Neither could Stephanie, though, so that might not mean anything." He paused in the entry and turned back to Lucian. "Could you read her?"

"Of course," the man said, as if that should be expected. "She takes some effort, though. I suspect she's been around an immortal for long periods of time in her past and gained some natural skills at blocking our thoughts.

Basil nodded. That happened to mortals who spent a lot of time around immortals, even if they didn't know about immortals and that they were in their presence. Their minds unconsciously sensed the probing, and they eventually, instinctively, learned to build up mental walls to block the intrusion. It made him curious, though, as to who the immortal was that Sherry might have been around.

"Try to read her again," Lucian said, distracting him from the question. The words weren't a suggestion. Neither were the orders that followed when he said, "And test the other symptoms too; food and so on. I need to know if she is or is not your life mate before I decide what to do about her."

Basil merely nodded.

"What?" Lucian asked with amusement. "No arguing or telling me to stop bossing you around?"

Basil smiled faintly. He usually did rebel when Lucian tried to boss him around. It was why he was a member of the North American council. People trusted he wouldn't just bow to his brother's bullying. It was also why he lived in New York. He was far enough away not to have to deal with his brother's bossiness too often, but close enough to see the family on special occasions and to fly in for emergency council meetings between the regular council meetings.

"Why bother arguing with you when it is exactly what I want to do anyway?" Basil responded. He then turned to head for the kitchens, eager to see Sherry again.

"This is Sam. She's Mortimer's life mate and a lawyer like Basil," Leigh announced, urging Sherry to one of the stools around the island in the large, bright white kitchen.

"Hi," Sherry said with a smile as the slender redhead at the stove set the lid back on a simmering pot and turned to greet them.

"Hi back," Sam said, wiping her hands on a dish towel before offering it with a warm smile of her own. As they shook hands, she said, "I hear you've had a bit of an ordeal. I'm sorry about that. Leonius has been a problem for a while now. Hopefully the boys will corner and catch him this time."

A snort from the end of the room drew Sherry's attention to the fact that Justin Bricker had his head in the refrigerator as he rummaged around for something.

"Not bloody likely," the man announced as he straightened with a bag of blood in hand. "Leo's a slippery bastard. He pops up in one place just long enough to get everyone rushing there, then disappears and pops up somewhere hundreds of miles away. Hell, the day before yesterday he was supposedly spotted in Florida. Today he's here. Tomorrow he'll be in Mexico."

"Is that true?" Sherry asked with a frown, watching Justin wave the bag of blood around as he spoke.

"I'm afraid so," Leigh admitted quietly.

"Yeah." Sam sighed. "Leo's crazy but smart. He never stays anywhere long. Sometimes he isn't even spotted, just his handiwork tells us he's been somewhere."

"*If* it's his handiwork," Justin said heavily. "He has a lot of sons, remember. And they aren't always with him. I'm guessing they cause some grief on their own and add to the myth that is Leonius Livius."

"Yeah," Sam said again, then shook her head and turned to hang the dish towel over the stove handle, saying, "But enough of this depressing talk. Sherry doesn't need to hear it. Her day has been rough enough. It's change-of-topic time." Turning back, she asked brightly, "So you're Basil's life mate?"

"Oh, I don't—" Sherry began weakly, relieved when Leigh patted her arm reassuringly and spoke up.

"She hasn't quite accepted that yet, Sam. You recall how hard it is at the start."

"Oh yeah," Sam said wryly and shook her head as she admitted, "I resisted like crazy, made Mortimer's life a living hell without intending to. Made my own life hell too, actually. It only got better when I gave in and went with it, but it took a bit to get me to that point."

"You were more than worth the wait."

Sherry blinked and glanced to the man who had entered the kitchen. Tall, with blond hair that had dark tips suggesting it had once been dyed brown, the man walked to Sam and slid his arms around her, and then pressed a kiss to her lips. Sherry supposed he must be Mortimer.

Straightening, Mortimer then glanced to Justin to say, "The dogs need to be fed before they're let out. Can you see to that for me?"

When the other man nodded and left the room, Mortimer glanced back to Sam and said, "Something smells good."

"I found a recipe online for that cheese and beer soup you liked so much when we went out to dinner last week. I'm making up a batch," Sam said with a grin.

"Really?" Mortimer asked with pleasant surprise.

"Yeah," Sam grinned.

"God I love you," he breathed and kissed her again, this time with enough passion that Sherry would have looked away if she'd been able. But her eyes seemed locked on the couple. At least they were until the sound of footsteps drew her attention to the door as Basil led Lucian into the room.

"You're with Basil," Lucian announced, spearing Sherry with his eyes. "The two of you have issues to sort, and the rest of us have some business to discuss, so go."

The man was definitely lacking in the communication department, Sherry decided, but then Basil held out his hand, and she forgot all about his brother as she moved to him like a moth drawn to flame.

Seriously, all he had to do was hold out his hand and she went like a whipped dog? Sherry would have been annoyed with herself except that Basil's warm clasp distracted her.

"Would you like to go to the living room and talk? Or shall we walk around outside?" Basil asked as he led her from the kitchen.

"Outside," Sherry decided, not sure what he wanted to talk about, but suspecting it was this life mate business. If so, she really didn't want this discussion to take place where someone could overhear.

Basileios nodded and led her along the hall to a back door and then ushered her outside.

Sherry glanced around curiously as he pulled the door closed behind them. The long driveway had told her it was a large property, but she was still surprised to see that it appeared to extend behind the house for quite a distance. The backyard was large and well treed. It was bordered on one side by woods and on the other by the driveway, and then she saw more yard followed by more woods.

Sherry eyed the driveway curiously, following it to a large outbuilding a good distance behind the house. The building appeared only to be one floor, but it was wider than the house itself, with several garage doors taking up more than half of it.

Basileios took her arm and urged her in the direction of the outbuilding.

Sherry, sure he'd brought her out here to discuss this life mate nonsense, waited patiently for him to begin. Unfortunately, he didn't appear eager to touch on the subject, or any subject for that matter. He didn't say anything at all as they walked, and before she could dredge up the courage to say something herself, they'd reached the outbuilding.

"I thought it might be best to introduce you to the dogs," Basileios explained, opening the door for her. "That way they will recognize you as a welcome guest when they are patrolling the yard."

Sherry's eyes widened at the suggestion, thinking it a good one. The last thing she wanted was a bunch of guard dogs to think she was an interloper and attack her.

He led her past an empty office, and then urged her down a hallway to the left. They passed through another door into a hall with what appeared to be jail cells running up either side.

"Rogues are held here until they are judged by the council," Basileios explained quietly as they passed the cells.

Sherry nodded, but wondered what council he was talking about. She didn't ask, however. Her curiosity had been caught by the murmur of a male voice from up ahead. It was accompanied by a sound she didn't recognize until Basileios commented, "It must be feeding time."

She realized then that it was the sound of dry dog food being poured into metal dishes and smiled faintly. "Yes. Mortimer sent Justin out to feed the dogs just before you and Lucian came into the kitchen."

Basileios nodded, and a moment later they reached the door of a small room where a man had lined up four metal dog dishes on a counter and was just finishing filling the last one. It wasn't Justin, however, Sherry saw with surprise as the dark-haired man glanced their way and offered a smile of greeting and a friendly "Hi."

"Hello Francis," Basileios responded. "Where is Justin? We expected to find him here."

The man shrugged. "I don't know. He left after passing on Mortimer's order for me to feed the dogs. I thought he went back to the house, but maybe he went to check on Russell at the gate."

Basileios nodded slowly, a small frown tugging at his lips, and then stepped forward to take two of the bowls the man had just filled. "You go ahead and get back to the gate. I shall take these in to the dogs. I wanted to introduce Sherry to them anyway."

Francis hesitated, but when Sherry picked up the

other two bowls, he nodded and headed for the door. "Thanks. If they aren't done eating when you're ready to leave, just give me a buzz at the gate and I'll come back and let them out."

"We will let them out," Basileios assured him as he led Sherry to a door at the side of the room. "These fellows do not take long to eat, as I recall. They will gobble this up in no time."

"Yeah, they will," Francis agreed on a chuckle, and slipped from the room.

"These are trained animals," Basileios warned Sherry, pausing at the door to turn back to her. "Do not try to pet them or—"

"No touch, no talk, no eye contact," Sherry interrupted with amusement, and informed him, "I'm a big fan of *Dog Whisperer*."

Basileios smiled faintly. "Well, I do not have a clue who that is, but he knows his business if those are his instructions."

"Oh, yeah, the guy's a genius with dogs," Sherry assured him.

"Hmm." Basileios turned back to the door and shifted one bowl on top of the other to free up a hand to work the doorknob. He then pushed the door open and led her into a large room with four kennels along the end, each with its own doggy door to the outside. "Just set the bowls in front of the doors. I shall open them after we have set them all down."

Sherry did as instructed, positioning herself close to but sideways to each door as she set down the food so that each animal could smell her. While she didn't look directly at either of the dogs, she did take quick surreptitious glances to see what they were. She wasn't terribly surprised to find that they were German shepherds.

Having set down both bowls, Sherry moved to stand beside Basileios, who had finished setting down his own bowls ahead of her. She then watched him push a button beside the light switch. All four doors on the kennels immediately rose as one, loosing the dogs. Sherry half expected them to charge out and rush around her, sniffing like mad at this new human in their midst, but the dogs were definitely well trained. Each animal stepped forward and then sat down in front of their dish before turning to peer at Basileios for permission.

"Go ahead," he said, and only then did they start to eat.

"Do they stay in here all day?" Sherry asked with a frown as she watched them eat. They were so well behaved it was almost scary. They were like furry soldiers under the watchful eye of their sergeant.

"No. I gather they spend the day in the house or out in the yard with Sam. That, or they follow Mortimer around, but he puts them in here for half an hour before dinnertime. Then they are fed and sent out to patrol the yard. Mortimer claims that the half hour in here beforehand helps them adjust from being spoiled house dogs to knowing it's time to work."

"Spoiled house dogs, huh?" Sherry asked with amusement, watching the dogs in question. They didn't seem spoiled at all.

"Oh yes, Mortimer says Sam is ruining them," Basileios said with a grin. "Apparently, they listen to her over him now, which annoys him no end."

Sherry chuckled and continued to watch the dogs eat, but her mind turned to the issue of this life mate business . . . as well as the fact that Basileios hadn't brought it up yet. It was the big pink elephant in the room and it was beginning to drive her a little crazy. So much so that after several moments had passed, she glanced to Basileios and blurted, "So, are we life mates or what?"

Basileios looked briefly startled and then smiled wryly. "You like the subtle approach, I see."

"Yeah." Sherry grimaced. "And here you probably thought I was the type to stomp about a subject like a bull in a china shop."

"Never," he assured her with a grin.

"Hmmm." She peered at him silently, and then raised her eyebrows. "So?"

"So," Basil murmured, his eyes skating over her before his lips twisted and he admitted, "I do not know."

That made her frown. "Stephanie said something about our having the same energy signature or something, but I haven't a clue what she's talking about. Is there another way to tell?"

"There are symptoms," he acknowledged.

"Like what?" she asked.

"Like not being able to read or control each other," Basil offered.

Sherry blinked several times and then frowned. "But Stephanie said she couldn't read or control me."

He merely nodded like that was no big deal, but Sherry was considering this with mounting alarm.

"Jeez. That doesn't mean I'm her life mate, does it? She doesn't think that, does she? 'Cause if so, she's going to be sorely disappointed. I am so not into girls. I mean, sure I've kissed one when drunk, but that's the limit of my experimentation in that area. I'm not into anything else. I like the cock."

Sherry realized what she was saying only as those words left her lips and it was far too late to call them back. Even worse, Basileios had definitely not missed them. His eyes had gone as wide as saucers and his lower jaw was nearly on the ground. Closing her eyes, Sherry pressed her hands to her suddenly hot cheeks and groaned, then opened her eyes and began to babble like the idiot she was.

"Sorry. One of the boys who works for me has a T-shirt that says that. Though I think it actually says, 'I love the cock,' not 'I like it.' And it has an arrow pointing to the side, which I just don't get because it's not like there's one floating in the air beside him . . . well, unless he has like a seven-foot boyfriend stand-ing beside him," she added with a frown, then shook her head and continued, "Besides he also has a T-shirt claiming he's the Vagina Fan Club President, so he's either bicurious or I'm not getting the meaning of the cock T-shirt."

A choked sound came from Basileios when she dared to pause briefly, and Sherry quickly added, "Of course, he doesn't wear them while working. He just wears them into work and changes before starting his shift. I would never let one of my employees wear a shirt like that on the floor. Heck, normally I wouldn't even ever *say* something like that. It's just been such a crazy day and I really think maybe my brain has been taxed beyond its limit by everything that's happened, and jeez I hope it doesn't mean there's something wrong with me that I said I like the cock, and not that I love it like the T-shirt says. I didn't mean—"

Sherry stopped her babbling abruptly when Basileios slapped his hand over her mouth. He didn't do it violently, but his hand was suddenly covering her mouth, preventing her from speaking, and really, she was grateful to the bottom of her heart that he did. Her words were still echoing in her own ears and making her cringe, and honestly, she had no idea why she'd said any of it. Maybe she was being controlled, she thought hopefully.

"I am very glad that you like . . . . men," Basil said carefully, "rather than females. Thank you for sharing that with me. However, the fact that Stephanie cannot read or control you does not necessarily mean you are a possible life mate for her. Some mortals are simply harder to read than others, either because of some physical ailment, or madness, or because—"

Sherry's eyes had widened as he spoke, but now she pushed his hand away. "You think I'm crazy?"

"What?" he asked with surprise. "No, of course not."

"Then I'm sick?" she asked with a frown.

"No," he assured her, patting her arm. "No, I am sure you are fine. I suspect you have unwittingly spent a great deal of time in the company of an immortal and have gained some natural skills in blocking our efforts to read your thoughts."

"Seriously?" she asked with surprise.

"Yes, seriously," he assured her, and then added, "Besides, Stephanie is young yet and she is used to being able to read everyone. She may have given reading you a cursory try and stopped when she encountered the first bit of blocking."

Sherry nodded absently, but wasn't really paying attention. She was now running through a list in her head of everyone she had ever known, trying to sort out who might have been an immortal. But she set aside that effort for later when Basil announced, "Lucian can read you."

Those words were enough to alarm her and make her try to remember what she'd been thinking while in Lucian's presence.

"And my being only a couple years younger than him, I should be able to as well," Basil continued, distracting her from that worry as well, and then he acknowledged, "But I cannot."

Sherry let her breath out on a slow sigh, unsure whether she should be happy about that.

"And that is usually enough to make it pretty certain we are life mates," he continued. "However, Stephanie's not being able to read or control you either does make that a little less conclusive . . . at least in my mind. Fortunately, there are other symptoms to help figure out if you are my life mate."

"Like what?" she asked curiously, thinking the man definitely talked like a lawyer.

"Well, after a while, immortals grow tired of food and other pleasures and refrain from them except on special occasions and family gatherings," he explained. "The arrival of a life mate can reawaken those hungers."

Sherry nodded. Stephanie had already told her that. Tilting her head, she asked, "And are you hungry?"

Basil grimaced. "Not yet, but I have not really encountered food with you either . . . unless you count dog food, which I do not."

"No, I don't think dog food counts," Sherry agreed with amusement, and then glanced down as she felt a nudge at her leg. Two of the dogs were done eating and had come to investigate. They were sniffing her lower legs with interest. Her gaze slid to the other two dogs as they both finished and came to join their friends. "It looks like they're done. Why don't we let them out and then go back to the house and see if food gets your interest?"

Basil nodded, his shoulders relaxing, and it was only then she realized he'd been a bit tense. She wondered about that because the feel she was getting off of him was a completely calm, mellow vibe. In fact, it was that vibe that had helped her relax so swiftly with him. Now it seemed he wasn't as relaxed about this situation as she'd thought. According to Stephanie, finding a life mate was epic, so if this was his excitement, the guy was a walking tranquilizer . . . . She liked it, Sherry thought as she followed him to the door, the dogs on her heels. She could do with a little tranquility in her life.

They were walking back up the hall when the first dog nudged her right hand, scooping his nose under it in invitation. Sherry gave him, or her, a quick pet as she walked, and then did the same to the dog on her left when that one nudged her as well. She supposed that meant she'd been accepted by the pack, which was a good thing. She didn't want to be nervous around these beautiful animals. Not that she planned to stay long, but walking out to a car when it was time to leave would be nerve-wracking if the dogs hadn't decided to like her.

The minute Basil opened the door, the dogs dropped back behind Sherry to let her exit first. They then followed, but stayed close until Basil said, "Go ahead. Guard."

All four dogs took off at once, headed around the house toward the front of it.

"Do they all guard the front yard only?" Sherry asked curiously as he closed the door to the outbuilding and ushered her away.

"No. They are probably heading up to the gate to greet Francis and Russell before they start their rounds," Basil explained, taking her arm and turning her toward the house. "Now let's go see if I have a sudden interest in food."

Four

"**W**hat is that god-awful smell?" Basil had just opened the back door of the house, and the most horrendous smell he'd encountered in a long time slapped him in the face as he did.

"What? I don't . . . Oh," Sherry said as the scent apparently reached her. She wrinkled her nose and said, "Something's burning."

"Yes," Basil agreed, hurrying for the kitchen, where the odor seemed to be coming from. He rushed into the room, surprised to find it empty, and then paused, and peered around trying to find the source of the smell. The scent so drenched the air it was hard to tell what was causing it. He'd expected to find the room on fire.

"The soup," Sherry said, pushing past him to get to the stove. She turned off the burner and quickly picked up the pot, intending to shift it to a cool burner, but just as quickly dropped it back down with a yowl of pain.

"Here." Basil was immediately at her side, urging her to the sink to run cold water over her hands. The pot had been hot, he guessed.

"It's all right, they aren't burned," she assured him, but didn't fight his putting her hands under the tap. "It just hurt and surprised me."

Basil nodded and patted her arm. He then moved to take care of the pot himself, saying, "Still, keep them under the water for a minute or two to be sure."

He moved the pot as she'd intended to do, wrinkling his nose with disgust at the stench coming off of it. The soup had smelled quite good when he entered the kitchen earlier, but now . . . Basil shuddered at the thought of anyone trying to eat it. Finished with the pot, he moved to the windows and began opening them to allow the smell out.

"How are your hands?" he asked as he worked.

"Good," Sherry assured him, and he heard the water shut off. "A little tender but that will go away."

Basil glanced over his shoulder as she finished drying her hands with a dish towel and leaned to open the windows above the sink to help him out.

"There," Sherry said a moment later when every window was open. "Hopefully the smell will leave quickly."

Basil nodded and hoped she was right. Immortals had a better sense of smell than mortals and this was just horrible to him.

"Oh no!"

That cry came from Sam as she rushed into the kitchen and hurried to her soup. "Damn," she cursed, grabbing a large spoon and checking the bottom of the pot before sagging with defeat.

"Maybe we can save it," Sherry said sympathetically as she moved to the woman's side.

"No, there's an inch of burnt crud on the bottom," Sam said unhappily. "The flavor will be all through the soup." Sighing, she set the spoon on the counter and carried the pot to the sink. As she poured the soup down the garbage disposal, she shook her head and muttered, "I only stepped away for a minute to go to the bathroom, but then little Gemma started crying and I stopped to check on her. Leigh came in then and I was about to come back down, but of course then Luka started fussing too and . . ." She shook her head helplessly. "The next thing I knew a really bad smell was drifting into the room. God, it stinks, doesn't it?"

Sherry smiled crookedly as the woman waved her hand in front of her face, but didn't want to insult her by agreeing. It did smell, though. To change the subject, she asked, "Who are Gemma and Luka?"

"They are Leigh and Lucian's babies," Basil explained, leaning against the counter next to her. "They are twins and their birth was part of the reason I came up for a visit. It gave me an excuse to visit Katricia without her thinking I was checking on her."

"Ah," Sherry said with amusement. "But you were? Checking on her I mean."

"Of course. I am a father," he said with a shrug.

Sherry smiled and then glanced back to Sam. Seeing the slouch to her shoulders and her unhappy expression as she ran the garbage disposal, Sherry patted her back sympathetically. "It smelled amazing the first time I came into the kitchen. I bet it tasted even better. I'll help you make more if you want."

Sam grimaced as she turned off the garbage disposal and tap. "I don't have the ingredients to make more. Well, I have the beer, I only used one of them in the recipe, but I don't have any cheese, or cream or . . ." She shrugged with disgust and dumped soap into the black-bottomed pot, and then began to run hot water into it. "I guess it's pizza again tonight."

Basil saw alarm cross Sherry's face, and then she moved to the refrigerator saying, "There must be something here to— Holy crap!"

Curious, Basil moved over to see what had brought that reaction. Sherry had the fridge door open but was standing in the opening, gaping at the contents, so he had to move up behind her and peer over her shoulder. He winced when he saw that aside from milk, butter, and one wilted celery stalk, the fridge held only a six pack of beer with one missing, and bags and bags of blood.

"Sorry," Sam said with a grimace. "Tonight is grocery shopping night. I usually go to the twenty-four-hour metro at around midnight to avoid lines. Besides, Mortimer likes to go with me and he's so not a morning person." She glanced around and added, "Justin is constantly eating. It makes it hard to keep food in this place, but there are some frozen meals in the freezer if you're hungry and don't want to wait for pizza."

When Sherry glanced his way in question, Basileios shook his head. "The smell has completely killed any possibility of my wanting food, but if you are hungry . . ."

Sighing, she shook her head and closed the door. "I'm not hungry. I had a couple bites of pizza at the restaurant. This was just to see if—" She broke off with a self-conscious glance toward Sam, and then asked in a near whisper, "Are there other ways to know?"

All immortals had superior hearing, so Basil wasn't surprised when Sam asked absently, "To know what?"

Sherry bit her lip and met his gaze briefly, and then admitted, "To know if he's my life mate . . . or if I'm his, I guess."

"Oh." Sam winced. "I suppose this has put a wrinkle in the enjoying food test, huh?"

"I fear so," Basileios said gently.

Sam nodded. "Well, then there's always the shared pleasure bit."

"Shared pleasure?" Sherry asked curiously. "What's that?"

Sam opened her mouth, closed it, blushed, then quickly dried her hands, murmuring, "I think I'll let Basil explain it to you, or show you. That's really more effective anyway. I'll leave you two alone."

Sherry stared after her with surprise when the woman rushed from the room. When she then turned to peer at him, Basil smiled weakly.

Clearing his throat, he began, "Food is not the only pleasure we lose interest in over time. Sex too, becomes . . . er . . . boring?"

"Boring?" Her eyebrows rose at this news. "You're

kidding, right? I mean Stephanie mentioned something about life mates making sex mind-blowing, but—"

"Even sex grows boring after several centuries," he assured her solemnly.

"No way! Sex is awesome," Sherry said with a laugh, and then added, "You must have been doing it wrong."

Basil stiffened slightly at the diagnosis, but then noted the twinkle in her eyes and realized she was teasing him again. He was beginning to recognize when she was, he noted, and found that fact reassuring. Even so, he answered her seriously. "Skill has nothing to do with it. All immortals eventually grow tired of it after a time. However, meeting a life mate stimulates a renewed interest in that just as it does food."

"Wow," Sherry breathed, and for a moment he thought she was amazed at what he'd just said . . . and she was, just not in the way he'd thought. He came to that conclusion when she added, "Only a lawyer could make passion sound so mundane. Seriously? A life mate 'stimulates a renewed interest'?" She tilted her head, and asked, "That translates to my presence should make you horny, right?"

The twinkle in her eye took away any offense from her question, and actually made him laugh. She certainly had a way with words he thought as he nodded.

"I see," Sherry said slowly, and then asked, "But what about this shared pleasure business?"

"Ah." He floundered briefly, and then simply said, "If you were my life mate and we . . . er . . . when I touch you I should feel the pleasure you experience and vice versa."

Sherry seemed to consider that, and then suddenly reached up on her tiptoes and pressed her lips to his. Caught by surprise, Basil didn't react at first, and before he could, she eased back to her feet to tilt her head and eye him with pursed lips. "Nothing. Maybe we aren't—"

This time Basil silenced Sherry by kissing her. He couldn't help himself. He'd been watching her lips as she spoke since meeting her, and they were full, and pouty and soft looking. Really they were quite the sexiest lips he'd ever seen, and he'd seen a lot of lips over the millennia since he'd been born. But he also did it because he didn't want to hear her say that she was not his life mate. Sherry wasn't petite and blond. She wasn't biddable. Actually, she was nothing like the woman he'd thought his life mate would be, but she felt right. It felt right to be with her. He had no other way to describe it. He'd expected to be nervous and even a little anxious with her. After all, she was believed to be his life mate, a woman he wanted to like and accept him, a woman he wanted to convince to spend the rest of her life with him. He *should* be nervous and anxious. Instead, he had immediately felt comfortable and at peace in her presence. He didn't feel he had to monitor himself around her; he didn't have to edit himself. He could just be himself and that was enough.

That being the case, it was something of a shock when his mouth covered hers and passion roared up through him like a back draft. He hadn't been prepared for that. He'd thought it would be a slow buildup, lips meshing, tongues dancing, and heat sliding up through him. Basil wasn't ready for the explosion of heat that stole his breath along with his common sense. He even forgot where he was and that anyone could walk in at any moment. Otherwise, he would have damned near ripped her clothes off and copulated with Sherry on the kitchen counter top.

He didn't . . . but he wanted to, and it came damned close. The moment the wave of passion rolled over him, it was as if a leash had been removed. Basil sprang on her like a slavering beast, his hands closing around her and pressing her close before lifting her off her feet so that he could bear her forward to the kitchen counter. He'd barely set her there when his hands were moving, trying to touch every available inch of her at once. They glided up her sides, slid around her shoulders to press her closer so that her breasts nudged his chest, then his hands slid down and around to find her breasts through the cloth of her shirt. But they paused there only briefly before dropping away and down and around to find her behind. He squeezed with delight as she sucked at his tongue, and he tugged her lower body tight against his own even as he urged her upper body back with his kiss.

Sherry was in turn gasping for breath and moaning, her body shifting, writhing, and arching, but she couldn't for the life of her figure out how she'd got there. One minute she was suggesting that perhaps she wasn't Basil's life mate, and the next his mouth was on hers and she was going up in flames. It all happened so fast. Caught by surprise as she was by Basil's kissing her so abruptly, Sherry didn't react at first. She remained completely still. But then his tongue urged her lips apart and . . . well, frankly, all hell broke loose in her body. Her brain shut right down and her body came to shuddering life in a way she'd never experienced before. And she couldn't get enough.

Sherry didn't fight when he lifted her off the floor and carried her back to the counter. She felt it press briefly into the small of her back, and then he was setting her on the countertop and bending her back enough that his hands could slide over her body. It was like those images she'd had flash through her head earlier, except that she wasn't naked.

But she wanted to be.

Dear God, she wanted to feel every inch of his naked flesh against her own. Her very skin seemed to cry out for it and her body was weeping for it. She could feel the passion gushing through her, eagerly shifting to where it could be of the most use. Moaning, as his hand found one breast and the other began to tug at her top, Sherry reached to help him with the task of removing the impediment to his touch.

"I would say you are definitely life mates."

Sherry heard Lucian's words, but they didn't really register until she realized that Basil had gone still against her. She didn't know if it was a result of his age, but he didn't act like a teenager and immediately jump away, all flustered and embarrassed. Instead, he broke their kiss and eased back just enough to give her the room to straighten her clothes and gather herself, sheltering her from his brother with his body as she did. Once she was done, he asked, "Okay?"

Sherry nodded, and—aware she was blushing, but unable to do anything about it—she decided to ignore it and forced her head up, determined to be as composed as he was.

"That's my girl," Basil murmured encouragingly, and gave her arms a squeeze before lifting her off the counter, slipping his arm around her waist and turning her with him to face his brother.

Sherry glanced at the man, grateful to find that he was at least alone, and then glanced to Basil as he said to Lucian with great aplomb, "It would seem so."

Lucian nodded. "Good. It saves us some manpower, which we are sadly short on lately thanks to Marguerite and her matchmaking." He scowled as he said that and then announced, "You will both stay here tonight and then accompany Stephanie and the girls back to Port Henry tomorrow. You'll be staying with them at Casey Cottage."

Sherry frowned. "I have a business to run. I can't just—"

"You cannot return to your business," Lucian interrupted firmly. "Leonius saw you with our Miss Stephanie. He knows where your business is, and is a crazy, vengeful bastard. When he cannot find Stephanie, he is likely to head back to your store to take it out on you and anyone else in the vicinity."

Lucian walked to the refrigerator and opened the door to retrieve a bag of blood before continuing, "We will place a couple of hunters in your store for now, to run it for you in the hopes that he returns and we can capture him. But you are to go nowhere near the place. You would be a liability if he showed up, and I will not have one of my people hurt or killed trying to protect you."

Sherry sighed and nodded reluctantly, understanding everything he'd said. Truthfully, she had no desire to return to the store right now if there was a chance that Leonius could return.

"Okay. I get that I can't go back to the store for now, and am willing to go with Basil and the girls tomorrow," she agreed, and then added, "But there's no need for me to stay here tonight. I have to go home and pack clothes and a toothbrush and whatnot anyway, and my purse is still at the store. I—"

"Justin will pack you a bag," Lucian announced. "And I shall have someone collect your purse from the store. But you are staying here tonight."

On that note, Lucian took his bag of blood with him, turned, and strode out of the room.

Sherry stared after him until he moved out of sight and then turned to Basil and said, "He does know the days of feudal lords and slavery are over, right?"

Basil grinned. "He is a high-handed bastard and bossy as hell, isn't he?"

"Definitely," Sherry said irritably.

Basil's expression grew serious. "But he means well, and he is right that it is safer for you to stay away from your store and home. If Leonius took it into his head to go after you, it would not take much effort for him to find out your name and where you live."

"How?" Sherry asked with a frown.

"He and his men have been inside the heads of your employees. He will know all sorts of things about them, be able to track them down and find out from them who you are and where you live." When he saw Sherry getting upset, he added soothingly, "Though, I am sure Lucian has people watching your employees. Still, it is better to stay here for now, rather than take risks."

"Right," Sherry said on a sigh, and thought that her eyes had been opened to a whole new world today, one that had more to do with *Fright Night* than *Leave It to Beaver.* The thought made her frown and mutter, "Today."

"Today what?" Basileios asked.

"It was mid-afternoon when Stephanie came into my store . . . and we were running around in the sunlight afterward." Turning to him she added, "And you and I walked to the outbuilding in sunlight too."

"Ah." Basileios nodded. "I gather Stephanie did not get the chance to explain our origins to you?"

"Your origins," she murmured, and then shook her head. "She said you weren't dead and soulless, but she didn't explain exactly how you are the way you are."

Basil nodded and then took her hand. As he turned toward the door to the hall, he said, "Well then let's go find a quiet corner and I shall explain everything now."

"Sherry? Are you all right?"

That question from Basil made her force a smile and nod. But Sherry wasn't at all sure she was okay after hearing the explanations he'd just given her about his people and their abilities. They were seated in a small parlor on the main floor and Basil had spent the last half hour giving her the explanations he had promised. Now she was trying to absorb what she'd been told.

"You are not speaking," Basil pointed out with a frown. "You have not spoken since I started explaining."

There was no denying the concern in his voice and on his face, and she supposed she could understand that concern. He'd just given her a lot of information, telling her things that would make most people call in the guys with straitjackets. However, after what Stephanie had told her earlier and the crazy stuff she'd seen . . . And then there was all the blood in the refrigerator, bags of it stacked on top of each other and filling a good portion of the fridge.

"Sherry?" Basil repeated, definitely worried now.

"I'm just processing," she assured him quietly, and then cleared her own throat and said, "So, let me be sure I have this all straight . . . Atlantis existed. It was technologically advanced, as the myths suggest. Scientists there developed a bio . . . er . . . something or other nano things that could be introduced to the body that were supposed to cure disease and heal wounds without the need for surgery or chemo and stuff."

When she paused briefly, he nodded. "Right."

"And these nanos run on blood."

"And use blood to make their repairs," he inserted.

"Right. But it means they need a lot of blood, more than your people can provide."

"More than a human can provide. We *are* human too, Sherry," he said quietly.

She thought that was debatable. Atlanteans may have started out human, but it seemed to her they were now a kind of cyber-vampire people.

"But no, the human body cannot produce enough blood to support the work the nanos need to do," he added when she didn't comment.

Sherry merely nodded and continued. "So, you're saying that in Atlantis they handled that small glitch with blood transfusions. But then Atlantis fell and those of you who survived climbed over the mountains to join the rest of society and—" Pausing, she tilted her head and frowned. "What did you mean when you said Atlantis fell? And did you really have to leave? Couldn't you have just stayed and rebuilt? Why did you have to join the rest of the world? How was the rest of the world separated from you? Surely it wasn't just the mountains? And how could the rest of the world be so far behind technologically? Why didn't your people share your technology with others? Heck, if the rest of the world had known about it they would have stolen it, but how could they not know? And—"

"Breathe," Basil instructed.

Sherry grimaced. "I'm sorry. It's just—"

"No need to apologize. I should have explained these things." He smiled wryly and then admitted, "This is the first time I have had to explain our origins."

"Really?" she asked with surprise.

Basil shrugged. "We are not encouraged to share our existence with others without good reason."

"Ah," she murmured.

"Atlantis was isolated from the rest of the world by mountains. I am sure there were some Atlanteans who traveled over the mountains to explore, but I did not personally know anyone who did. Most I think were happy to remain in Atlantis. Until the day Atlantis was no more," he added sadly, and then took a deep breath and continued, "When I said it fell, I meant that literally. It suffered a series of earthquakes and crumbled, sliding into the sea. There was nothing . . . and nowhere, to rebuild. And precious few to rebuild it. The only survivors were those who had the nanos."

"Everyone in Atlantis didn't have the nanos?" she asked with surprise.

"No. It was only tested on a dozen or so people who were mortally wounded or fatally ill before the scientists realized the flaw. My parents were among them, and my brothers and I inherited the nanos."

"The flaw?" she asked.

"The nanos were programmed to return their host to their peak condition and then self-destruct and disintegrate, to be flushed from the patient's system."

"So get cancer, get a shot full of nanos, they kill off the disease and then disintegrate and you're normal again?" she asked.

Basil nodded. "That was what they expected to happen, yes."

She arched an eyebrow. "So why didn't that happen?"

"Because rather than have to program individual groups of nanos with different programs, like programming one group for cancer, another for damage to the kidney, another for damage to the arteries, etcetera, they went the lazy route and programmed the nanos with all the information on the human body," he explained. "And, as I said, they then gave them the prime directive to return their host to their peak condition."

She shook her head, still confused.

"While it may have been given to patients with fatal diseases or who had internal trauma, etcetera, the human body is at its prime in the early twenties."

Her eyebrows rose. "So rather than just curing or repairing, it acted like the fountain of youth, sort of, making anyone older than that young again."

"Yes, but even that was not the problem. Returning us to our prime is an unending process. Between damage from the sun, pollution, or even simple aging, our bodies are constantly in need of repair."

"So once they repair one thing, something else needs repair," Sherry said with understanding. "The nanos are always working and never dissolve."

"Exactly," he said, sitting back, and then he shrugged and added, "Once the scientists realized that, they stopped their trials and went back to work on the nanos in an attempt to find a way to handle that problem."

"I'm guessing they never succeeded," Sherry said quietly. "Otherwise you and the others wouldn't be—"

"No," he agreed solemnly. "The fall happened before they managed to do that, and the only survivors were the Atlanteans with nanos, the patients who had been given them in the trials, and their offspring. And then only about sixty percent of us survived."

"So only seven or eight of you survived?"

"No. There were more than that by then. As I said, it was originally tested on twelve subjects, but those twelve married, had children . . ." He shrugged. "I am not sure how many made it out exactly. I know of at least twenty, but we did not all come out together. Others took different routes. For instance, no one knew the no-fangers had made it out. We are not even sure how they did. The conclusion we came to was that they were either released by one of the scientists, or perhaps just escaped and climbed out when the buildings began to crumble."

"Released?" she asked with confusion.

"No-fangers were dangerous, crazy and sadistic, basically a bunch of Jack-the-ripper types. They were locked up," he said quietly, and then admitted with distaste, "I suspect the scientists experimented on them, trying to remove the nanos."

"So Atlanteans were enlightened-type people," she said sarcastically. "Willing to experiment on the victims of their own inventions."

"They were just people, Sherry," he said quietly. "And as with every society, we had good people and bad people too."

"Right," she said on a sigh, then commented, "So if not all of you made it out, then your kind *can* die?" It had been sounding like they couldn't.

"Oh yes, we can die. It is just harder to kill us. As far as I know, only decapitation or being consumed by fire can kill us," he said quietly.

"I see," she murmured. Sherry paused for a moment

to consider that, and then went back to the original conversation. "So sixty percent of the Atlanteans with nanos survived—"

"That does not include no-fangers," he inserted.

She nodded. "But those of you who survived were left with nothing. No home, no homeland, no transfusions."

Basil nodded.

"So the nanos gave you fangs and . . . stuff," she ended lamely.

"Fangs, extra strength, night vision, abilities and skills that would make us better able to get the blood we needed."

"Okay, but I don't understand how the nanos . . ." she hesitated, searching for the right words, and finally settled on, "*knew* to do that, I guess. I mean, you said they were programmed to repair injuries and stuff, but who programmed them to give you fangs and the other things?"

"I am very sure no one programmed that into them," he said. "I believe it was just their solution to the problem when Atlantis fell and we found ourselves without any way to get blood transfusions to gain the blood they needed. Getting that blood was the only way they could carry out the directive to keep us at our peak. Without those abilities, we would have died. In fact, some of us did die without evolving."

"So these nanos can think?" she asked with a frown.

Basil frowned too and started to shake his head, but then his eyes widened slightly and he said, "I guess they must."

He seemed shocked at the idea, and for a moment they were both silent, and then Sherry let out the breath she hadn't realized she'd been holding and said, "So, Atlantis fell, your people joined the rest of the world, grew fangs and— Oh, hey!" she interrupted herself suddenly. "Stephanie said Leo and his men were no-fangers. She said she was an Eden something or other too and then said she was immortal, so I'm not sure—"

"Edentate," he explained. "It is an immortal without fangs."

"Wouldn't that be a no-fanger, then?" she asked with confusion.

"No. No-fangers are from the same batch of nanos as Edentates, but while the no-fangers were insane, the Edentates are the ones who survived the turn with their sanity intact. They are very like us, just without the fangs."

"There was more than one batch of nanos?" she asked with interest.

"Yes. The first round of experiments with nanos were much less successful. One-third of the patients died, one-third came out of the turn insane, and only one-third came out seemingly fine. However, those who survived the turn from the first batch—insane or not— well, they never developed fangs after the fall. Most of them who survived the fall died when they didn't produce fangs."

"And Stephanie—?"

"Was turned by Leonius Livius, a no-fanger," he explained quietly. "So was her sister, Dani. Fortunately, they both survived the turn with their sanity intact."

"Leonius is the Leo from my store?" Sherry asked, and he nodded.

"Anyway," Basil said, "when the first batch of nanos showed such poor results, they changed the programming, and the new improved nanos were the ones that immortals who later produced fangs came from. It's very rare for a turn to die in the process, and no one comes out of it insane . . . well, unless they were insane beforehand," he said with a smile.

"Right," Sherry said quietly. "You're an immortal . . . with fangs?"

He nodded.

Sherry hesitated, and then asked, "Can I see them?"

He blinked in surprise, and she suspected he wasn't often asked that. Maybe even never, she thought wryly. Sherry doubted vampires ran around playing "You show me yours and I'll show you mine."

"Basil! Sherry! Pizza's here!"

He stood abruptly, offering her his hand as he said, "I guess I shall have to show you later."

Sherry accepted his hand and stood, but she glanced at him curiously as they left the sitting room. She got the definite feeling he was relieved to put off showing her his fangs. She wasn't sure why, though. The man was reacting as if she'd asked him to strip naked for her.

But then, she thought suddenly, maybe for vampires, fangs *were* like genitals. Certainly he wouldn't have been encouraged to flash them around anymore than mortal men were encouraged to whip out their penises at a party. Perhaps that's all it was, she thought, and then let the worry go as they reached the kitchen and she saw all the people there. Lucian, Leigh, Stephanie, Bricker, Sam and her Mortimer. There were also two other couples there she didn't know. A dark-eyed and dark-haired man who she would have guessed was Italian was leaning back against the counter with his arms around the waist of a woman leaning back against him. The woman was beautiful, with silver-blue eyes and dark brown hair laced with red, and she looked familiar. Sherry suspected she'd waited on her in the store a time or two.

"That is my sister-in-law, Marguerite, and her mate, Julius," Basil murmured, noting where she was looking.

Sherry nodded and turned her attention to the other couple, who were sitting at the big kitchen table at her end of the room. Well, the man with dark hair and silver eyes was sitting at a chair at the table. The woman was sitting in his lap. Sherry peered curiously at her, noting the chestnut-colored hair up in a ponytail and her golden-brown eyes, thinking she'd seen her before too.

"You have, Sherry," Bricker said suddenly.

"Excuse me?" she asked, glancing to the young man with confusion.

"You have seen Nicholas and Jo before," he explained with amusement. "Just not up close and probably not clearly. They were in the—"

"SUV," Sherry finished for him, recognizing the names now. They'd been the hunters in the SUV that followed Leo and his boys. She glanced to the pair with concern. "Were you able to catch those men? Is the woman all right?"

Nicholas's mouth turned even grimmer at the question, and it was Jo who said, "No. Leo crashed the car and then he and his boys fled on foot in different directions. But we had to stop and help the woman. She was pretty banged up."

"Will she be okay?" Sherry asked, recalling the terror on the woman's face when she'd found her friends dragged out of the car and herself trapped in that backseat with Leo's boys.

"Yes," Jo assured her, and then grimaced and added, "Eventually. She really was badly banged up. The emergency room doctor thought she would need months of physiotherapy." She forced a smile and added, "But that's better than what Leo and his sons would have done to her."

"And what he will do to his next victims," Lucian said grimly.

Jo frowned and scowled at the man. "I know you think we should have left her and chased after Leo, but she was trapped in the car and it was on fire. She would have burned alive if we hadn't stopped."

"It was in downtown Toronto," he said heavily. "There were plenty of mortals there to help her."

"They couldn't have got her out of the car, Lucian," Jo snapped. "Nicholas had to bend metal to get her out. Mortals couldn't have done that."

"So you saved one woman and let Leo run free to claim numerous other victims," Lucian said grimly. "I doubt the families of his future victims will think it was a fair exchange."

"You were not there, Uncle," Nicholas growled. "We did what we thought was right at the time."

"You mean you knew you should have followed Leo, but did what your softhearted wife thought was right," Lucian snapped.

"No, of course he didn't," Jo said at once. "I didn't ask him to stop. I was going to do it myself."

"But he feared you are not strong enough yet to bend the metal and get the woman out," Lucian informed her. "So he reluctantly stopped to help because he feared your soft heart, combined with your stubbornness, would keep you trying right up until the car exploded and took the lives of both the woman and yourself."

"No," Jo protested, and then turned to peer at the man whose lap she sat in. "That's not why you stopped, is it?"

"It is," Lucian assured her when Nicholas merely avoided her gaze. "And that is why I do not think life mates should work together anymore."

"Well then, you will lose a hunter," Nicholas said grimly. "Because Jo is not working without me to watch her back."

"You'll lose two hunters," Jo corrected firmly. "Because I don't want Nicholas hunting without me there to watch *his* back."

"Honey," Nicholas said gently, caressing her cheek. "I have been a hunter for a long time, I would be fine."

Jo didn't soften. "If you go out hunting without me there to watch your back, then I will work with someone else."

"She can work with me!" Leigh said cheerfully. "I've been practicing my marksmanship and fighting. I'm ready to be a hunter."

"No!" Nicholas and Lucian barked together, the sound a small explosion in the room.

"No offense, Leigh," Nicholas said into the silence that followed. "It is not you. I simply will not have Jo work without me."

"Then either we work together or we don't work at all," Jo insisted, and when he scowled, added, "Otherwise, I guess Leigh and I will be teaming up."

"Over my dead body," Lucian growled.

"That could be arranged if you like," Jo said sweetly.

Much to Sherry's amazement, Lucian's lips twitched with amusement at the words, but he said, "Leigh is not going to be a hunter."

"I'm not?" Leigh asked gently. "And who says so?"

Lucian opened his mouth, closed it, and then reasoned, "You are far too busy to take on any kind of job right now, my love. You have two babies to look after."

"*We* have two babies to look after," Leigh pointed out firmly, and then smiled and added, "And we could manage. You could take them during the day while Jo and I work, and then I can watch them at night while you work."

Sherry wasn't sure which horrified the man more. He turned green at the mention of him looking after the babies, but then paled terribly at the part about Leigh working with Jo. The women had obviously chosen their threat well. Neither man would want their wives—two newly turned immortals and relatively inexperienced hunters—working together without more experienced backup.

"Or," Leigh said now, "you could just let Nicholas

and Jo continue to work together, and I can get in a little more practice and wait for the babies to start walking and talking before I consider day care." She frowned now and asked, "Is there such a thing as day care for immortal babies?"

Rather than answer his wife's question, Lucian turned a fierce scowl on Nicholas and Jo. "You can continue to work together." Shifting his focus onto Jo completely then, he added, "But you are completely responsible for every- and anyone Leo kills from here on out."

"Lucian," Leigh said with a frown when Jo paled. "That's harsh."

"Perhaps," he agreed wearily. "But it is also true. And perhaps next time, knowing that will help Jo ignore what her soft heart wants her to do, and do the right thing instead." He turned back to Jo and added quietly, "If given the choice between one life or captur- ing Leo, you have to remember that you cannot save everyone, and that letting Leo go means many more deaths. Deaths that are on your head."

All the fight seemed to go out of Jo then. Nodding, she sank against Nicholas's chest and buried her face in his neck. Nicholas promptly stood and carried her out of the room.

"Well," Sam said dryly. "Anyone still hungry? Or shall I put the pizza in the refrigerator until later?"

Bricker snorted at the suggestion and grabbed one of the six pizza boxes. "Screw that. I'm starved."

"So am I," Stephanie announced, grabbing a second box and carrying it to the table. "Come on, Sherry, Basil. Grab some before Bricker eats it all."

Sherry smiled faintly, the tension that had claimed her during the previous exchange easing, and then she turned to Basil questioningly. Did he have an appetite for food again? It was apparently one of the signs of having met a life mate, along with shared passion. But while she'd certainly experienced a great deal of passion earlier with Basil, Sherry wasn't sure if she'd actually experienced the shared pleasure he'd mentioned. She'd just sort of exploded with desire when he kissed her. His suddenly having an appetite would be more of an indicator to her than what had passed between them earlier.

He smiled and opened his mouth to say something, but before he could, Lucian barked, "Basil. The council meeting is in fifteen minutes. We have to go."

"Oh. Right." Basil glanced at his watch. Sighing, he turned to Sherry and said apologetically, "I have to go. Will you be all right?"

"Of course she will," Stephanie said cheerfully, catching her hand and pulling her toward an empty chair at the table. "I'll look after her. You go ahead. She'll be here when you get back."

"Right." Basil hesitated, and for one minute Sherry suspected he was going to kiss her good-bye, but in the end he merely nodded and turned to follow Lucian out of the room. She watched him go, surprised at how disappointed she was that he had to leave her.

"Don't worry. He'll be back," Stephanie said cheerfully. "He won't be able to stay away from you for long from now on. In the meantime, have some pizza. It's really good."

Five

"**I** am amazed at how well you seem to be accepting all of this."

Sherry glanced up from washing her hands to meet Drina's gaze in the bathroom mirror. They were in the women's washroom of a service center about forty-five minutes from their destination of Port Henry. On spotting the sign that they were approaching the rest stop, Stephanie had announced a need to use the bathroom, so Drina had taken the off ramp when they reached it. Once they got here, however, everyone had decided that using the bathroom was a good idea.

"You do not seem to be overly distressed about us, and that is rather rare," Drina continued with a wry twist of the lips. "Most mortals have at least a mini nervous breakdown when they find out about us."

Sherry smiled faintly as she retrieved her hands from under the automatic tap and moved to the sensory paper towel dispenser. "Believe me, I'm freaking out inside. I just hide it well."

"She is," Katricia announced, coming out of one of the booths and moving to a sink. Smiling kindly at Sherry, she added, "But it is not a serious 'freak' out. Just a sort of is-this-really-happening-or-did-someone-slip-me-a-mickey-and-I-am-having-some-drugged-out-hallucination 'freak' out."

Sherry glanced to the girl with surprise. That exact thought had run through her mind several times since Stephanie had rushed into her office.

"No way!"

Startled, Sherry turned to the line of booths when Stephanie screeched that from inside one of them. A flush sounded and then a door opened and the teenager rushed out, her eyes immediately seeking out Katricia.

"You can read her?" she asked with disbelief.

Katricia nodded. "Yes. She is hard to read, though. You have to concentrate and focus and then it is still a bit fuzzy."

Stephanie turned to Drina. "What about you?"

"Yes."

Sherry was actually surprised at the answer. Since the woman had thought she was handling all of this well, she'd assumed she couldn't read her somewhat scattered thoughts.

"Your thoughts are a bit scattered," Drina acknowledged, as if she'd spoken aloud. "But trust me, it is nothing like how some people react."

Katricia nodded. "You really are handling this well."

"Thanks," she murmured, looking the woman over.

This was Basil's daughter . . . who was born in 411 AD. Sherry hadn't really got the chance to do more than utter a quick hello to the girl as she'd been hustled into the van when they'd left the Enforcer house that morning. The start of her day had been rather rushed. After a restless night as she tossed and turned, fretting over everything that had happened the day before and everything she'd learned since, Sherry had been roused from sleep that morning by Stephanie bursting into her room to tell her they were leaving in half an hour and if she wanted coffee and breakfast before they left she'd best get up.

Sherry was out of bed and pulling on her clothes even as the girl whirled and rushed back out. They were her clothes from the day before. There had been no choice. Lucian had arranged for her purse to be collected from the store and returned to her the night before. He'd then requested her keys and given them to Justin with the order to go pack her a bag. However, Justin hadn't returned by the time she'd gone to bed.

She'd spotted her suitcase by the front door when she got downstairs and briefly considered dragging it back up to her room to find her toothbrush, brush her teeth, and change her clothes, but the smells from the kitchen had convinced her to put it off until after she'd eaten. She'd found Sam, Mortimer, Justin, Stephanie, and Basil already eating in the kitchen and had eagerly joined them. But she'd regretted that decision when Katricia and Drina arrived just as she was finishing her breakfast and she found herself rushed out of the house and into the van without the opportunity to change first.

Her introduction to the two women had been a brief,

"Sherry this is my daughter, Katricia and my niece Drina," as Basil handed her into the van behind Stephanie. Sherry had murmured a "Hello, nice to meet you" almost over her shoulder as she climbed inside and then they'd been on their way. With Drina driving, Katricia in the front passenger seat, and Stephanie alone on the first bench seat in the back, Basil and Sherry were left to take the back bench seat. It made conversation difficult, and all Sherry could see of Katricia was the back of her head.

Now Sherry took note of Katricia's blond hair, athletic body, fine facial features, and silver-blue eyes and thought she definitely took after her father in looks. Katricia seemed nice too, as far as Sherry could tell, and that made her wonder if the girl knew that she was supposedly her father's life mate.

"There is no supposedly about it," Katricia said with amusement, finishing at the sink and moving to the paper towel dispenser. "Uncle Lucian said it was certain. He also mentioned catching the two of you being naughty in the kitchen, and my father has never forgotten himself so much as to do something like that. You must be life mates."

"We were just kissing," Sherry said at once, blushing brightly as she assured herself that was really all it had been. Okay, maybe there was some groping and stuff too, she acknowledged vaguely, but being naughty made it sound like they had actually been doing the dirty on the kitchen counter, and while things might have been heading in that direction, Lucian's arrival prevented it.

Thank God, she thought, but not with much conviction. As embarrassing as it would have been to be caught further along in their passionate exchange, she couldn't help but think it very well might have been worth it. Basileios had knocked more than her socks off with his kisses and caresses, and she'd been jonesing for more ever since, but Basil hadn't done more than give her a peck on the cheek when he saw her to her room the night before.

"The passion between life mates is rather powerful," Drina said quietly, making it known that she at least was still in her thoughts. "But Uncle Basil is old-school."

Sherry wasn't sure what that meant exactly. She knew the man was old, but—

"He was raised in Atlantis," Katricia added gently. "They were taught to always be respectful, especially to women. He will try to fight his urges in order to give you time to adjust. It is the gentlemanly thing to do."

"Oh," Sherry said, doing her best to ignore that she was blushing and that this was the weirdest conversation she'd ever had. The daughter of the man she was lusting after was reassuring her that his lack of jumping her was out of respect, not any lack of desire. Weird.

"Yes, you could say we are weird," Drina said suddenly with amusement. "But then over time I have learned that normal is kind of overrated . . . and really boring."

"Yeah, I guess it is," Sherry said with a grin. Certainly, her life had been going along in a nice, normal fashion before Stephanie burst into her office. Comparing it to her life now, just a day later, her life before did seem kind of boring.

"Oh, come on," Stephanie said suddenly with disgust as she finished drying her hands and tossed the paper towel away. "This is so unfair. I can't hear what she's thinking so I'm only getting half the conversation."

"Ah, poor Steph," Drina teased lightly, slinging an arm around the girl's shoulders and steering her toward the door. "I guess you will just have to try harder to read her. I suspect if you do, you will find you can read her too."

"Really?" Stephanie asked, glancing over her shoulder as Sherry and Katricia followed the pair out of the bathroom.

"Really," Drina assured her, urging her to the side to avoid a collision with a supporting column. "But try doing it when you are not walking, so you do not run into a wall."

"You wouldn't let me walk into a wall," Stephanie said on a laugh, but turned and faced forward and then shrugged out from under Drina's arm. "I'm going to Wendy's to get a pop before we go."

"Hang on." Drina collared the teenager before she could take off. Pausing, she glanced around, smiling when Basil moved away from the wall to join them. Glancing from him to Sherry, she asked, "Do you guys want anything?"

"Coffee from Timmy's for me, but I'll get it," Sherry said at once, glad she had her purse back and didn't have to depend on these people for money, at least. Realizing that Drina wouldn't allow Stephanie to go to

Wendy's stall alone after what had happened the last time she'd gone off on her own, Sherry asked, "Do you want a coffee or something too? I'll get it for you while you go with Stephanie."

"You will not," Basileios said calmly. "I shall take care of the drinks. Just tell me what everyone wants."

"I will let you guys fight it out with Katricia while I take Steph to Wendy's," Drina said with amusement. Turning to head for the fast food counter with the impatient girl, she added, "But I would appreciate a medium coffee, double, double . . . and maybe a chocolate dip donut."

"Oh, me too, please," Stephanie said over her shoulder.

"Got it," Sherry said with amusement, but was perplexed by the bit about fighting it out with Katricia. It was she and Basileios who were—

"I am paying," Katricia announced interrupting her thoughts, and when Basileios opened his mouth to argue, she held up a gold card. "It is on the council."

Basil's eyebrows went up. "Are we handing out credit cards now?"

Katricia shrugged. "Uncle Lucian gave it to me this morning when we stopped to pick up his van. I gather Enforcers are being issued cards to use on the job." She glanced to Sherry and explained, "Enforcers used to get cash for expenses on the job, but there were some lost receipts and stuff, and Bastien was bitching about needing them for taxes, so Lucian has decided credit cards are the way to go."

She turned to lead them toward the coffee shop stall then.

Sherry followed, but asked curiously, "Who is Bastien and who pays for them?"

"For the credit cards?" Katricia asked.

"For the cards, and the house and vehicles and the hunters," Sherry clarified. "I mean I assume you all get wages?"

"I am actually a deputy in Port Henry now," Katricia told her. "I mainly work for the town, but I sideline on occasion for Uncle Lucian, like now . . . and yes, Enforcers are paid."

"Everyone on the council contributes to the funds needed to run the Enforcers," Basileios said, answering her initial question as they started toward the long lines of customers waiting at the Tim Horton's counter.

"So you basically pay for the decisions you make?" Sherry suggested, recalling that he'd told her last night that he too was on the council that ran the Enforcers who kept immortals in line.

"I suppose you could say that," he agreed wryly.

"And does that influence your decisions?" she asked curiously as they stopped at the end of the shortest line, one that still had a good twelve people in it. Sunday was a prime day for travel, with people returning from weekends away or day visits.

"If you mean do we tend to choose cheap alternatives over what is right but expensive, then no," he assured her.

"Most of the immortals on the council are at least a couple thousand years old," Katricia explained, turning to face them so that she could speak quietly and not be overheard by the person in line in front of them. "They have had more than enough time to amass enough wealth that the money used to run the Enforcers is little more than a drop in the bucket. Certainly cheaper than mortal taxes."

Sherry raised her eyebrows, but kept her voice down when she asked, "So all older immortals are crazy rich?"

"Most," Basil acknowledged. "Although there are some who simply do not care enough to bother amassing a fortune and make little more than they need to get by."

Sherry tilted her head at this news and asked, "You're kidding, right? I mean, surely not every immortal is smart enough to amass a fortune. You have to have one or two who—"

"Stupid immortals do not usually live centuries, let alone millennia," Katricia interrupted quietly, and then added, "At least they did not use to. Now that there is not a battle around every corner, they have a longer life expectancy."

"Last I heard there were several battles going on," Sherry said dryly. "Afghanistan, Somalia, Pakistan, Iraq . . ."

"Yes, but those are only taking place in certain parts of the world, and those places can be avoided. Besides, the weapons are different now," Katricia countered. "In the Middle Ages in Europe it seemed like everyone was fighting everyone, country with country, but also neighbor with neighbor . . . and they used swords and battle-axes and other things that often took off a head."

"Which is one of the few ways your kind can die," Sherry said with understanding.

Katricia and Basileios both nodded.

"So you lost a lot of stupid immortals to battle-axes and swords?" she muttered, shaking her head. She couldn't believe she was having this conversation. Immortals, beheadings, people who lived centuries or even millennia.

"A good many stupid or impetuous ones, and a few who were simply unlucky," Katricia said with a shrug, and then added gently, "You will get used to the idea of us and stop feeling like you are in the twilight zone. It just takes a bit of getting used to."

"Are you having trouble coping with all of this?" Basileios asked with a frown of concern. "I thought you were handling it well."

"She is," Katricia assured him. "But it would throw anyone for a loop."

"Yes, I suppose it would," Basileios agreed quietly.

Feeling like a child whose parents were discussing her, Sherry cleared her throat and pointed out, "It's our turn."

"Our—? Oh!" Katricia said with surprise as she glanced around to see that the line in front of them was gone and it was their turn at the till. She moved forward at once, and then paused to glance back at Sherry and her father. "What would you like?"

"A small coffee regular and a Boston cream donut," Sherry said, smiling at the server.

"The same for me," Basileios murmured as the girl began punching keys on her cash register.

Katricia nodded and turned to finish giving the order,

and Sherry glanced at Basileios, a slow smile crossing her lips.

"You ordered food," she said softly, and then her smile widened as she recalled that he'd been eating breakfast that morning when she joined them. She'd been so kerfluffled by the rush that she hadn't noted it at the time, but now she recalled that he'd had a plate heaped with bacon and scrambled eggs when she settled at the table.

"I am feeling a bit peckish," he said, smiling in return. But the heat in his eyes as he slid his arm around her waist and drew her to his side suggested food wasn't what he was thinking about.

Sherry grinned despite the blush she could feel rising over her face at this sign of his reawakening appetites. She still wasn't sure that what she'd experienced with him the day before was this shared pleasure business he'd mentioned. The passion had been crazy strong, but it seemed to be her own, not his and hers combined. Still, he couldn't read her and his appetites were definitely in evidence. She probably was his life mate . . . She just had to decide what she wanted to do about it, she acknowledged, some of her inner glow dimming a bit. So far she liked the guy and had a serious compulsion to jump his bones, but this life mate business was like marriage, as far as she could tell, and she'd only known him a day, not even a full twenty-four hours.

While she was known to be spontaneous and impulsive, jumping into this seemed a bit crazy rather than just impulsive. She really needed to think about her future and what she wanted . . . which didn't mean she wasn't going to jump the guy at every opportunity while she was doing so. He had some serious mojo going for him. Sherry was incredibly aware of every inch of male body pressed against her side and had to fight the urge to run her hands over his chest and kiss him. Closing her eyes, she bit her lip and imagined just that, sliding her hands up his chest as she shifted to press against his groin. Claiming his lips with her own and nipping at, then sucking on, the lower one as she—

"Why don't you two go wait in the van?" Katricia suggested suddenly. "I will take care of this."

"Good idea," Basileios said, swinging Sherry away and urging her toward the exit.

Sherry went willingly, but couldn't help peering at him curiously. He'd practically growled the two words, and the only time she'd heard his voice go that raspy was during their shared passion experiment in the kitchen at the Enforcer house last night. One look at the silver flaring in his eyes told her that his thoughts were running along the same line as her own, so she wasn't surprised when he hurried her into the back of the van, tugged the door closed and then dropped onto the bench seat and pulled her into his arms. He didn't have to do much pulling, she was already shifting closer, her arms reaching for him.

His kiss was as exciting as she recalled from the night before. It hadn't simply been the situation and high adrenaline after the escape from Leonius, which was something she'd considered last night while trying to get to sleep. Any possibility that it was hormones or events that had raised her passions so high fled as his tongue lashed her own.

Dear God, the man was one hell of a kisser, she thought, and moaned when his hand found her breast through the silk of her blouse. When he then undid the top four or five buttons and tugged the shirt and bra aside so he could cup her breast unimpeded, Sherry gasped into his mouth and blinked her eyes open. Groaning as he squeezed and kneaded, she stared blindly out the window behind him, some small part of her mind thinking it might be a good idea to watch for Katricia and the others.

Glimpsing blond hair across the parking lot, she tried to focus, but it wasn't Katricia. She didn't think the person was even a female, but someone who looked a great deal like Leonius. Frowning, she focused on the man, trying to see if it was him or not, but in the next moment a semi drove past, blocking her vision, and then Basileios broke their kiss and dropped his head to claim the nipple he'd bared. Sherry glanced down with a gasp as he closed his lips over the already hard nub and began to suckle.

"Oh, God, Basileios, don't do that. They'll be back any minute," she moaned even as she cupped his head to urge him on.

He mumbled something around her nipple and then added an exclamation point to whatever he'd said by sliding one hand down to cup her between the legs through her skirt. Sherry cried out and covered his hand, pressing it more firmly against herself, all thoughts of the blond man in the parking lot slipping from her mind.

In the next moment, she was on her back on the bench seat with Basileios on top of her, his groin grinding against her own through their clothes as his hands replaced his mouth at her breast and he returned to kissing her again. Every nerve in Sherry's body was clamoring now and straining toward the explosive release she was sure was coming. Her legs were wrapped around his hips for a better angle and her hands were alternating between pulling at his clothes and squeezing his behind to urge him on, and then the sound of the door sliding open hit her ears and she heard Stephanie saying, "So try to remember to use contractions more often. You know, *he's, she's, they're,* and stuff like that and— Hey, how come the windows are all fogged up?"

Basileios froze and then broke their kiss and lifted his head to give her an apologetic smile.

Sherry stared back wide-eyed as it slowly occurred to her that she'd been dry humping in the back of the van, something she hadn't done since she was a teenager. And they'd been caught, she realized as Basileios eased off of her and shifted to sit on the end of the bench as she heard Stephanie say, "Oh, there you are." There was a pause and then she offered, "We can go back inside for five or ten minutes if you like. But I'm not dressing you guys and buckling you in when we come back to find you both passed out and naked."

"Get in." Drina's voice sounded half amused and half exasperated as she gave the order, and Sherry felt the van shift as Stephanie climbed in. Realizing that she was laying there with her top open and her breast still out of her bra, Sherry quickly straightened and did up her clothes, then ran her hands through her hair as she shifted her legs off the seat and sat up.

"Hungry?" Stephanie asked with a grin as she settled on the bench seat in front of them. She raised the Tim Horton's bag she carried and added, "For food I mean."

Sherry responded with the maturity she was known for and stuck her tongue out at the girl.

Stephanie just burst out laughing.

"I like her."

Basileios turned from watching Sherry disappear up the curving staircase to the second floor of Casey Cottage, and smiled at his daughter. "I do too."

"Good thing since she's your life mate," Katricia said on a laugh.

"Yeah," he agreed, and then raised his eyebrows. "Are you heading back to Teddy's now?"

"Nope. He's actually on his way here," she said wryly, and then explained, "Lucian asked us to stay for a day or so until they have a better handle on the Leonius situation. I talked to Teddy, he agreed, and was going to pack bags for both of us and meet us here. He should arrive any minute."

Basileios didn't hide his surprise at this news and asked dryly, "What? Lucian didn't think six rogue hunters in the house were sufficient?"

"Actually, Teddy and I will make four immortals in

enforcement here," Katricia told him. "Hazel and D.J. are on vacation in BC at the moment, and Elvi and Harper are not hunters, so it's just Drina, Victor, Teddy, and myself."

"And me," he added quietly.

Katricia crinkled her eyes and said, "Yeahhhh." It was a long drawn-out sound that was more dubious than anything. "No offense, Father, but just having met your life mate, you are not going to be much use for the next little while. I fear you are going to be a little distracted and not very dependable when it comes to vigilance and stuff."

"She means your brain is going to be firmly lodged in your drawers for the foreseeable future," a deep male voice announced, and Basileios turned to see his younger brother, Victor, stepping into the house through the back door. Elvi had been the only one to greet them when they all arrived in the van, and said that Victor had made a run to the grocery store for her. Katricia then offered to show Sherry to the room they'd set up for her. Victor was back now, though.

"Drawers?" Stephanie asked. "Nobody uses that word anymore, Uncle Vic. At least not in that way," she announced, closing the refrigerator door and moving to hug Victor in greeting.

"Well excuse me, Miss Know-it-all," Victor said, giving the girl an affectionate squeeze with the hand that wasn't holding four grocery bags. "I'll try to remember that in future so as not to offend your delicate sensibilities."

"Good, 'cause you're too handsome to sound like an

old fuddy-duddy," Stephanie said with a grin as she slipped out of his one-armed embrace. "Did you get anything good?"

"Scads of chips and other junk food," Victor said with dry amusement as she began to relieve him of the bags. "Your Aunt Elvi thought you might want comfort food after your close encounter."

"Ooooh, brownie mix!" Stephanie squealed, dragging the bags to the counter to begin removing the contents.

Shaking his head, Victor left her to it and moved around the counter to approach Basileios and Katricia. He gave Katricia an affectionate hug, then turned to Basileios and did the same, the two men slapping each other's back. When the hug ended, Basileios arched an eyebrow. "Uncle Vic?"

"Well I cannot be Dad, she has one," Victor said with a smile. "But she is our girl . . . and Drina and Harper's, and Hazel and D.J.'s," he added wryly, then glanced to Katricia and said, "And on occasion she's even Teddy and Katricia's."

"She is a lucky girl," Basileios said quietly.

"We are all lucky," Victor assured him, and then arched one eyebrow. "So where are Drina and Harper?"

"Harper was taking a nap when we got here," Katricia announced. "Drina went up to wake him and tell him we have arrived."

Victor nodded and glanced to Basil. "And where is this life mate Lucian was telling me you found? Sherry, is it?"

"Yes. Sherry." Basil realized he was grinning at the mere mention of her name and tried to tamp it down a bit. "Elvi took her up to show her to her room." Basileios glanced toward the stairs now, disappointed to find them empty. Turning back, he added, "But I did not find her, Stephanie did."

"Ah." Victor nodded. "Yes, she did say she could tell who were life mates to each other when she met them and who was not. It was just a matter of time before she turned into a mini Marguerite," Victor said lightly as he turned and headed around the counter that separated the kitchen from the dining room. Pausing at the refrigerator, he glanced around at the others as he opened the door and asked, "Blood?"

Basileios hesitated, his glance shifting to the stairs again.

"Has she not seen you feed yet, Father?" Katricia asked, either reading his expression or reading his mind.

"'Dad,' Tricia," Stephanie corrected with amusement. "Call Basil 'Dad.' You can't keep calling him Father."

"Why not?" Basil asked with a frown.

"Because it makes her sound old," Stephanie said dryly.

"She *is* old," Basil pointed out.

"Thanks . . . Dad," Tricia said as dryly.

"We are all old," Basil said quietly. "Compared to mortals, that is. Though you are just a pup to me."

"I didn't mean old like in years," Stephanie said with exasperation. "Like you say, you're all old. But you look young, yet you guys all talk like you're from another century."

"We are," Basil pointed out.

"Yeah, but—"

"Stephanie thinks we draw attention to ourselves with our antiquated speech," Victor said calmly.

"I don't think it, I know it," Stephanie said, and shook her head. "I don't understand it either. I know you guys avoid mortals as much as possible, but you do see and speak to them on occasion. Why is your speech still so old fashioned?"

"Because speech patterns and accents are learned while you are young and tend to stick," Katricia said with amusement, and then added, "Surely you have met transplanted foreigners who still have heavy accents after years living over here?"

Stephanie nodded. "Yeah, our neighbor, old Mrs. Marcetti, had a really thick Italian accent and she moved to Canada when she was like fifteen."

"Yes, well, she still has it because she was old enough that it was ingrained by the time she moved here," Katricia announced. "It's difficult for her to change it now, and so it is for us."

When Stephanie scowled at this, Victor quickly said, "However, Stephanie is right and our speech probably does make us stand out, so we are trying to modernize our speech pattern . . . with her help, of course."

"Ah," Basil said with amusement as he noted the way Stephanie relaxed. "I see."

"So?" Victor asked, arching an eyebrow. "Yes or no to blood?"

Basil hesitated. As far as he knew, Sherry hadn't seen anyone feed yet. She hadn't even seen fangs yet either, at least not his. She hadn't asked again when he'd returned from the council meeting and he hadn't reminded her. He was concerned about how she would react. It was one thing to be told vampires or immortals exist, but another entirely to actually see their fangs and witness them sucking blood up like pop through those pointy little fangs.

"She has to see it sometime," Katricia said quietly. "I think she will be okay with it."

"Yeah," Stephanie agreed, "She might be a little weirded out at first maybe, but in the end I think she'll be fine too."

"Right," Basileios murmured, and then glanced to Victor. "Yes, I guess I shall—"

It was as far as he got, Victor had already retrieved four bags and was now tossing him one as he kicked the refrigerator door closed.

Basileios easily caught the bag. As he slapped it to his fangs, Victor tossed a second bag to Katricia, and then set a third on the counter beside the pile of goodies Stephanie was still unpacking. He then walked around the counter, saying, "Blood before junk food, Steph."

"Ahh," she complained. "Can't I just—"

"You know the rules, kiddo," Victor interrupted, before slapping the last bag to his own fangs.

Basileios smiled around the bag at his mouth. He was aware that Stephanie still found consuming blood difficult. It didn't help that she had no fangs, so had to drink it out of a cup like red milk. But the exchange just seemed so much like one between a father and daughter

that he couldn't help smiling. Also, he was glad to see
his brother so happy again. It had been a long while
since he'd seen Victor so content.

"You've got your own en suite bathroom," Elvi chat-
tered, opening the door to show Sherry the bathroom.
"And this room is away from the road, so the sounds of
traffic shouldn't bother you."

"Thank you so much, Elvi," Sherry said sincerely as
Elvi closed the bathroom door. "I appreciate this."

"You're more than welcome," Elvi said sincerely.
"Besides, while we offered to have you stay here on the
house, the Enforcers will pay, so you really don't have
anything to thank me for."

"Oh, I see," Sherry said on a chuckle, and then
shrugged and added, "It's the thought that counts,
though, and you did offer to put us up."

Elvi smiled. "I like the way you think."

Sherry grinned and turned to open the suitcase Elvi
had set on the bed. She now knew why the woman had
insisted on carrying it up for her. Elvi felt she had to
because Sherry was apparently an official guest.

Aware that Elvi was moving toward the door to leave
her alone, Sherry quickly asked, "So what's Basileios
really like?"

Glancing over her shoulder, she saw that Elvi had
stopped by the door and turned back with surprise on
her face.

"I only met him yesterday," Sherry pointed out quietly. "Yet apparently I might be his life mate, but, really,

I don't know him from Adam. I'd appreciate anything you can tell me."

Elvi hesitated, but then nodded with understanding and moved back, settling on the bed beside her suitcase before admitting, "This is the first time I've met him." Before Sherry could comment, she rushed on, "But Victor says he's a lot like Lucian, which is why the two constantly butt heads."

"They butt heads?" Sherry asked with interest, forgetting all about unpacking.

"Apparently," Elvi said with a shrug. "Victor said the two were always at loggerheads when they were younger. Until Basileios moved away. Victor said it was to get away from Lucian, who likes to boss people around."

Sherry frowned. "Does that mean Basileios likes to boss people around?"

"That's what I asked," Elvi admitted on a laugh, and then said wryly, "I mean, Lucian is great, but I don't think the world is ready for two tyrants like him. But Victor said no, Basileios has more of a live-and-let-live kind of personality. But that he's got a strong character like Lucian and an even stronger sense of right and wrong. The problem was that while Basil doesn't try to boss others around, he also doesn't like to be bossed around . . . and that was an issue with Lucian as a big brother."

Sherry nodded, not surprised to hear this. She didn't know Lucian any better than she did Basileios, but it didn't take long to come to the conclusion that the guy thought he was a feudal lord and the entire population of the world were his subjects.

"He's not quite that bad," Elvi said solemnly, proving that she too could read her.

"I thought I was supposed to be hard to read, and probably impossible to read for new turns," she said with a frown. "Are you an old turn? I got the feeling you were newer."

"Really?" Elvi asked with interest. "Why is that?"

"I don't know," Sherry murmured, and then after a moment to consider it, said, "I think because you don't speak as stiffly as the older ones. You use short forms like *don't* and *aren't*, while they tend not to shorten their words as often. You sound more today compared to Basileios, Katricia, and Drina."

"Yes, they speak more formally. Though Stephanie is trying to change that," Elvi said with a faint smile, and then admitted, "And you may have been harder to read at first, but once you were put together with Basileios . . ." She shrugged. "I'm afraid you will become easier and easier to read for a while."

"Why?" Sherry asked curiously.

"I think it's the sex, or maybe the sex hormones," Elvi said, and then added dryly, "They certainly seem to scramble the brain for the first little while." She shrugged. "I think they lower your ability to guard your thoughts."

"Hmm," Sherry muttered, and lifted a sheer black top out of the suitcase to hang up in the closet. It was a dressy top and she supposed it would come in handy if they went out to dinner or something. But only if Justin had packed the black camisole she liked to wear with it. The thought of his pawing through her lingerie drawer, though, was kind of embarrassing. To get her mind off of it, she asked, "So, as far as you know, Basileios is an okay guy?"

"According to Victor, Basileios is a good man. In fact, he's Victor's favorite brother, so I've been looking forward to meeting him."

"Oh." Sherry turned back from hanging up the top. As she crossed to the suitcase, she said, "I'm sorry. Go on down and get to know him, then. I didn't mean to keep you from——"

"It'll wait," Elvi said on a laugh, and then standing up, offered, "But why don't I help you hang up your clothes. It will speed things along so we can go downstairs and make tea or something. Victor should be back by now with goodies to have with tea."

"Thank you," Sherry murmured, and picked up another shirt, frowning as she noted it was her sheer white blouse, similar to her black one but a different cut. Still, it too needed a camisole. Holding it in one hand, she began to dig through the clothes with her other and released a mutter of dismay.

"What's wrong?" Elvi asked.

"Other than two see-through tops, everything in here is negligees. There are no socks, no slacks, not even any panties and—— Oh wait, he packed my black lace bustier and the matching thong," she said with disgust.

"I gather you didn't pack the bag?" Elvi asked carefully, obviously trying not to laugh at her predicament, which Sherry supposed would be funny to others, but wasn't to her. She couldn't walk around in peignoirs all the time. In fact, she couldn't walk around in them at all except in her room. What the devil was she supposed to wear?

"No," she said, tossing the silky dressing gowns back in her bag with irritation. "Lucian sent Justin to do it."

"Ah, it was probably his idea of a joke, then," Elvi said soothingly. "Don't worry, we can nip down to Walmart and buy you anything you need. Or we can even go into London and hit the nicer shops." She patted Sherry's shoulder and then grinned. "And, since Justin messed up, we can just charge it to the room and let the council pay for it. Their mistake, they foot the bill."

Sherry smiled slowly at the suggestion, then closed the suitcase and nodded. "Sounds like fun."

"Good. Let's go down and make some tea, then, I'm parched," Elvi said, heading for the door. Halfway there, though, she mused, "Or maybe a glass of wine would be nice."

"It isn't even noon yet," Sherry pointed out with amusement.

"Yes, but alcohol doesn't affect me anymore anyway," Elvi assured her. "The nanos clear it away too quickly. I just like the taste . . . and it might help you relax. You're practically vibrating with tension."

Sherry stopped walking and peered at her wide-eyed. "Am I?"

Elvi nodded, a sympathetic smile on her face. "Your mind is just racing. Am I a life mate? What does that mean? Would this Leo person really come after me?

Will my life ever return to normal? Was it shared pleasure or just lust?"

Sherry was pretty sure she was blushing brightly by the time Elvi finished listing the thoughts she was reading from her. And those *were* the worries running around inside her head. It was terribly disconcerting, though, to think everyone was hearing these worries . . . especially the one about shared pleasure and lust.

"I know," Elvi said on a little sigh. "It's terribly embarrassing and distressing to know that every single person in this house will know exactly what you're thinking for the next while. Unfortunately, there isn't a thing you or I or anyone else can do about it. We aren't listening in so much, as you're shouting your thoughts at us. It's another sign of life mates," she explained.

"Oh dear," Sherry breathed, horrified at the thought that her mind was shouting out things like "Was it shared pleasure or lust?" to everyone.

Elvi nodded. "That's why I thought wine might be nice. Hopefully, it will help you relax and worry a little less."

"Yes, then wine sounds good," Sherry decided firmly.

"Come along, then, we'll go see if we have some," Elvi said, turning back to open the door. "If not, we'll make the boys take us shopping and then out to lunch. You can't worry about all these things while debating between which blouse to buy."

Smiling faintly, Sherry followed her out of the room. She suspected she and Elvi would be good friends. Certainly, she already liked the other woman.

Six

"**D**o you have to go into the restaurant today, my love?" Victor asked.

Sherry glanced to Elvi in surprise. They were seated at the dining room table enjoying coffee. Sherry had passed on the wine in the end, feeling awkward about drinking it so early. She, Basil, Elvi, Victor, and Katricia were there. Drina and Harper still hadn't come downstairs, and Stephanie slipped away to her own room shortly after Sherry and Elvi had come below.

"You work in a restaurant?" Sherry asked curiously. For some reason she'd just assumed Elvi had her hands full with running Casey Cottage.

"My friend Hazel and I own a Mexican restaurant in town. It's called Bella Black's," Elvi explained. She then glanced to her husband and said, "I might go in later, but after Lucian called last night, I asked Pedro and Rosita to open today, and to call in one of the girls for an extra shift." She smiled wryly and shrugged. "I thought I should stay here to greet Basil and Sherry."

"Ah." Victor nodded.

"I'm glad I did too, since Bricker didn't pack anything but lingerie for Sherry and we need to take her shopping," Elvi added dryly.

"I'd rather you wait a day for that shopping trip."

Sherry glanced around with surprise at that comment and stared at the man who stood in the open kitchen door. Tall, dark-haired, and really rather gorgeous, the man wore a police uniform and carried two duffel bags that he now set on the floor. It could only be Katricia's Teddy, she decided when Basil's daughter stood and moved around the counter to greet him with a kiss that made her eyebrows rise. It looked like it started out and was meant to be a gentle kiss of greeting and nothing more, but best intentions and all that, it quickly caught flame and turned into much more. Sherry was about to turn away when Teddy suddenly broke the kiss and tucked Katricia's head against his chest to avoid temptation.

"God, woman, I hope you found a dress because I surely missed you and don't want you to have to leave again," he growled, holding her close.

"I did," she assured him, and then raised her head to add, "I didn't get the chance to buy it, but I can call in the order and have it delivered."

"Good," he said, and kissed her forehead, then released her to remove his shoes.

"So, why do you want Sherry and I to wait a day to go shopping?" Elvi asked now. "Is there trouble?"

"No," Teddy answered, finishing with his shoes. Straightening, he added, "I'd just rather Sherry and Stephanie stay close to the house for a day, to make sure they weren't followed from Toronto." Slipping his arm around Katricia, he then urged her around the counter to join them in the dining room, saying, "Once we're sure there isn't going to be trouble you can take her shopping."

"Drina and I kept an eye out, I am pretty sure we were not followed," Katricia said, and then added, "But it is better to be safe than sorry."

When Victor and Basil both nodded in agreement, Elvi sighed and cast Sherry an apologetic look. "Tomorrow, then. But I'll loan you clothes until we can go shopping."

Sherry seriously doubted she'd fit in Elvi's clothes. The woman was a little shorter than her, and definitely thinner. Sherry had more of a Marilyn Monroe type figure than she liked.

"Sherry, this is Teddy Brunswick, Chief of Police in Port Henry and a very old and dear friend," Elvi said, making the introductions.

"Hello," Sherry murmured, smiling at the man, and then taking his hand when he held it out.

"It's a pleasure to meet you, Ms. Carne," Teddy said politely as he shook her hand. "Welcome to Port Henry. I'm sorry your visit couldn't be under better circumstances."

"Thank you," Sherry murmured as he released her hand.

Nodding, Teddy turned to Elvi then. "If you'll tell me which room we're in, I'll take the bags up and get them out of the way."

"Top floor next to Harper's room," Elvi announced, standing up and gathering empty coffee cups. As Teddy turned to head back to the bags by the door, she asked, "Do you want a coffee, Teddy? There's still some in the pot."

"Maybe later, thanks," he said as he bent to gather the bags.

"I'll help you take them up," Katricia said with a grin as she quickly scooped one up herself. She then caught Teddy's free hand to lead him to the stairs.

"That's the last we'll see of those two for a while," Victor said with amusement as he watched the pair hurry upstairs.

Elvi grinned and then glanced to Basil and Sherry before saying, "Well, I may as well head in to the restaurant after all. Then I can take tomorrow off instead for our shopping trip."

Sherry smiled at the suggestion and then shifted her gaze to Victor when he stood as well.

"I'll take you to the restaurant, love," Victor announced, and then glanced to Basil. "There's a sunroom off our bedroom with a television and whatnot. You two can go there and talk in private if you like. I am sure you have a lot to discuss."

Basil nodded. "Thank you."

"I had a security system put in when they renovated after the fire," Victor added. "We'll lock up and turn it on, on our way out. I'll show you how to work it when I get back, but in the meantime, the others know what to do if it goes off."

"Okay," Basil murmured.

Nodding, Victor turned to Elvi. "Shall we?"

Smiling, she took the hand he held out and headed for the door.

"Well," Basil said once the door closed behind the other couple. "Would you like to go see the sunroom?"

Sherry nodded and stood up. There didn't appear to be much else for them to do at the moment. Besides, she had a lot of questions she'd like answered. She lined them up in her head as they walked upstairs.

Elvi and Victor's room was at the opposite end of the house from hers. It was a large, beautiful room done in shades of cool blue, she saw as they walked through the short hallway next to it, leading to the sunroom.

"Wow," she said as they stepped out into the sunroom itself. It was lovely, furnished with a large comfortable couch and a chair along the outer walls, and a large television, PlayStation, and music system on a shelving unit against the wall backing onto the house. That wall and the bottom halves of the outer walls were all painted a pale yellow, while large glass windows made up the upper halves of the outer walls, leaving a three-sided view. Sheer blinds covered the windows, allowing sunlight in, but she guessed not allowing anyone to actually see in. She smiled as she peered out at the pretty tree-lined street and the big backyard with its garden and old trees.

"Very nice," Basil agreed, taking it all in with a smile. "It makes me envy my brother his home."

"Tell me about it," Sherry said on a laugh as she moved closer to the back window to look down on the deck in the backyard. She had an apartment in Toronto. It was owned, not rented, and a nice size, but there weren't a lot of trees anywhere near it or near her store. She didn't see this kind of greenery often and hadn't realized how much she missed it until just this moment. Glancing to Basil, she asked suddenly, "So why is this your first trip down here?"

Basil turned to arch an eyebrow. "Who says it is?"

"Elvi said she hadn't met you before," Sherry explained, turning her gaze back to the window. "So either you only came when she wasn't here, or . . ." She shrugged, leaving the rest unsaid.

"Very good deductive reasoning, Dr. Watson," Basil teased lightly, and then admitted, "I have been meaning to fly up to meet Victor's new life mate, but business or family always intervened."

"Fly up?" Sherry asked.

"I live and work in New York."

"Oh." That surprised her. She'd just assumed he was from Toronto like her.

"Anyway, I should have met Elvi at the wedding, but I got detained in Europe," he said wryly.

"Detained?" Sherry asked. "Like pulled over by airport security detained?"

"No," he said on a chuckle. "I was supposed to fly back the night before the wedding, but a big storm hit.

No one was flying. We left as soon as we could but still ended up hitting New York a good four hours after the wedding. By the time we got through traffic into the city, even the reception was over."

"Elvi and Victor got married in New York?" she asked with surprise.

Basil nodded. "It was a big multi-wedding. Several couples married at the same time. Elvi and Victor were among them."

"Ah," she murmured, but then asked, "So what do you do in New York?"

"Ride herd on my children, harass my brother Lucian with long distance calls, and make money for both myself and the council," he said with a shrug.

She grinned at the harassing his brother bit, but asked, "And working as a lawyer makes you that much money?"

"While I am presently a lawyer, I also run half a dozen companies under one large umbrella company, and manage several investments I have built up over the years."

"Right," she said slowly. "I forgot, you're old so you're stinking rich."

"I have a lot of money, but have not noticed it giving off any kind of unpleasant odor," he assured her.

If she hadn't caught the twinkle in his eye, Sherry would have thought he'd taken her literally. However, she did see it, so merely smiled and asked, "What kind of lawyer?"

Basil hesitated and then turned and moved to sit on the couch before answering, "Business law mostly at the moment, although I am licensed in criminal, civil, and immigration law as well."

"Of course, you are," she said dryly, and shook her head as she moved to sit on the other end of the couch. "I suppose living so long allows you to diversify a bit."

"Yes," he agreed. "I have not always been a lawyer. I only took it up the last century or so."

She peered at him curiously. "What were you before you were a lawyer?"

Basil grimaced and then smiled and admitted, "I have been many things over the centuries. I was a Rogue Hunter at one time, a warrior, a doctor, a sous chef, a musician, an artist, a—"

"Artist?" she asked with interest. "And a doctor?"

"I was a bad artist," he admitted, "and just an okay musician, but I was a pretty good doctor."

"Well, you definitely seem to like variety," she said wryly.

"It helps relieve the boredom of living so long," he said quietly.

She nodded and peered out at the passing cars on the street in front of the house for a moment before changing the subject, and asking curiously, "You said run herd on your children. How many children do you have?"

"Twenty-two," he answered easily.

Sherry froze, and then turned to stare at him wide-eyed. "What?"

Basil glanced at her, noted her expression and said a little more warily, "Twenty-two."

"You have *twenty-two* children?"

Basil nodded slowly, appearing perplexed by her dismay.

"Why?" Sherry asked.

His eyebrows rose with surprise. "Why what?"

"Why twenty-two children?" she clarified. "I mean, I can see three or four, but . . . twenty-two?"

"Actually, we had twenty-six altogether, but only twenty-two still live," Basil said quietly. "And we had so many because . . . well, Mary and I both like children. We are allowed to have one every hundred years, and so we have. Our youngest is twenty-five and just got called to the bar. We are quite proud of him."

"*We* are?" Sherry asked with dismay. "Your wife is still alive? I mean I knew you must have been married at one time to have Katricia, but she was born back in—well, ages ago, for heaven's sake. I thought your wife must have died by now. But she's still alive? You're still married?" Sherry was shrieking by the end, she was so horrified at this news. Here everyone was squawking about her being his life mate, and shared pleasure and blah blah blah, and the man was *married,* for God's sake.

"Breathe," Basil said soothingly, reaching out to clasp her hand gently. He allowed her a moment to regain her calm and then said, "Mary and I are not now, and never have been, married or even involved. We are nothing more than friends."

Sherry blinked repeatedly at that and then snapped, "Friends who have had twenty-six kids together, but you're not involved? That sounds pretty damned involved to me."

Basil winced and shook his head. "You have to understand—"

"Understand what?" she bit out, and then said sarcastically, "No, let me guess. She doesn't understand you. Or she's cold and won't let you touch her, but you stay together for the kids. Or, oh, she's having a relationship with the plumber but won't agree to divorce because she's Catholic. Puhleeze," she growled. "You—"

"We are not married, by law or even common law. We do not now, and never have, lived together. We have only ever been friends and co-parents. The children were . . ." He seemed to struggle for the words to explain, and then sighed and tugged at her hand, urging her to sit beside him. Once she settled stiffly on the couch next to him, he said solemnly, "Sherry, living so long sounds grand and wonderful. No one thinks they want to die, but the truth is, it gets pretty damned repetitive. You get up, you feed, you work, you sleep, and then you get up and do it all over again."

Mouth tight, he turned to peer out of the window and then said, "I have been alive 3,538 years. That means I have seen roughly 1,291,370 sunrises and sunsets. I have eaten and slept and worked and . . . Quite frankly, it's boring as hell. That is why some of our kind go rogue and start misbehaving. They are exhausted and bored and need something to make them feel alive again. A life mate can ease that. But waiting to find that life mate is hell. I was in that place. I needed something to give me a reason to look forward, something to capture my interest and hold it.

"Mary and I grew up together. We were more buddies than anything else. We can read each other, and as the older one I imagine I can control her, although I have never tried. So, when she admitted she was growing tired of living, I understood completely. And then when she said she thought having a child might ease that, that it would give her someone to think about and care about besides herself, I thought . . ." His mouth tightened and then he said, "Well, I thought it was worth a damned try. It was certainly better than suicide by Rogue Hunter, so I agreed.

"We did not think," he admitted quietly. "We did not plan anything, we simply did it. And it worked. Gabriel was our first child, a beautiful baby boy. He gave us both a reason to get up in the evenings. He reinvigorated us. We are both alive and relatively healthy all these centuries later because of Gabriel, Katricia, Crispinus, Marius, Flavia, and all the others. And I did not regret it. I do not regret it. I love my children, every one of them, and I am also grateful to them because they saved my sanity and my life . . . and Mary is too."

Sherry was silent for a minute, and then asked, "You didn't live with Mary? Even when the children were little?"

"No," he assured her. "We are not life mates, Sherry. You do not understand what that means. We can read each other's thoughts. It is difficult to live with someone who can read your thoughts. You have to guard every little thing that goes through your mind, even one stray thought could unintentionally wound them. You can start the day with everything fine, one stray thought hits, and boom, it is a world war in the middle of your home."

She smiled faintly and said, "It can't be that bad."

"Trust me, it is. Think about some of your thoughts through the day. Is every one of them complimentary?"

Sherry frowned, considering her thoughts. As far as she knew, she didn't run around having insulting thoughts.

"You are shaking your head. You cannot think of anything insulting you might have thought?" he asked, and when she shook her head again, he nodded. "We are often not even aware of it." He hesitated for a moment and then said, "Okay, you walk into the office, or in your case, your store, one of the girls comes in looking a little peaked, gray-faced, bags under their eyes, etcetera . . . Have you really never thought, 'Wow, she looks like hell'?"

Sherry bit her lip. She actually had thought that. She never would have said it, of course, but she had thought it.

"Or you have never looked at someone and thought they have put on a couple pounds, or those pants make their behind look huge?"

Sherry grimaced. Yes, she'd thought that.

"Or, you are training a new employee and she seems slow to learn, you briefly lose your patience and think, 'Good Lord, she is so dense sometimes,' before you take a breath and try again?"

"Ah," Sherry breathed on a sigh.

"Or you think someone's laugh sounds like nails on chalkboard. Or someone is humming off-key and you think they are tone deaf. Or—"

"I get it," Sherry interrupted, and grimaced as she admitted, "Yes, I guess I probably have thoughts that could be considered insulting, and more often than I realized."

"You do not mean them as insulting. They are your thoughts, after all, no one can hear them," Basil said quietly.

"But immortals can," Sherry said on a sigh. "I guess that would make it hard to live with one."

"It is a little more complicated than that," Basil said quietly. "Younger immortals usually cannot read older immortals if we are guarding our thoughts, but it is impossible to constantly guard your thoughts. Well, not impossible, but it is stressful and that guard can slip. And of course, mortals cannot read immortals, but they also do not guard their own thoughts at all, and being constantly bombarded with stray thoughts, insults, and fantasies can be exhausting."

"I can imagine," Sherry said quietly, bit her lip anxiously and then asked, "But you cannot read my thoughts, right? Or can you now? Stephanie can now."

"No, I cannot read you," Basil assured her. "Which makes you the most restful person in Casey Cottage."

"Restful?" Sherry asked with a wince. That sounded about as sexy as snot.

Basil chuckled at her expression. "Believe me, it makes you the most attractive woman in the world. I can relax with you, Sherry. Usually the only time I can relax is when I am alone, but being alone is . . . well, lonely," he said dryly. "It is nice to be able to enjoy company without having to be on my guard. I have not enjoyed that since Acantha."

"Acantha?" Sherry asked. "Where is that?"

"Acantha is not a place, she was my first life mate," he said quietly.

"Your first life mate?" she asked with surprise. "So I'm not the first?"

"No," he said solemnly. "I was fortunate enough to meet a life mate while I was quite young. Sadly, I did not have her long."

"What happened to her?" Sherry asked.

"Atlantis fell six months after we were mated. She did not survive." He was silent for a moment and then added, "Acantha was a teacher. The school where she taught exploded during the first quake that hit. She was caught in the flames and . . ." He swallowed and then explained, "For some reason the nanos make us very flammable. She did not have a chance."

"I'm sorry," Sherry said quietly.

"As am I," he said solemnly, and admitted, "At the time, it felt like the end of the world, and I am ashamed to admit it, but I basically sat down and . . ." He shrugged. "I was not exactly motivated to struggle to survive. I would have died there with everyone else, but for Lucian. He basically dragged me out of Atlantis, me and our brother Jean Claude both, though I do not know where Lucian found the will or desire to live himself. He lost not only his life mate in the fall, but his children as well."

"That's awful," Sherry murmured.

"Yes." Basil sighed the word and then glanced her way with a wry smile. "And this is some terribly depressing conversation. Besides, it all happened a very long time ago. We have all had more than three thousand years to grieve the loss of Atlantis and all those who died with it, family and friends, home, a life that can never be replicated."

Sherry nodded and peered down at their entwined hands, trying to think of another topic, something less depressing to discuss. After a moment she said, "If Atlantis was that advanced back then, imagine how much further ahead it would be now."

"Hmmm," Basil murmured, and then pointed out, "On the other hand, they might eventually have found a fix for the nano issue and then I would not be here to meet you."

She nodded silently at that, acknowledging it was true. She hadn't known the man long, but she was definitely glad to have met him . . . so far.

"So . . . why a kitchenware store?" Basil asked suddenly.

Sherry glanced to him with surprise and then grinned at his somewhat baffled expression. She supposed to a man, opening a kitchenware store would be the last thing he'd think to do. Especially a man who hadn't eaten in forever. Shrugging, she said simply, "Because I love food."

Basil considered her answer for a moment, but his expression didn't clear and he finally asked, "Well, then why not a restaurant?"

"Because I suck at cooking," she said honestly, and chuckled at the dismay this brought to his face. After a moment she assured him, "I don't really suck at it, but I'm not good enough to run a restaurant. Besides, I love all the gadgets and whosits in my store; pasta makers, ice cream makers, the gadget that peels, cores, and slices your apples . . ." She shrugged. "There are so many nifty things out there now that make cooking easier for women like me who are busy and want to save time. And then there are lovely serving sets, pretty wine decanters, cool stone ice cubes, and so on. There are so many innovations and new ones almost weekly."

"And you probably have every one of them in your own kitchen," he guessed with amusement.

"I do," she confessed with a self-deprecating smile, and then confessed, "I have pretty much everything and anything necessary to throw fabulous dinner parties. Sadly, I never get to use them. I never have the time, and even if I did, I haven't had the time to make much in the way of friends. I have a couple, but I've been so busy getting the store up and running that I let a lot of friendships drop."

"So a social butterfly who is held back by work?" Basil suggested gently.

Sherry considered that, then smiled with self-deprecation and said, "That or a wannabe social butterfly who hides behind her work."

Basil appeared surprised by her candor, but merely asked, "How long have you owned your store?"

"Three years," Sherry answered.

"And you're thirty-two now?" he asked.

"Yes, I opened it on my twenty-ninth birthday."

Basil raised his eyebrows and gave a silent whistle. "Impressive."

Sherry smiled faintly and shook her head. "Not that impressive. While I worked hard and saved every spare penny after university, I still couldn't have opened the store that young on my own."

"Then how?" he asked curiously.

Sherry shrugged, and avoided answering by telling him, "I could have opened it six or seven years earlier than that. Luther offered me the money to open a store when we graduated, but I refused."

"Luther?" Basil asked, obviously curious.

"Oh." She gave a slight laugh. "A friend. His name is really Lex, but I used to call him Lex Luther as a joke and then somehow it just became Luther." She shrugged and then smiled reminiscently before saying, "He's the best friend I ever had. We met in university, ended up both renting rooms in the same house when I moved off campus after my first year, and we're still friends today, though I don't get to see him anymore.

"Anyway, he comes from a rich family," she added. "So when graduation came, he offered to bankroll me on the store. We'd be partners. But—" She paused and grimaced. "I wanted to do it on my own. I wanted to prove to myself I could do it, and I had a plan. Besides, I didn't want to gamble on his money. I'd have never forgiven myself if the store failed and I lost his money."

"Is this Luther the man you were dating but were not exclusive with?"

Sherry noted that he was talking about it in the past tense, as if she'd agreed to break off her casual relationship with the man she'd been dating. But she let that go and shook her head. "No. Luther has only ever been a friend." She smiled and added, "Actually, I haven't seen him for years. He was offered a really good position with a company in Saudi Arabia about the time I opened my store, and other than the occasional e-mail, we hardly talk anymore. But before that he was kind of like a combo girlfriend and older brother all in one. And I think he's gay, although he hasn't admitted that to me yet." Sherry paused to ponder that briefly, wondering why Luther wouldn't admit it to her. It wasn't like she'd care.

Shrugging that concern away, she continued, "Anyway, he offered me the money to open the store, but I said no and set out to do it on my own. According to my big life plan, I would have saved enough to open my own store by the time I was thirty-four, and I would have owned it free and clear, no loans or anything."

"But instead you were able to open it at twenty-nine," he murmured, and then asked, "What happened? Did you win a lottery?"

"I wish," Sherry said softly, and shook her head. "No. I'm afraid my mother died. A heart attack at fifty-four."

"I am sorry," Basil said quietly.

"As you said about your wife, so am I."

"I presume you used your inheritance to start your store early?" he guessed.

Sherry nodded. "Mom had an insurance policy. I put it toward the store. I think it's what she would have wanted. She was always supportive of my dream."

Basil nodded. "And your father? Siblings?"

Sherry shrugged. "I had a brother, Danny. He was a year younger than me, but . . . ."

She paused and swallowed and then it suddenly came

out. Tumbling over her lips like wine out of a bottle, she blurted the whole story of how she'd lost her brother.

"He drowned when I was eight. We were on a boating trip to Cedar Point. We went with several other families we often boated with. We arrived just before dinnertime and were supposed to visit the park the next day. The boaters decided to barbecue at the dock that night, to save money for the next day, I guess. There were picnic benches and stuff on the shoreline for boaters to use. Us kids were playing while the adults barbecued on hibachis . . . hot dogs and hamburgers. Mom forgot the hot dog buns. Dad sent Danny back to the boat to get them." She glanced out toward the backyard again and said, "It took a while for anyone to realize he hadn't returned with the buns. When they went to check on him, Danny was floating between the boat and the dock. He was a good swimmer. We both were, but there was a gash on his forehead. They think he must have slipped getting on or off the boat and hit his head."

"So young," Basil said sadly, shaking his head. "That must have been hard on you all."

Sherry nodded. "My parents never got over it. They blamed each other and themselves. If she hadn't forgotten the buns, if he had gone for them himself . . ." She shook her head. "It wasn't long before they divorced. Dad moved out West, met and married a woman with two kids and had two more with her, and I haven't seen him since."

Basil frowned. "He never contacts you or—?"

"He called a couple times. E-mailed too," she admitted. "But I wasn't very receptive. It felt like I lost my brother and then he abandoned us. It also felt like he didn't care about me, like Danny was all that had mattered to him and I wasn't enough to keep him there," Sherry admitted quietly.

"I am sure that is not true," Basil said quietly.

Sherry shrugged. "He didn't try very hard to see or speak to me when I stopped taking his calls," she pointed out, and then sighed and said, "But that's okay. It was a long time ago."

"So, you are alone in the world?" Basil asked.

"No. I have three aunts on my mom's side and their families. They gathered around me and were very supportive when Mom died. They still are. They always include me in holidays and birthdays. And I have friends."

Basil merely nodded and asked, "So what did you take in university? Business?"

"Yes." She smiled. "It seemed the sensible degree if I wanted to own my own business one day."

"Very sensible," he agreed. "And did you use it before starting your business?"

"Of course. I worked in the offices of a large international building contractor based in Toronto. It was a good job, the pay was excellent, otherwise I never would have been able to save money as I did. And they were willing to pay all the overtime I wanted to work." She grinned. "I worked a lot of overtime.

"Ah." He nodded. "You never married, then?"

She glanced at him with confusion. "What has overtime to do with marriage?"

"Spoken like someone who has never been married," he said with amusement. "A husband would protest at so much overtime."

"Oh." She shook her head. "No. I've not been very lucky in love. I have terrible taste in men. It's been all losers and louses for me," she said wryly, and then added, "I was engaged once, though, for a bit."

"What happened to end the engagement?" Basil asked, curious.

Sherry shrugged. "It just didn't work out. These things happen. It's better this way."

He nodded and then smiled faintly. "Well, it is certainly better for me."

"How's that?" she asked.

Basil hesitated and then said, "Ask me that again a week from now."

Sherry stared at him curiously, but then turned to peer outside again as movement caught her eye. A woman had just come out of the house next door with gloves and a sun hat on and a basket in hand full of gardening tools. As Sherry watched, the woman moved to the rosebushes lining the front of her house, set down the basket, picked up pruning shears and set to work on her rosebushes.

"It's a beautiful day," Basil said quietly.

"Yes, beautiful," Sherry sighed, and then pointed out, "When I brought up sunlight and your people not seeming to have any problem with it, you explained about the nanos. Does that mean that, unlike Stoker's vampires, you don't have problems with sunlight?"

"No."

She raised an eyebrow. "But traditional vampires can't stand sunlight . . . or garlic . . . or religious symbols like the cross."

"Ah." Basil smiled faintly as he watched the woman work. "Well, while we won't burst into flames or anything when struck by sunlight, it does damage our skin, just as it does mortals. Traditionally we did, and still do, avoid sunlight as much as possible. You will not find any sun worshippers among our people. The more damage we take, the more blood we need. The need for more blood at one time meant more risk of getting caught. Now it just means wasting blood, which is a precious commodity. Our blood banks have as much trouble replacing stock as the Red Cross and mortal blood banks do." He shrugged. "So we avoid it as much as possible. In the past, that meant staying indoors much of the day and living mostly at night. Nowadays, though, we are much freer. We have UV protective glazing put on windows in both our homes and cars, so it's just a matter of getting from the vehicle to a building or vice versa, which does little enough damage."

Sherry shifted her attention to the actual glass of the window she was looking out of, supposing they probably had that UV protective glaze.

"As for churches and religious symbols," Basil continued. "They are not a problem for us."

Shifting her attention back to him, she asked, "And garlic?" The question was more teasing than serious.

"I personally love garlic," he assured her. "Well, I would not eat it before a date, but otherwise . . ." He shrugged. "It does us no harm." He pursed his lips and then added, "My brother Jean Claude loathed garlic, though, which may be where the whole garlic thing came from."

Sherry glanced doubtfully at him, wondering how one man's dislike of garlic could turn into the whole myth of garlic being detrimental to the health of vampires. But Basil merely shook his head, and muttered, "Long story."

"You've mentioned your brother Jean Claude a couple of times. Does he live in Canada or the U.S.?"

"He lived in Canada at the end, but passed away some years back," Basil answered.

"Oh." She grimaced. "Sorry."

Basil shrugged. "That is one of life's drawbacks, death is a constant companion."

"Less so for your kind than mine," she pointed out dryly.

"Perhaps I should have said loss is a constant companion to life," he said solemnly. "For while I have lived a very long time, I have witnessed and grieved the loss of countless family members, friends, and acquaintances."

"Wow, you're really trying to sell this immortality business," Sherry teased with amusement. The man was not making it attractive.

Basil grimaced. "Salesman is one career I never tried. I knew I would not be good at it."

Sherry shrugged. "I'm not good with sales either."

Basil laughed at that. "You own a store. Sales *is* your business."

"That's different. People come in looking for something and we help them find it. We don't drag people in off the street and try to sell them something."

"Ah," he smiled. "Yes, I can see the difference."

They were both silent for a minute, and then Sherry asked, "Do you like living in New York?"

Basil shrugged. "It is all right. But it would certainly be nice to see more trees and grass. That is probably the only thing I miss in New York. There are parks, of course, and I have a couple of potted trees on my terrace, but it is not the same as living somewhere like this."

"No. That's how I feel about living in an apartment in Toronto," Sherry agreed.

Basil nodded. "On the other hand. I am usually working, so would not get to enjoy the trees much anyway."

"Yeah," Sherry agreed with a wry smile. "It's the same with me. I seem always to be working as well. Not that I mind," she added quickly. "It's my dream. A labor of love, so . . ." She shrugged.

"But it leaves precious little time for a social life?" he suggested.

"Oh, I don't mind that either," she assured him, and he looked surprised.

"Really?" he asked. "No biological clock ticking? No pining for marriage and little ones?"

Sherry shook her head and then frowned. "I used to. When I was younger I often thought about finding a man I loved, marrying and settling down. But now I just want the store to be up and running and doing well."

"You started it three years ago?" he asked.

Sherry nodded.

"Is it not self-sustaining by now? It usually takes about three years for a store to find its footing."

"Yes," she agreed.

"And yours has not?" he asked.

"Oh, yes. It did surprisingly well from the start, and since I paid for it outright and had no loans, we started turning a profit almost right away," she admitted.

"Then it shouldn't need all the extra work anymore," he reasoned.

"Yes, but I just want the store to be up and running and doing well," she repeated as her gaze settled on the Keurig coffee machine beside the television. "I wonder if they'd mind if I had a coffee? All this talk is making me thirsty."

Basil was silent for a minute, watching her, but then he gave his head a small shake, stood, and walked over to the coffee machine. "Of course they would not mind."

Sherry stood and joined him, noting that the machine sat on a black metal holder for the small K cups, similar to the one she had in her own office. Opening the drawer, she found various types of coffee in it. Drinking cups were lined up next to the machine and a silver canister held spoons. There was even sugar. Her gaze slid to the water cooler standing next to the shelving unit and she smiled. "I bet there is cream in the cooler's refrigerator."

"Refrigerator?" Basil echoed dubiously.

Smiling, Sherry knelt and opened the lower front of the water cooler base, revealing the small refrigerated compartment inside and the cream it held. There were also some soft drinks there. "I have the same setup in my office. Water cooler with fridge. It supplies the water for my Keurig, and I can keep my milk cold so I never have to leave my office to grab a coffee while working. Saves time."

"Clever," Basil commented as she retrieved the cream and stood up.

"Or lazy," she admitted with amusement. "It's also cheaper than installing a sink and fridge in my office."

"I am quite surprised Victor drinks coffee," Basil said as she selected a vanilla hazelnut K cup and set it in the Keurig machine. "Actually, I've noticed all the hunters seem to drink it, which surprises me."

"Why?" Sherry grabbed a coffee cup next and set it on the silver grill, then hit the middle button. She shifted to lean sideways against the shelf as she waited for Basil to answer.

"Caffeine can make immortals a bit . . ." He hesitated, obviously searching for the right word. Finally, he shrugged and said, "Well, I believe the modern term is wired."

"Enough of it can make anyone wired," she said with amusement, and then raised her eyebrows and asked, "The nanos don't take care of the caffeine in your systems?"

"Oddly enough, no. Instead, the effects appear to be amplified in immortals."

"Hmm. Weird," she commented, and turned to collect her coffee as the machine finished dripping it into her cup. "Does that mean you don't want coffee? They have cider and hot chocolate in the K cups up here too, I noticed."

"No, I shall have the coffee. I quite enjoyed the one we had on the ride down," Basil said, opening the drawer. After a hesitation, he selected a vanilla hazelnut as well.

Sherry grabbed him a cup and set it on the silver grill even as he popped the K cup in. Then she left him to hit the middle button and turned her attention to adding cream and sugar to her own coffee.

"So, this man that you are casually dating . . . ?" Basil asked a moment later as he began to doctor his own coffee.

Sherry turned to walk to the couch, aware that her eyebrows had risen. She didn't know why, but his broaching the subject surprised her. Although, she supposed she shouldn't be surprised. He'd asked if Luther was the one she was dating when he'd come up in conversation. Sitting on the couch, she set her coffee on the side table and glanced to him in question. "Yes?"

"Tell me about him," Basil suggested.

Sherry shrugged. "There isn't much to tell. Barry owns the sporting goods store next to my store. He's newly divorced and going through the slut stage."

"Slut stage?" Basil asked with a sort of horrified bewilderment.

Sherry chuckled slightly at his expression. "I've noticed that when couples break up, one or the other often goes through either a crazy period or a slut stage. The slut stage is dating and sometimes even sleeping with everything that moves. The crazy period is the weeping, wailing, bitching, and can't-stand-to-be-alone thing. Barry is going through the slut stage."

"And you are dating him?" he asked with dismay.

Sherry rolled her eyes. "I did say it was casual. We go out to movies or dinner and stuff. I'm not stupid enough to sleep with him when he's sleeping with half the women in Toronto."

"Oh." Basil settled on the couch next to her and set his own coffee on his end table. He then glanced to her with a confounded expression and asked, "But why even date him?"

Sherry sighed. "Because it's easy. He has no expectations. He doesn't want commitment. Doesn't get angry when I work late, or when I cancel at the last minute because something has cropped up at the shop. He just calls one of his other friends." She pursed her lips and then admitted, "I suppose we aren't even really dating so much as going out on dates once in a while."

"But why even do that?" he asked, truly appearing bewildered. "Courtship is undertaken in the hopes of finding a mate, and yet you don't appear to consider him mateworthy."

"Maybe, but I don't really have time for a mate right now," Sherry said with a shrug. "I need the store up and running and doing well before I can take the time out for a husband and family."

He blinked. "But the store is doing well. You said it started turning a profit almost right away," he pointed out.

Seven

"What?"

Sherry grimaced. The man looked rather bewildered
by her question. She couldn't tell if that was because
he genuinely didn't understand what she'd meant when
she said, "Are you ever going to kiss me again"—which
seemed rather unlikely. It was a pretty straightforward
question, after all—or whether he was just befuddled
that she had been brazen enough to ask it. She suspected it was the latter. She supposed she'd somehow
shocked his old-world sensibilities.

Self-conscious under his unblinking stare, she
shifted uncomfortably and began to babble. "I mean
we're alone here, something that probably won't
happen often. And we do have to find out if we experience that shared pleasure business you mentioned. For
one thing, I'm really quite curious about that myself. I
mean I can't even begin to conceive of what that might

be like. But we also need to find out if we experience it so that we know for sure that I truly am a possible life mate. Because I'm not at all sure—"

Much to Sherry's relief, Basil ended her little babble-athon by kissing her . . . and it was as amazing as the last two times he kissed her. She liked to think she was a good kisser, but the man was a master at the art. There was no hesitation, he was just suddenly beside her on the couch, his hand at the back of her head, pulling her forward as his mouth descended to cover hers.

She sighed her relief into his mouth, and then opened to him when his tongue slid forward to demand entrance. Passion immediately roared up through her like a freight train, and she gave up analyzing his kissing skills. It was impossible to think when your body suddenly felt like liquid fire. Sherry felt as if she was bubbling and melting wherever he touched her, and his hands were everywhere. The hand at her head dropped down to her back, pressing her closer even as his other hand found and covered one breast, cupping and squeezing the soft globe before gently pinching her nipple through the cloth of her blouse and bra.

Sherry groaned and clutched at his shoulders, her body arching to thrust itself into the caress. She then groaned again when he released her to work on the buttons of her shirt. She tried to help him, but her hands were suddenly clumsy stumps. It didn't matter, though, the man was skilled in more than kissing. He had the buttons undone and the front clasp of her bra unsnapped so fast it was enough to leave her gasping with shock. It was a sound she repeated when both his hands suddenly closed over her breasts.

Moaning into his mouth, Sherry arched and twisted into his caresses by turn as his fingers played over her. Then she groaned with disappointment when he broke their kiss, only to gasp, "Oh, God," when his mouth replaced one hand and he drew the nipple between his warm wet lips and began to suckle.

"Basil," she gasped, clutching at his head to urge him on. Sherry felt his displaced hand briefly clasp her knee. When it then began to slide up her leg under her skirt, she instinctively let her legs spread a little for him, shocked to find them trembling like a virgin's as his hand continued its journey.

Basil lifted his head to kiss her again as his fingers brushed against the silk cloth of her panties. It was just a feather light touch the first time, but became firmer the second time, and Sherry groaned, her legs clasping around his hand and squeezing eagerly. Basil nipped her lip in response and withdrew his hand to urge her legs apart again. He then hooked a leg over her knee, keeping the one leg still and preventing the other from closing as well. Once that was done, he deepened their kiss again, his tongue thrusting into her mouth as he found her silk panties again. He brushed over the cloth once, then quickly tugged the material to the side and began to caress her without the cloth in the way.

Sherry cried out into his mouth and then began to suck on his tongue, her body writhing where he had her pinned to the couch as her need grew in mounting waves that were becoming almost unbearable. She needed release, she needed him inside her, thrusting and—

Tearing her mouth from his, she cried, "Basil please!" and reached for his pants. Her hands were not clumsy stumps anymore. Suddenly they were working again and she quickly had his dress pants undone. She would have reached in and found him then, but Basil immediately broke off what he was doing, stood up even as he caught her legs to turn her sideways on the couch, and then came down on top of her. His kisses then turned almost violent, his tongue thrusting out to spread her lips even as he reached down between them, freed himself, and then shifted his hips and thrust his erection into her.

Sherry cried out, her hips bucking to welcome him, her body clasping his hardness, reluctant to release him as he withdrew a bit before plunging back in. Some part of her mind was aware that it was all happening extraordinarily quickly, that foreplay had pretty much been neglected altogether, but she didn't care. She wanted him, needed him to do exactly what he was doing. Foreplay could wait for the next time, she thought, and then cried out in shocked pleasure as an orgasm exploded through her with darkness hard on its heels.

Knocking at the door woke Sherry sometime later and she peered around with confusion at the room she was in. Windows, blinds, a television . . . Oh yes, the sunroom, she recalled, and remembered what had happened here at the same moment as she became aware of the man slumped on top of her. Basil. Good Lord, they'd—

Another knock interrupted her realization of what had gone on, and she quickly grabbed the afghan off the back of the couch and pulled it over them both as the door began to open.

"Oh, sorry folks," Teddy said, turning his head away as he realized what he'd walked in on. "Just checking to make sure you two were still here and okay. For a bit we thought you'd left. This was the last place I thought to look. But I'll let you be." He started to pull the door closed again, but paused with it still cracked open. Eyes still averted, he added, "Katricia and Drina are making supper if you want any. Don't worry if you don't. We've all been where you are, so we'll understand. But we'll put some away in the fridge for you to grab later when you surface."

"Thank you, Teddy," Basil murmured, and Sherry glanced down to see that he was awake now and had tugged the afghan off of his head to look around. It left her chest bare, and his sleepy eyes were lighting up and turning bright silver as they roved over her naked flesh.

"You're welcome," Teddy said, drawing her gaze back to his averted face. "And if I don't see you before bedtime, good night."

He pulled the door closed then, and Sherry glanced back to Basil. "He doesn't think we'll want to eat?"

"As he said, he's been where we are. He knows the hunger between life mates will hold more sway," Basil murmured, tugging the afghan off of them both and letting it slide to the floor.

"Is this life mate hunger?" Sherry asked uncertainly. Basil stiffened, his eyes shooting to meet hers with surprise. "You still are not sure? Even after what just happened?"

"Well, it was pretty amazing," she admitted. "But I still didn't experience anything that could be described as shared pleasure. At least, I don't think I did. I mean, it's never been this intense before, but . . ." She let her words trail off when Basil dropped his forehead to rest on her shoulder, and then asked, "What?"

"This is my fault," he acknowledged, raising his head. "I was just so—it has been so long and—I pretty much attacked you and—"

"You didn't attack me," she interrupted with a smile. "Heck, I asked you to kiss me, and I was the one who—"

"No, I meant that I did not give you the chance to do much. I was all over you and did not give you the chance to do more than hold on for the ride."

Determination filling his expression, he shifted to a sitting position, forcing her to do the same. Once they were seated side by side, he kissed her again, and Sherry moaned as desire immediately reignited within her. Honest to God it rose up fully formed, as if they hadn't already sated it once but had merely stirred it to life and then taken a short break.

Sherry's whole body was humming just from the kiss. She hardly noticed when Basil caught her hand and drew it toward him . . . until he wrapped it around his already hard erection and squeezed her fingers gently, urging her on. Rather than respond to the silent request, she froze with shock. Something had zinged through her when Basil wrapped her hand around himself. Some sort of . . . She squeezed him gently, and then eased her hand his length and gasped into his mouth when it happened again. Excitement shooting through her like—

"That is shared pleasure," Basil growled, breaking their kiss. "What you are experiencing is what I feel when you touch me. I also feel your pleasure in the same way when I touch you. And the reason it is all so intense is because your pleasure and mine bounce back and forth between us, all the while amplifying and building to an unbearable level so that we lose consciousness."

"I fainted," Sherry realized with amazement as she continued to touch him. She had been so startled at Teddy's waking them, she hadn't recalled or considered what it meant that she lost consciousness while in the throes of orgasm. She also hadn't realized he'd lost consciousness too. She'd thought him just sleeping.

"Yes," he said through gritted teeth, then caught her by the waist and lifted and shifted her to straddle his lap with a muttered, "I am sorry. I cannot take that anymore."

Since she was experiencing his pleasure along with him, Sherry understood completely and didn't protest. She simply released her hold on him and grabbed for his shoulders. She already knew it was going to be a hell of a ride.

It was fully dark when Basil woke up. He glanced at the streetlamps and the headlights of passing vehicles, and then shifted his glance to where Sherry lay slumped with her head on his shoulder and wondered what time it was . . . and how soon Victor and Elvi would return. He didn't want Sherry to be embarrassed by their getting caught like this.

"Sweetling," he murmured, brushing the hair back from her face so he could see her eyes. "Sherry?"

Murmuring sleepily, she tightened her arms around his shoulders and turned her face into his neck, releasing a little sigh as her pelvis shifted against his. That small action was enough to wake the beast in Basil and cause his cock to begin to swell between them. He closed his eyes briefly, trying to maintain control of himself. Dear God, he'd forgotten how all-consuming and damned inconvenient life mate passion could be, he acknowledged, grinding his teeth together. After a moment where they both remained still, it eased again and he let his breath out.

Now all he had to do was get them up, out of this room and into hers, or even his, without waking the beast again. A much harder prospect than one would think since all he really wanted to do was roll her onto the lambskin rug on the floor and thrust into her over and over until they passed out again.

"And thinking that way is not very helpful at all," Basil muttered to himself with disgust. Damn, life mate sex was bloody addictive.

"What?" Sherry murmured sleepily, lifting her head and sitting up in his lap.

"Oh, God, no," he gasped with alarm, clasping her hips to hold her still. "Do not move."

Sherry froze at once, confusion and alarm her first reaction, but those were quickly overridden by hunger as his response to her body moving against his hit her, his pleasure transmitting itself to her body.

"Do not look at me like that," Basil hissed, closing his eyes. "Do not move and do not look at me like that. I am trying to resist you."

He knew at once that was the wrong thing to say by the way Sherry immediately relaxed in his lap.

"Don't," was all she said, and then she was nibbling at his lips, her hands moving over his skin, caressing his shoulders, his chest, and pausing to flick at his already erect nipples as she shifted her body, rubbing herself along his growing erection.

"Sherry," he growled, turning his head away. "I do not know what time it is, but it is dark out. Elvi and Victor could come back at any moment."

"Then we should move to my room," she murmured, licking and nibbling at his neck even as she shifted herself over him again.

Basil growled and then turned to catch her mouth with his, kissing her punishingly even as he caught her behind in each hand and stood up.

As punishments went, it wasn't very successful, he decided when Sherry immediately wrapped her legs around his hips and kissed him eagerly back. She was obviously too caught up in the life mate madness to see sense. He would have to think for both of them. Getting her dressed for the coming trip through the house wasn't likely, he decided when he broke their kiss and she turned her attention to licking and nibbling her way around his neck and ear.

Although she wasn't really undressed, he noted. The

passion had overwhelmed them quickly enough both times that they hadn't got around to undressing. She still wore her skirt, it was just up around her hips, and her blouse was on, just open. Come to that, he still wore his shirt, it was merely unbuttoned as well, and his pants were on, just—

Okay, they weren't on anymore, he acknowledged as they suddenly slipped down around his ankles. Maybe they wouldn't run into anyone, Basil thought hopefully as he stepped out of the pants and headed for the door.

Sherry was aware that they were moving. She also knew she should probably be more helpful in this situation, have him put her down so she could straighten her clothes and walk to her room on her own two feet. Unfortunately, she just couldn't seem to do that. She didn't want to. She wanted Basil to go back to kissing and caressing her and she wanted him inside her again. And while she knew she should care that Elvi and Victor might be back at any moment and find them doing the nasty in their sunroom, she couldn't seem to manage to care about that. She just wanted Basil. Her mind was full of what she had experienced with him. Her body ached for him. She hungered for him like no one and nothing she'd ever before experienced. It was bad, really bad. Being deprived of oxygen was the only thing she could compare her need for him to. Every nerve ending in her body was aware of him and screaming for him. She felt like she would die if he didn't make love to her again.

It was madness, Sherry acknowledged, and didn't

care about that either. If she was mad, they could lock her up, so long as they locked her up with Basil, she thought, and then glanced around when he abruptly stopped. They had reached the door and he'd pulled it open and was now surveying the dark hall and listening.

Sherry could vaguely make out voices, but they sounded far away. Probably downstairs, she thought, and lost interest. Her attention returned to Basil and she began to nibble his lobe and then run her tongue around the rim of his ear.

"Stop that," he hissed, and then moved forward to the end of the short hall to peer cautiously out into the main hall.

Sherry didn't stop that, started to let her hands roam, running them over his back and shoulders and up into his hair. But when she tightened her legs around his hips and used her hold to try to lift and shift herself onto the erection she could feel pressed between them, Basil cursed and started quickly up the empty main hall.

They were perhaps halfway to her room when Basil suddenly froze. It took another moment for Sherry to become aware of the footsteps coming up the stairs . . . and quickly. They would never make it to her room.

Sherry barely had the realization when Basil bolted for a door a few steps ahead of them and pulled it open to duck inside with her. Just before he pulled the door closed, she caught a glimpse of shelves and neatly folded towels and sheets. They were in the linen closet, she realized, and for some reason that made her laugh.

When Basil immediately covered her mouth with one hand to silence the sound, Sherry jerked her head back in surprise, slamming it into the wall.

"Ow," she muttered when he removed his hand and whispered, "Are you all right?"

"Hello?" someone said outside the closet door before she could respond.

Sherry stilled and glanced toward the crack of light around the door. It sounded like Stephanie's wary voice, she noted, but took her cue from Basil and remained silent.

"Sherry? Basil? Is that you two in the closet?"

Basil sagged with defeat, and it was Sherry who said, "No," on a laugh.

"Yeahhhh . . . rrrrright," Stephanie drawled, and then sighed with exasperation. "You do know you're in a boardinghouse, right? I mean, there are a ton of bedrooms in this place and you both have one. Why are you in the linen closet?"

"Because Basil has no pants on," Sherry admitted with a wicked grin.

Basil groaned at her announcement, but he wasn't alone. Stephanie groaned too and then said, "Oh, that's just gross. He isn't touching any of the linens is he? I don't want Basil's bare butt prints on the next face towel I use. Gawdddddd. You life mates are all crazy."

"I am not touching the linens," Basil announced with what Sherry considered great aplomb considering the situation. "And we shall be moving along just as soon as you leave the hall. I simply did not wish to alarm you . . . and possibly ruin your dinner," he added dryly.

"Too late," Stephanie announced. "Well, you can come out. I'm going to my room to get something. Please, please, please move the party to Sherry's room or yours before I come back."

"Certainly," Basil responded with dignity.

"Good. I'm going now," Stephanie announced. "Count to ten before you come out so I can get to my room."

"Of course," Basil said on a sigh.

"Where is her room?" Sherry asked curiously.

"The back right corner if you are facing the house. On the other side of the small hall to the sunroom," Basil answered as they listened to her footsteps move away.

"Oh," Sherry murmured, and then smiled wryly when she heard a door slam shut from that direction.

"I believe it is safe, if you could get the door?" Basil said in a ridiculously polite voice.

Sherry reached for the doorknob, quickly opened the door and then closed it again after Basil carried her out. She wrapped her arms around his shoulders again as he carried her to her room.

"You do know you are a menace, do you not?" Basil asked conversationally as he walked.

"Am I?" Sherry asked with amusement.

"First seducing me in the sunroom, then trying to keep me in the sunroom when I very chivalrously tried to bring you to somewhere safe from prying eyes and then, 'Because Basil has no pants on,' " he quoted back to her dryly. "Was that punishment for not letting you have your way with me in the sunroom and insisting on moving to another room?"

"Yep," she admitted.

"Yep?" he echoed, apparently surprised she'd admit as much.

Sherry shrugged unrepentantly and then reached out to open the door to her bedroom when he stopped in front of it. "Guess I'm just a naughty girl," she said as the door opened. Turning back, she grinned and asked, "What are you going to do about it?"

"I'll think of something," Basil muttered, carrying her into the room and kicking the door shut with one foot.

Eight

"So then I look out the window, and the shed's on fire," Victor said, shaking his head. "And who do you think is locked inside?"

"Elvi?" Sherry and Basil guessed together, both grinning with amusement.

"Exactly," Victor said, and reached out to squeeze his wife's hand affectionately as he added, "The woman nearly got herself killed half a dozen times after we first met. If it weren't for the nanos, I would have hair as white as snow now."

"Fortunately, you do have nanos," Elvi said dryly, and then pointed out, "Besides, you were the biggest threat to my life. You were here hunting me."

"What?" Sherry squawked, dropping her fork onto her plate with a clang that drew as much attention from the other guests in the restaurant as her shocked cry did.

"Victor was a Rogue Hunter," Elvi told her with a

nod. "He was sent to hunt me down and bring me in for judgment."

"I was," Victor agreed mildly. "But the moment I realized you were my life mate, I knew I could not do it."

"You were a *rogue*?" Sherry breathed, staring at Elvi with disbelief. The woman was so nice, so kind, so . . . *nice*. It was hard to imagine she was ever a rogue anything.

"I wasn't rogue," Elvi assured her. "Well, I suppose I was, but only because my friends made me one."

"Your friends?" she asked curiously.

"Yes. Teddy and Hazel. My best friends," Elvi said dryly. "Not on purpose. How were they to know advertising in the personals section of the newspaper to find me a male vampire might get me hunted down and executed?"

Sherry's eyes widened incredulously. "They put an ad in the personals?"

"They did," she assured her. "And, without warning me ahead of time, mind you."

"Oh my," Sherry said with amusement.

"Mmm." Elvi smiled faintly. "It's funny now, but it was not funny then. I was mortified."

"I can imagine," Sherry said sympathetically. "I hate setups too. Stephanie is just the latest in a long line of people who have tried to set me up with someone over the years. It's like people can't stand to see a woman on her own or something. But the setups never work. They are always a disaster."

"Over the years?" Elvi asked curiously. "Have you never been in a serious relationship?"

"Yes. I was engaged once," she admitted.

"But you didn't marry?"

"It just didn't work out. These things happen. It's better this way," Sherry said with a shrug, and then asked. "What made Teddy and Hazel decide to put an ad in the personals?"

"Oh." Elvi smiled faintly. "It was really very sweet. Teddy and Hazel were my best friends from childhood on. They were getting old, though. All our friends were, and they were starting to pass on around us. Teddy and Hazel started to worry about dying themselves and leaving me alone, so they decided they had to find me a vampire who could keep me company once they were gone."

"Oh, that *is* sweet," Sherry said.

"I know," Elvi said on a little sigh. "Teddy and Hazel have always been the most amazing friends."

"Teddy." Sherry smiled faintly. "It's such a rare name and yet there are two of them here in Port Henry. Katricia's Teddy and your Teddy."

"No. There's only the one," Elvi assured her. "Katricia's Teddy *is* my friend Teddy."

"But he's not old," Sherry protested with amazement. "Why would he be worried about . . ." Her voice trailed away as understanding set in.

"Yes. He was mortal before Katricia turned him as her life mate. He was sixty-four when they met last Christmas," Elvi told her.

"Wow," Sherry breathed, thinking of the good-looking, dark-haired, silver-eyed man at the house. Like everyone else, he seemed no more than twenty-four or twenty-five. He was also gorgeous, and looked damned fine in the police uniform. "He looks good for sixty-four."

"Sixty-five now," Elvi said with amusement.

"Oh." Sherry nodded and then glanced at her sharply. "He was your best friend and was mortal?" When Elvi nodded, she asked, "Does that mean you were?"

"Mortal? Yes," Elvi admitted. "So was my other friend, Hazel. She's immortal now too, though."

"So Katricia was born a vamp— immortal." Sherry corrected herself quickly when she noted the way Victor and Basil winced as she started to say *vampire*. Stephanie had said older immortals didn't like the term, and it appeared she was right. "So Katricia was an immortal and Teddy a mortal. Victor was born immortal and you were mortal. Hazel was mortal . . ."

When she hesitated, Elvi said, "Yes, D.J. was immortal."

Sherry nodded. "What about Drina and Harper? Which of them was mortal?"

"Neither," Basil announced. "Both were born immortal."

"Oh," she said with surprise. "So a life mate can be an immortal too?"

"Yes," Basil assured her. "Though it is more often a mortal, but that's probably a function of population ratios. There are a lot more mortals than immortals."

"Right," Sherry murmured. "But mortal life mates are expected to become . . ." She just couldn't say it, and didn't have to. Elvi smiled sympathetically and nodded.

"Yes, an immortal's life mate usually becomes immortal too."

"Of course," Sherry murmured, and sat back. She'd known that, of course. In some part of her mind she'd realized that would probably be the case. All the people she'd met at the Rogue Hunters' house were immortals and most had been couples. Besides, it just made sense. She peered at the people at the table with her. Every one of them looked to be in their early twenties. Anyone looking at them would think she was the oldest one here at thirty-two, but not one of her companions was actually younger than her. Elvi was in her sixties, and she had no idea how old Basil and Victor were, but Basil's daughter had been born in 411 AD so he had to be older than that.

And that was just madness, no one lived that long, she thought faintly. But then it was all madness. Vampires, drinking blood, reading minds, controlling mortals . . .

But the maddest thing of all was that she believed it all. She'd obviously lost her mind . . . or maybe she was dreaming, or they'd dosed her with LSD or something and she was hallucinating the entire thing.

That had to be the answer, she thought now, because . . . well, frankly, it was all kind of hard to swallow. It was like suddenly being told that Santa really did exist . . . or the tooth fairy. Even the extreme passion, or perhaps especially the extreme passion she'd experienced with Basil, was hard to accept as a reality. She was not a virgin, she'd had sex, good sex, great sex, even, over the years, but nothing like the mind-blowing madness she'd experienced with Basil. All he had to do was touch her and she went up in flames. When he kissed her, all she could think about was taking him into her body and riding the pony to unconsciousness again.

Hell, he didn't even have to be conscious for her to want him like a drug addict in serious need of a fix. After they'd escaped the linen closet and made it to her room last night, they had another very fast round before passing out from pleasure again, but this time Sherry had woken up first. She'd blinked her eyes open, found herself lying on his chest, smelled the combination of spice and woods that was his cologne mixed with his natural odor, and then found herself licking her way down his body. After passing out that time, she woke to find that Basil had decided turnabout was fair play and buried his face between her legs. She'd barely woken up in time to enjoy the orgasm he gave her before she was sent back to unconsciousness again.

Sherry had lost count of how many times she orgasmed and passed out through the night. Like a drowning swimmer, she'd come up for air, gasped as pleasure filled her body and mind, and then sank under the waves and passed out before surfacing once more to do it again . . . and again.

They'd probably still be there in her room, she thought, if Elvi hadn't woke them with a knock at the door and a call that breakfast was ready and they could go shopping afterward. It was only after Basil kissed her cheek and slipped from the room to shower and dress that she'd become aware of the state of her body. Sherry had hickeys and love bites everywhere and was swollen and sore as hell in places that were never swollen and sore. The worst part was the realization that as sore as she was, if he so much as kissed her, she'd spread her legs and welcome the man again in a heartbeat, even here on the tabletop with Elvi, Victor, and the whole restaurant watching. She wanted and needed him that badly, and that just was not her. Even thinking this way was madness. So this couldn't be real. It was a dream or drugs or something, but it was not real, she thought, and could have wept because she wanted so much for it to be real.

"Well, I need to visit the ladies' room before we leave," Elvi announced suddenly, getting to her feet. "Join me, Sherry?"

"Oh," Sherry said, blinking away her thoughts. "Uh . . . sure."

Standing, she forced a smile for Basil and Victor and then followed Elvi to the ladies' room, stopping abruptly when the door closed behind them and the other woman halted, swung around and pinched her.

"Ow! What—?" Sherry said in confusion, and then Elvi opened her mouth and her incisors shifted and slid down, making two sharp fangs. Sherry staggered back a startled step and stared at the pointed teeth blankly for a moment, watching as they simply slid up and shifted again, becoming what appeared to be two normal incisors. A heartbeat later they slid back down into view once more. Fangs.

Elvi let them recede again and then arched an eyebrow. "Do you want to touch them and feel that they are real? That all of this is real?" she added meaningfully.

Sherry blinked, but shook her head.

Elvi nodded. "Do you want me to bite you so you can be sure they work?"

She shook her head more swiftly at that.

"Will you now stop trying to convince yourself that you're dreaming or drugged and accept that what's happening is really happening and that what we've told you about immortals, nanos, and no-fangers is true?"

When Sherry merely stared at her with confusion, Elvi sighed and took one of her hands in both of hers.

"Dear, I know this is a lot to take in," she said solemnly. "I also know that right now you're grasping at alternate solutions because you're terrified of what this means to you."

Sherry blinked as those words struck a chord in her body.

"You're afraid that you'll be expected to turn and become immortal like the rest of us," Elvi said quietly.

Sherry bit her lip but didn't say anything. While she'd been fascinated at first and eager to believe, now that she realized that as Basil's life mate she'd be expected to become an immortal too . . . well . . . she *was* scared. Terrified even. This wasn't like being expected to switch to Catholicism or some other religion to be with the man you loved. This was a permanent physical alteration. This was huge . . . and she didn't know what she actually felt for Basil yet. Sure, she lusted after the man something awful, but—

"Sherry," Elvi said gently, drawing her from her thoughts. When Sherry met her gaze, Elvi patted her hand and said, "You are scaring the wits out of yourself and there is no need for that. I really don't think you should even worry about having to become an immortal. You have enough on your plate at the moment. Why not just enjoy getting to know Basil and let the future take care of itself?"

Sherry let her breath out slowly. "You were reading my mind at the table."

"Yes, I was," Elvi agreed. "Although, as I said, you're pretty much shouting your thoughts right now, and what you were shouting at the table was that you were on the verge of a full-fledged panic attack over the possibility of having to become an immortal."

Sherry nodded, and then blurted, "I don't think I could drink blood."

Elvi didn't appear surprised. Smiling wryly, she shrugged. "It is not exactly something we, as mortals, ever expect to have to do."

Sherry let her breath out on a little sigh, relieved that the woman was being so understanding.

"Of course I understand," Elvi said with a crooked smile, obviously still reading her thoughts. "Sherry, I know this is all very scary. But, my dear, you don't have to do anything you do not want to," she said firmly. "Right now, you're our guest and under our care and protection while the Rogue Hunters take care of Leo. Anything beyond that is up to you, so just relax and enjoy your stay with us. Consider it a free vacation."

"And Basil?" she asked.

Elvi shrugged. "That is up to you too. He can either be a vacation romance, or he can be your future, but you will be the one to decide which."

"Right," Sherry breathed. Elvi was right, of course. She'd been reacting as if she didn't have a choice in any of this, and she did. There was no need to panic. She should just relax and, as Elvi had suggested, enjoy the free vacation. There were people running her store, she was at a lovely bed and breakfast, and was about to enjoy a shopping spree on the council members. She was also enjoying the best sex of her life. What happened after they caught this Leo person was up to her.

"That a girl," Elvi said with a smile, obviously still listening in on her thoughts. "Now let's go spend some council money on a pretty new wardrobe for you."

Managing a shaky laugh, Sherry nodded and followed her out of the ladies' room.

"Are we ready?" Elvi asked as they reached the table where the men waited.

Victor nodded and picked up the bill as he stood. "Just have to pay this on the way out, my love."

"Council credit card?" Basil asked with amusement when he spotted the card his brother took out of his wallet.

"Yeah, so I guess you're really paying," Victor said with amusement. "Or at least part of it."

"Then I do not have to offer to pick up the tab myself," Basil said with a smile.

Sherry stared at him silently, her gaze sliding over his clothes and watch. He looked good. He also looked expensive. She didn't see any obvious insignias to suggest he wore designer clothes, but she'd stake her life on the fact that he did. Dear God, she was dating a man with fangs, immortality, and who wasn't just well off, but was thousands-of-years-of-amassing-a-fortune rich. Dear God, he—

"Breathe," Elvi whispered by her ear, slipping her arm through hers to urge her toward the exit. "He is just a man . . . well, an immortal man," she added wryly. "But a man just the same."

"Who is a man?" Basil asked curiously, stepping up next to Sherry when Elvi turned to say something to Victor as they reached the register.

"You heard that, did you?" Sherry asked dryly. That was just her luck. Shrugging to herself, she admitted, "Elvi was just reminding me that you're just a man."

"I am," he assured her solemnly, opening the door for her.

"Right," Sherry said as she led the way outside. "A man who's immortal and has more money than God." She shook her head. "Nothing intimidating about that."

"Sherry." Basil caught her hand and brought her to a halt in the parking lot. "First of all, I am quite sure God does not have or care about money, and frankly, neither do I, really. I've simply amassed a lot because I've been alive a long time and don't spend a lot of it on unnecessary luxuries. Money is not important."

"You wouldn't say that if you didn't have a lot of it," she assured him. "I mean, I make a good wage off my store, but I scrimped and saved for a long time to scrape the money together to start it. So it wasn't that long ago that I was without . . . by choice, true," she admitted. "But whether by choice or not, when you don't have it, money carries a lot more importance than—"

"Sherry," he said solemnly. "I have been alive a long

time, and like to think I have learned a little something over that time. What I have learned is that people are what is important . . . family and friends. They are the only thing of any real value in life. They see you into this world and they see you out, and they are your only real support in between. Money buys food, clothing, and a roof over your head. Food lasts minutes in your mouth and then you're hungry again hours later. Clothing changes with each season, and a roof over your head is just that, a roof. It's family that makes it a home and family that lasts a lifetime. Whether it's the family you're born into, or a family you choose from among friends or loved ones. They are all that really matter."

Sherry shook her head, pretty sure Basil had been wealthy for so long that he just didn't recall what it was like to be without it, and how important it really was.

Basil considered her expression and then asked, "Did you not scrimp and save, as you say, and give up all those luxuries you could have had to save the money to start your store?"

"Well, yes," she admitted with a frown.

"And would you not give up your store and all the money it has made you to have your mother back?" he asked.

"In a heartbeat," she said without having to think about it.

"You see? Money is not really that important. It is merely our society that makes it seem so. The corporations, magazines, and television commercials with their advertisements and chants to buy this and this and this and you must have that."

"Well, sure, if you have enough money, then—"

"How much is enough?" he asked with amusement. "Because I know many wealthy mortals who have millions, and instead of relaxing and enjoying it, waste their short lives on acquiring more millions," he said wryly, and then added, "Do not get me wrong, the wealth I have allows me to do things I could not otherwise do. I could not visit my daughter here in Canada when I wish, I could not help bankroll the Enforcers and so on. But it was not the money I have that kept me alive all these centuries, it was the love of my family and children.

"Money is not the secret to happiness," he assured her. "And it is not as important as the present culture claims it is. Unfortunately, those who are without money and unhappy think that money will fix all their woes, and those who do have a bit of money and are unhappy, think more money will make the difference. But their thinking is wrong," he said solemnly, cupping her shoulders. "And I know this because with all the money I possess, in all the millennia I've lived, I have not been truly completely happy except for twice in my life . . . when I was with my Acantha, and since meeting you."

Sherry stared at him, wide-eyed. They'd known each other a little less than two days . . . and she didn't have a clue how to respond to that, so was actually grateful when Victor called out, "Sorry, bro."

She and Basil glanced around to see him walking toward them, his arm around Elvi.

"I should have given you the keys to the car so you

weren't left standing around waiting for us," Victor said, and raised his key fob to push the button to unlock the car doors. "Hop in. Time to shop."

Nodding, Basil urged Sherry to the car and opened the door for her. She slid in without protest and then busied herself doing up her seat belt as the others got in. Much to her relief, Elvi began chattering away about her restaurant, saving Sherry from responding to Basil's words, which was a relief since she still didn't have a clue what to say.

It turned out that the entrance to Masonville Mall was just across the street from the restaurant where they'd had lunch. Inside, it took about two and a half minutes for Sherry to notice that most of the stores were geared toward the younger crowd, and that the shoppers milling around them were mostly young too.

"This mall is close to the university," Elvi explained as they paused to look in a store window. "It's where most of the university students shop."

"Ah," Sherry said with a nod. "So, why are we shopping here?"

"Because it has good stores and lots of selection . . . it also has a Rocky Mountain chocolate store, which I love," the other woman added with a grin.

Sherry chuckled at the admission.

"You'd look good in that," Elvi commented, eyeing a mannequin in a store window that wore a cropped burgundy sweater and ripped jeans.

"It's kind of casual," Sherry said uncertainly, and then asked, "Don't you think it's a little young for me?"

"You're on vacation, casual is what you need. You're

also thirty-two and single, not sixty-two and a granny," Elvi said with amusement. "Come on. You need to at least try it on."

Sherry shook her head, but allowed the woman to drag her into the store, aware that the men were following docilely along. Ten minutes later Sherry found herself in a changing room with scads of totally inappropriate clothing hanging on the rods all around her. Short skirts, cropped tops, tight jeans . . . There wasn't a thing there that she would normally wear. She was a businesswoman, she wore business clothes . . . always. But then she was always working and had been doing so for a long time. She had spent years working overtime and skimping and saving to start her own store, and since opening it she'd worked just as long and hard to get it up and profitable.

Come to think of it, she led a pretty boring life, Sherry acknowledged with a frown. Or had before this anyway.

"I don't hear any sound coming from in there," Elvi said from the other side of the door. "Have you even started to undress?"

"No," Sherry admitted.

"Well, get to it. Start with that short leather skirt and the cropped sweater while I go grab those snakeskin pants we passed on the way here. I'll be right back."

"Snakeskin?" Sherry muttered, and shook her head. She was thirty-two years old. Responsible, hardworking . . . boring. She did not wear snakeskin *anything*.

"What the hell," she muttered to herself. She wasn't paying for these clothes, so it wouldn't matter if she never wore them again. Why not wear some of these things while she was here? It would certainly be a new experience. She had been a jeans and T-shirt girl with her nose stuck in books in university and then graduated directly to business suits. She'd sort of bypassed the whole experiment with the slutty clothes stage.

"I've lost my mind," she told her reflection in the mirror, and began to strip.

The brown leather skirt and cropped burgundy sweater looked kind of cute together. Or would if her muffin top wasn't showing between where the cropped sweater ended and the skirt started, she thought with a grimace. She really needed to work out or something. Diet too. She was probably killing herself with all the takeout she ate and the hours she spent sitting at her desk hunched over the books. She was certainly killing anything approaching a figure.

"Muffin tops and saddlebags," she breathed with a sigh as she peered at herself. "Nice." And was she getting a double chin? Ugh!

Well, at least the skirt hid the saddlebags, she noted, turning a bit from side to side. She had okay legs too. Her thighs were a bit chunky, but you couldn't see that under the skirt either.

"Well?" Elvi asked, outside the door.

Sherry reached for the doorknob to the changing room and then hesitated. "Are the men out there?"

"Yes."

"Then I'm not coming out," Sherry said, letting her hand drop from the doorknob.

Elvi clucked with exasperation and then said, "Basil,

go see if there's anything you'd like to see her in. Victor, go with him."

Sherry heard the men's voices rumble and then silence.

"Okay, they're gone," Elvi announced.

Sherry opened the door and stepped out. All she said was, "Muffin top."

"Hmmm." Elvi eyed her thoughtfully. "The skirt is cute, though."

Sherry glanced down at it. The skirt *was* cute. Too young for her, but cute. "We should have brought Stephanie. She'd have loved this place."

Elvi smiled sadly and nodded. "Unfortunately, she can't take a lot of shopping in crowded places. She won't even go out for lunches or dinners anymore except to nip in and grab takeout."

"Really?" Sherry arched her eyebrows. "Why?"

"She can't block out people's thoughts yet," Elvi admitted quietly. "Being out in public for her is like standing in a room with a hundred blaring radios all playing different stations. Even being in the house with all of us is a bit much for her. You'll find she spends a lot of time in her room to give her head a rest." She explained, "Harper had all sorts of insulation and soundproofing put in her room when the renovations were done after the fire. It doesn't block everyone completely, but reduces it to a dull roar and makes it bearable for her."

"So after you turn, you can't block out other peoples thoughts?" Sherry asked with a frown. That didn't sound very attractive.

"Usually it's the opposite. New turns usually can't

read thoughts even if they try. It takes a while to be able to do it. Stephanie is . . . gifted," she ended finally, though her expression suggested it wasn't much of a gift. "She has been able to hear everyone from the start, even older immortals, which is rare, and she picked up on controlling mortals quickly too."

"Stephanie mentioned something about controlling mortals . . . can you really do that?" Sherry asked, not liking the idea that any one of the people in the house might be able to make her do something against her will.

"I'm just starting to be able to do that," Elvi admitted. "But Stephanie could very early on, and without training."

"Then why didn't she take control of me when we met?" Sherry asked, and then explained, "She kept shushing me and I kept talking, but she didn't take control of me and make me stop."

Elvi shrugged. "When she had trouble reading you, she probably just assumed she wouldn't be able to control you either."

"Oh," Sherry murmured. "You say she's gifted, but—"

"No, it really isn't much of a gift at all," Elvi admitted unhappily. "It would be if she could shut it off, but she can't."

"And you're worried about her," Sherry said quietly.

Elvi nodded. "Stephanie started out attending high school here and trying to lead a normal life, but bit by bit she's retreated. We home-school her now. She has dropped the friends of her own age because she can't stand to go out, and she spends a lot of time locked up in her room, alone. That's why Dree and Tricia insisted on the girls' weekend with her, to try to get her out."

"But shopping?" Sherry asked with a frown.

"It was a very exclusive dress shop. By appointment only. They were promised there would only be themselves and a couple of salespeople to help them."

"Ah," Sherry nodded.

"Then they were going to stay at Harper and Drina's apartment in the city. Harper put in a specially insulated room there just like the one Steph has here in Port Henry, so she could spend time there if she wanted to get away," Elvi explained. "And then Lucian sent another drug for her to try, one they hoped would muffle the voices. But, like the others, it only works until the nanos clear it out."

"Drugs?" Sherry asked with a frown.

"It's bad," Elvi said solemnly. "Bad enough that we're afraid if we don't find a way to silence the voices for her, she could go no-fanger."

"Stephanie?" Sherry asked with dismay.

Elvi nodded. "For all we know, this kind of thing is what actually makes the no-fangers crazy."

Sherry stared at her with horror, trying to imagine Stephanie acting like Leo had in her store. The idea was not a pleasant one. She liked Stephanie. The girl seemed like a relatively normal kid—well, for being a vampire. She hadn't even realized there was anything wrong with her.

"It will be fine," Elvi said with a forced smile. "Drina, Harper, and Victor are trying to train her to block thoughts. Once she's able to do that, she'll be fine."

"I'm sure it will," Sherry murmured, although it seemed obvious to her that, despite her words, Elvi wasn't at all sure.

"Anyway, enough of this talk. We need to find you clothes. Try that skirt with a different top and then try these on," Elvi said, handing her the snakeskin jeans. "I'm going to go find you a couple more tops."

Sherry nodded and watched her walk away, then turned and moved back into her changing room. The thought of Stephanie going no-fanger continued to bother her, though, as she stripped off the cropped top and switched it for a longer sweater with holes at the shoulders. She eyed the results with surprise. This one covered her muffin top but also looked rather sexy.

A knock at the door announced Elvi's return, and Sherry turned and pulled it open with a smile. "This one is much better, I . . .." Her voice died as she realized it wasn't Elvi.

Nine

LYNSAY SANDS

"You need to convince Sherry to let you turn her."

Eyebrows rising at that announcement, Basil glanced to Victor and then back to the glittery and very skimpy halter top he held in his hands. Trying to imagine Sherry in it, he pointed out, "I have only just met her. Can we not enjoy getting to know each other before we get into—"

"No. With Leonius around, you cannot afford to dally," Victor said firmly. "Especially since I think you will have some trouble convincing her to turn."

"What?" Basil dropped the top and rounded on him.

Victor shrugged. "The woman was panicking in the restaurant at the mere thought of becoming immortal. She started trying to convince herself that this was all just a dream or the result of drugs." Scowling, he asked, "What the devil have you been saying to her to make her so afraid of becoming one of us?"

Basil frowned and then admitted reluctantly, "I may

have mentioned that living so long without a life mate was difficult."

Victor narrowed his eyes on him and then gasped with dismay, "Suicide by Rogue Hunter?"

Basil grimaced. "Stay out of my head."

"I will if you start using your head," Victor countered grimly. "Dear God, how could you tell her all of that?"

"She seemed upset, perhaps even a little horrified, that I have had so many children with Mary, and I was trying to explain—"

"Oh God, you told her about Mary and the kids too?" Victor asked, looking alarmed.

"Of course. She is my life mate, Victor. I have to be honest with her," he pointed out.

"Yes, but you could have saved that little nugget of information for *after* you convinced her to be your life mate," Victor said grimly. "Good Lord, man. Telling her how depressed and miserable you were to live so long? And you think that is going to make her eager to become immortal?"

Basil turned his back and began to rifle through the tops on display, but he was worrying now that he'd blown it with Sherry. Maybe it hadn't been a good idea to tell her—

"I'm sorry, brother," Victor said suddenly. "Of course you had to tell her about the kids. And perhaps it's only fair that you warned her about how long and lonely life can be when you live so long alone," he added solemnly. "I just wish it wasn't. I do not want to see the same thing happen to her as happened to Stephanie and her sister, Dani."

Basil stiffened at the thought of Sherry somehow being turned by Leonius and becoming an Edentate. It presented worries that being an immortal wouldn't. They would have to worry over any children she bore, that it might grow up to be a no-fanger, if it even survived to birth. Frowning, he said, "That should not be a worry. We brought her to Port Henry to keep her away from Leonius. She is supposed to be safe here."

"Yeah, well Dani was supposed to be safe at the Enforcer house too," Victor pointed out. "But Leo still got his hands on her."

Basil nodded slowly, and then asked, "How? I was told about it at the time but now do not recall how exactly. They were away from the house, were they not?"

Victor nodded. "They went shopping. She got separated from the others for a couple minutes and that was all the time Leo needed."

Basil glanced around and spotted Elvi sorting through a rack of tops about ten feet away. Sherry was alone. Cursing, he headed for the entrance to the dressing rooms.

"He could not get past us and to her unseen," Victor said soothingly, following in his wake. As they stepped through the arch to the cubicles, he added, "I have been watching. She's perfectly— Shit!" he muttered even as Basil barked an alarmed, "Sherry!" and rushed toward the crumpled figure at the end of the hallway full of dressing room doors.

Reaching Sherry's side, Basil knelt and anxiously turned her over to search for wounds.

"She's unharmed," Victor said with relief next to

him, even as he noted there were no obvious wounds. "She is okay."

"She is *not* okay, she is unconscious," Basil growled, scooping her up into his arms.

"I just meant there are no serious injuries," Victor said soothingly, straightening beside him.

"What happened?" Elvi asked with concern, rushing to join them. "I heard you shout her name. What—? Why is she unconscious?" she asked with alarm as Basil turned toward her with Sherry in his arms.

"We do not know. She—" Victor paused as Sherry moaned and stirred in Basil's arms.

Blinking her eyes open, Sherry peered around at the three of them.

"What happened?" she asked with confusion, and then began to struggle as she realized Basil was carrying her. "Put me down, I'm fine," she muttered with embarrassment. "You'll hurt yourself carrying me. I'm too heavy."

"You are not heavy, and I am not going to hurt myself," he said dryly, but set her carefully back on her feet. He continued to hold her by the arms, though, as she regained her feet.

"What happened?" she asked again.

"We do not know," Victor said grimly. "We found you unconscious on the floor. Do you recall how you got that way?"

"What?" She peered at him blankly and then shook her head. "No, I was trying on clothes and then . . ." She frowned, briefly, and finished, "I guess I fainted."

Basil glanced to his brother, silently telling him to search her memory for what had happened, but then looked sharply back when Sherry shook off his hold and moved into the dressing room again.

"I better get back to it. I still have a load of clothes to try on." She closed the dressing room door. There was no way Victor could read her now. He needed to see her to read her.

"Perhaps we should leave shopping for another day and head back to the house," Basil suggested to her through the door.

"No. Elvi can't keep taking days off to shop with me," Sherry responded, sounding a bit exasperated. "Besides, I need clothes."

"But if you are not feeling well—" Basil began.

"I'm fine. I feel fine," she insisted, definitely exasperated now.

"We can come back tomorrow," Basil said soothingly. "Right now I think—"

"Basil, I've worn the same outfit for three days now. I'm not wearing it a fourth time," she said firmly. "If you don't like waiting while I try on clothes, go grab a cup of coffee in the food court. I'll be as quick as I can."

Basil frowned at the door, then turned to glower at his brother when Victor began to chuckle.

"What the hell is so funny?" Basil asked with irritation.

"My apologies, brother," Victor said, making an obvious effort to kill his smile and failing miserably. Shaking his head, he gave up the effort and said, "I am sorry, I just—" He shrugged helplessly. "The nanos chose well. She is perfect for you."

"Perfectly stubborn," Basil muttered.

"Exactly," Victor said, and laughed again, louder this time.

"*I* am not stubborn," Basil grumbled, leaning against the wall next to the dressing room door and crossing his arms grimly.

"You are," Victor countered at once. "It's why you and Lucian drive each other crazy. You are both as stubborn as the other."

"So you're saying Sherry and I will drive each other crazy?" Basil asked archly.

"Well, that hardly sounds like life mates," Sherry said from inside the dressing room, her voice drenched in disgust.

"No, I'm sure Victor didn't mean you'd drive each other crazy," Elvi said quickly, raising her voice to be sure Sherry heard her.

"No, I did not mean it that way," Victor agreed, raising his voice as well. "But you will not let my brother boss you around either, which would be easy for him to do with most women. He needs someone with a solid backbone, and you appear to have one."

"Yeah, except for the fainting like some Victorian miss bit," Sherry muttered, her voice somewhat muffled, which suggested she was in the process of taking off or pulling on something over her head. The idea caught Basil's imagination, and he found himself picturing that in his mind. Sherry pulling off the sexy sweater she'd been wearing, revealing a lacy scrap of cloth barely covering burgeoning breasts.

"Her breasts are not that burgeoning," Victor said with amusement, apparently catching the stray fantasy.

"Her breasts are perfect," Basil said staunchly.

"Yes, but they are not as large as you are picturing them in your mind," he assured him.

"Yes?" Elvi asked her husband. The tone was sarcastic, but she had a twinkle of amusement in her eyes. "Yes, Sherry's breasts are perfect?"

"Yours are more perfect, of course, my love," Victor said with a grin.

"Oh, for God's sake," Sherry muttered. The door to the dressing room burst open and she stormed out, a mountain of clothes caught up in her arms, the hangers sticking out every which way. "I'll just take these, now let's go."

She strode past them and stormed out of the dressing area, charging for the register.

"You'd best hurry and catch up to her, Victor," Elvi said. "You're paying."

"The devil he is!" Basil snapped, rushing after his brother as he strode after Sherry. "If anyone is paying, I am."

"You are," Victor assured him with amusement, and then added, "At least part of it. The council is paying, remember? Bricker packed nothing but lingerie for her, so the council gets to pay."

"Oh right, nothing but lingerie," Basil murmured, and wondered if he could control himself long enough to allow Sherry to change into one of the outfits Bricker had sent.

"He also packed see-through tops, bustiers, and thong panties," Elvi announced, amusement clear in her voice.

"What else does she need, eh, brother?" Victor asked with amusement.

Despite himself, Basil smiled at the words as he followed Victor to the cash register. See-through tops and lingerie. He couldn't fault Bricker for taste. He was quite sure all of that would look lovely on Sherry. But in the next moment, Basil scowled as he realized that this meant the other man had been going through—and handling—her lingerie, bustiers, and panties.

"Pervert," he muttered, and scowled at Victor when his brother burst out laughing at the comment.

"Tacos! Yum!"

Sherry glanced up from the cheese she was grating and smiled at Stephanie when the teenager charged into the kitchen on that happy note. While Sherry shredded the cheese, Elvi was dicing onions, Drina slicing lettuce, Katricia chopping tomatoes, Victor cooking the meat, Harper heating the shells—both hard and soft, and Teddy and Basil had taken on the task of setting the table and fetching the salsa, sour cream, and guacamole. With all of them working, it was going to be the fastest meal ever made, Sherry thought with amusement, but it was nice to be part of such a large group. The closest thing she'd had to this, aside from holidays with her families, was when she and Luther used to hold their "dinner and a movie" night. The pair of them would team up to make supper, and then settle in front of the television and watch a movie. It had always been nice and relaxing.

"Who is Luther?" Stephanie asked, pinching a bit of the grated cheese and popping it into her mouth.

"An old friend," Sherry answered with a faint smile.

"He doesn't look old," Stephanie said, pinching some more of the cheese from the bowl.

Sherry wrinkled her nose at the girl. "Poking through my memories?" she asked dryly. When Stephanie just shrugged, she added, "Well, stop it."

"I wish I could," Stephanie muttered unhappily.

Sherry glanced back to her task and then said, "Luther isn't old, old. He's my age. But we've known each other a long time. We went to university together and I still consider him a friend, even though we don't get to see each other anymore."

"Sooooo, he's like a girlfriend but a boy," Stephanie said slowly, and Sherry glanced to her with amusement, and then noted that her gaze was on Basil, who had stopped setting out forks to turn and look at them.

Sherry turned her gaze back to the cheese and continued shredding. "Yes. He's a friend, not a boyfriend."

"I could tell," Stephanie said lightly.

Glancing up with surprise, Sherry arched an eyebrow. "How?"

"'Cause you think of him with his clothes on and don't strip him like you do Basil."

Sherry's jaw dropped open and she was sure she was

about as red as the tomatoes Katricia was chopping as the others all chuckled at the words.

"Stephanie," Elvi reprimanded. "Don't tease her."

"Sorry," Stephanie said sincerely. "I was saying that for Basil's benefit. He was getting all jealous."

Sherry glanced sharply toward him, to see that Basil was now studiously back to setting out the silverware, but he was also beet red.

"How long until supper?" Stephanie asked abruptly, and Sherry noted with a frown of concern that the girl was absently rubbing her forehead. It reminded her of what Elvi had said about Stephanie being unable to shut out voices, and that the more there were, the worse it was for her.

"Five minutes," Elvi said gently. "Do you want to wait in your room? We can call you when it's on the table."

"No. I'm okay." Stephanie lowered her hand and managed a smile, but her gaze turned back to Sherry. "I'm not having trouble reading you anymore."

"I gathered," she said wryly.

"It's the life mate thing. You and Basil really are life mates," Stephanie informed her.

Sherry didn't comment and kept her gaze firmly fixed on what she was doing.

"You should see what Sherry bought today, Steph," Elvi said. "She got some pretty nice outfits."

"I like the one she has on," Stephanie said with a nod, and Sherry glanced self-consciously down at herself. It was the ripped jeans and the sweater with the large holes baring the shoulders. She thought they looked good too, but she still wasn't used to wearing such casual clothes, or clothes that were this overtly sexy either. Business dressy didn't exactly lend itself to sexy. Well, okay, business dressy *could* be sexy, but she didn't usually think of herself that way in business clothes. She wore them to look professional. These did look good on her, though, and on the plus side, if she'd damaged them at all when she'd fainted, you couldn't tell.

"You fainted?" Stephanie asked, and Sherry glanced to her as the girl's eyes narrowed and then suddenly widened. "You saw Leo!"

"What?" Sherry squawked with amazement, even as everyone else in the room froze and barked the same word.

"Sherry?" Basil asked with concern, moving toward her. "You saw Leo today? Here? In Port Henry?"

"No," Sherry assured him. "I would have told you if I'd seen him."

"You *did* see him," Stephanie insisted. "But not in Port Henry, in London, while you were shopping. It's the last thing in your head before Basil was waking you up on the dressing area floor."

Sherry shook her head. "I didn't. I'd remember that."

"Not necessarily," Basil said quietly, concern evident in every line of his body.

"Of course I would," she insisted.

"He could have wiped himself from your memory," Elvi told her gently.

"Then how could Stephanie be reading it?" Katricia

asked with a frown. "If he wiped it from her memory, it shouldn't be there for Steph to see."

"Unless there's a trace image of it in her mind and Stephanie's able to pick up on it," Drina suggested, and Sherry could feel the anxiety that suggestion caused in the room. She knew they were all worried sick about Stephanie already. Suggesting she had more skill would only increase those fears they had for her.

"Or maybe Sherry is blocking the memory," Teddy said quietly. "Victims often block horrifying memories. But it would still be there for Stephanie to find."

"Or maybe I had a nightmare while I was in my faint," Sherry suggested. "I mean the man is like some kind of Freddy Krueger character and certainly featured in my nightmares last night, so I wouldn't be surprised if I dreamt about him while I was unconscious. But I definitely did *not* see the man." She stared around at the people in the room, all of them staring back with varying degrees of concern, and then sighed with exasperation and demanded, "Well, can any of the rest of you see Leo in my head?"

"Sherry, we can only read what you think of," Elvi said quietly. "If you've blocked it from your mind or had it wiped, the rest of us won't be able to see it."

"Maybe you can," Basil countered, and caught Sherry's arms to turn her toward him. "What were you thinking just before Stephanie said you had seen Leo?" he asked.

Sherry frowned and tried to recall, but frankly, after all the excitement of the past few minutes, she couldn't remember what she'd—

"I said I liked your outfit," Stephanie said suddenly, prodding her memory.

"Oh, yes," Sherry murmured and recalled wondering if it were a little young for her and then thinking that with the holes and threadbare state, no one would be able to tell if she'd done it any damage in the fall when she'd fainted and—

"I saw it," Dree cried. "It was just a flash, but Stephanie is right. Sherry opened the dressing room door and Leo was there."

"I saw it too," Katricia said quietly.

"But how could that be? How did he get past you two unseen?" Elvi asked with dismay. "Victor, you said you were watching the entrance to the change room."

"I was," Victor assured her firmly. "That's why I didn't try to read Sherry's memory to see if anyone had caused her faint when we found her. No one had come or gone. She was alone."

"I did not see anyone enter or leave the dressing area either except for Elvi," Basil added, backing him up. "But if the girls are seeing the same memory . . ."

"I saw it too," Harper said solemnly.

"So did I," Victor admitted. "But I do not see how he could have got to her. It doesn't make sense."

They were silent for a moment and then Teddy shifted and said, "He could have followed you to the store, saw her choosing clothes, and slid into one of the empty dressing rooms, knowing she'd probably try them on." Mouth tightening, he pointed out, "Then all he had to do was wait for you to leave, approach her, and then slip back into whatever dressing room he was hiding in until you left. That way, he wouldn't have had to pass you two at all."

"Damn," Basil breathed, goose bumps rising on his skin at the thought of Leonius alone with Sherry. He could have done anything to her.

"And if that's the case, he probably followed you back here from London," Teddy pointed out now. Expression grim, he moved to peer out the kitchen window at the dark backyard.

Drina and Tricia moved to the front windows to peer out, and Harper turned to head out of the room. Sherry supposed he was going to look out the side windows of the house, but noted that he retrieved his cell phone from his pocket as he went.

"No!" Elvi protested, sounding almost desperate. "Leo couldn't have followed us back. We'd have noticed."

"Sweetheart," Victor said quietly, turning off the burner under the meat and moving to slip his arms around his wife. "He could have. We weren't watching for him. We thought he was in Toronto."

"Yes, but—" Her gaze shifted anxiously to Stephanie, and she said with frustration. "What was he doing in London? He's supposed to be in Toronto."

"Who knows?" Victor said wearily, pulling her against his chest.

"There are hunters crawling all over Toronto looking for him," Katricia said quietly, continuing to look out the window. "He probably got out of town to avoid them."

"But London? Why London of all places?" Elvi asked

almost plaintively, and Sherry frowned, sure there was something going on here that she wasn't quite getting.

"Could he have followed you girls down from Toronto?" Teddy asked, and Sherry's eyes widened as she recalled spotting someone she'd thought might be Leonius in the service center parking lot.

"No," Drina assured him. "I was watching for—"

Sherry blinked her thoughts away and glanced to Drina curiously when she abruptly went silent. The woman was peering at her, dismay on her face. She wasn't the only one. Everyone in the room was staring at her with expressions that varied from surprise, to horror, to anger. Only Basil wasn't. He was glancing from expression to expression, his eyes narrowing.

"What is it?" he asked finally.

"You *saw* him?" Elvi asked Sherry, accusation in her voice. She pulled away from Victor and stalked toward her, growling, "And you didn't say anything?"

"I wasn't sure it was him," Sherry said at once. "And then a truck went by and he was gone and . . . ." Her gaze slid to Basil as she recalled how she'd been distracted by his kisses. By the time the others had returned to the truck, Leo was the last thing on her mind. Shaking her head, she sighed. "I'm sorry. I—"

"You're *sorry*?" Elvi interrupted in a voice that shook with a rage and grief that left Sherry bewildered. "We are about to lose our daughter because of you and you're 'sorry'?"

Sherry stared at her wide-eyed. "I don't understand. Your daughter?"

"Stephanie," Victor said quietly. "She was sent here

because it was a safe place Leo couldn't know about. But now—"

"But now he knows," Elvi said grimly. "Because *you* didn't say anything about seeing him in that service center parking lot. If you'd said something, Drina and Tricia could have kept driving, or turned back to Toronto, or *something*. Anything but lead him here to Port Henry. But you said nothing and now he knows about this place. She'll never be safe here again until he's caught. She'll have to leave. We'll lose her . . . because of you."

"Elvi," Victor said wearily, pulling her into his arms again. "This is not Sherry's fault. Leo is the villain here."

Elvi pushed at his chest, trying to break out of his hold. "But if she'd just *said* something."

"She was not sure it was him, and did not even remember it once Basil got done kissing her," Victor pointed out quietly, rubbing her back. "Not until now. You remember what it is like when you first meet your life mate."

"Yes, but—"

Sherry didn't stay to hear more. Turning on her heel, she hurried out of the kitchen and upstairs to her room. But when she tried to push the door closed behind her, it bounced off of something. Swinging around, she stared wide-eyed at Basil as he followed her inside.

"I—" she began, but it was as far as Sherry got before Basil pulled her into his arms and kissed her. As usual, her body responded at once, flooding with passion and overwhelming need, but he broke the kiss quickly and rested his forehead on hers. They were both silent for a minute, trying to catch their breath, and then Basil raised his head and peered her in the eye.

"None of this is your fault," he said solemnly.

"But—"

"None of it," he repeated firmly, and then said, "Sherry, the day before yesterday you were just a store owner with a normal life, friends, and family. Then Stephanie charged into your store, Leo and his men followed, and everything changed. This is all down to Leo."

"But if I'd told them that I thought I might have seen him at the service center—"

"You did not remember it, Sherry. You could not tell them something you did not remember," he reasoned.

"Yes, but I *should* have remembered," she said grimly. "That's the point. I *should* have remembered. It's not like forgetting where you put your keys or where you parked your car. Leo is a monster. I should have remembered seeing him. In fact, I can't believe I didn't."

"Victor said you were not sure it was Leo in your mind. Is he right?"

Sherry sighed. "I suppose. Still—"

"How close was he?" Basil interrupted.

"What?" she asked with confusion.

"How close was the person you saw that you thought might be Leo?"

Sherry hesitated and shook her head. "I'm not sure. He was on the other side of the parking lot, by the service center."

"And we were in the van, about two hundred feet away," he said dryly. "Sherry, you are mortal, with mortal eyesight. There is no way you could have been able to tell more than that someone with blond hair was there. From that distance it would have been hard to tell if they were even male or female unless they were very curvy or wearing gender appropriate clothes. What were they wearing?"

"Jeans and a T-shirt," she said unhappily.

He arched one eyebrow at that. "In today's society everyone seems to wear jeans and T-shirts. For all you know it could have been a woman you saw at the service center," he pointed out, and then asked, "Was he alone?"

"Yes. No. I don't know," she said with frustration. "I didn't see anyone with him."

"So you saw someone with long blond hair?" he asked. "And immediately thought of Leo?"

Sherry nodded.

"That is not surprising. He would have been firmly on your mind after what happened the day before in your store. But it might not have been him," he pointed out.

"But he's here," she countered. "At least, he was in London. It has to have been him."

"Actually, no, it doesn't," Victor said from the door, and Sherry glanced to the man sharply.

"Victor," she breathed unhappily. "I'm sorry. I—"

"There is nothing to apologize for," he assured her, moving into the room and easing the door closed. "That is why I came up, to apologize for what Elvi said. She does not mean it. She is just upset."

"Of course she is," Sherry said wearily. "You two basically adopted Stephanie, from what I can tell, and now she'll have to leave and it's all my fault."

"No," he said solemnly. "It isn't, and Elvi will realize that and feel bad for what she said the moment she calms down." He hesitated and then added, "And Basil is right, it may not have been Leo you saw at the service center. We know his sons are always with him. According to Basha, he never travels without at least a couple of his sons at his side. In fact, the only time he has been without them was when we captured a handful of his boys and he was trying to free them. So, if you did not see any of the other Leos at the service center, then it probably was not him that you saw, just someone who looked like him or reminded you of him."

Sherry bit her lip, but then pointed out, "Maybe, but then if I'd just remembered seeing him at the mall today, you would have known not to come back here, and Stephanie wouldn't have to leave."

"You are determined to take responsibility for this, aren't you?" Victor said with a faint smile, and then shook his head. "You did not remember seeing him when you regained consciousness, Sherry. You still do not recall it. How could you tell us something that you do not remember?" He shook his head. "No, Sherry. You hold no fault here. Leo is the only one at fault. Now," he added, his smile fading. "You two need to pack."

"Pack?" Basil asked.

Victor nodded. "Harper sent for his helicopter. He and Drina are taking Sherry and Stephanie back to Toronto to the Enforcer house. I assume you will want to accompany Sherry?"

"Yes, of course," Basil said at once.

"Then pack and come downstairs. If you are quick, you might even have enough time to eat before the helicopter gets here." Smiling wryly, he turned to the door as he added, "Otherwise the rest of us are going to be eating tacos for a week."

Ten

"All right?"

Sherry glanced back at Basil as he followed her into Harper's apartment. She forced a smile and nod but couldn't resist adding, "I really don't think I like helicopters, though."

Stephanie patted her arm sympathetically as she moved past her into the large entry. Shrugging out of her jacket, she said, "Yeah. I didn't care for it myself at first. But you get used to it. Sort of." She grimaced and then admitted, "Well, not really. I still get nauseous myself, just less nauseous."

"That sounds encouraging," Sherry muttered, taking both her overnight bag and Basil's from him and then moving past him and out of the way as he removed his overcoat. She didn't have a jacket to remove. Bricker hadn't packed her one and it wasn't something she'd thought to buy on their trip, so she'd done without. It hadn't been that big a deal. While it had been nice out that day, it was fall, and the temperature had dropped at night. Fortunately, she didn't have to walk far, merely crossing the street from Casey Cottage to the school-yard where the helicopter collected them, and then crossing the roof to enter the building here, when they landed.

"Sherry," Drina called, following them into the apartment with Harper on her heels.

Pausing, she glanced back questioningly.

"Don't jump out of your skin in surprise if Lucian is in the living room," Drina warned.

"Lucian?" she asked with confusion.

Drina nodded. "Harper called and left a message that we were coming back. Last time he did that, we found Lucian waiting here when we arrived." She shrugged. "I just didn't want him giving you a scare if he's done that again."

Nodding, Sherry turned and continued forward, taking the four steps that led down into a large open living room. This time she looked around curiously as she went, expecting to find the grim-faced Lucian Argeneau somewhere, his hard eyes full of accusation and inspecting her as if she were a bug under a microscope. Instead, she found a glorious room empty of people, but filled with beautiful furnishings. Most of the large space was set up as a seating area by a large fireplace, but the far end held a dining room table and chairs.

"Wow," she breathed, setting the bags down beside one of the couches and moving to the windows. The apartment was apparently the whole top floor of the building, but this large room took up at least one corner of the floor. Windows made up the wall in front of her and the wall to her right, presenting a view of the city that was absolutely stunning.

"Nice," Basil commented behind her, and Sherry turned to peer at him with disbelief.

"Nice?" She turned back to look out over the city skyline and asked, "You think this is just 'nice'?"

"It's hard to beat the New York skyline at night for making an impression."

Sherry glanced to her right at that dry comment, to see Lucian coming out of what was obviously the kitchen. The man had a drink in one hand and a wax-paper-wrapped submarine sandwich on a plate in the other. He carried both to the sunken sofa in front of the fireplace and set them on the coffee table as he sat down.

"Sit," he ordered, and then glanced back the way he'd come and barked, "Bricker! Do not forget the—" He ended on a grunt of satisfaction as a bag of potato chips flew through the kitchen doorway and sailed across the room toward him. Lucian caught the bag and dropped it on the table next to his plate, then glanced to Sherry as Basil urged her to sit on the sofa opposite.

Lucian's gaze was sharp and direct. It was also penetrating. The man didn't mess about. He went straight into her thoughts. Sherry could feel him ruffling about in there, sorting through memories and thoughts and raking up what he was looking for. When he found it, he grunted with seeming displeasure and immediately turned his attention to opening the chips.

"Dinner?" Basil asked with amusement.

"Leigh had just put dinner on the table when I got Harper's message," Lucian said. "So I had Bricker stop for sandwiches on the way here." He blinked and wrinkled his nose as the chip bag opened, and Sherry could only assume the smell that wafted out surprised him. He tilted the bag to read the label. A curse slipped from his lips then and he glanced toward the kitchen door and barked, "I said barbecued chips, Bricker."

"They didn't have barbecued chips," Bricker announced, coming out of the kitchen with a drink, a sandwich on a plate, and a bag of chips of his own. "So I got you Salt and Vinegar. Trust me, Salt and Vinegar rock with subs. You'll like them."

Lucian growled something under his breath and set the chips down to pick up his sandwich.

"You didn't have to pick up anything," Harper said, ushering Drina and Stephanie into the room now. "There is food here, Lucian. And I told you to make yourself comfortable. That included eating whatever you want."

Lucian shrugged and merely unwrapped his sandwich. "I did not feel like cooking."

"No need," Harper assured him. "I told Ms. Parker to get in some frozen meals and to cook up a couple of meals a week in case you dropped in."

Basil raised his eyebrows. "Why would Lucian need to eat here? I understood Leigh was an amazing cook."

"She was," Lucian said, sounding glum. "But she saw some damned thing on the Internet about cruelty to farm animals and she's gone vegetarian."

"Oh dear," Basil said with a wince. "So she only cooks vegetarian now?"

When Lucian merely grunted and shook his head, it was Harper who said, "Leigh still cooks main dishes of meat for Lucian."

Basil raised his eyebrows. "Then what is the problem?"

Lucian swallowed and repeated in dry tones, "She's vegetarian now."

He said it as if that should clarify the matter. It didn't. Basil simply stared at him blankly, not comprehending.

"Leigh no longer tastes what she's cooking if it has meat in it," Bricker explained with amusement. "So it's a coin flip as to whether it will be good or not. Sometimes it's underspiced, sometimes it's overspiced, and sometimes it tastes like tonight's dinner." He glanced to Lucian and asked lightly, "Cow patties in cream sauce, wasn't that what you said it was?"

"Country chicken," Lucian corrected grimly. "But it tasted like cow patties in cream sauce."

"Oh dear," Basil said, sounding suspiciously like he wanted to laugh.

"Hmmm," Lucian muttered, and glanced to Harper. "I was glad to get your message."

"Gave you an excuse to avoid eating Leigh's cooking, hmm?" Harper asked with amusement.

He nodded, and picked up his sandwich again. "Which is why I am not as angry as I should be."

"Leo makes all of us angry," Basil said quietly as Lucian took another bite of his sandwich.

Lucian didn't even look at him. His gaze was locked

on Drina as he chewed. Once he swallowed, he asked, "Why did you bring the girls back?"

"I explained everything in my message," Harper said with a frown.

When Lucian didn't even glance his way, but continued to stare at Drina, she said, "Leo found the girls."

"No. He didn't," Lucian said, and took another bite of his sandwich.

"Yes, he did," Drina assured him. "At least he found Sherry. He approached her at a mall in London. We were concerned that Leo might have followed them back to Port Henry."

Lucian nodded as he swallowed and then said, again, "He didn't."

"He didn't follow them back?" Drina asked with a frown. "How can you know that?"

"Because he didn't approach her at the mall," Lucian said grimly.

"What?" Drina asked with confusion.

"It's Susan all over again," Lucian announced.

"Susan?" Sherry murmured, glancing to Basil questioningly. However, he merely shrugged, apparently not knowing what the man was talking about either.

"I don't understand," Drina said slowly.

"Port Henry," he reminded her. "The attacks there. You all assumed it was Leonius."

"But it wasn't," Drina pointed out. "That time it was Susan."

"Yeah," he agreed. "And this is the same thing all over again."

Drina shook her head. "This is nothing like the last

time, Uncle. There haven't been any attacks. And this time it *is* Leo. He approached her at the mall. We *saw* him in Sherry's memory."

"Did you?" Lucian asked mildly, peering into the bag of chips and picking one out to sniff suspiciously before popping it in his mouth.

"Yes, we did." Stephanie spoke up now, scowling at the man as he winced, his cheeks sucking inward as if he'd bitten into a lemon. "We all saw it in her memory."

Lucian didn't even glance at the girl. Returning his gaze to Drina, he chewed, swallowed, and said, "Look again . . . and this time really look . . . as you would if you had no idea who it might be."

Sherry wasn't surprised when Drina immediately turned to her. She was a little dismayed, though, that everyone else did too. Well, everyone but Lucian. He turned his attention back to eating as Drina, Harper, Stephanie, Bricker, and even Basil turned to eye her. Basil was the only one who wasn't staring at her with that weird concentrated expression, but then he was the only one there who couldn't read her.

Resigning herself to it, Sherry recalled the moment they were looking for and simply waited.

"See," Stephanie said with a nod. "She was wearing the outfit she has on now. Someone knocked at the dressing room door. She opened it and it was . . ." Stephanie shook her head with frustration. "It looks like Leo, except—"

Sherry tilted her head at what Stephanie had said. It twigged a memory for her. She recalled exactly what Stephanie described. She had been wearing the jeans she now had on and the sweater. A knock sounded at the door. She'd opened it, expecting it to be Elvi, but . . . Sherry frowned and shook her head. It was all very fuzzy. She saw Leo standing outside the dressing room, but another face kept trying to replace his, and the image was overlaying his, or perhaps his image was overlaying the other so that it was a confused picture, like a double-exposed photo.

"It was a dream," Stephanie said suddenly, her eyes wide. "It was fuzzy the first time, but I can see it better now. It's like a digital recording that's gone whacky. It must have been a dream we've picked up on."

Sherry let her breath out with a little sigh of relief. That made sense. As she'd suggested back at the house, she'd been having nightmares about Leo and his little trio of monsters since the attack in her store. Why wouldn't she have one during her faint?

"It's not a dream," Lucian announced, and took another bite from his sandwich.

"It has to be," Stephanie protested, scowling at Sherry as if she were deliberately remembering it all wrong and confusing her on purpose.

"I am afraid Lucian is right," Drina said, sounding weary. "I have seen this before. What you are seeing is the result of someone trying to make her see something that wasn't there."

"What?" Stephanie asked, turning to peer at Drina.

"Whoever knocked on that dressing room door wanted Sherry to think it was Leo," Drina explained. "But she's built up that resistance to mind control. It didn't work properly." Drina grimaced and glanced to

Sherry again, adding, "I suspect he realized that and tried to erase it altogether. Only that didn't work fully either, which is why we can read it from your memory despite it being veiled from you. The attempt to bury it is probably why you fainted, though." She glanced to Lucian and admitted, "I would have realized that the first time I picked up on the memory, but I didn't look hard enough. I saw Leo, and it was what I expected, so I didn't trouble myself over the fact that the image was garbled. I am sorry, Uncle. I let you down and did exactly what they wanted."

"What who wanted?" Sherry asked with a frown.

"Whoever wanted us to think Leo was at the mall," Drina explained grimly.

"Why would someone want that?" she asked with confusion, and then before anyone could answer, she added, "And this might be a good thing. It could help us narrow down who it might be. There can't be that many people who know about Leo and what he looks like, right?"

Stephanie snorted at the question. "Everyone knows that he's being hunted and what he looks like. He's been the Blood Bag Boy for months now."

"The Blood Bag Boy?" Sherry asked with confusion.

"Yeah," the girl said dryly. "You know how they used to put missing kids' pictures on milk cartons?"

Sherry nodded.

"Well, it's kind of like that," Stephanie announced. "Only it's Leo's face glued on blood bags from the blood bank. Every immortal orders blood, and so every immortal has seen his picture, knows he's Immortal

Enemy Number One, and knows they are to call if they see him in their vicinity."

"Oh," Sherry murmured with disappointment.

"The problem is, Leo has now become a handy go-to-guy whenever there's trouble," Lucian explained. "He's a bad guy we know, so the first suspect."

Harper nodded. "He's become the bloody bogeyman. Something happens, it must be Leonius."

"We need to take care of the bastard," Bricker said with a shake of his head.

Lucian merely grunted and then shrugged. "That is not the problem here, though."

"What problem?" Stephanie asked with a frown. "This is good news. It means Leo didn't find us. We can go back to Port Henry."

"*You* can," Lucian said quietly.

Stephanie frowned. "And Sherry and Basil too, right?"

Lucian merely shook his head.

"But—"

"Wait," Sherry said with a frown. "I don't understand. Why would anyone want me to think Leo was in London?"

"My guess would be they knew it would put everyone in a panic and make us bring you back here," Harper said. "Which is exactly what we did."

"So someone wanted me *out* of Port Henry?" she asked with confusion. "Why? I don't even know anyone there."

"It doesn't have to be that someone wanted you out of Port Henry. It could be that whoever it was wanted you back in Toronto."

"Isn't it the same thing?" she asked.

There was silence, and then Lucian asked, "Who is the immortal in your life?"

"Basil," Sherry answered promptly, and then added, "And the rest of you, I guess."

Lucian shook his head. "Your resistance to being read and controlled suggests long-term exposure to an immortal, or perhaps more than one."

"How long would it take for a mortal to build up that kind of resistance?" Bricker asked curiously.

"At least twenty years," Drina murmured, eyeing Sherry curiously.

She immediately shook her head. "There is no way I have had an immortal in my life for twenty years without my knowing. You guys don't age. I'd notice that."

"Hair dye, older clothes, maybe some padding and a little makeup could make it appear like they were aging," Drina said quietly.

"Seriously?" Sherry asked with surprise.

Drina nodded. "It will be someone you spend a lot of time with. Almost daily for twenty years, I should think. They . . ." Her voice trailed off when Sherry began to shake her head again.

"You can stop there. I haven't had anyone in my life for that long."

"No one?" Basil asked with a frown.

"Well, my mother was around for my first twenty-nine years, but she died three years ago of a heart attack. Your people wouldn't die of a heart attack."

"It's not your mother. If your mother was immortal, you would be too. It's passed on through the mother's blood."

"Unless her mother was turned after Sherry was born," Drina pointed out.

Sherry shifted impatiently. "Hello. Heart attack. Dead. You people only die by decapitation and fire, from what I understand."

"Did your mother have a partner?" Drina asked.

"Just my father. She never dated after they split up."

"No one?"

Sherry started to shake her head, but then hesitated.

"Who is Uncle Al?" Lucian asked sharply, apparently picking up on the thought that had crossed her mind unspoken. "Your father's brother?"

Sherry shook her head. "No. He wasn't really an uncle. He was a family friend. He used to spend a lot of time with us, and he was very supportive of Mom when she and Dad split." She shrugged. "For a while I thought they might start dating or something, but nothing came of it."

"You're sure about that?" Basil asked, and pointed out, "They might not have told you they were dating."

"No. They didn't date," Sherry assured them. "I would have known. Besides, he wasn't in my life that long. He came around after my brother Danny died, when I was seven. As I said, he wasn't really an uncle. By the time I started university he was little more than a fond memory."

"So was he a friend of both your parents or not?" Bricker asked with a frown, and when she glanced to him questioningly, pointed out, "You said he was a family friend of your mom and dad's, but then you said he came around after your brother died when you were seven. Did he show up when you were seven or before that?"

Sherry hesitated and then shrugged helplessly. "I don't know. I was a kid."

"It doesn't matter if he hasn't been in her life since she was a teenager," Drina interrupted. "We're dealing with an immortal who is obviously still in her life. This Uncle Al would hardly disappear for fifteen years and then suddenly show up to scare her out of Port Henry all this time later."

"Well, there isn't anyone in my life who fits the bill of an immortal," Sherry said. "The only people I even deal with on a daily basis, who are in their early twenties, are my employees Emma, Joan, Allan, Zander, Sarah, and Eric . . . and I didn't know any of them before I opened the store three years ago. So if one of them is an immortal—"

Drina shook her head. "Three years isn't long enough. But it doesn't have to be someone who looks like they're in their early twenties. As I said, hair dye, makeup, and clothing could make them look older."

"It doesn't matter how old they look," Sherry insisted. "I just haven't had anyone in my life that long. The longest anyone has been in my life is my mother, who as I said is dead. After that, my buddy Luther was in my life for the longest at nine years, and he got a job in Saudi Arabia and moved there just before I opened the store three years ago. I haven't seen him since."

"Aunts and uncles?" Drina asked.

"My relatives are not vamp— immortals," Sherry said with certainty.

"You cannot be certain—" Drina began, but Sherry cut her off.

"I *am* certain," she insisted firmly. "No amount of makeup and hair dye could make a twenty-something look sixty to seventy years old. My mother was the youngest, an afterthought, born fifteen years behind her eldest sister. All my aunts have varicose veins and are wrinkled from their foreheads down to their feet. As for my uncles, one is bald with a little sprout of gray hair on his crown, the other has that donut thing happening where the top of the head is bald and the hair grows around the sides, and the third one has a belly that actually does shake like a bowl full of jelly when he laughs. I'm telling you, they are not immortals."

Silence filled the room briefly, and then Lucian crumpled up the empty wrappings of his sandwich, tossed it on the plate with his now empty chip bag, picked up his plate and drink glass and stood to leave the room for the kitchen. They heard him banging around in there, presumably disposing of the wrappings and putting the plate in the dishwasher, then he returned with a notepad and a pen.

"Write down everyone you have ever known in your life and how long they have been or were in your life," he instructed, handing the notepad and pen to her.

"Everyone?" Sherry echoed with alarm.

"Everyone who has spent a lot of time around or near you while they were in your life," he clarified. "Friends, family friends, that sort of thing."

"That's a lot of people," Sherry warned, accepting the notepad and pen.

"You have until morning," Lucian said firmly, and then turned to Harper. "You can take Stephanie and Drina back to Port Henry, or stay for a couple days, as you like. But if you stay, Stephanie doesn't leave the apartment."

Harper nodded, but asked, "And Sherry and Basil?"

"They stay here until we sort out who the immortal is in her life and why they didn't want her in Port Henry," he announced.

Sherry couldn't help noticing that nobody protested his dictating everyone's life like this. Even she was keeping her mouth shut, she acknowledged wryly as Lucian continued.

"If you're staying tonight," he said to Harper and Drina, "they can stay here too. Otherwise, Bricker will take them to the Enforcer house after he drops me off."

Harper nodded and glanced to Drina when she caught his hand. She tugged him to the side to whisper in his ear, and his eyebrows rose slightly. But he nodded and then straightened and said, "Sherry and Basil can stay here. We'd like to stay a couple days and try to help sort out who this immortal might be before we go."

"To make up for my mistake," Drina added quietly. "It can't hurt to have more minds working on the puzzle of who the immortal in Sherry's life might be."

"I like puzzles," Stephanie announced, dropping onto the couch next to Sherry and grinning at her good-naturedly.

Sherry smiled back and then glanced to Lucian as

he headed for the entry, announcing, "We're leaving, Bricker."

Bricker paused with his sandwich halfway to his mouth and gaped after the man, then sighed and quickly wrapped up the second half of his sandwich, muttering, "Of course, we are."

Sherry bit her lip as they all watched Bricker scramble after Lucian. No one spoke until they heard the telltale sign of the elevator door opening and closing, and then Drina glanced to Sherry and smiled.

"I'll make some coffee and see if Mrs. Parker made brownies or anything to help fuel your brain while you make the list."

"I'll help," Harper offered, moving to her side.

Sherry jumped in surprise when Stephanie suddenly squealed, "Brownies!" and leapt off the couch to hurry after the couple. She watched the girl go with wry amusement. Sometimes Stephanie seemed sixty, and sometimes she just seemed sixteen . . . or even six, she thought, and shook her head.

"Are you all right with staying here?"

Sherry glanced to Basil and started to nod, then frowned and said, "Oh, God, I'm sorry, Basil. You came to Canada to visit your daughter and now—" Biting her lip, she shook her head and said, "You don't have to stay here, you know. I'll understand if you want to return to Port Henry and continue your visit with Katricia."

He smiled faintly at her words and reached out to caress her cheek, then tucked a strand of hair behind her ear. "We can visit Katricia after we resolve this. I meant are you okay with staying here as opposed to the Enforcer house? This is the third new place in almost as many days. I wondered if you would prefer someplace you've already been."

"Oh." She smiled weakly and glanced around. "No, this is fine. It certainly has a great view," she said, then frowned and added, "As long as we aren't putting Drina and Harper out. I wouldn't want to inconvenience them."

"You aren't," Harper announced, returning to the room with a tray of sugar, cream, sweetener, and spoons. "Actually, it's nice to get some use out of this place. We spend so much time in Port Henry, this apartment is really a waste. Thank God I own it and don't pay rent," he added dryly. Harper smiled at her reassuringly as he set his tray on the coffee table. "There are several guest rooms, or the two of you can share one. It's up to you."

"Thank goodness my room is soundproofed," Stephanie said now, carrying out a second tray, this one bearing a pan of brownies and several plates. "At least I won't have to listen to you four going at it tonight. I don't know how the others sleep with all that racket."

"So says she who snores like a lumberjack," Harper teased.

"I do not!" Stephanie gasped with dismay, and then asked worriedly, "Do I?"

"No, honey," Drina assured her with a reproving look at Harper as she entered the room with a tray of coffee cups. "Harper's just teasing you."

"Hmmm." Stephanie scowled at him as Drina set

down the brownies and plates, then she slumped on the couch next to Sherry and eyed the notepad. "Would it be easier for you to make your list at the dining room table?"

"Oh!" Drina paused, her own tray still in her hand. Clucking her tongue, she turned in that direction. "I should have thought of that. We can have coffee and brownies at the table so you can write. The coffee's on, by the way, it won't be a minute."

"Oh, you don't have to . . . ." Sherry let her voice trail away. Drina was already halfway to the table, and Harper and Stephanie were grabbing up the trays to follow. Shrugging, she stood and followed too, leaning into Basil when he slipped his arm around her as he joined her. It really would be easier to work at the table anyway.

Sherry and Basil settled there as Stephanie cut and distributed plates of brownies and Harper passed out the coffee cups. Drina busied herself giving everyone spoons and forks and placing the coffee fixings in the center of the table. She then collected the trays and returned to the kitchen to check on the coffee.

Sherry had opened her notepad and had the pen poised at the first line but hadn't written anything when Basil suggested, "Maybe start from your earliest memories. Write everyone you can remember when you were a child, put down how long they were in your life, and then continue on until today."

"Right," she said, peered at the page, and then wrote down her mother's name followed by the date she died.

"If she has to list everyone from school friends to

teachers, this is going to take a while, huh?" Stephanie commented, slipping a generous slice of brownie onto a plate.

"Why do you think Lucian gave her till morning?" Harper asked dryly.

"I thought you guys slept during the day," Sherry murmured as she followed her mother's name with her father's.

"Some do, some don't," Basil murmured, rubbing her shoulders as she wrote her grandparents' names down. "We all avoid actually going out in daylight, but that doesn't mean we can't be up and about. Lucian will probably take a nap when he gets home, so he's fresh in the morning."

Sherry merely nodded and continued with her list. The faster she finished, the faster they could go to bed and the more sleep they'd get before Lucian was back to harass them.

"Like you two will do any sleeping," Stephanie said dryly.

"Steph!" Harper growled.

"What?" the girl asked, and shrugged. "You know it's true. You two won't get much sleep either, and Basil and Sherry are newer at this life mate thing than you guys. I doubt they'll sleep at all other than the brief bouts of unconsciousness." She carried a plate with a slice of brownie around and set it in front of Basil, then patted Sherry's arm and suggested, "You should really let Basil turn you. The lack of sleep won't affect you as much that way. All you have to do is suck up some more blood. Besides, with Leo prowling around out there . . ." She hesitated and then finished sadly, "Well, you just don't want him to be the one to turn you."

Sherry raised her gaze from the notepad and glanced around when sudden silence fell over the room. Drina stood in the kitchen doorway, a large, full coffeepot in hand and a stricken look on her face. Harper stood at the head of the table peering down at his feet, his expression a combination of frustration and sadness, and Basil was eyeing Stephanie with pity. As for Stephanie herself, the teenager had returned to her place in front of the pan of brownies, but now simply stared down at the squares, her shoulders slumped.

"Didn't someone promise me brownies?" Sherry asked with forced cheer. "Here I am slaving away at my list and yet I'm the only one without a brownie."

"Right." Stephanie stiffened her shoulders and returned to cutting, muttering, "We can't have that."

Sherry swallowed back a sigh and peered at her notepad again, but her vision was a bit blurry, her eyes glazed with tears.

Eleven

Sherry finished brushing her teeth, set her toothbrush on the counter next to Basil's and then turned to the door, only to pause. It was late, after 2 A.M., and Lucian was supposed to come in the morning, so they weren't likely to get much sleep, and still she was dithering about going to bed. She'd already brushed her teeth three times.

Grimacing, she turned back to the sink and eyed the woman who peered back. A nervous woman in a short, rose-colored lace nightgown that she might as well not be wearing since everything showed through it. Still, it wasn't like Basil hadn't seen everything already.

"Seriously?" she whispered to her reflection. "You've already had sex with the man multiple times, but now you're nervous because you're sharing a room with him?"

Her reflection didn't respond, and Sherry rolled her

eyes and lectured, "All you have to do is open the door, walk out there and climb into bed. Preferably without tripping and breaking your neck or otherwise humiliating yourself."

"Sherry?"

She turned sharply to the closed door. "Yes?"

"Are you okay?" Basil asked with concern, and then sounded confused as he added, "Who are you talking to?"

Sherry glanced back to her reflection and whispered, "Now see what you've done?"

"What did I do?"

Muttering, "Damned immortal hearing," she opened the door. Basil stood just outside in light blue cotton pajamas and a dark blue robe. He looked so damned debonair . . . like he was used to being in strange bedrooms with women he'd only met days ago.

"Nothing," Sherry assured him when she realized she hadn't responded to his comment, and then she admitted with a little chagrin, "I was just talking to myself."

"Oh." He looked relieved at this news and smiled, his gaze sliding down over her with pleasure. "You look lovely."

"Thank you," she squeaked, and moved past him to hurry to the bed, her only thought to hide herself under the covers. God, she was such a ninny.

Sherry climbed quickly to sit in bed and tugged the covers up to her neck. She then held them in place with one hand and forced a smile for him.

Basil still stood across the room, a rather bemused

look on his face. She supposed she couldn't blame him. She was acting like a terrified virgin on her wedding night. Clearing her throat, she patted the mattress next to her with her free hand and asked, "Aren't you going to come to bed?"

Basil eyed the spot but shook his head. "No, I think it's probably better if I don't."

"What?" she squawked with surprise.

Turning to pace to the chair that sat in the corner of the room, he settled himself in it and said solemnly, "Honey . . . we need to talk."

"Oh, God, really?" Sherry groaned, closing her eyes and rubbing her forehead with the fingers of one hand. According to the movies, "Honey, we need to talk" was code for "I'm about to dump your ass."

"Really what?" Basil asked uncertainly.

"The breakup speech," she said grimly, dropping her hand to scowl at him. "Let me guess, this is all going so fast and we need to slow it down."

"What?" he asked with bewilderment. "No, of course not. Honey, you are my life mate, I will never break up with you."

Sherry narrowed her eyes, but he looked so earnest, she actually believed him. Relaxing a little, she asked, "Then why are you way over there?"

He smiled crookedly and admitted, "Because if I come any closer I fear I will not be able to refrain from ravishing you, and we need to talk first."

Refrain from ravishing? He was so cute, Sherry thought, and let the blankets slip a little so that it rested just above the neckline of her nightie. Basil's gaze immediately dipped to follow the movement and she saw his hands clench on the chair arms. Suddenly feeling more cheerful, she said, "Sure. What do you want to talk about?"

Basil hesitated and then forced his gaze back to her face. "Do you recall what Stephanie said earlier tonight?"

"Which time?" she asked, letting the blanket drop a little more so that the top half of her breasts, visible through the lace nightie, were on display. She might as well have been bare from the nipples up, she noted with a quick glance down, so wasn't terribly surprised when Basil seemed to find it a little harder to pull his attention upward this time.

He did, though, eventually, and then cleared his throat, frowned and asked, "What was I—?"

"Stephanie," she reminded him sweetly, feeling incredibly powerful in that moment.

"Oh yes." Basil nodded, his gaze slipping down to her lace top as she let the blanket drop altogether. She was pretty much fully exposed now, her breasts visible through the lace, her nipples a darker rose than the nightie itself. They were also erect, she noticed, and felt a blush curl up over her cheeks. It was amazing how quickly you could go from feeling like a ninny, to feeling powerful, to feeling like a shy schoolgirl, Sherry thought.

A tearing sound drew her gaze back to Basil to see that he was clutching violently at the chair arms now and had apparently done some damage to the material. More importantly, though, her nipples weren't the only thing in the room that were erect. Basil had popped a mini-tent in his lap.

Confidence restored and the sense of power surging back within her, Sherry slid out of bed, and this time she did not scamper, but walked with slow and what she hoped were sexy steps to stand in front of Basil.

He was reaching for her before she'd even stopped walking, his hands clasping her upper hips and pulling her forward when she would have halted.

Sherry grabbed for his shoulders to keep her balance, and then gasped in a breath of air when he closed his mouth over her nipple through the lace. She felt his tongue move, rasping and shifting the cloth across her nipple, and she moaned as heat instantly poured through her. So distracted was she that she didn't even notice that his hands had left her hips until she felt cool air on her stomach. Just as she realized that he'd pushed her nightie up to just below her breasts, Basil released her nipple and ducked his head to lick her stomach above her belly button.

Suddenly self-conscious about her body again, Sherry started to retreat, but Basil let the nightie drop over his head and grabbed her hips again to hold her in place. He murmured something as well, but she didn't have a clue what it was. Words could get a bit garbled when you tried to talk while licking your way down a woman's body.

Gasping, Sherry grabbed for his head to keep from falling when Basil suddenly forced her back a step and slid to his knees in front of the chair. His tongue never once left her skin as he made the maneuver, and she would have been impressed but was too busy gasping again, this time in shocked pleasure as he ran the fingers of one hand lightly across the damp flesh between her legs. Even as her body responded to the caress, he withdrew his hand to grasp her left leg and shift it over his shoulder. Basil then dipped his head between her legs to caress her with his tongue instead.

Sherry was pretty sure her heart stopped then. She was also pretty sure she wouldn't be able to keep her balance long and so was relieved when he suddenly lifted her off her feet, turned on his knees and dropped her in the chair he'd just vacated. That relief only lasted until he reached out to grasp her knees and raise and spread her legs, draping one over each arm of the chair. The position left her open to inspection. Sherry immediately tried to sit up and close her legs, but he was having none of that. Planting his hands firmly on each thigh, Basil held her in place, then bent his head to minister to her again.

The first rasp of his tongue this time brought a cry of pleasure, and Sherry had the inane thought that it was certainly a good thing that Stephanie's room had soundproofing. But it was the last sensible thought she had as Basil reduced her to nothing more than a trembling mass of moans, groans, and cries that ended in a shout that could probably be heard twenty floors below. It was followed by darkness.

Sherry opened her eyes slowly, at first confused as to what she was doing sitting in the corner of the bedroom. But then she realized she was splayed there like an abandoned doll and quickly shifted her legs together and sat up, tugging her nightie down to cover her decently.

"I would have done that for you, but I was afraid if I touched you I wouldn't stop."

She glanced across the room at that announcement and spotted Basil standing, staring out of the window. He must have turned at some point to see her straightening herself, but right now he had his back to her, his hands clasped behind him.

"Er . . ." she said weakly, and then shook her head when nothing followed.

Apparently, she was not the most brilliant of conversationalists at the moment.

"The turning," Basil said suddenly, and she glanced to him with confusion.

"What?"

"That's what I wanted to talk to you about," he explained with his back still to her. "I wanted to talk to you about the turning and what Stephanie said about it."

"Oh," she breathed, and then tried to recall what the girl had said. Oh yes. "That I didn't want Leo to turn me."

"Yes," he said solemnly, and finally faced her. She couldn't help noticing, though, that he avoided looking below her neck. The man was still hot for her . . . and she liked that about him.

"Your face," Sherry gasped, standing up with alarm as she noted the red round circle on his left cheek.

Basil waved away her concern. "Apparently when we passed out after . . ." He waved again rather than say what he'd been doing to her, and then continued, "I think I fell back and smacked myself in the face as I did." He smiled wryly. "At least it is the only conclusion I can come up with . . . and my hand was on my cheek when I woke up."

"Oh," Sherry murmured and settled back in the chair again, supposing there were more embarrassing positions he could have found himself in.

"That was very naughty of you, by the way," he said suddenly, and Sherry glanced to him again.

Managing an innocent expression, she asked, "Whatever are you talking about?"

Basil snorted, apparently not buying it, and accused, "You deliberately distracted me."

"All I did was cross the room," she said with a shrug. "It's not like I pulled my nightgown down and did the boobie dance in your face."

"The boobie dance?" he asked with a frown.

"You know, jiggling my boobs in your face."

Basil licked his lips, a faraway look on his face that suggested to her that he was imagining just that, and then his expression cleared and he scowled once more. "You are distracting me again."

Sherry stared, the sudden urge to hug him briefly overwhelming her.

"Why are you looking at me like that?" he asked warily.

"Like what?" she asked softly.

He hesitated and then admitted, "I'm not sure how to

describe it. Either as if you want to eat me up or slap me."

Sherry burst out laughing at that. Talk about not being able to read expressions. Shaking her head, she smiled and said, "I'd be happy to eat you up. It only seems fair to return the favor."

Basil groaned. "Sherry we have to talk about this."

Relenting, she stood and moved to the bed. This time she laid down in it rather than sit, and then she pulled the covers up to her armpits and rested her hands on top. "All right. Talk."

Basil breathed out a sigh and moved to perch carefully on the bottom corner on the opposite side, about as far away as he could get in the bed. When she simply waited patiently, he finally said, "I think Stephanie is right."

"That I don't want to be turned by Leo?" Sherry asked.

"Yes."

"Okay. I understand that, and you're right, I wouldn't want Leo to turn me," she admitted.

Basil nodded, and then took a deep breath and blurted, "So, perhaps I should turn you to prevent that happening."

Sherry froze. She was quite sure her heart actually stopped, or at least skipped a beat. She hadn't been expecting this. She was supposed to be able to just enjoy what was happening between her and Basil and worry about the rest of it later. This wasn't worrying about it later.

"Sherry?" he queried solemnly.

"I . . ." She paused, licked her lips and then admitted, "I don't think I'm ready for that yet, Basil. Everything has happened so fast. We need to slow down and think about this."

"That sounds eerily like the breakup speech you mentioned," he said dryly.

She grimaced and sat up in bed, not caring that the blankets fell away. "Basil, we only met a couple days ago and you're asking me to do something that can't be undone."

"To prevent you from suffering Stephanie's fate, which also cannot be undone," he said quietly.

"Yes, but . . ." Frowning, she peered down at her hands and then bit her lip and asked, "But what if we don't work out? What if you grow tired of me?"

"Sherry," he began, and then paused and stood to move around the bed to sit next to her hip and take her hands. "I know that all of this is a lot to take in. That until a couple days ago you did not even know we existed in your world let alone that there was such a thing as life mates, but please believe me when I tell you that this *will* work out and I will *never* tire of you." Squeezing her fingers, he said firmly, "We are life mates. That is a bond that cannot be undone and will not fade with time. It will live and thrive for as long as we do. So long as we are both alive, no one and nothing can come between us. It is as simple as that."

Sherry stared at their entwined hands for a moment, but finally shook her head. "I need more time."

Basil sat still as a statue, his mouth tight, and then he

said, "You don't have to agree to be my life mate now. Just agree to let me turn you."

Her eyes widened incredulously. "But what if you did that and we split up?"

"I am willing to take that chance to keep you safe. I would rather have you alive and immortal and not with me, than dead and never mine," he said grimly.

Sherry stared at him for a moment, amazement overwhelming her. She didn't know what to make of his offer. What did it mean? She needed to think. "Can you please just give me a little more time?"

Basil closed his eyes and then confessed, "I am afraid of losing you. I have waited for you for what feels like eons, and I am terrified that Leo will snatch you away from me and either kill you or turn you himself, which could also kill you or make you insane." Eyes opening, he said, "I am afraid that if I don't turn you, you could be lost to me forever."

Sherry met his gaze squarely as she said, "I'm sorry for that. But when I make the decision, I don't want it to be for the wrong reasons. I want it to be based on our feelings for each other, not because we're afraid of what Leonius Livius might do." She hesitated and then said, "Please tell me you understand."

Basil was silent for a minute, and then, rather than answer, he slid one hand around her neck, pulled her face forward and then kissed her. It was a deep, hungry kiss, and felt very like the ravishing he'd mentioned earlier.

Sherry was so relieved that he wasn't stomping out

of the room in a snit, she immediately responded, her upper body molding itself to his as her hands glided up his chest, around his neck on either side and into his soft, short hair. When he tightened his arms around her and stood up, taking her with him, she went willingly. Her legs slid out from under the covers and fell against his, then took her weight when he set her down.

Basil reached for the hem of her nightie then, and Sherry raised her arms so he could tug it off over her head. Once it was a crumpled heap on the floor, though, she reached for the tie of his robe. She'd barely started to tug on it when he caught both her wrists in one hand and held them firmly as he removed the undone tie himself. She didn't resist when he quickly bound her hands with one end of it, but simply watched with curiosity.

He kissed her again then, his tongue thrusting almost violently into her mouth, and then pushed her backward. Sherry fell across the bed with a surprised gasp, and then glanced up as he knelt one knee on the top of the bed by her head and laced the other end of the robe tie through the wooden slats of the headboard. She glanced to his face worriedly when he finished, half afraid he intended to turn her anyway, without her permission. But he merely stood up and began to undo his pajama top, his eyes feasting on her as he did.

Once finished with the buttons, the top hit the ground next to her nightie. Sherry bit her lip as her gaze skated over his chest. Then her eyes dropped to watch him hook his thumbs beneath the waistband of his pajama bottoms as he shoved them down.

Basil stepped out of them and then crawled onto the bed and up her body to kiss her again. He then leaned up on one hand, hooked his other arm under her back and lifted her upper body until he could close his mouth over her breast.

Sherry moaned as he suckled and laved at first one breast and then the other, and then she gasped in startled surprise when he nipped at the sensitive tip of one before releasing it and easing her back to the bed. His eyes were glowing silver and turbulent as he straightened and let his gaze slide over her, and she knew he was as affected by what he was doing as she was. He was feeling her pleasure, it was bouncing between them, expanding with each pass, and she thought he was struggling with it, trying to prolong their pleasure. Or perhaps he was trying to torment her for refusing his offer and agreeing to the turn. If so, he was torturing himself as well.

Distracted as she was with her thoughts, Sherry was caught by surprise when he suddenly leaned forward to brush his hand lightly against the core of her before thrusting a finger inside her with a vigor that startled a yelp from her. That yelp was followed by a moan as his thumb found her sensitive nub and began to run lightly back and forth over it, and then around it in circles.

Panting, she pushed her feet into the bed and lifted herself into his touch, watching the struggle taking place on his face through almost closed eyes. She had to marvel at his self-restraint. If her hands weren't tied, she would be trying desperately to push him down on his back so she could climb on top of him, take him into her body and end this torment.

"Oh God," Sherry cried when he eased his finger out and thrust back in again, hard, this time using two fingers and stretching her. She tugged at her bindings, her body arching, hips pressing down into the thrust, seeking the release she was so close to finding. And then Basil stopped caressing her and removed his hand from between her legs.

"No, no, no, please," she moaned, and then sagged with relief when Basil shifted to kneel between her legs. There was sweat on his forehead that told her how much that little bit of foreplay had cost him, how hard he'd had to fight their growing passion to try to draw this out. But she didn't care. At that point all she wanted was to feel him thrusting into her, so she was relieved when he grabbed her by the hips, lifted her off the bed so that she was strung from the headboard like a hammock, and plowed into her with the vigor they both needed.

"God, yes," Sherry cried, and wrapped one leg around his hips. She kept her other foot planted on the bed for leverage and used both to thrust back, meeting each thrust with her own eager passion. And then Basil released her hips, leaving her to ride him as she would while he leaned forward to fondle her breasts.

Sherry bucked against him on a cry of excitement as he pinched her nipples, then bucked again when he shifted one hand down between them to run his thumb roughly over her excited nub. As sensitive as she was, her pleasure was almost painful under the bold touch, and she went wild, thrusting and bucking and screaming obscenities as she rode his erection to her own pleasure . . . and his.

Sherry woke up first this time. Her memory of what happened didn't come to her immediately. It wasn't until she tried to sit up and her bound wrists and Basil's body prevented it that she recalled. Blushing all the way down to her toes then, she closed her eyes briefly.

Jeez, who knew she had such a potty mouth? she thought as she recalled the things she'd been yelling at the end. Biting the inside of her lip, she glanced down at Basil's head and tried to imagine what he must think of her now . . . and what was going to happen when he woke up. She'd have to ask him to untie her, she realized, and closed her eyes as she imagined suffering through his knowing looks as he did it, and—

Sherry's eyes blinked open as he shifted. When she peered down this time it was to see that his eyes were open and he was watching her.

"Hi," she said weakly, and then cleared her throat and asked, "Do you think you could untie me?"

Basil gave her a lazy smile, and then shifted off of her and crawled to the head of the bed to examine the robe tie.

"I think you'll need to come up higher so the tie has a little give," he said with a frown as he examined the stretched material.

Sherry hesitated, and then rolled onto her stomach and shifted to her knees, murmuring "Thank you" when he reached back to take her elbow and help her crawl to the top of the bed on her knees. They were both upright and kneeling on the pillows now, side by side, and Basil rubbed his hand briefly down her back before setting to work on the tie.

"Thank you," she whispered again when he managed to untie the end attached to the bed.

"My pleasure," he assured her, and then turned and kissed her.

Sherry kissed him back, sucking eagerly at his tongue, before thrashing it with her own. She felt one of his hands claim a breast and pressed into the caress, then moaned as his other hand ran down her back to caress her bottom, before slipping between her legs from behind to find the wet heat building there.

"Oh, God," Sherry moaned when he broke their kiss to run his mouth to her ear and nibble at it. She was riding his hand, her excitement back and burning bright, and then Basil suddenly cursed and stopped what he was doing to shift behind her and grab her hips. He paused then, though, and took a deep breath.

"I should finish untying—"

She raised her hands over her head for him to get to them, and he quickly set to work, groaning when she rubbed her bottom against his erection. It was madness and she knew it. They'd just done this twice, well not this exactly, but they'd both reached fulfillment twice now and yet all he had to do was touch or kiss her and she was burning as brightly as a Roman candle, desperate to find that release again.

"Hurry," she urged, rubbing harder against him, and gasping at the pleasure it sent through them both. When her hands suddenly broke free, Sherry grabbed the top of the headboard and rubbed back against him a final time before he clasped her shoulder with one hand and her hip with the other and pulled her back even as he thrust forward.

She moaned as he filled her, her body clenching around him and trying to hold him in place. She then reached down between her legs to caress herself, her fingers playing over her slick skin as he thrust in and out of her. She was just teetering on the edge of orgasm when he suddenly reached around to find and pinch one of her nipples. It was what she needed. In the next moment they were both screaming as pleasure overwhelmed them.

Twelve

The next time Sherry woke up she was alone in bed. Shifting sleepily, she turned on her side, intending to go back to sleep, but then paused when she saw the readout on the digital clock on the bedside table. It was 9 A.M. . . . and Lucian was supposed to be coming back this morning. Sighing, she reluctantly pushed the blankets aside and climbed out of bed, then made her way to the bathroom. She'd opened the door and started in before it occurred to her that Basil might be in there.

Fortunately, he wasn't. Although the room was warm and a little steamy, suggesting that he'd showered not long ago. Deciding a shower was a good idea, and hoping it would wake her up and make her feel less like death warmed over, Sherry closed the door.

Fifteen minutes later Sherry was showered, teeth brushed, and her damp hair brushed neatly away from her face. She peered at herself in the mirror and grimaced at the circles under her eyes. Reaching for her makeup, she acknowledged that they should have gone right to sleep last night instead of—

Color came into her pale cheeks as she recalled what they'd done, and she picked up her makeup with a little shake of the head.

"You're an animal," she told her reflection quietly, and that's what it had felt like. Unrestrained, wild, give it to me now. If her hands hadn't been restrained the first time and if she hadn't had her back to him the last time, his back and maybe even his front would have been a mass of scratches today.

Maybe that's why he tied her, she thought suddenly. She was pretty sure she'd marked him up during their first go-round at the house in Port Henry . . . although, fast healer that he was, there had been no proof of it by the time she'd seen his back the next morning. For some reason, with Basil . . . she couldn't help herself. She became this mindless wild thing, interested in only—

"God, I do love the cock rather than just like it, after all," she muttered with self-deprecation, and then added to herself, Well, at least Basil's. None of her previous lovers had driven her mad as he did. Not that she'd had hoards of them or anything. She could count how many lovers she'd had on one hand, which was pretty moderate for a thirty-two-year-old woman in today's world. Still, she'd thought she'd had hot sex before, but this was beyond the norm.

Having done all the damage control she could with the makeup, Sherry headed out to the bedroom to dress.

As she was reaching to take a top off its hanger, she noticed her wrists were chapped and bruised from her attempts to pull free of the robe tie. She had not healed overnight, like Basil would have. Grimacing, she left the shirt she'd originally intended to wear and reached for a long-sleeved blouse instead.

The sound of voices drifted up the hall when she opened the bedroom door. She recognized Drina's and Harpers, and then Basil's, but then another female spoke and she didn't recognize this new voice. Frowning, Sherry slowed as she reached the end of the hall and then stopped to survey the people in the living room.

Lucian, Bricker, Drina, Harper, and Basil she all knew. She didn't, however, recognize the second woman in the room or the man standing with her. The woman—tall, slender, dressed all in black, and with several weapons strapped to her waist and legs— certainly made an impression. But her hair was the most notable thing about her—ice blond from the scalp and for three inches down, it then switched to a darker color, which was a mixture of brown and red for the next six inches or so. Sherry couldn't tell if it was a dye job that was growing out or if it had been deliberately dyed with dark ends, but it was striking just the same, and oddly attractive. The man was fair-haired and equally attractive.

"That's Basha Argeneau and Marcus Notte."

Sherry glanced around at that quiet announcement and raised her eyebrows at Stephanie, who now stood at her elbow. "Who are they?"

"Basha is Lucian and Basil's niece," Stephanie explained. "Marcus is her life mate."

"Okay, but why are they here?" Sherry asked, clarifying her previous question. "Are they hunters like Drina?"

"Oh," Stephanie said with a grimace. "No . . . well, sort of. At least they are right now," she added, and told her, "Basha is Leo's mom."

"What?" Sherry gasped with amazement, her eyes widening incredulously.

"She said I am Leo's mother."

Sherry's head whipped back at that smooth announcement, alarm racing through her when she found Basha had crossed the room and now stood directly in front of her. Even as she noted that, the man Stephanie had said was Marcus stepped up behind Basha and slid his arm around her waist in a protective manner.

Sherry simply eyed the pair silently, unsure what to say. Should she apologize? Offer her sympathies? Ask the woman to please get her son in hand so she could go back to her life?

"An apology is unnecessary," Basha assured her quietly. "The sympathies are appreciated, though, and if I could get my son 'in hand,' as you put it, I would have done so long ago rather than have to be the one who now has to put him down like the rabid dog he is."

"Ah," Sherry murmured, and then frowned. "Lucian is making you handle your son?" That seemed harsh.

"Not as harsh as what could have been done," Basha said quietly. "They had Leo a couple years ago. I helped him escape. I didn't know what he'd done and was doing," she added quietly. "But it doesn't matter. The fact is, he killed again after that and I'm responsible for those lost lives. The council could have held me responsible for them and punished me. Instead, they expect me to clean up my mess . . . and I intend to do that."

"*We* intend to do that," Marcus said in a solemn rumble, pulling the woman back against him.

"Yes," she sighed, and tilted her head back to offer the man a grateful smile.

"If you're done introducing yourselves," Lucian said dryly into the brief silence.

Basha smiled faintly at Sherry's alarmed expression. "His bark is worse than his bite."

"No, it's not," Marcus said dryly, shifting his arm around Basha to turn her back toward the couch.

Sherry and Stephanie followed silently, both moving toward Basil when he shifted to make room for them on the couch he occupied alone.

"Good morning, love," he whispered, leaning toward her to kiss her briefly as Sherry settled next to him.

"You should have woken me," she murmured, covering his hand where it rested on his leg and squeezing gently.

"You looked so peaceful sleeping, I didn't have the heart," Basil said solemnly, and then smiled wryly and added, "I was also afraid that if I did, we'd never get out of the room."

Sherry smiled faintly, silently acknowledging that he was probably right.

"I've brought Basha and Marcus up to speed on the situation since Leo showed up at your store," Lucian announced, garnering everyone's attention.

Her gaze immediately moved to Basha at this news, and she wondered how the woman must feel, knowing that her son was such a monster. All of this had to be difficult for her.

"Harper made copies of your list, Sherry," Drina said now, gesturing to several stacks of paper on the coffee table. "Do you want coffee and something to eat before we go through them?"

Sherry hesitated and then stood up. "It's okay. You go ahead, I'll just grab myself a coffee while you go through the names. I already know them."

Drina nodded and started to hand out the stacks of paper, saying, "There are bagels in the cupboard and cream cheese in the fridge, or there's bread, peanut butter, honey, and jam if you'd rather have toast."

"Thanks," Sherry murmured as she eased between Basil's knees and the coffee table and headed for the kitchen. She went straight to the coffeepot first. It was nearly empty. She poured herself the last cup and then put on a fresh pot, considering what to have for breakfast as she did. She'd never been much of a breakfast eater, but had expended a lot of energy last night, so decided to have a bagel.

Sherry ate at the island rather than take it out to eat in front of the others. When she finished, the fresh coffee was done as well, so she grabbed the pot to take with her in case anyone wanted a refresher.

"Anyone up for more coffee?" she asked as she rejoined them at the couches. "I can bring cream and sugar out when I take back the pot."

Lucian nudged his cup on the table without glancing up from the list of names he was perusing, which Sherry guessed was his version of "Yes, please." But Basil, Bricker, Basha, and Marcus actually said the words.

"Sherry?" Drina murmured thoughtfully, glancing up to watch her pour coffee into Basil's cup.

"Yes?" Sherry moved on to Basha and Marcus, refilling their cups.

"I have done a quick once-over and there's no one here who has been in your life for more than ten or eleven years," Drina pointed out with a frown.

"No, there isn't," Sherry agreed, stopping to fill Bricker's cup.

"That cannot be right," Drina informed her. "For you to build up the resistance you have, there has to have been an immortal who was an integral part of your life for a good twenty years at least."

Sherry raised her eyebrows at this news as she moved on to Lucian's cup. Shrugging, she said helplessly, "Well, I don't know what to tell you. The only people who have been in my life for twenty years or more are aunts and uncles and cousins and my mom's friends."

She straightened with the nearly empty pot in hand. "I'm quite sure none of them are immortals. But aside from that, none of them have really been integral, if by that you mean they spend a lot of time with me. I only see my family on holidays and birthdays, and that's the way it's always been. As for my mom's friends, the last time I saw any of them was at her funeral three years ago, and I didn't see them more than once every year or two before that." She shrugged. "There really is no one who has been in my life on a daily basis for twenty years."

"There is," Lucian announced, reaching for his coffee. The words were spoken with unshakable certainty, but then Sherry suspected the man always spoke that way. He was that kind of guy.

Having learned that it was a waste of time to argue with people like that, she turned away, saying mildly, "If you say so."

"Was that sarcasm?" she heard Lucian growl as she escaped into the kitchen.

"No," Basil assured him with a smile in his voice. "I believe she is humoring you."

Sherry didn't hear Lucian's response, but he was scowling when she returned to the room with spoons, cream, and sugar.

"You mention Uncle Al here, that friend of your mother's," Drina pointed out as Sherry settled on the couch again. "But you didn't put down his last name."

"Because I don't remember it," Sherry admitted, noting the surprise on the expressions of those around her before she continued, "I always just called him Uncle Al. But, as I said, he wasn't really an uncle. He was a family friend. He used to spend a lot of time with us, and he was really supportive of Mom when she and Dad split, but then he just stopped visiting and stuff. By the time I started university, he was little more than a fond memory."

Drina blinked and slowly sat back.

"She has a couple of instances of that," Basil said quietly.

"Of what?" Sherry asked, turning to him with confusion. "Family friends whose last names I can't remember?"

Basil shook his head. The notepad with her original list was on the coffee table beside the pen she'd used. He picked up both now, quickly scribbled something down, and then closed the notepad. Setting it on his knee, he turned to Sherry and asked, "You said you don't date much?"

"No," Sherry admitted. "I don't really have time. I can date later. Right now I just want the store to be up and running and doing well."

Basil nodded. "But you were engaged once. To an artist."

Sherry nodded.

"What happened there?"

Sherry shrugged. "It just didn't work out. These things happen. It's better this way."

Basil handed the notepad to Drina. "Open it and read what I wrote."

The woman's eyebrows rose, but she opened the notepad and her eyes widened as she read what he'd written.

"What is it?" Sherry asked with a frown, and Drina turned the notepad so she could read it. She did so out loud, a frown beginning to pull at her lips: " 'I just want the store to be up and running and doing well . . . It just didn't work out. These things happen. It's better this way.' "

Sherry sat back after reading that, then glanced to Basil with confusion. "What . . . ?"

"It's what you say each time those subjects are broached. I noticed the part about getting the store up and running when we were talking on the porch at Casey Cottage. It wasn't making sense. You said the store was doing well and even making a profit, but then kept repeating that you needed the store up and running and doing well before you could take the time to date. The exact same phrase each time." He grimaced. "I thought maybe it was just a one-off, but you said the same thing when the subject came up at lunch with Elvi and Victor. You also had another phrase that you repeated when the subject of your love life came up at lunch. You mentioned your broken engagement, and when she asked why, you explained—"

"It just didn't work out. These things happen. It's better this way," Sherry said, and then covered her mouth with horror as she realized she was saying exactly what he'd written. It had just slipped out, like a knee-jerk reaction.

"Those thoughts were put in your head," Drina said quietly. "As was your response to questions about your Uncle Al."

"He wasn't really an uncle. He was just a family friend. He was really supportive of Mom, but then—"

"He just stopped visiting and stuff. By the time I started university he was just a fond memory," Drina said with her.

Sherry sat back, sure all the blood had drained out of her head. "Someone's controlling me?"

"No," Basil assured her. "At least not directly. Those are explanations that were put into your head. But for you to repeat them so faithfully, they must have been put in your head firmly and often . . . and reinforced over a long period of time." After a pause, he commented, "The fact that there's an automatic response to questions about her Uncle Al—"

"He's not really my uncle. He was very—" Catching herself repeating the phrase, Sherry cut herself off so abruptly she nearly bit her own tongue. Grim now, she muttered, "Sorry. You were saying?"

"I was merely going to suggest that it might point the finger at your—at this Al person," he finished.

"But he hasn't been in my life for fifteen or sixteen years," she pointed out with a frown.

"Are you sure?" Basil asked. "What did he look like?"

Sherry glanced to him with surprise and shrugged. "He was . . ."

"What color was his hair?" Drina asked when Sherry fell silent, a frown claiming her face.

"It was . . ." She frowned and then shook her head. "I don't . . ."

"How tall was he?"

"Was he fat or thin?"

"How did he dress?"

Sherry stared at them all blankly. The answers to their questions simply weren't coming. She couldn't remember. She couldn't visualize the man at all. She kept trying to draw up moments in her life when she knew for certain that he had been there; her brother's funeral, her birthdays, her graduation . . . But all she saw was a fuzzy outline of a man, as if someone had erased the image.

"It's all right," Basil said quietly, taking her hand gently in his. "Breathe."

Sherry concentrated on her breathing for a minute, but her head was spinning. Good old Uncle Al.

"This is awful," she breathed with horror.

"No. This is good," Basil assured her. "We are a step closer. Uncle Al was the immortal."

"But he hasn't been in my life for—"

"He very well may have been, Sherry," Basil said quietly, and then pointed out, "Why else would he erase your memories of what he looked like?"

"Are you suggesting he erased my memory of what he looked like as Uncle Al so that he could be in my life as someone else?" she asked with a frown. "Is that even possible?"

For a moment no one spoke, but Sherry couldn't help noticing that several glances were exchanged, and then Drina sighed and said, "He would have had to work it carefully. Withdraw from your life for a couple of months to allow the memory to fade a bit naturally, and then simply add to it with some mind control when he reappeared."

"And he probably would have changed his look when he did come back into your life," Basil added quietly. "Different hair color and cut, different style of dress, facial hair or no facial hair, as opposed to how he looked as Uncle—your uncle," he caught himself quickly, and then added, "Perhaps even a different context."

"Different context?" Sherry asked uncertainly.

"Someone connected to the university or work rather than home and family," Drina explained. "People often keep the three separated mentally. We automatically compartmentalize our lives into home, school, and work. We don't usually mix the three."

Sherry shook her head, confusion and bewilderment rife within her, and then finally asked with frustration, "But why? Why would an immortal go to all that trouble to spend time with me?"

There was silence for a moment as everyone exchanged glances, and then Basil sighed and took her hands in his. "There are only two possible reasons. One, you may be a possible life mate to him or her, they recognized this when you were quite young, and so have been a part of your life since, waiting for you to get older before approaching you."

Sherry blinked in surprise at the suggestion, and then asked with exasperation, "Well, for heaven's sake, how old is old enough with you people? I'm thirty-two, not jailbait."

"Yes, well, it's possible he or she was waiting for you to succeed at your endeavors so that you would have more confidence and be your own woman first," he said quietly. "With a mating between a mortal and an immortal who has seen centuries or even millennia, it is possible the mortal will look up to and defer to the immortal and never really come into their own."

"Well, that's just silly," Sherry said with annoyance.

"Is it?" Basil asked with a faint smile. "You may think so now, but you have lived a bit and had some successes. Imagine yourself when you were fresh out of high school. Imagine finding out there were immortals and that you were a possible life mate to one." He let her think for a minute and then said, "If they were older like myself, and wealthy, there would be no need for you to work. You might not have gone on to higher education and got your business degree. You might not even have pursued your dream to open a store. Or you might have, using money your mate gave you, which wouldn't have given you as much confidence as having saved and done it all on your own."

Sherry frowned, reluctantly admitting, if only to herself, that he was right. In fact, she would guess it would have gone further than that. Knowing her mate had lived so long, and seen and experienced so much, she probably would have developed a sort of hero worship for him, deferring to him in everything rather than trusting in her own intelligence and instincts. She supposed it truly could have hampered her developing into her own woman.

"Still," she said, "I achieved my dreams and started my store three years ago. Surely if there is someone, he would have approached me by now?"

"Yes," Lucian said, joining the conversation for the first time. "Which is why I suspect the immortal in your life is your father."

Sherry turned on him with amazement. "My parents split up after my brother died. My father then moved to BC. He hasn't been in my life since I was eight years old."

"I wasn't speaking of your mother's husband," Lucian said.

For a moment his words didn't make sense to her, and then Sherry sat back as if he'd hit her. She began to shake her head.

"I was sifting through your memories when you were talking to Drina about the fact that you have no one on your list that has been in your life more than ten or eleven years," Lucian said. "You ran over the list in your head as you talked and were recalling everyone from childhood on," he informed her.

Sherry wasn't surprised that he'd sifted through her thoughts, and she knew she had run quickly through the list of people in her life.

"From the memories that slid through your head, you have your mother—Lynne Harlow Carne's—eye shape and lips," Lucian said. "But everything else—your eye color, skin color, your nose, the shape of your face . . ." He shook his head. "Nothing like your mother, and nothing like the man you knew as your father, Richard Carne, either."

Sherry felt the breath slip out of her. What he said was true. He wasn't the first to comment on it. She had none of her father's traits. Her parents had both been fair and blue-eyed, where she was dark-haired and dark-eyed and her skin was more a buff beige than the ivory they'd both had. And while she had her mother's large doe eyes and full lips, her nose was almost Roman in its straightness and her face was oval instead of long and thin. She was also short and curvy in comparison to her tall, svelte parents. Her aunt Vi had even once commented on it and joked that she was a changeling.

Sherry shook her head, forcing those thoughts out.

They were crazy. Madness. It couldn't be true. Heck, if her father was an immortal—

"I'm not immortal," she said abruptly, sure that disproved the theory.

"You wouldn't be," Basha said quietly. "As I've recently learned, the child takes on the mother's nature. If she is immortal, the child will be. If she is Edentate, the child will be. And if she is mortal—"

"The child will be," Sherry finished for her. "But if my mother was the life mate of an immortal, why wouldn't he have turned my mother and made her one too?"

"She wasn't his life mate," Lucian said with certainty.

"Or, maybe she was, but he'd already used his one turn and couldn't turn her," Basil said quickly, giving Lucian a look that made it obvious he thought he was being insensitive.

Lucian scowled in response. "You are not saving her feelings by suggesting there was a relationship that did not exist. You are merely dragging it out for her. She will come to these conclusions herself eventually." He turned to Sherry then and said, "While he may have cared for your mother in some small way, she was not his life mate. If she were, he would have been incapable of staying away from her."

"But if you're right and he's been in my life all these years, then he didn't stay away," Sherry pointed out. "Maybe he was her life mate and—"

"He stayed in your life, not your mother's," Lucian interrupted.

"She was there too," Sherry said quickly.

"She was also married to and sleeping with her mortal husband," Lucian said grimly. "A life mate could not stand by and suffer that."

Sherry scowled now and shook her head. "Well, this is all stupid speculation anyway. My parents were married a full year before I was born. My mother was not the type to be unfaithful. And she would have told me if my dad wasn't my father."

"Are you sure about that?" Lucian asked, obviously not agreeing with her.

"It would explain your father's absence in your life," Basil pointed out gently. "If he knew you weren't really his child . . ."

Sherry simply stared at him with dismay for a moment, and then lurched to her feet and stumbled past Stephanie's legs to hurry to the hall leading to the bedrooms. She was suddenly desperate to be alone.

Thirteen

"Let her go. She wants to be alone."

Basil tore his gaze from Sherry's retreating back to scowl down at his brother's restraining hand on his wrist. Her stricken face at the possibility that Richard Carne might not be her father had set him back a bit, and he'd been slow to follow. But now he wanted desperately to go to her and help her through this.

"Take your hand off me, or I shall remove it for you, brother," Basil said coldly.

Lucian considered him briefly and then shrugged and released him. The moment he did, Basil slipped around the coffee table and made his way to the bedroom he had shared with Sherry last night. His gaze scanned the empty room quickly as he entered. The sheets were tousled, their night clothes from the evening before strewn everywhere, but she was nowhere in sight. However, the door to the bathroom was closed.

Pushing the bedroom door closed, he crossed the room and then hesitated and pressed an ear to the door. All he could hear was her heartbeat and breathing.

"Sherry?" he called softly. "Are you okay?"

There was a brief silence and then, "Yes."

Basil reached for the handle and found the door was locked. Releasing it, he asked, "Can I come in?"

"No."

"Sherry—" he began worriedly.

"I'm fine, Basil. I just . . . I'm going to curl my hair and straighten my makeup. Go on back and help with the lists. I'll be out in a bit."

Basil shifted his feet, peered at the door and then back to his feet. She was hurting. He knew she was hurting. What they had suggested shocked her, rocked her world, in fact. He wanted to comfort her, but it seemed she didn't want comforting. She really wanted to be alone.

Turning away from the door, he glanced around the room again and then gathered up their clothes. Folding them neatly, he set them on the chair, then turned his attention to making the bed. The entire time he did so, he listened for sounds from the bathroom, determined that if he heard what even vaguely sounded like a sob or weeping, he would break in and comfort her whether she wanted it or not.

He didn't hear that, though. Instead, he heard the occasional metallic click and a clatter that he suspected came from her curling iron being used and then set on the counter while she gathered fresh strands of hair to wrap around it. She really was curling her hair, he realized, and shook his head. As he gave in and headed out of the room to leave her in peace, Basil acknowledged that he had no clue when it came to women.

A man would have beaten the hell out of someone or something after such news, but a woman? His woman? She didn't weep and wail or beat up anything, she curled her hair.

"I told you she wanted to be alone," Lucian said as Basil returned to join them.

"Shut up, brother," Basil muttered.

In the bathroom, Sherry unplugged the curling iron and left it on the counter to cool as she began to brush her hair. Her mind was an utter blank. She'd wanted to be alone to absorb the possibility that her father wasn't her father, and she'd known she wouldn't be able to do that with Basil there. He would have hugged her, offering comfort, but it would have turned into passion and— It had just seemed better to be alone. But even alone, her mind didn't seem to be absorbing it. It was like someone telling you that the sky was yellow when you have known and seen it as blue all your life. It just wasn't computing.

Sherry turned and opened the door to walk out into the bedroom. She'd heard Basil moving around in the room so wasn't terribly surprised to find it tidied up. Her gaze slid to the bed and she considered lying down, but Basil *had* just tidied the room. Besides, she wasn't tired. In fact, she was actually feeling quite restless . . . and her mind was racing. Her father was not her father.

She didn't even know how to feel about that. Basil was right, it would explain why he had so easily withdrawn from her life, because while she'd been unresponsive to his few attempts to speak to her, he hadn't tried very hard to overcome that . . . which had always hurt her. But if it was true, why had she not been told? She could understand why it might have been kept from her as a child, but once she was older . . . and especially when her mother was on her deathbed. She would have expected her mother to at least tell her then.

Her mother had been weak and hospitalized after her first heart attack, but survived a week before a second one had taken her life. Sherry had spent every night of that week with her, the two of them talking, sharing memories and so on. During those talks there had been many opportunities for her mother to tell her that Richard Carne wasn't really her father. Why wouldn't she do that?

Because it wasn't true, Sherry decided. It couldn't be. Her mother would have told her.

But Basil was right, it would explain a lot, she thought in the next moment. Why she was such a changeling. Why she'd grown up pretty much without a father from the age of eight on.

But Sherry just couldn't believe that her mother wouldn't have told her.

Unless her mother had been afraid that she would be angry or think less of her on learning it.

This not knowing one way or the other could make her crazy, Sherry thought grimly. She needed to know the truth . . . . But the only one with the answers she needed was the immortal they all thought had been such an integral part of her life for so long.

And who the devil was that? she wondered with frustration.

The others seemed to think it was her Uncle Al during her younger years, and it was true that he had spent a good deal of time in her life. She'd seen him daily after her parents had split. Sherry's mother had worked for social services, and while she'd dropped her off at school every morning, it was Uncle Al who collected her afterward while her mother was still at work. When she'd started ballet at nine, he was the one to take her to her classes after school. When she'd switched to gymnastics at twelve, again it was Uncle Al who had taken her. He even took her to dinner a couple times a week on nights when her mother worked late.

In fact, now that she thought about it, most of her time with Uncle Al had been spent without her mother there. Although there were occasions when he'd taken both her and her mother on outings, to the science center or the zoo on a Saturday or Sunday. Actually, he'd sort of stepped in and taken her father's place, at least in her life if not her mother's.

Funny how she'd forgotten that, Sherry thought now with a small frown.

But Uncle Al had faded from her life during her high school years, seeing her less and less often, until she'd hardly seen him at all the last two years before she went to university, and she hadn't seen him at all that last summer. Wrapped up in school, prepping for university while enjoying a blossoming social life, she hadn't really noticed his absence at the time . . . or perhaps she hadn't because he'd messed with her head, she thought grimly now.

Lucian seemed to think that Uncle Al was the immortal in her life and that he had changed his appearance and then reappeared while she was at the university.

The thought made her sift through the people she'd known there. She'd had a couple of good male friends through university and afterward. She'd also had a couple of professors who mentored her. But the only person she'd seen daily during that period and for several years afterward was Luther.

They'd met during her first year of university, had several classes together and ended up hanging out, and then went in with several other people to rent a five-bedroom house during second year. They'd remained roommates throughout the rest of her time at university. While their other roommates had changed, they both stayed in that house until they got their MBAs, and then continued to be roommates after graduating into the work world. Luther had been her best friend and confidant. She'd cried on his shoulder, listened to his advice, and shared her life with him. He'd been rather like an older brother. Luther had worked a couple years before starting university and was twenty-four when they met, five years older than her.

At least he'd claimed to be twenty-four, she thought now. And then after her mother's funeral, while Sherry had been busily settling her mother's accounts and then buying and stocking her dream store, Luther had got the offer of a job in Saudi Arabia that paid so much money it would have been mad for him to refuse it. He hadn't, of course, and disappeared from her life, just like Uncle Al.

The only males she'd seen daily since then were Allan, Eric, and Zander, who all worked at her store and had done so since she'd opened three years ago.

Sherry paced back to the bathroom, walked inside, checked that her curling iron was cool and bent to tuck it back in her bag where it sat on the floor. It was as she was straightening, everything finally clicked into place.

"Son of a bitch," she muttered, and stared at her reflection briefly, then whirled and hurried out and across the bedroom to the hall. She was moving quickly, eager to get to the others to tell them that she knew who the immortal must be, but slowed and then stopped as she heard what they were saying in the living room.

"Well . . ." Basil said, glancing over the notes he held. "According to the dates Sherry listed here, her university friend Luther and this Uncle Al are the people who have been in her life the longest, and as far as she can recall, her uncle was only in her life from seven to eighteen, and the roomie was around from eighteen to twenty-nine."

"So both of them were in her life for eleven years," Harper said thoughtfully.

"I suspect this Uncle Al is the father, and that he was around probably from the day she was born," Basha said thoughtfully.

"Yes, but it's doubtful he was in her life on a daily basis before her brother Danny died and the man she knew as her father left Lynne," Drina said with a frown. "Richard Carne would have hardly welcomed him."

"True," Marcus commented. "No man wants his wife's old lover hanging around."

"Even if he's the girl's birth father?" Basha asked.

"Especially if he fathered her," Marcus assured her. "There's a reason lions eat the offspring of previous mates of the lioness when they take over a den. Mortals may not kill the woman's offspring, but many resent a child that isn't theirs. It's a constant reminder that she had a previous mate."

"Is there a male she sees daily now?" Lucian asked.

Drina glanced through the list. "Eric, Zander, and Allan. They're all employees at the store."

"Seems easy enough," Bricker said now. "Uncle Al is now Allan."

"Wasn't the roommate's real name Lex?" Stephanie asked suddenly, and Basil glanced to where the girl sat, feet up on the couch and arms wrapped around her knees, eyeing them all with eyebrows raised. She looked pale and her eyebrows were drawn together as if she were in pain. Katricia had told him that Stephanie not only could hear the thoughts of mortals, young immortals, and even older immortals, but she couldn't shut their voices out, that it seemed to her as if they were shouting their thoughts in her ears. He suspected that having so many of them there, their minds all screaming at her at once, was causing her a great deal of distress.

"Yes, Lex Brown," Drina answered when no one else spoke. "What about it?"

Stephanie raised her eyebrows, uncrossed her arms and sat up. "Seriously? You don't see it?"

Basil glanced around. The others were peering at each other, looking as blank-faced as he probably did . . . all except Lucian, who was almost smiling. If Basil were to guess, he'd say Lucian had seen whatever Stephanie was talking about. And probably long ago. The bastard had just been sitting around waiting to see who would sort it out first.

"And it was the child rather than one of the adults who sorted it out first," Lucian said dryly, obviously having heard his thoughts.

"I am not a child," Stephanie said with annoyance.

"Can we skip to whatever it is the rest of us aren't seeing?" Basil asked impatiently.

Stephanie glared at Lucian for a moment longer and then turned to Basil and shrugged. "Think about it . . . Uncle Al? Lex? Zander?"

Basil frowned at her briefly and then his expression cleared and he breathed, "Alexander," with sudden understanding.

"So . . . he's been around since she was seven at least. That's twenty-five years. Definitely long enough for her to have built up a strong resistance," Basha realized.

"I suspect he's been there since she was born," Lucian said quietly.

"Then you don't think he's another life mate?" Basil asked, feeling relief slide through him. That possibility had bothered him.

Rather than answer directly, Lucian asked, "Could you have refrained from claiming her all this time if you'd met her at seven or younger?"

"I'd have had to. I'd have hardly tried to claim her as a child," Basil pointed out dryly.

"True, but once she was sixteen or so it would become very difficult to *not* claim her. You might want to do the honorable thing and allow her to mature without interference," he said solemnly. "But your mind would remind you she was mortal and an accident could steal her from you. You'd want to watch her, keep her safe, and doing that would make it very difficult to refrain from bedding and claiming her." He shook his head. "This Alexander is her father."

"Great!" Stephanie said brightly. "Now that I've solved that for you, does anyone else have a hankering for a shake? I could really use one of your famous chocolate shakes about now, Harper . . . and I'm sure the milk is good for my growing bones," she added in wheedling tones.

"One chocolate shake it is," Harper said with amusement, standing to lead her to the kitchen.

"Does anyone else want one?" Drina asked, getting up.

"Oh, yeah. I'll take a chocolate one too, please,"

Bricker said at once, but everyone else merely shook their heads.

"So . . ." Basha said as Drina headed for the kitchen to tell Harper that Bricker wanted one too. "Now that you know or think you know who the immortal in her life is . . ." She raised her eyebrows. "What next? Go question him and find out why he wanted her to think she ran into Leo in London?"

"We already know the answer to that," Lucian said, and then pointed out, "It was because he wanted her back in Toronto."

"Yes, but why?" Basil asked, and then tilted his head and eyed him suspiciously. "You know the answer to that as well, don't you?"

"Sherry gave us the answer when she said she was born a year after her parents married," he said mildly.

"I don't see what the one has to do with the other," Basil admitted.

"That's because you're old," Bricker put in, understanding clear on his face.

Basil scowled at the younger man. "What has that to do with anything?"

"It means you haven't had the least interest in sex or dating in forever until now," Bricker said dryly.

"What has that to do with—"

"When you're without a mate and still young enough to be interested in sex and dating . . ." Bricker paused as if to consider his words, and then shrugged and said, "Well, frankly, the world is a smorgasbord. Pretty women are everywhere, and with our ability to read their minds and know exactly what they're thinking and what they want to hear, etcetera . . ." He shrugged again. "Every single one is yours for the taking if you want her." He paused and then added solemnly, "Unless they are married."

"Ah." Basil nodded slowly. Life mates were a serious business with immortals, and while mortals were not blessed or cursed with them, as the case might be, marriage was the closest thing they had. Marriage was a binding contract to spend their lives with each other. It was as close as a mortal could get to a life mate. It was considered more than shameful for an immortal male to use their unfair advantage to get a married female mortal to sleep with them. They had even made a lesser law to prevent it from occurring. Lesser laws were not punishable by death, but by various lesser penalties. For instance, fines, sanctions, shunning or incarceration for a stated term. Basil couldn't recall what the penalty was for dallying with a married mortal, but he was quite sure it was unpleasant. There had been a time when a wife could be murdered for getting caught in an adulteress relationship. In some countries that was still allowed. The penalty had to be a strict one to prevent it from happening.

"I'm afraid I don't understand," Basha admitted quietly, and Basil recalled that she was newly returned to the fold and probably didn't yet know all their laws.

"It is against one of our lesser laws to interfere in a mortal marriage," he explained now, and Bricker snorted.

"Lesser, my ass," Bricker muttered. "Most men would prefer to be staked and baked than having their ding-dong shredded once for every year of their life when they made the indiscretion."

Basha blinked. "So if you were a century old when you did it . . ."

"They'd shred it one hundred times, letting it heal between each," Bricker said dryly.

"How do they shred it?" she asked curiously.

"I don't know," he admitted grimly. "Never wanted to know either, so I stay well clear of married women."

"Well then, it seems to be effective," Lucian said dryly.

Bricker snorted. "It's barbaric."

"What about women?" Basha asked. "What if an immortal woman interfered in a mortal marriage?"

Obviously not knowing the answer to that, Bricker blinked and glanced to Lucian questioningly, but it was Basil who said, "Actually, at the time the law was made, mortal men were the power brokers in the world. They were free to have mistresses without fear of it interfering in their marriages, so there was no sanction for a female immortal who dallied with a male mortal."

"Ah, man!" Bricker cried. "That is so unfair."

Basha just grinned and brought them back to the subject at hand. "So, it would have been against the law for an immortal to have dallied in Sherry's parents' marriage?" she said. "But we think he fathered Sherry, who was born a year after her parents got married."

"Which means the immortal had a relationship with

a married woman and is subject to the punishment," Basil said, pointing out the obvious.

"What if he didn't use his immortal abilities to have the affair?" Marcus asked. "What if he didn't use influence, or mind reading, or mind control? Is the punishment the same?"

"It doesn't matter," Basha said before anyone could answer to that. "If she was born a year after her parents married, then she was conceived during the third or fourth month of their marriage. They would have been in the honeymoon stage still, and probably still madly in love. He had to have used influence and mind control."

"Unless Sherry's mother was a ho," Bricker pointed out.

"I didn't get that impression from Sherry's memories of her mother," Basha said dryly.

Bricker shrugged. "Well, she'd hardly be a ho when she was older. That doesn't mean she wasn't when she was younger."

"It's doubtful she was willing," Lucian said quietly. "I suspect he used undue influence."

"You think he raped her?" Stephanie asked with shock, drawing their attention to the fact that she'd re-entered the room and stood several feet away, listening, with Harper and Drina behind her.

"He wouldn't have had to rape her," Bricker said quietly. "We are oddly attractive to mortals. Bastien once told me it was thanks to special pheromones the nanos produce in us. He thinks they were originally meant to assist us when we needed to feed off the hoof."

"That wouldn't have been enough," Basha said with certainty. "Especially when they were so newly married. He must have used some mind control to overcome her conscience and any reluctance she felt."

"Which is rape," Stephanie said grimly, and scowled around at them as if they were each responsible as she added, "I know he probably made her enjoy it, and I know you guys are so used to controlling mere mortals and making them do what you want that you probably don't think it's rape, but it is."

Silence filled the room briefly, and then Harper cleared his throat and placed a soothing hand on her shoulder before saying, "But that doesn't really explain why he'd want her away from Port Henry. If we're even right about all of this—it is all guesswork after all," he pointed out. "And we wouldn't have guessed any of it if he hadn't scared her back here."

"I guess we'll find that out when we talk to him," Lucian said grimly, and glanced to Basil. "Sherry will know Zander's address."

"Doesn't he work at the store?" Drina pointed out. "It's daytime. He should be there if he's assistant manager. Especially with Sherry away."

Lucian shook his head. "We've got hunters in the store and sent the workers home in case Leo and his boys returned. He should be at home, or at least not at the store."

"Right." Basil stood and moved silently out of the room to head up the hall to the room he shared with Sherry. All it took was a quick glance inside for his

Fourteen

"Here you are, lady."

Sherry glanced around to see that they were stopped in front of her store. As it turned out, it hadn't been far from Harper's apartment after all. She could have walked, but she hadn't recognized where she was when she'd left the building, so she'd flagged down the cab . . . and then spent the entire short ride trying to grasp the fact that she might be the daughter of an immortal rather than the man she'd grown up calling Dad, and if that was the case, that she was a child of rape.

"Lady?" the driver prompted.

"Oh, sorry. What do I owe you?" Sherry muttered, and reached for her purse when the driver told her how much. That was when she realized that she didn't have her purse. She was pretty sure she didn't have any money in her pockets either, but desperately began to check them anyway as she searched her mind for a solution to her problem. She then glanced sharply to the front passenger door when it opened and Basil asked, "How much?"

Sighing with relief, Sherry slid out of the backseat as Basil paid the driver.

"Thank you," she murmured when he closed the door and turned to her. "I wasn't thinking straight I guess. I forgot I left my purse behind."

"You left me behind too," he said quietly, taking her arms and peering solemnly into her face. "Why?"

"I . . ." Sherry shook her head helplessly. "Like I said, I wasn't thinking. I just ran." She grimaced and then added, "I heard what you guys said about his raping my mom. I didn't want to face anyone . . . and then I didn't want someone else to talk to him. I want him to tell me himself. I need him to explain, Basil."

"I know," he murmured, and pressed her head to his chest with one hand while with the other he rubbed her back soothingly. "I understand, but I'd like to go with you."

Sherry didn't respond for a moment, and then she suddenly pulled back and peered up at him with a frown. "How did you know I'd come here?"

"I didn't. I came out of Harper's building just as your taxi pulled away and followed."

"In another taxi?" she asked, looking around for one.

"No. I ran," he admitted dryly. "Fortunately, it was only five blocks and your driver managed to hit every red light."

She stared at him wide-eyed for a moment and then shook her head. "I'm sorry. I should have—"

"It's okay," he said firmly, squeezing her arms.

Sherry gave up her apologies and lowered her head.

"Are you okay?" Basil asked, and she could hear the frown in his voice, though she couldn't see it. She was staring down at the ground, and supposed that was why he was worried. She supposed she looked as lost and scared as she felt.

"Yes." She forced her head up and managed a smile. "Of course."

"Okay." Looking somewhat relieved, but still a little concerned, he slid his arm around her shoulders and then turned toward the building. "So, I take it this is his— It's your store," he realized. "Honey, he won't be at work. The Enforcers sent all of your employees home in case Leo and his boys return."

"I know. I came here to get his address off my Rolodex," she explained.

"Oh." He glanced around warily now, and then abruptly urged her forward. "Let's get inside, then. If Leo does return, I do not want him to find you out here."

Nodding, Sherry moved quickly, glancing around as she did. She expected people in black to be in every corner, instead her gaze found and stopped on one of her own employees behind the cash register.

"Joan?" she said, approaching her slowly. "What are you doing here? I thought you and the others had been sent home until it was safe to come back?"

"We were," Joan Campbell said with a bright smile. "But they called last night and said the gas leak had been repaired and we could come back today."

"Gas leak?" Sherry echoed with confusion, turning to Basil.

"A cover story they would have used. They probably removed your employees' memories of what really happened, if they had any, and replaced them with that too," he assured her.

Sherry nodded, recalling the blank expressions on everyone's faces that day. She glanced toward Joan again when Basil asked the girl, "Who called you?"

"Zander," she answered.

"Zander did?" Sherry asked, glancing around now in search of the man.

"Yeah. I gather some inspector guy called Allan last night with the news because he couldn't get a hold of Zander. But Allan was able to get ahold of him, so Zander called everyone with their shift schedules for today. He said you were out of town, though," she added.

"I was," Sherry admitted. "Is Zander here now?"

"In your office," Joan said. "He was going to call in some orders that got put off while we were shut down."

Nodding, Sherry turned sharply and headed toward the back of the store, but paused when the front door opened. For one second she feared it would be Leo and his boys stalking into her store as they had the other day. Instead of him and his blue-jean-clad compatriots, there were two men in black jeans and leather jackets.

"Enforcers?" she asked Basil, quite sure she was right. They were dressed like Bricker, Basha, and Marcus.

Basil nodded. "Anders and my nephew Decker. Wait here, I'll just have a word with them."

Sherry nodded, her gaze shifting over the two men again as Basil approached them. Both were tall, but one had dark hair and silver-blue eyes, while the other had skin the color of dark mocha, and brown eyes with gold shot through them. Sherry was guessing the first man was Basil's nephew. Not only did he have the same eye color, but the shape of their faces were similar.

"What's going on?" Basil asked. "I understood the employees had been sent home and Enforcers were manning the store until we cleared up this Leo business."

Sherry moved closer to hear the men's response.

"We're short-handed and this could drag out for a while," the darker man said. "So Mortimer thought it would be a good idea to bring the employees back and watch the building front and back with two men instead of having to man it with four or five."

"So who's watching the back?" Basil asked pointedly.

"I was," Decker announced. "But I came around front when Anders said you were here with a woman. I figured it was this life mate Aunt Marguerite mentioned."

"And you wanted to see her," Basil guessed.

"Of course," Decker said with amusement, and then added, "But also because Uncle Lucian called me a few minutes ago and said if you came anywhere near here, we were to call him at once."

"Then you'd better call him," Basil said, and turned to move toward Sherry, adding, "Tell him Zander is here and Sherry and I are going to her office to talk to him."

"Will do," Decker said, retrieving his phone from a pocket to begin punching buttons.

Pausing in front of Sherry, Basil squeezed her shoulders gently. "Let's get this over with."

When Sherry nodded, he took her elbow and urged her toward the back of the store.

Sherry moved forward, but now that she was here, she was reluctant to see the man who might or might not be her father. Once she talked to him, her whole life would be changed. Well, her past would be changed anyway.

They were both silent as they walked, but all too soon they reached the door to her office and Basil was opening it. Sherry hesitated when he paused to peer at her. But there was no going back now. Taking a deep breath, she started up the eight steps leading into her office.

She could see into the room before she'd ascended all the steps, but she didn't see Zander until the last step. He stood at the window overlooking the floor, his back straight and stiff.

Sherry glanced back at Basil, and then realizing he was still on the stairs because she was blocking the way, she moved farther into the room to make way for him. She then glanced around. It was her own office, and yet it felt alien somehow. It felt like she'd been away for years rather than a few days.

Her gaze slid back to Zander as he finally turned to look at her. He didn't appear surprised to see her there. In fact, he looked resigned.

For a moment Sherry simply stared at the man. She had known him as Zander for three years, but it felt like she was seeing him for the first time. While he was taller than her, he was shorter than Basil. Shorter than her own fath—than the man she'd thought of as her father all these years. His hair was ginger, but it was the same dark color at the roots as her own, as if his hair had been dyed ginger and was growing out. He also had a Roman nose and oval face like her . . . and he couldn't seem to meet her gaze. Turning away toward the counter behind her desk, he said, "I shall make you both coffee."

"I don't want coffee," Sherry said before he could move.

Zander paused and then turned reluctantly back, a sad expression on his face. "No. You're here for answers, aren't you."

Despite the way the words were couched, it wasn't a question, but Sherry nodded anyway. At the same time, she was aware that his words told her he wasn't simply the nice guy she'd hired to manage her store and then had become friends with.

"Of course." Zander hesitated and then straightened his back. Expression grim, he spread his arms. "Fire away."

Sherry hesitated, unsure where to start, and then blurted, "Are you my father?"

"Yes," he answered.

Simple as that, yes. One little word that rocked her world, literally. Sherry swayed on her feet. She felt Basil's steadying hand on her arm and took a shaky breath, but continued to stare at the man who had just admitted he was her father, unsure where to go from there.

It was Basil who asked, "And you're Uncle Al?"

He nodded solemnly.

Sherry closed her eyes. Now that she knew he was Uncle Al, those memories of him from her childhood that had been so fuzzy became clear and she could recall everything. He'd had hair as dark as hers then, and a full beard and mustache. She would best describe his appearance back then as a young Grizzly Adams.

Lex, on the other hand, had been clean-shaven, his dark hair shorn to the point of being nothing more than a constant state of five o'clock shadow on his pate. He'd also sported an earring in one ear, though it had been a clip-on rather than pierced, which she'd teased him about mercilessly when she realized it. It had been a clever earring, impossible to tell it was a clip-on until it was taken off.

Now, as Zander, he had ginger hair and a goatee. Three completely different looks, but it seemed obvious that all three men were the same. Still, she asked, "And Lex?"

"Yes," he said solemnly. "My true name is Alexander, and it's been my privilege to be in your life in one capacity or another from the day you were born."

"Because you're my father," Sherry murmured slowly, struggling with this news. Her mother was not the sort to have an affair, but then she wouldn't have imagined that her wonderful Uncle Al, or her best friend in the world, Lex, or even her friend and store manager, Zander, could rape a woman.

"I did not mean to rape her," Alexander said quietly, no doubt reading the thought from her mind. Raising his hands helplessly, he added, "It was an accident."

"What?" Sherry squawked with amazement. Well that was a new one. Certainly it was the first time she'd heard that excuse . . . and of course she didn't buy it for a second. "Let me guess, you tripped and fell on top of her, your dick falling out of your pants and into my mother through her clothes?"

"No, of course not," he said sharply, and then sighed and ran his hands through his hair. "Sherry, I'm your father——"

"You're my store manager," she interrupted grimly. "And apparently you were my sperm donor, my affable doting uncle, and at one time my supposed best friend, but you were never my father. And," she added coldly, turning toward the stairs, "I guess I've heard what I came here to hear, so——"

"Please," Alexander said, stepping quickly forward and reaching out as if to take her arm. He paused and let his hand drop, though, when Basil stiffened and stepped closer to her.

"Sherry," he said, his voice soothing and pleading all at the same time. "You're angry. I understand that, and you have every right to that anger, but please, let me explain what happened. Surely you owe me that much?"

"I *owe* you?" she asked with a disbelief underlined

by anger, and then turned to Basil when he touched her arm.

"Perhaps you should hear what he has to say," he suggested quietly, and then pointed out, "Otherwise you'll always wonder."

Sherry frowned, wanting to refuse and simply walk out. But she knew he was right. She *would* wonder. Taking a deep breath, she nodded and turned back, but found now it was she who couldn't meet his eyes. She couldn't even look at him. She merely stood, staring at her store logo on his shirt as she waited for him to talk.

"I met your mother in a bar," Zander began slowly, and when she glanced quickly up, smiled wryly and added, "Actually, *at* the bar in the bar. I was holding up the end corner and she came up to order drinks for herself and some friends who were there with her.

"She was a beautiful woman, your mother," he added with a smile of remembrance. "Tall, willowy, with long fair hair and a winsome smile. Put wings on her and she could have passed for an angel walking the earth."

Sherry felt her mouth tighten, and glanced down to her hands again. She'd seen pictures of her mother when she was young, and she *had* been lovely. Many was the time Sherry had wished she looked like her. Now she was imagining that beautiful young woman being turned into nothing more than a blow-up sex doll, made to do what this man wanted.

"I have always had a weakness for beauty," Alexander said solemnly. "I flirted shamelessly with her."

When he fell silent, Sherry glanced reluctantly to him and saw that he was running his hands through his hair, his expression guilty. After a moment he let his hands drop and shook his head.

"That first trip to the bar, her response to my flirting was rather cool. But it seemed like she'd barely left with that round of drinks before she was back for another and then another. I thought she was . . . I mean, why weren't one of the other women she was sitting with coming up to fetch them? I assumed . . ."

"You thought she was coming back because she was interested," Sherry said when he fell silent.

He nodded.

"But you're an immortal. You can read minds," she said accusingly.

"I *did* read her mind," he assured her. "Unfortunately, all I did was dip in far enough to see that she found me attractive too. I don't know if it was ego or . . ." Alexander shook his head. "I didn't bother to go deeper into her thoughts and find out anything else about her. I was attracted, she was attracted, and that was all that mattered to me. She was mortal," he said, trying to explain. "She wasn't a possible life mate. There couldn't be more than . . ."

"A one-night stand," Sherry suggested grimly when he faltered.

He gave a slight nod, and then admitted solemnly, "I should have looked deeper. If I had, I would have realized that while she found me attractive, she would never have pursued that attraction because she was newly married and loved her husband."

Alexander scrubbed a hand through his hair again and then said, "Unfortunately, that quick dip is all I bothered to take, and from there—arrogant fool that I was—I decided she was playing hard to get and just needed a little mental nudge to help her along."

Grim now, he continued, "So I ordered a round of drinks for her table and joined her party. There were five young women, all but her were a little the worse for drink and out celebrating the upcoming wedding of one of the other women. Your mother was the maid of honor and she was playing mother on this outing. They'd pooled their money and she was purchasing the drinks but wasn't drinking herself, and was to see them all safely home."

"Which explains why she was the one who kept going up to the bar," Sherry pointed out.

He nodded. "Yes. Although I didn't really clue into that at the time."

"Of course you didn't," she said dryly.

"I have mentioned that I was arrogant back then," Alexander reminded her quietly. "I realized that later, much too late to prevent what happened."

Sherry frowned, but before she could ask what that meant, he said, "Your mother was silent when I approached the table and asked to join them, but a couple of the other girls were drunk, single, and eager to welcome me. They also made it obvious that they would welcome my attentions, but I preferred your mother."

"Who wasn't interested," Sherry said coldly.

"I thought she was just—"

"Playing hard to get," Sherry said wearily. and then waved it away with annoyance. "Just go on."

Zander shrugged. "At the end of the night your mother called for two taxis. She sent half the girls in the first one that arrived, leaving herself and two others for the second taxi. When it hadn't arrived ten minutes later, I offered to drive the three of them home. Again your mother was reticent, but the other two were more than happy to accept, and she was supposed to be seeing to their safety and so went along with it. I dropped off the other two first and then took her to her place. Or what I thought was only her place. I later found out she and your father shared the small bachelor apartment. He was in his last year at business college and your mother was working to support them both. The following year he was going to work and support them while she finished her degree."

Alexander was silent and then said, "Your father was out of town that night for the bachelor party. Apparently the men had gone camping overnight for their version of the celebrations."

He paused and raised his eyes to meet hers. "I didn't know all of that then. I really thought she was just playing hard to get . . . and she *was* attracted to me . . ." Alexander shook his head and then lowered it again, staring at his hands as he admitted, "I didn't slip into her head and take control. If I had, I would have read that she was married. Besides, I knew she was attracted . . . so all I did was push the thought at her that it was okay. That she should spend the night with me. That there was nothing wrong with it. That she could do what she wanted without guilt or repercussions and—"

"Without guilt? I thought you didn't know she was married," Sherry snapped.

"I didn't," he assured her. "I just thought she was a good girl who didn't have one-night stands. That's the guilt I meant," he explained, and then lowered his head briefly before looking at her again. "I know you consider what I did rape, but at the time I didn't . . . which I suppose speaks to my character. But, in my defense, I had been raised to think that we, immortals, were superior to mortals. And I guess I'd had too many years of getting whatever and whomever I wanted. But it was the eighties. Sex was cheap, and it was everywhere."

When she didn't say anything, he continued, "Anyway, because I thought she was just playing hard to get, I didn't erase her memory afterward. I just thanked her and went on my merry way. I never expected to see her again."

"But you did," she pointed out.

"Yes," he acknowledged. Mouth twisting wryly, he said, "Thanks to a little boy who broke away from his mother and ran out in front of my car. It was two months later, a rainy evening. I couldn't stop in time to prevent hitting him. Fortunately, I did slow down enough that he merely got knocked down, but he hit his head pretty good, there was a lot of blood and his mother was in a panic. It seemed easier and more expedient to simply drive them to the hospital than to wait for the police or an ambulance, so I piled mother and son in my car and took them to the nearest hospital emergency.

"The boy's head injury turned out to be more show than real damage, and I was just leaving when an ambulance pulled up. I stepped back to make way for the EMTs to get their patient in, and as the gurney rolled past I glanced down and . . . it was your mother."

Sherry stiffened. "My mother?"

He nodded. "I recognized her at once and dipped into the minds of the EMTs to find out what had happened. I was rather shocked and even more troubled to learn that she had slit her wrists."

Fifteen

Sherry's jaw dropped at this announcement and her legs went suddenly weak, so she sat on the corner of her desk, uncaring of the items poking her in the bottom. No one had ever told her that her mother had tried to commit suicide. In fact, she found that hard to believe. Her mother just wasn't the sort. Sherry had always known her to be the optimistic sort. For cripes sake the woman used to sing "Tomorrow" while she washed dishes and did other household tasks.

"As I say, I was shocked too," Alexander said solemnly. "Enough that I wanted to know what had happened, so I turned around and followed them in, taking control of anyone who tried to stop me. But of course, no one at the hospital knew why she'd done what she'd done and she was unconscious." He paused briefly, and then said, "It came as quite a shock when a young man arrived and I read his mind to learn he was her husband.

"Between his thoughts and your mother's when she woke up, I learned she had only been three months married, and very happily so when I'd encountered her. That while she was indeed attracted to me, she loved her husband and would never have been unfaithful if I had not controlled her mind and pushed her past her resistance. That after I left her, she suffered terrible guilt and shame over what had happened. But she was terribly confused by the whole thing too. In her memory, she was polite to me but resistant and then suddenly . . . wasn't . . . and she didn't know why or how it had happened.

"She'd been struggling with her guilt and shame for the two months since I'd last seen her, but when she found out she was pregnant, she knew it wasn't her husband's. They'd always used condoms. She and I hadn't. She was sure it was my child, and couldn't live with the knowledge that not only was she unfaithful, but she was now pregnant as a result. She couldn't do that to her husband, so she . . ."

"Tried to kill herself," Sherry said quietly.

Alexander nodded with shame. "I'd taken a beautiful, vibrant young woman and made a mess of her life. Both their lives. I had to fix it, of course. But it wasn't as easy as that sounds. I erased what had happened between the two of us from her memory, put the thought in both their heads that perhaps they hadn't always been as careful to use protection as they could have been—besides, protection is never one hundred percent—and that the child was his. But your mother had lived with the memory for two months, and a simple mind wipe doesn't always prevent the memory from resurfacing. So, I stayed in their lives, befriending her husband and becoming his buddy."

"Uncle Al," she said, standing up again and crossing her arms.

"I was just Al then, and never intended to be Uncle Al," he confessed apologetically. "I thought I might be able to leave once you were born and she saw you as their child, but the moment I saw you . . ."

There was stark emotion briefly in his eyes, and then he said, "I wanted to be a part of your life. So, I became good old Uncle Al, the family friend, on the fringes of your life but at least still able to see you a couple times a week."

"Until my brother died," Sherry said thickly.

Alexander nodded. "Until your brother died and your parents' marriage fell apart. That wasn't my fault," he added quickly.

"I know," she said quietly. "He blamed her for my brother's death and she blamed him."

"They couldn't get past it," he said sadly. "Your father eventually moved out and your mother filed for divorce."

"And you started seeing me daily," Sherry said. "Picking me up after school, taking me to ballet, gymnastics, or just playing baseball with me."

"They were the best years of my life," he said solemnly. "And the scariest."

Her eyebrows rose. "Scariest?"

"You are mortal," he said quietly. "So fragile. Your brother's death drove that home to me. A fall, illness, fire, drowning, a car accident . . . anything could take you from me in a heartbeat. I became obsessed with keeping you safe. I was watching you even when you didn't know I was watching you." Alexander swallowed and admitted, "I even considered using my one turn on you. The only thing that stopped me was that it would mean having to tell you what I had done, how you'd come to be born, and I knew you'd hate me for it."

Sherry merely ducked her head, unsure how to respond to that. Did she hate him? The truth was, she wasn't at all sure how she felt anymore. Her emotions were in complete chaos. She was recalling her adoration of her wonderful Uncle Al, her sisterly love for her best buddy Lex, and the friendship she had with Zander, and then putting that next to her revulsion and rage at the thought of her mother being controlled and used like a blow-up sex doll. She wanted to hate the man before her for what he'd done to her mother . . . but her mind was arguing that he had tried to make amends for it. After the encounter at the hospital, he'd stuck around to ensure that everything was all right. Another man might not have done that, or another immortal.

Still, he'd nearly destroyed her mother. She'd nearly taken not only her own life but Sherry's as well when she'd tried to kill herself—and he'd driven her to it with his selfish, arrogant, and uncaring use of her. On the other hand, if he hadn't done it, she wouldn't even exist.

Basil slid his arm around her back and pulled her closer, and Sherry glanced to him. He offered her a gentle smile and then turned to Alexander—her father, she acknowledged—and asked, "I presume it was you who approached her in the dressing room in London?"

"Yes," Alexander said solemnly.

When he didn't explain himself, Basil asked, "Why did you want her to think she'd encountered Leo? I presume it was to get her to leave Port Henry and come back to Toronto."

"Yes," he admitted. "Joan called me after the upset at the store and before your people got there to wipe minds and clean up the mess. Between what she said and what I know of Leonius Livius, I knew Sherry would have been taken into protection . . . and I knew . . ." He paused and then said with frustration, "I knew the hunters would realize that she'd had an immortal in her life for a lot of years and would want to find out who it was and why. I knew that eventually everything would come out if I didn't get her away, and I just panicked."

"How did you follow us to Port Henry?" Basil asked.

"I knew where the Enforcer house is, most immortals in the area do," he added, and then continued, "I parked down the street and watched the gate from there with binoculars. When the SUV came out with Sherry, you, and the others in it, I followed you to Port Henry."

"And watched the house there, and then followed us to London the next day?" Basil guessed.

Alexander nodded. "I didn't know, though, that she was your life mate when I first approached her in the changing rooms and started to put the idea that she'd seen Leonius in her mind," he assured Basil. "I read that in her thoughts as I was rearranging her memories, and once I realized it, I tried to undo the rearranging." He grimaced and added, "I gather I made a bungle of the whole thing."

Basil grunted in the affirmative, and Alexander—her father, she thought grimly—sighed unhappily.

"I'm sorry," he said now. "I was just trying to look out for you, Sherry."

"Were you?" she asked dubiously, her eyes narrowed.

"Yes," he assured her. "It's all I've ever wanted to do since the day you were born."

Sherry merely stared at him for a moment. She was recalling those phrasings she kept repeating when certain subjects came up. The one about Uncle Al had obviously been to protect him, to keep anyone from questioning her too deeply about an uncle who was no longer around. Probably even to explain it to her should she have questions about his absence. But what about the other two? The one about her broken engagement. And the one about not having time to date until her store was up and running?

Now that she was thinking about her breakup with Carl, the artist, she couldn't recall why they had broken up exactly. Even worse, she didn't even remember actually doing it.

"What are you thinking about?" Alexander asked quietly, and reached toward her, but Sherry backed up a step, out of his reach. They had said she'd built up a resistance to having her mind read in general, but more specifically to whomever was the immortal in her life. This man. He had to touch her to read her, she suspected, and definitely to control her, and she was beginning to suspect he'd controlled a lot of her life.

Lifting her chin, she glared at him. "It just didn't work out. It's better that way."

Alexander stilled, alarm flashing across his face.

"You put that thought in my head, just like you put the thought about Uncle Al just fading from my life there," Sherry accused.

"Yes," he confessed quietly, and then rushed on, "It was for your own good, honey. Carl was a waste of space. All he did was smoke pot and strut around with a paintbrush in hand. You were so much better than that. You were hardworking and had ambitions and he was an anchor dragging you down."

"I loved him," Sherry cried, but wasn't sure she really had even as she said it. Her memories of that time were foggy at best.

"Sherry, he was getting you into pot and other drugs. You were losing the thread of your life," he said quietly.

"I was not," she gasped with disbelief. "I've never done drugs in my life."

"You did with him," Alexander argued. "Not at first, but then one night after a party where you'd had too much to drink you had a couple tokes with him, and then it happened again and again. And then he got you to try acid, and mushrooms . . ." His mouth tightened. "You were going off the rails. Buying his nonsense that no one should have to work, that the birds don't dress up in suits and go to an office every day and people shouldn't have to either."

"I wasn't," Sherry denied, but with a little less fervor.

That phrase sounded vaguely familiar. Frowning, she argued, "Birds may not put on suits, but they do work. They build nests, and they have to hunt food."

"Exactly, and that's what you said when you were sober. But once he started getting you into drugs, you started slipping. And the day you repeated his nonsense line about the birds to me as if it were gospel, I knew I had to intervene."

Sherry was silent, confusion rife in her head as memories began to flood her now. Chilling on the couch in a marijuana haze, dancing through the park watching the light trails of fireflies on acid, hallucinations after eating mushrooms.

"Your mother was worried sick about you, and tried to talk you around, to get you to see what was happening. But in your heart you blamed her for your parents' divorce. If she hadn't blamed him, if she'd just tried to talk to him, you thought, they might still be together. So the more she criticized and talked, the more rebellious you got and the more you let him convince you to do," he said grimly.

"You started to skip classes. Your grades started to drop. Your whole future was going up in smoke and I debated what to do, and then the day you caught him in bed with your next door neighbor—"

"What?" Sherry squawked, even as an image flew into her head.

"You were pissed, and when you came to me and told me, I hoped you'd finally end it, but then he showed up and started giving you some nonsense about man not being naturally monogamous, that most animals weren't and it was all cool, he still loved only you but why shouldn't you both have some fun. I could tell you were confused. I was afraid you were going to go back to him, so I . . ."

"So you took control of me, broke us up, and erased all of this from my head," Sherry said slowly.

"It was better that way," Alexander assured her. "You got back on track right away. Your grades came back up, you were more studious and determined than ever."

She nodded slowly and simply asked, "And the part about wanting the store to be up and running before bothering with dating?"

"I . . . it was what you wanted. And you wouldn't take money from me. I thought if you were stable, with a steady income, I could worry less about you. And you have such poor taste in men, honey."

He reached toward her again and Sherry again jerked back.

"How many mistakes like Carl, the artist, did you prevent?" she asked grimly.

"What?" he asked warily.

"How many times have you intervened in my life?" Sherry asked, her voice steel now. "How many 'wrong men' did you stop me from going out with? How many bad decisions did you keep me from making or change for me? How much of my life was actually my own?" she ended heavily.

"I . . ." Alexander shook his head helplessly. "I was just trying to keep you from making mistakes."

"They were my mistakes to make," Sherry snapped. "It was my life. It's a part of growing up and maturing."

"I was just doing what any parent would do," Alexander said impatiently. "Every parent tries to keep their kid from making mistakes."

"They do," she agreed, "But every parent can't take control of their child, erase or replace memories and make them do what they want. You literally ran my life. I don't know now what was me and what was you. Did I even want to own my own business or is that something else you put in my head?"

"You did," he assured her. "It was what you wanted from when you were little. I just helped you get that."

"By keeping me from going off the rails," she suggested.

"Exactly. I kept you on track," Alexander said with relief, now that she appeared to understand.

"You steered the goddamned train that was my life," Sherry snapped. "You took over my life and ran it the way you decided it should be."

"You wanted to own your own business," he argued desperately.

"And before that I probably wanted to be a ballerina or a singer," she said dryly, and then remembered, "When I got to university I didn't care as much for business courses as I thought I would, but I loved the psychology courses I took and considered switching my major. Did you have anything to do with my staying in business?"

"No one gets a job with a degree in one of the ologies unless they go all the way to get their doctorate," he said impatiently.

"One of the ologies?" Basil queried.

"Psychology, sociology, archaeology," Alexander rattled them off. "B.A.'s in any of them is basically toilet tissue."

"That's your opinion," Sherry snapped. "And who says I wouldn't have gone all the way to get my doctorate?"

"Your mother couldn't afford to put you through all the way to a doctorate," he said with irritation.

"I was getting one hundred percent on my exams. The university pulled me aside and offered to help. They said there were grants for people who did as well as me," she reminded him coldly. "You know that. I told you when you were Lex Luth— Dear God, you really are my Lex Luther," she realized suddenly. "You're the bad guy in my life."

"No," Alexander protested. "I was just trying to help."

"Help me to be what you wanted me to be," she snapped, and turned to Basil. "I've heard enough. I—" She stopped abruptly as she spotted someone to her right. Turning, she stared at Lucian Argeneau. She almost asked him when he'd arrived and how long he'd been there listening, but it didn't really matter. Even if he hadn't heard it all, a quick read of her mind would tell him everything that had been said.

"If you're done speaking with your father, I'll have Bricker take him to the Enforcer house," Lucian said mildly.

"Why?" she asked uncertainly.

"Because I broke one of our laws and interfered in a mortal marriage," Alexander said quietly, moving past her to Lucian's side as Bricker stepped off the stairs and approached him. "It's time to face the music."

"He will be held until the council can gather, hear his case, and pass judgment," Basil said quietly in explanation.

"We don't use handcuffs, buddy," Bricker said when her father held his wrists out. "Immortals can just break them anyway. I'll just trust you not to try to break and run and walk you out to the SUV."

Alexander let his arms drop, but then turned back to Sherry. "I've made a lot of mistakes with you, Sherry. I'm sorry. My only excuse is that you are my first child and I . . ." He sighed and shook his head, and then said, "I know what the punishment is and I'll take it. And while I regret that I hurt your mother emotionally, I don't regret what I did, and knowing everything I know now, I would do it again. If I hadn't done it, your mother and I wouldn't have had you, and I think she'd agree with me that you are worth the emotional pain she suffered, and you're certainly worth the physical pain I am going to suffer." He raised a hand as if to caress her cheek, but then let it drop and sighed. "I hope after it's done we can talk and I can still be a part of your life. I do love you, sweetheart. You're my daughter."

He turned back to Bricker then and nodded. Justin took his arm and urged him toward the stairs leading down to the door that opened into the alley.

"Fortunately for you, we parked in the alley rather than take the time to try to find a spot on the street," Bricker explained to her father as they paused at the back door and he unlocked it.

"Why is that fortunate for me?" Alexander asked dryly.

"Because Victor and Elvi drove up today and are in the front of the store," Bricker explained as he unlocked the door. "And I'm pretty sure Elvi wants to kick your ass for showing up in London and scaring the hell out of her with that trick you played in the dressing rooms," Bricker said dryly.

"I didn't go anywhere near Elvi," he said quietly.

"Yeah, but just the hint that Leo was in the area had them pulling Stephanie out of Port Henry, and Elvi's a mama bear who now wants to tear apart the immortal who got between her and her baby bear," Bricker said wryly.

"Right," Alexander said with a sigh as Bricker opened the door and urged him out of the office.

The back door swung closed and Sherry stared at it in utter confusion. She was angry, and hurt, and so very unsure who she was anymore. She had no idea how much of her life was made up of her own decisions and how much had been Alexander's. It just wasn't a problem she'd ever imagined having before learning about the existence of immortals.

"I need a word," Lucian said to Basil.

Basil hesitated and then turned to Sherry and clasped her face in his hands. Peering into her eyes with concern, he asked, "Will you be okay for a minute alone?"

Sherry nodded and cleared her throat. "Of course. I'll just . . ." She waved vaguely toward her desk, unsure what she would just do. Sit around and think about everything she'd learned, probably. Try to sort out how many of her life decisions were her own and whether she really wanted to be where she was, or if instead she was where Alexander had wanted her to be.

"Are you sure?" Basil asked with a frown.

Obviously, she hadn't been convincing, Sherry thought wryly, and straightened her shoulders. "I'm fine. Go ahead and talk to Lucian. I'll be waiting here when you're done."

Basil still looked concerned, but he kissed her gently and then released her face and followed Lucian down into the store. Sherry watched them go, then started to turn toward her desk, but paused as the sound of a vehicle starting and driving away drew her gaze back to the door. Bricker had unlocked it to leave, but couldn't lock it from the outside. She should do that now, she thought, but paused and glanced toward the door to the store when it opened.

"Sherry?" Elvi called, and then said, "Oh," when she spotted her at the top of the stairs. "Can I come up?" she asked uncertainly.

"Of course," Sherry said quietly.

Nodding, Elvi slipped through the door and hurried up the steps to join her on the landing between the two sets of stairs. She hesitated once there, and then pulled her into a hard hug. "I'm so sorry, Sherry. I shouldn't have said those things. I was just scared that we were going to lose Stephanie. That's no excuse, I know, but I really am terribly sorry."

Sherry hugged the woman back without hesitation. "I know. It's okay. I understand."

"But can you forgive me?" Elvi asked, easing back. "I was cruel and nasty, and I'm never cruel or nasty."

"You were a mama bear protecting her cub," Sherry said, recalling Bricker's words. She patted Elvi's shoulder. "Victor explained everything, and I really do understand. Stephanie is like a daughter to you."

"Yeah. I guess it's a parent thing," Elvi said wryly. "We occasionally do stupid things because we care so damned much. But somehow we never expect our parents to be human and mess up too. I mean I don't know what I would have done if I found out Stephanie was doing drugs. Well, if she was mortal and I could control her, I'd probably do what your father did and just take control and make her stop. Which I suppose is a horrible thing to admit," she added.

Sherry narrowed her eyes slowly, and then asked without anger, "Reading my mind again?"

"Actually, no," Elvi said, and when Sherry didn't hide her disbelief, added, "The intercom was on in the store. We could hear everything."

"What?" Sherry gasped, and whirled toward her desk. She spotted the intercom panel at the corner of her desk . . . and it was still on. She must have sat on it when she'd perched there early in the conversation with her father, she realized, and now rushed over to shut it off.

"It's okay," Elvi said soothingly when Sherry ran her fingers into her hair with a moan. "Decker and Anders took control of your employees and sent them to lunch, then locked the doors and put the Closed sign up so no customers entered and heard anything."

"But they heard everything," she said on a sigh. "And so did you and whoever else is down there."

Elvi nodded apologetically. "Sorry. If I were a better person I would have walked out of the store and waited until it was over before coming back in, but . . ." She shrugged helplessly. "I guess I'm not as good a person as I always thought I was."

"That or you're as curious as the rest of the world and couldn't resist," Sherry said, and then patted her arm. "Don't worry, I'm not mad. I probably wouldn't have been able to make myself leave either. It's like a wreck on the side of the road—no one can resist slowing to look as they pass."

"Hmmm." Elvi nodded, but then pointed out, "On the bright side, though, none of us will be reading your mind on your way out to see what happened."

Sherry gave a half laugh at that, knowing it was exactly what would have happened if the intercom hadn't been on. There seemed to be no such thing as privacy among these people. It made her wonder if they had to be better people because of it. She was certainly finding herself editing her thoughts a lot . . . and she didn't even consider herself a bad person, but she did have thoughts once in a while that could be hurtful or rude if spoken aloud.

"How are you doing?" Elvi asked after a moment. "Finding out all of that stuff about your mother, your conception, and your father . . ." She shrugged. "Are you okay?"

"I don't know," Sherry admitted. "The truth is I don't even know how I should feel."

"There is no 'should,'" Elvi said quietly. "You feel how you feel."

Sherry nodded solemnly.

"I imagine you're feeling all sorts of things right now. Anger at what he did to your mother, yet confused because it's the reason you were born."

"My poor mother," Sherry said unhappily.

"He didn't rape her," Elvi said soothingly. "At least not in the violent, violated way. She was attracted to him and he just mentally veiled her reasons for not sleeping with him, and subdued her conscience. And," Elvi pointed out, "she got *you* out of the deal. And while your mother apparently wouldn't have had an affair with him without his influence, I'm sure she was glad to have you as a daughter, Sherry. Any mother would be. Especially after your brother died."

"Yes, but maybe if I had really been my dad's daughter, maybe they wouldn't have divorced. I mean, that could have been part of it. Maybe he sensed I wasn't his. If I had been his, maybe they would have worked harder to stay together."

"Sherry, you could never have been his daughter. There is no way for you to exist but as the daughter of Alexander and your mother," she pointed out gently, and then added, "And that isn't a guarantee the marriage would have worked anyway. From what I understand, a lot of couples don't survive the death of a child. Especially when the couple blame each other for the death, and it sounds like your parents did that."

"They did," she admitted, and then added resentfully, "But Alexander also controlled me. Made me do things I didn't want to do."

"Isn't that kind of the job of a parent?" Elvi asked, and then said, "Not the controlling part, but making the kid do things they don't want to do. Although," she said thoughtfully, "even the controlling part is something parents have to do too, only it's usually done with rewards, grounding, and threats of punishment rather than straight-up taking control."

Elvi let that sink in and then asked, "Do you really resent that you're now a self-made, successful businesswoman and not smoking dope in a little hovel with someone who thought monogamy and work were both for idiots and dupes?"

"No, but—"

"I'm sorry, sweetie," Elvi interrupted. "But I don't know many parents who wouldn't wish they could control their child when they saw they were making a huge mistake. And in Alexander's defense, he had your best interests at heart."

"Okay," she allowed. "But how self-made am I if he was taking control and making me do what he thought I should?"

"You told me your friend Lex, who is your father Alexander, offered you the money to start your own store when you graduated, but you refused," she reminded her.

"Yes."

"And he allowed you to do that rather than take control of you, and make you think it was a good idea to accept it," she pointed out. "Then you saved the money yourself to open the store."

"My mother's insurance money helped," Sherry pointed out.

"It allowed you to open it a couple years earlier than your plan," she acknowledged. "But you still saved the rest of it yourself. And I'm guessing you designed and stocked the store yourself."

"I did," Sherry admitted with a faint smile. "Lex had flown off to his supposed job in Africa and I hadn't hired Zander yet."

"Then your success is all your own," Elvi assured her. "You did an amazing job. No wonder Marguerite loves it so much."

"Marguerite?" Sherry asked, recognizing the name from her first night at the Enforcer house. "Lucian's sister-in-law? I thought I recognized her."

Elvi nodded. "She was going on about this store and how lovely you and everything in it were the last time I saw her. She said it was bright and airy and welcoming and . . . how did she put it? 'Even in the middle of winter it feels like a warm spring day when you walk into the store,'" she recounted, and then smiled. "She was right. I love it."

Sherry smiled. That was exactly the effect she'd been hoping to produce, and it appeared she'd succeeded.

"I'm quite sure your father had nothing to do with that," Elvi said solemnly, and then grinned. "Men are rather useless when it comes to decorating and kitchen stuff." She considered it briefly and then added, "That's probably why your father felt he could leave you alone so soon after your mother's death. He knew he would be no help with preparing and opening the store, and knew it would keep you occupied."

"If he even actually left town," Sherry said.

"Well, he probably didn't," Elvi acknowledged. "He was probably watching over you even then, just from a distance, as he did when your parents were still married. I think he really does love you and want the best for you, Sherry," she said quietly. "And I hope you'll give him the chance to be a part of your life after everything is settled."

When Sherry remained silent, her thoughts circling, Elvi patted her hand and said, "I don't know about you, but I could do with something to drink after all this talk."

"I have a Keurig," Sherry said, glancing around.

"I'm feeling more like one of those cold cappy frappy things, and I'm pretty sure I saw one of those fancy coffee shops around the corner that sell them."

"Actually, that does sound good," Sherry agreed.

"I'll just go see if I can get one of the boys to get us a couple, then. Be right back!"

Sherry nodded and watched her go, then turned to peer out the window over the store. Basil and Lucian were in a huddle, talking with Decker, Anders, Victor, Basha, and Marcus. As she watched, Elvi rushed to the group. After a couple minutes, Basha and Marcus were the ones who broke away and headed for the door. Sherry supposed they wanted a couple of the drinks themselves. That, or Decker and Anders couldn't leave the store.

Elvi turned to head back, but Victor caught her and swung her back for a kiss. Sherry smiled when Elvi threw her arms around him and kissed back, one foot leaving the ground to hang in the air. Sherry had always thought that only happened in classic movies. Apparently not. It made her wonder if she'd ever done that when Basil kissed her.

"Ah, isn't that sweet? It must be true love, huh?"

Sherry turned with a start to find Leonius standing beside her, watching the people below.

Sixteen

Sherry stumbled back with a gasp, nearly tripping over her own feet in her clumsy effort to get away. But Leo caught her arm, steadying her. His hold also prevented her from escaping.

"Careful, clumsy Cathy," he chided, drawing her to his side. "I wouldn't want you to fall and hurt yourself."

"My name's Sherry not Cathy," she said defiantly.

"Yeah, but clumsy Cathy sounds better than stumbling Sherry, don't you think?"

Glowering, Sherry ignored the question and asked, "How did you get in my office?"

Leo raised his eyebrows and said, "There's this little thing called a door . . ." He tilted his head. "You should really lock yours. I mean I know you have to keep the front door unlocked for customers, but the back door? Into an alley, no less. You really should have locked it behind Justin and your daddy."

"You saw them leave?"

"Yeah. I was hiding in your Dumpster. Fortunately, you don't sell foodstuffs, so I was only crouching amidst cardboard boxes and stuff. Still, it's a pretty undignified thing to have to do," he pointed out. "However, when I heard Bricker say the SUV was in the alley and realized he'd be coming out that door, there was nothing for me to do but jump in your blue bin."

"You heard him?"

"I heard loads of stuff. You people do like to talk, and I've been out there ever since Decker gave up his position watching the back of the store and ran around to the front," he informed her. "In fact, I was about to come in after Basil and Lucian left, but then Elvi—is that her name?—she came in, so I waited. I must confess, though, that I was losing patience and considering taking both of you when she finally left."

He glanced past her and clucked his tongue. "Speaking of Elvi, I do believe she's about done making out with her husband and is about to come up here. We should go. Otherwise, we'll have to take her with us." Using the hold he still had on her arm, Leo swung her toward the door leading out to the alley. "And you know that old saying, two's company and three's mass murder."

"And here I thought it was three's a crowd," Sherry muttered, pulling uselessly on her arm to distract him as she grabbed the letter opener off her desk in passing and concealed it against her side.

"Only when you're talking Argeneaus. Three of them is definitely three too many," he assured her as he dragged her down the stairs. "Speaking of which, I hear you're a life mate for my mother's uncle Basil."

"Wouldn't that make him your great-uncle?" she asked as he paused to crack the door open and peer warily out into the alley.

"Nah. I am not an Argeneau. At least not by blood. A great disappointment to my mother, I'm sure."

Sherry glanced at him curiously as he pushed the door wide-open now and dragged her out. His voice had gone tight with either pain or anger when he'd said that.

"Speaking of disappointing your parents." Pausing outside the door as it swung closed, Leo arched an eyebrow at her. "Smoking weed, Sherry? Really? Naughty, naughty."

"I was a kid," she said through her teeth as he turned to start moving again.

"Actually, you were twenty," he corrected. "News flash, it's ridiculous to lie to a man who can read your mind, so don't bother."

"Fine, I was twenty. That's still a kid," she said defensively.

"Only to someone over thirty," he assured her, and then pointed out, "After all, the army thinks eighteen-year-olds are old enough to take a life. Personally, I started killing much younger. So twenty is definitely old enough to know better."

"Whatever," Sherry said wearily, giving up on her tugging. "What does it matter anyway?"

"It doesn't," Leo assured her. "It's just nice to know I'm not the only one who disappointed my parent." Grinning, he added, "The good news is you can do all the drugs you want now that you're with me. I like feeding off stoned women. Much less screaming that way, and as much as I enjoy the terror, the screaming tends to give me a headache. Besides, I do like the buzz I get when their drugged blood hits my system. But drugs are so bad, really. Don't you think?"

Sherry shook her head, finding it too much work to follow his conversation and try to think of a way to get away from him at the same time. "I thought you liked drugs."

"Well, sure, but it always leads to bigger and not always better things. Like for you, it'll start with drugs and move on to finding yourself tied up in a dilapidated building with big nasty me slicing you up and slowly draining away your life." Pausing again, he turned to smile at her and added, "Oh, and don't bother trying to use that pig sticker you grabbed off your desk. I'll stop you, and it wouldn't do much good anyway. I may not have fangs like the others, but I heal just as quickly as any immortal." Leo winked and then added, "Hold onto it, though. I'll get a kick out of using your own letter opener on you."

"You're a sick puppy," Sherry said grimly, trying again to free her arm.

"Surprisingly, you aren't the first woman to say that," Leo told her, and then turned to glance toward the end of the alley, a frown suddenly pulling at his lips. "Speaking of puppies . . . where the hell are the boys?"

Sherry followed his gaze to the mouth of the alley some ten feet ahead of them. Not only were his boys not there, but no one was there, she noted with a frown.

The alley opened onto a busy side street. There should have been people passing and—

"Mummy!"

Sherry blinked at that startled cry from Leo as Basha suddenly stepped out in front of them. She then gasped with surprise as she was tugged behind Leo as if she were a chocolate chip cookie and he was trying to prevent Basha from seeing he'd nipped her from the cookie jar.

It was a ridiculous reaction, of course. She wasn't a bloody cookie and Basha could see her, especially when she leaned to the side to look around Leo's arm.

Basha wasn't alone, she saw with relief. Marcus, Bricker, and her father—Alexander— had stepped out behind Leo's mother.

"You killed your own grandsons," Leo said suddenly with dismay.

"Only two of them," Basha said calmly.

"Leos Four and Six," Leo growled. "My oldest and my favorites."

"Eleven and Twenty are still alive," she offered.

"Not for long, I'm sure," he said dryly. "Mortally wounding them and tossing them trussed up into the back of an SUV was very ungrandmotherly of you. Especially when it would have been kinder to just kill then. You know the council will order their deaths. Hell, there's a standing KOS order on all of us now."

"What's a KOS order?" Sherry asked, glancing from Basha to Leo.

"Kill on sight," Leo said with a scowl.

"You have the right to go before the council," Basha said grimly. "If you—"

Basha paused as her son spun back the way he and Sherry had come, but then Leo halted abruptly again and Sherry saw that Decker, Lucian, Basil, Anders, and Victor were spread out across the width of the alley behind them, in that order from left to right. Lucian had a hand on Basil's arm as if he had been holding him back, and Elvi stood a few feet behind them, looking worried.

Cursing, Leo spun back to face Basha, dragging Sherry up beside him. "So what are you waiting for? I'm in your sight. Kill me."

Basha shifted, her hand tightening on the sword she held and raising it slightly before she lowered it and shook her head. "It doesn't have to be like this, Leo. You have the right to go before the council too."

"Over Sherry's dead body," he growled, dragging her in front of him.

"Leo," Basha said, taking a step forward. "Don't do this."

"Do what? Snap her neck like a twig?" he asked, catching Sherry's chin with one hand and turning her head to the right. "Or maybe I'll just rip her throat out with my less than immortal teeth. With no fangs, it would seriously hurt, huh? Or maybe . . ." he said suddenly, with what Sherry was sure was a smile in his voice, "Maybe I'll just turn her right here and now with you all watching, helpless to do anything."

"Crap," Sherry muttered, thinking, Who was the

stupid idiot who had refused to let Basil turn her last night to prevent just this kind of thing from happening?

"You," Leo said, and Sherry glanced around, wondering who he was talking to and why he'd stopped.

Leo sighed wearily, gave her chin a jerk to get her attention, and said in an undertone, "I was talking to you, Sherry. You are the stupid idiot who refused to let Basil turn you last night."

"Yes, I am," she whispered in agreement, and in that moment regretted it with all her heart. And not just because it probably would have saved her life, but because in that moment when she didn't know if her neck was going to be snapped, her throat ripped out, or she would be turned by a no-fanger, Sherry saw herself and her life with a clarity she had never before experienced.

She'd had a good childhood . . . even after her brother's death. Her mother and Alexander were always there for her, offering support and love. And yes, Alexander had been controlling and done things she now didn't appreciate, but hadn't he done them to ensure that she didn't make mistakes and fail? Didn't all good parents do what they could to try to help their children have the best life they could?

And then there was Basil. He said they were life mates and wanted to turn her so they could spend the rest of their lives together. But last night he'd offered to turn her just to ensure that she was safe. His giving up his one turn was an even bigger deal than her agreeing to the turn, yet he was ready to do it despite the fact that she hadn't yet agreed to be his life mate. She could have let him turn her and then gone on with her life without him, leaving him high and dry. Yet, he'd been willing to do that to keep her safe. If that wasn't love, she didn't know what was.

She'd been offered love by two wonderful men, welcomed by all the others now standing around her, and she hadn't appreciated any of it until this very moment, when it might be too late to do so. She was more than an idiot, she was a moron, and it was time to stop acting like a helpless idiot and do something.

Clenching her hand around the letter opener, Sherry suddenly jammed it back into Leo's leg. He shouted in pain, and when his hand loosened on her chin and arm, she pulled away and stumbled several steps to the side until she collided with a hard chest.

"Sherry, thank God," Basil gasped, his arms closing around her.

She started to lift her head, but then swung it around to peer back toward Leo as a whizzing sound cut the air behind her. What she saw was Leo, bent forward, clutching at the handle of her letter opener. It hadn't hit him in the leg, as she'd thought, Sherry realized. More like his groin. Basha was taking advantage of his bent position, and as Sherry watched, she brought down the sword she'd just raised, beheading Leo in one clean motion. At least, Sherry suspected she beheaded him. She never really saw. Basil grabbed her head and turned her quickly back to face him and she missed the actual blow.

She wasn't sorry about that. The sounds that accompanied the act, and the blood that rained out over them and across the wall behind her and Basil . . . well, the combination was quite disgusting enough. She was more than grateful when Basil scooped her into his arms and hurried back toward the store's back door with her. She didn't want to see what Leonius Livius's expression was like in death. Was he surprised that his mother actually ended his miserable life? Or grateful for it?

Personally, Sherry was quite sure he'd come looking for his mother to have her kill him. Why else would he be stupid enough to come to Toronto, where the Enforcers' base was situated?

Despite not wanting to see Leo, Sherry found herself shifting her head to peer back at the scene behind her. She was in time to see Basha collapse into Marcus's arms, weeping. Sherry supposed the woman was weeping for the child she'd raised rather than the man he'd become, and knew this was probably the hardest thing Basha Argeneau had ever had to do. She hoped it was, anyway, and felt for the poor woman.

As Sherry watched, Marcus scooped Basha up into his arms just as Basil had done with her. Only he carried the woman out of the alley in the opposite direction.

Sherry's gaze shifted over the others. Victor was ushering Elvi after her and Basil, but the others—including her father, Alexander—all stood around the body in the alley, talking quietly.

"I don't know his name."

Basil glanced to Sherry and saw that she was peering over his shoulder at the scene he'd just taken her from. "Livius," he said. "His name was Leonius Livius."

She shook her head. "Not him. My father. I know his first name is Alexander, but I have no idea what his last name is." She stiffened suddenly, her eyes shooting to his face as she asked, "He isn't an Argeneau, is he?"

"No. We are not related," he assured her at once.

Sherry relaxed with a little sigh. "Good. I mean what would it make us if you were my cousin or an uncle or something?"

No Problem *Incestuous*

"It would make us most unfortunate," he said dryly.

"I'll say," she muttered, and then glanced around when he stopped. Seeing that they had arrived at the door, she reached out to pull it open for him without being asked. Basil caught the bottom of it with his foot and kicked it open wider, then ducked inside with her. When she sighed and leaned her cheek on his shoulder, he held her a little tighter, wanting to keep her there, just like that, forever.

Basil had never been more scared in his life than when he'd rushed out of the store and spotted Sherry in Leo's grip. The moments before it had been stressful as well. First, Bricker had called in to say he'd spotted Leo's boys in a coffee shop directly across from the mouth of the alley behind the store. Lucian had ordered him to park and pursue them.

Bricker had headed across the store then, intent on reaching Sherry and making sure she was okay. Lucian had followed, calling Basha as they went, and getting ahold of her just as she reached the entrance to the coffee shop and spotted the men inside. Bricker had heard him order her to wait for him and Alexander and then to help them handle the four men. Basil had barely hung up when Elvi suddenly burst out of the door to the office ahead of them. He hadn't needed her to shout that Sherry was gone or to tell him there was a problem—the woman's pale face and horrified expression had been enough to make him race past her and up into the office. He'd come to a shuddering halt on the upper landing, however, when he saw that Sherry was indeed gone.

"The back door," Lucian had barked right behind him, and Basil started moving again, charging down the stairs and out into the alley. He would remember the moment when he'd spotted Leo and Sherry for the rest of his life. It was burned into his mind, into his very heart. The monster had his woman, and he was helpless to do a damned thing to save her. Still, he would have tried. He'd rushed forward, intending to tackle the bastard, which probably would have gotten Sherry killed or at least hurt, but he hadn't been thinking. Fortunately, Lucian was, and had caught his arm to stop him.

Reaching the office now, Basil moved to the chair behind Sherry's desk. He'd intended to set her in the chair, but once he got there, he settled in it himself with her on his lap. He wasn't ready to let her go. He might never let her go again.

"What do I do?" Sherry asked, and he peered down into her face.

"You let me turn you like I wanted to do last night," he said firmly, and when her eyes widened in surprise, he found himself suddenly angry. "You could have died, Sherry. Leo had you and there wasn't a damned thing I could do about it. You could have died."

Sherry hesitated, but then pointed out gently, "Being immortal doesn't really protect against that, Basil. Leo was immortal and he's dead now."

When Basil stared at her blankly, she sighed and admitted, "I was actually asking what I should do about not knowing my father's last name."

"Oh." He frowned, and then glanced toward the door as it opened and Victor ushered Elvi inside.

"Are you okay?" Elvi asked anxiously, rushing around the desk toward them.

"Yes. I'm fine, really." Sherry started to sit up, but Basil held her in place. She glanced toward him with surprise, and then turned back when Elvi began to speak again.

"It scared the crap out of me when I came back in and realized you were gone, and then I saw that the back door was cracked open, and I just knew Leo must have got in," Elvi babbled. Squeezing her hands, she added, "Thank God you're all right."

"Yes, but more importantly, Stephanie is safe now," Sherry pointed out with a smile, and Basil could have crushed the woman's bloody neck. Who cared if Stephanie was safe? Stephanie had been safe in Port Henry. *She* was the one who had nearly died, dammit!

"Oh, my," Elvi breathed, her eyes widening. Apparently, that hadn't yet occurred to her. Now that it had, Basil couldn't tell if she was going to burst into tears or shout with glee. The tears won out, and Elvi turned to Victor and buried her face in his chest, her shoulders shaking.

Much to Basil's amusement, Victor peered down at his woman as if she'd lost her mind.

"Honey, this is a good thing," he pointed out, his arms automatically going around her.

Elvi lifted her head to sob, "I knowwww," and then buried her face in his chest once more.

"She's just happy and relieved," Sherry said, rubbing the other woman's back sympathetically. "She must have been terribly scared for Stephanie. It must have killed her to let her out of her sight to come to Toronto."

"It diddddd," Elvi cried, burrowing deeper into Victor's chest.

Victor peered helplessly from his woman to his brother. "I . . . er . . . I think I should . . . er . . ." Giving it up, he scooped Elvi into his arms and turned toward the stairs, only to pause to allow Lucian and Bricker to pass him and come into the room. The moment the way was clear, though, he headed down the stairs that led into the store.

"What the hell is going on?" Bricker asked with amazement as they watched Victor carry Elvi out. "First Basil's carrying Sherry away, and then Marcus is carting a blubbering Basha off, and now Elvi's sobbing to beat the band and Victor is playing he-man too. Have the women gone crazy or is this an immortal caveman convention?"

Lucian reached out and biffed the younger man in the back of the head.

"Ow," Bricker complained, rubbing the spot. "What?"

"Show some respect," Lucian snapped. "Basha just killed the man she's thought of as her son for two millennia. There was no shame in her weeping over that."

"Yeah, okay," Bricker agreed. "I get that."

Lucian grunted and turned back to peer at Basil, only to scowl when the young hunter said, "But what about Elvi and Sherry?"

"I wanted to get Sherry away from the scene as quickly as possible. She is not crying," Basil pointed out. "But she *is* mortal. Watching a man beheaded and dealing with the aftermath is not a common occurrence for her."

"Okay, I can see that too," Bricker allowed, and then glanced from Basil to Lucian and asked, "But what was Elvi's deal?"

Lucian scowled when the young man settled his gaze on him. It seemed obvious to Basil that his brother had no idea why Elvi was crying, but rather than say so, he simply said, "She is a woman. They don't need a reason to cry. They just do."

Sherry released what sounded suspiciously like a snort, her body jerking against his, and then she explained to Bricker, "Elvi is just relieved that Stephanie's life is no longer in danger. It has been a great strain on her to worry about the girl for so long."

"Ah," Bricker said with understanding. But now Lucian was scowling even harder.

"She should be happy now then. Stephanie is safe," Lucian pointed out.

"She *is* happy," Sherry assured him patiently. "That's why she was crying."

If anything, that seemed to confuse Lucian more. Shaking his head, he turned to Bricker and said, "You see? It's as I said, women don't need a reason to cry. They just do."

"Yeah, right. You'd best not be suggesting Leigh is the crybaby type," Bricker said with amusement. "She's the strongest woman I know. She has to be to put up with you."

Lucian glowered at the man. "She cried when she was pregnant. A lot. Hormonal, Marguerite called it," he added morosely, and then shuddered and confessed, "It made me glad we can only have children every hundred years."

Basil smiled widely. He knew Lucian adored his wife as much as he himself adored Sherry, and it was so damned fine to see him acting like a human again. His smile faded as he tuned into his own thoughts. He adored Sherry?

Yes, Basil acknowledged. He did. At the start, he had simply noted that he couldn't read or control her, and accepted that she was his life mate. It had been that simple, like A + B = C, his inability to read plus the inability to control, equaled life mate in his mind. End of story. But that was then. Now he'd gotten to know her.

Basil knew Sherry's ambitions, her determination, even how she'd briefly lost her way. He enjoyed her sense of humor, her intelligence, and her kindness. She had a decency that made the world a better place and a passion equal to his own. She also had courage. In the penultimate moment, when Leo had held her life in his hands, no one could have saved her from him without a high risk of getting her killed instead. Whether she had known that or not, she had not stood as a victim to the man, helpless to his whims and waiting to be saved, but stabbed him in the balls and got the hell away from him. Sherry had saved herself in the end.

Even if no one else had been there, and if Basha had not stepped up to lop off his head the moment Sherry was out of the way, Basil was quite sure Leo would not have got up quickly from the wound Sherry had given him. The man had been about to collapse on the ground screaming in agony when Basha forever silenced him with her sword. Had Sherry been there alone, he was quite sure that she would have had a good deal of time to escape before Leo healed enough to follow. And Basil was damned proud of her. But more than that, he loved her for it. And now he wanted more than for her to accept the turn and agree to be his life mate. He wanted her to love him back. Needed it, even.

"Is my father still out in the alley?" Sherry asked, breaking into his thoughts.

Basil glanced to Lucian at her question and noted that he was staring at him with silent concentration. No doubt Lucian had been listening in on his revelations. He didn't care. He would be happy to shout from the rooftops that he loved this woman.

"No," Bricker answered when Lucian simply continued to stare at Basil. "Decker and Anders took him back to the Enforcer house with the others."

"Oh no. We have to do something." Sherry began to

struggle to rise, and Basil again held on at first, but then he let her go and stood as well. He knew she wanted to find out her father's last name. She'd probably hoped to ask him before he was taken away.

"Actually, at the moment she is more worried about his ding-dong than his last name," Lucian growled, proving he had been not only in Basil's thoughts, and still was, but in Sherry's as well.

"His what?" Basil asked with a start.

"The punishment for interfering with a married woman," Lucian reminded him. "They shred his ding-dong. Bricker's term, not mine, if you'll recall," he added with dignity.

Basil glanced around, intending to soothe Sherry, but she'd somehow disappeared during the few seconds he had been distracted.

"Where the hell did she go?" he muttered, moving to the landing between the stairs that led down to the store, and the ones leading down to the door to the alley. Both doors were closed and he had no idea which way she'd gone.

"She dragged Bricker out through the store," Lucian said calmly, following Basil when he plunged down the stairs. "She intends for him to drive her to the Enforcer house."

The store appeared empty when Basil came out into it, but he glanced around to be sure. He saw no one, though, so rushed out onto the sidewalk and peered first one way and then the other. Cursing when he didn't see either Sherry or the young Enforcer, he spun back to the store impatiently and then hurried back to the door and opened it to shout, "Will you hurry up, dammit! Which way is the truck?"

"Relax," Lucian said dryly. "Bricker will not leave without me. The SUV is—"

"What?" Basil asked when his brother paused with his arm half raised, shock crossing his features.

"The little shit just drove away without me," Lucian said with amazement.

Looking in the direction Lucian had started to point, Basil saw the black SUV that was even now merging with traffic. The word he used then was much worse than the little shit Lucian had called Bricker.

Seventeen

"You know, Lucian is going to be seriously pissed at our taking off like this," Justin warned as he pulled into traffic.

"I don't care," Sherry assured him. "This is urgent. My father's ding-dong is in my hands."

"Yeahhhhh, that just sounds wrong," Bricker drawled.

"What?" Sherry asked with bewilderment, then realized what she'd said and clucked her tongue impatiently. "You know what I mean."

"Actually, I don't," he informed her. "The council decides these things, Sherry. His ding-dong is not in your hands at all."

She bit her lip at this news and then asked, "Well, surely if I tell Mortimer that I don't want them to shred his ding-dong a hundred times or whatever, he'll let him go? I mean I am the victim here. Well, my mother was, but she's dead, so that leaves only me to care one way or another. Besides, isn't there a statute of limitations or something? It happened thirty-two years ago, for heaven's sake."

"Yeahhhh, I'll just drive around the block and pick up Lucian and Basil now," Bricker decided.

"What? Why?" Sherry asked with a frown. "I wanted to get back to the house before them to convince Mortimer to release my father to me."

"Yeah, but it's not going to work, honey pie," Bricker informed her. "You can plead with Mortimer until you're blue in the face and he won't release your father without Lucian's say so. And," he added dryly, "all our leaving them behind would do is piss off Lucian and make him less likely to listen to your pleas."

Her eyes widened in dismay as she realized what he said was probably true. "Turn around. Go back."

"I am," Bricker said soothingly as he took the next corner.

Sherry bit her lip and began to wring her hands, worrying over whether the men had come out yet, and realized that they had left. As Bricker took the next corner, she muttered, "I wished you'd said that earlier. Why did you agree to leave them in the first place?"

"Because I wanted to know what you were up to, whether you planned to try to break your father out of jail or what," he admitted with a shrug, and then paused as he negotiated the next corner before pointing out, "I'm an Enforcer. It's my job to make sure you won't be a problem."

Sherry turned on him with dismay at this news.

Bricker caught her expression, grinned and admitted,

"I also couldn't resist seeing what Lucian's expression would be when I pulled out and left him behind." His grin widened into a full-blown savoring smile, and he assured her, "Believe me, that was priceless."

Eyes narrowing, Sherry growled, "You're a shit disturber."

"That I am," he agreed easily.

"Ass," she muttered with disgust.

"Oh, don't be like that, Sherry. Look on the bright side, this way you can nag the hell out of them all the way to the house," he pointed out brightly as he took the next turn. "They'll be captive listeners, unable to escape your arguments. See how this all works out so well?"

Sherry merely scowled again. It was pretty obvious that Bricker had a bit of a twisted sense of humor. It made her wonder just what kind of woman the nanos would pick out for him.

"I think Lucian wants the front seat," Bricker said with amusement.

Sherry glanced around to see that they'd stopped in front of the store and Lucian now stood outside the passenger door, scowling unpleasantly. She considered locking the door and making him get in the back, but it didn't seem the smart thing to do when she wanted something from the man.

Unsnapping her seat belt, she slid out of the seat and crawled into the back as Basil opened the door to get in beside her.

"We thought you'd left without us," Basil admitted as he closed the door and claimed the seat next to her.

"We drove around the block," she muttered as she did up her seat belt. When she finished and straightened, she found Lucian in the front passenger seat, peering from her to Bricker with a glowering expression. He, of course, could read her. Grimacing, she pointed out, "We came back for you."

"Bricker always intended to. You, however, only agreed because you are concerned about your father's family jewels," Lucian said dryly.

"You are?" Basil asked with concern, taking her hand.

"Er . . . actually, the family jewels aren't what are imperiled," Bricker announced. "Family jewels are the testicles, Lucian. Not the ding-dong."

"Well then give me another name for the item in question, because I am not saying ding-dong again. It's ridiculous."

"You just did . . . say it again, I mean," Bricker pointed out with amusement, and when Lucian scowled at him, he shrugged. "Okay, well let's see, there's ankle spanker."

Sherry blinked at the name. "Ankle spanker? Seriously? No man is that big."

Justin considered for a minute. "Okay then, how about disco stick, or bed snake?"

When Lucian merely scowled at him, he shrugged and offered more suggestions.

"Winkie? Flesh flute? Tallywhacker? Baby maker? Quiver bone? Joystick? Fun stick? Lap rocket? Love muscle? Wedding tackle? One-eyed wonder weasel? Helmet head? Wang? Trouser snake? Giggle stick? Schlong? Mushroom head? Love rod? Pecker? Thundersw—"

"Enough!" Lucian barked, and when Bricker paused and glanced to him questioningly, he said, "I do not know what alarms me more, that you have so many names for cock or what it means in regard to how much time you spend thinking about cock." And then arching an eyebrow, he asked, "Is there something you wish to tell us, Bricker?"

"What?" Justin said with dismay, and then he squawked, "No! I read them online once. This Web site had, like, a hundred and seventy or eighty names like that. Those are just the ones I remember off the top of my head."

"Hmm," Lucian muttered dubiously. "Well, since you just went through a red light, I suggest you stop thinking about cock and pay attention to the road."

"Fine," Bricker snapped, and then muttered, "Jeez, try to help a guy out . . ."

Lucian ignored him and turned in his seat to peer at Sherry. "So . . . you are concerned about your father's equipment."

"Yes, of course," Sherry said with a frown. "Wouldn't you be?"

"I could not care less about your father's equipment," Lucian assured her dryly.

"What if it was *your* father?" Sherry asked grimly. "And stop talking about his equipment. According to you guys, it would heal, but I'm concerned about the pain punishing him like that would put him through."

"You don't think he deserves it?" Lucian asked mildly. "Your mother did nearly kill herself, *and you*," he added heavily, "because of what he did to her."

"But she didn't," Sherry said quietly. "And he has spent the last thirty-two years trying to make up for it. Don't you guys have a statute of limitations on your crimes?"

"Honey," Basil said quietly, taking her hand. "If we let him go unpunished, we could be accused of favoritism, because he's your father. We can't have one law for us and another for those who aren't connected to the families."

"Aside from that," Lucian said, "others might think we are softening and may commit the offense, expecting we will let them get away with it too."

Sherry ground her teeth with frustration, but it was Justin who said, "It's a pretty barbaric law anyway. I mean, times have changed. Divorce is more common, and husbands don't usually kill wives now for infidelity . . . well, not in most countries."

"So, that makes it all right for an immortal to use our abilities to interfere in a marriage that otherwise might have been fine?" Lucian asked. "To make a woman have sex when she otherwise would not have?"

"No, I suppose not," Justin said on a sigh, and then rallied and added, "But if that's the concern, then the law should apply to immortal women now too. A wife is just as likely to divorce her husband if he is unfaithful as a man is now. At least here."

"He's right," Basil said solemnly. "When we made

the law, mortal men had mistresses by course. The wife not only often knew that, but expected it. Now . . ." He shrugged.

Lucian nodded. "We shall have to revisit the law."

"I don't care about your law, I care about my father," Sherry said with frustration. "He has tried to make amends. As far as I know, he's never even dated since then."

"What?" Bricker asked with amazement, meeting her gaze in the rearview mirror. "Seriously?"

"As far as I know, he never dated anyone as Lex or Zander. And while I was young at the time, I don't think he did as Uncle Al either."

There was silence for a moment and then Lucian and Basil exchanged a glance, before Lucian said. "We shall talk to your father when we get to the house. I will read him and see what he has or hasn't done."

"And then?" Sherry demanded.

"And then we shall see," he said simply.

"Maybe you could give him a suspended sentence," Sherry suggested. "You know, permanent probation or whatever. If he never does it again, he's fine. But if he does, he receives the punishment for this time plus that time."

"We shall see," is all Lucian said, and then he turned and faced front, making it obvious the conversation was closed.

Sherry sat back in her seat with a little sigh and then glanced to Basil when he squeezed her hand.

"You don't seem to be as angry with your father as you first were," he pointed out solemnly.

Sherry grimaced, and then admitted, "Elvi said some things that made me think, and then when Leo had me . . ." She bit her lip as she recalled her fear then, but pushed past it and said, "I remembered the good about him instead of the bad. He was basically my father as a child after my brother died, taking me to classes and the science center, helping me with my homework . . . He even cooked my dinner for me on occasion when Mom worked late. He was lousy at it," she admitted with a crooked smile. "But he tried."

"It sounds as if he tried to fill the hole Richard Carne left behind when he separated from your mother," Basil said quietly.

"He more than filled it," Sherry said on a sigh. "He paid me more attention and was more of a father than Richard Carne ever was."

"And then he left and came back into your life as Lex," Basil said gently.

Sherry nodded. "As Lex he was my best friend, but . . . Well, I thought of him as an older brother of sorts, but the truth is he was still more of a father figure. He was still doing all the things he had before, advising me on what courses to take, helping me with assignments when I ran into difficulty, making sure I ate when I got wrapped up in studying and stuff."

"And as Zander?" Basil asked.

"The same again. He was my employee and supposedly younger than me, but he was there for me, offering me support and encouragement and helping out however he could."

"It sounds like he devoted a lot of his time to you," Basil said quietly, and then added, "As a father myself, I know how hard it is to get it right, Sherry. We are human, we make mistakes, but he appears to have tried very hard to be a good father to you under the circumstances."

Sherry nodded and then glanced down at their entwined hands and admitted, "You're right. He did." She grimaced and then added, "I'm not happy that he controlled me, but I realized after talking to Elvi that it's what parents do. Mortal parents use punishments and groundings and stuff to control their kids, not actually taking control of them. But it's a parent's job to keep their child away from drugs or other things that might hurt them, and to make them decent, self-sufficient people. And I know that's something that is harder and harder to accomplish in this society. Some parents don't even bother, but Alexander, at least, tried, and he was always there for me."

She fell silent, and when Basil didn't say anything, raised her gaze to him uncertainly, and then paused at his expression. He was staring at her, a softness in his eyes that she'd never seen before. Biting her lip, she tilted her head and then asked, "What?"

"God, I love you Sherry Harlow Carne," he growled, and then kissed her. It wasn't the usual passionate devouring, but a tender caress, and Sherry felt her heart swell and her eyes glaze with tears, and then his tongue slid between her lips and her pants were on fire. Dear God, the man was a match to her tinder. All he had to do was kiss her and she was ready to crawl into his lap and ride him down the highway . . . and she didn't particularly care that Lucian and Bricker were there.

"If you two can untangle yourselves, we have arrived," Lucian said dryly from the front seat.

Sherry moaned with disappointment and leaned her forehead on Basil's chest when he reluctantly broke the kiss. They both remained still as they regained their composure, and then Sherry eased back into her seat and glanced around to see that they had passed through the gates and were coming to a halt in front of the house.

"I expect you'll want to talk to your father," Lucian said, unsnapping his seat belt. "Basil can take you. You have ten minutes."

Sherry scowled at the autocratic man, but was beginning to see that it was impossible to argue with him, so she didn't bother. Instead, she quickly unsnapped her seat belt and scrambled out of the SUV.

"Where is he?" she asked Basil as he closed the door. "In those cells by the dogs?"

When Basil nodded, Sherry caught his hand and started in that direction at a jog.

"Did you want to talk to him alone?" Basil asked when she reached the door to the outbuilding behind the house and suddenly stopped, without reaching to open the door.

"No," she said quickly, spinning to face him. "No, I want you there," and then blurted, "I love you," and spun to open the door.

Sherry was halfway up the first hall when she realized Basil was no longer with her. Frowning, she rushed back to the door and pushed it open to see him standing where she'd left him, looking as if he'd been pole-axed.

"Basil?" she said impatiently.

His gaze flickered up to her face. "You love me?"

Sherry frowned, her gaze going over her shoulder to the building housing her father, but then sighed and stepped back outside. Pausing in front of him, she reached up to cup his face and said, "Yes, Basil. I love you." She followed that up with a gentle kiss, but pulled away before he could deepen it and spun back to the door, adding briskly, "Now let's go. We can talk about this later. We only have ten minutes."

"Right. Later. Ten minutes," Basil muttered, sounding dazed, but when she started up the hall and glanced back this time, he was right on her heels. He was also wearing a goofy grin now, she noted, and found herself donning one as well. Damn, she loved him.

Shaking her head, Sherry took the left hall just past the office and hurried forward. She couldn't hear the dogs this time so supposed they were up at the house being spoiled rotten, or ruined, as Mortimer put it, by Sam. That thought made her smile, and then she pushed through the door leading to the hall of cells and her smile faded.

She found her father in the second cell on the right. He was seated on a cot, a book in hand. But he quickly closed it and got to his feet when he saw her.

"Hi," he said uncertainly when Sherry just stared at him.

"Hi," she murmured back, finding herself backing up until she bumped up against Basil's chest. She relaxed a little when his arms slipped around her, and then blurted, "What's your name? You're my father and I don't even know your name."

Alexander sighed and dropped the book on the bed, then took a couple steps closer to the bars. He paused, though, when Sherry stiffened again.

"I told you, my name is Alexander," he said gently.

Sherry shifted impatiently and moved forward a step, unintentionally moving out of Basil's arms. "I know that. But Alexander what? You were Lex Brown and Zander—"

"Marrone," he answered before she could finish.

"Oh," Sherry said, and then tried out the name. "Alexander Marrone. I suppose it's okay."

"I'm glad you approve," her father said with amusement, and then glanced to Basil when he shifted beside Sherry.

"You aren't Reg's son?" Basil asked with a frown. "The one who's been missing for . . ."

"Thirty-three years," Alexander finished for him dryly when Basil paused with sudden realization. "Now you know where I disappeared to and why."

"Your father's still alive?" Sherry asked Alexander with surprise, and when he nodded, turned to Basil and said, "And you know his father?"

Basil nodded. "Alexander's father, your grandfather, is on the council, Sherry."

Her eyes widened incredulously when he said the word grandfather. She had family besides the aunts and uncles she saw only a couple times a year? She had no idea how to feel about that.

While she turned that over in her mind, Basil eyed her father and said, "I know where you disappeared to, but not necessarily why."

Alexander grimaced. "My father is a very controlling man, and—"

"Shocker," Sherry interrupted dryly, and her father's expression filled with chagrin.

"Yeah, I guess the apple really doesn't fall far from the tree, honey," he said with a sigh. "I am sorry about controlling you. I couldn't think of anything else to do at the time, and I was so worried about you, but today, when you got upset . . ." Alexander shook his head. "What you said wasn't unlike what I said to my own father before storming out of the house the last time we argued," he admitted.

Sherry raised her eyebrows at this and asked, "How old are you?"

"Fifty-two," he answered quietly.

"So you were twenty when you met my mom?" she asked with surprise. Every immortal she'd met until now had been over a hundred. Her father was a baby in comparison, practically like a mortal.

"Nineteen, actually," he admitted, flushing, and then added, "A very arrogant, ignorant nineteen who thought he knew everything, and as it turns out, didn't know a damned thing."

Sherry turned to Basil. "He was just a kid. I mean, practically a baby for you guys. Surely the council would take that into account?"

"Sherry," Alexander said quietly. When she turned back to him, he shook his head. "I don't want you to worry about the council, or my punishment. That isn't your concern, and," he added firmly when she started to protest, "I am willing to take whatever they decide is my punishment." He paused and smiled wryly. "I mean, I'm not looking forward to it, but . . ." He shrugged. "I earned it."

"But—"

"Listen to me. I need you to understand," he interrupted quietly.

Sherry sighed but closed her mouth, then glanced around and smiled in gratitude when Basil shifted behind her to pull her back against his chest and hold her again.

"As you said, I was a kid, but I was headed down the wrong road. I had a friend, Ben, who got me into mixed bloods, and—"

"What are mixed bloods?" Sherry asked with confusion.

"Blood from mortals who have ingested alcohol or drugs," Basil said quietly.

Sherry's eyes widened. "You were biting mortals?"

"No," he assured her. "I hadn't gone that far off the rails. It was bagged blood, and only alcohol mixes. They sell it at the Night Club or you can order it by the case if you want it for home."

"Oh." Sherry relaxed.

"Anyway," Alexander continued, "I started overindulging, going a little wild, doing stupid things. Just petty things, really, but it was enough. My father pulled me in to rake me over the coals. I decided in my arrogance that he was a stupid old fool who didn't have a clue, told him to go to hell and stormed out."

"I find it hard to believe Reg took that well," Basil said dryly.

"Yeah, I figured you knew him when you called him Reg the first time," Alexander said with a wry smile. "He makes most people call him Regulus. Only his friends call him Reg."

"We have served on the council together for a long time," Basil said with a shrug.

Alexander nodded. "To tell you the truth, I don't know how he took it. I wanted to get as far away as I could, somewhere he wouldn't find me."

"And you chose Canada?" Sherry asked with a wince. "Why not somewhere warm and balmy like Florida?"

"Honey, you have an hour and a half more darkness here in southern Ontario in the winter than Florida. For a couple of young vamps eager to party, the longer the darkness lasted meant the longer the party. Besides, someone told us the girls here were . . . er . . . friendlier."

"Those were your deciding factors?" she asked dryly. "Darkness and hos? Really? God, you *were* young."

"We all were once," he said with amusement.

Shaking her head, she waved at him to continue. "So you and Ben came to Canada, and . . . ?"

"Yeah." He sighed. "I was away from home, my father wouldn't know what I was up to and so couldn't chastise me, and I went a little crazy. We were always partying. We bought bagged mixed blood by the case, and to tell you the truth, I think Ben might have slipped in a couple of black market bags, stuff we shouldn't have been touching. There were a couple of times when I know I had more than an alcohol buzz." He paused briefly, his expression reflective, and then he sighed and shook his head. "Anyway, that's the state I was in when I met your mother."

Alexander met her gaze and admitted, "I said I didn't know she was married, that I merely dipped into her head to see that she was attracted to me and that was it. And that's true, but the fact is, I was in no shape to dip deeper than that. I was so out of it, I'm not even sure I didn't get some whiff that she was married. I mean, it's possible one of the other girls said something, isn't it? If so, I was too far gone to pick up on it."

Basil shifted behind her, and Sherry glanced over her shoulder to see that he was now frowning. After a hesitation, he said, "The nanos would have cleared your system relatively quickly. You said you sat with them until they left. You should have been clear-headed by then and— Oh," he ended on a sigh.

"What 'oh'?" Sherry asked, frowning now herself as she turned back to her father.

"Basil just read my mind," Alexander explained to her, and then said, "What he found was that, like I said, we were buying it in boxes. We had a box in the back of our car most nights, including that one, and we would excuse ourselves saying we were going to take a leak, but instead of going to the men's room we would slip out to suck back another bag or three. We did that any time our buzz showed the least sign of wearing off."

"You were a mess," Sherry said solemnly.

He nodded. "To tell you the truth, if your mother hadn't been so exceptionally lovely, I'm not sure I would have recognized her in the ER when they rolled her in. I didn't remember most of the women I slept with during that time."

Sherry bit her lip. His being drunk didn't excuse what he'd done, but surely it mitigated it somewhat? Maybe?

"I didn't tell you this to give you an excuse. Being in that state does not take away my responsibility for my actions. I chose to be in that state, and then I went out and did exactly what my father said I would do and hurt someone," Alexander said quietly now. "I didn't know it until two months later, but I did. And when I realized . . . well, it was a wake-up call. I haven't touched mixed blood since the day I saw your mother being wheeled into the ER."

"Sherry said she didn't think you've dated since then either," Basil said, and it was a question.

Alexander nodded. "It wasn't because . . . well, I just devoted all my time to Sherry and didn't have time for women." He shifted his gaze to Sherry and moved forward to grip the bars as he said, "So you see, I really did earn my punishment. And it won't be so bad. I was only nineteen, and I'm still young so I heal fast. It'll be over in no time," he said with false bravado.

His expression turned serious then and he said, "I just . . . You're my daughter. I love you, Sherry, and I have since the minute I laid eyes on your wrinkled, red little face in the hospital. And I hope you'll come to forgive me for what I did to you as well as your mother. I want to continue to be a part of your life."

She had a father. One who had always been there for her, and always would, Sherry realized. Tears blurring her eyes, she started to nod and then whipped her head around at the sound of a door opening. Lucian came into the hall with Mortimer on his heels. Her ten minutes were up.

Turning to her father, she reached through the bars to squeeze his hand, blurted, "You've always been here for me. I love you too," and turned to hurry past Lucian and Mortimer with her head bowed so they wouldn't see her tears.

She didn't slow until she was outside the building, and then she spun to grab Basil by the front of the shirt and asked, "He was lying when he said it would be over in no time, wasn't he?"

Basil grimaced. "I'm afraid so. Even though he was only nineteen, it takes time to heal between each . . . er . . . round of punishment," he finished finally.

"Then you need to do two things for me," Sherry said firmly.

"What's that?" he asked warily.

"You need to get me a couple bags of one of those black market blood mixes, the blood of someone who has taken morphine maybe. And you need to get me in to see him right before the punishment, and I mean like right before."

"Honey," Basil said on a sigh. "The nanos will remove the morphine from his system long before the punishment is done."

"Maybe, but maybe not. If the nanos are busy healing him, they might leave the morphine until they're done," she pointed out, and when he paused to consider that, Sherry added, "And it's better than doing nothing."

He peered at her silently for a moment, and then sighed and nodded. "Fine."

"Really?" she asked with surprise.

Basil nodded. "I love you, Sherry. And I don't want to see you unhappy or worried about your father's punishment, so if it will help you, I'll do it."

"You really don't think it's going to work, do you?" she asked on a sigh.

"I don't know," he admitted solemnly, and she believed him.

Which meant it might work, Sherry thought hopefully, and then allowed her mind to move on to what was trying to crowd out worries for her father, "You said in the SUV and then again just now that you love me? Do you mean it?"

"Yes," he said simply, his expression certain.

"But we haven't known each other long, and—"

"You didn't mean it then when you told me you love me?" Basil interrupted with concern.

"Oh, yes," she assured him, slipping into his arms. "I realized that when Leo had me. You're perfect for me,

Basil. You're a gentle soul with so much love to give. You're kind and have a great sense of humor. I've never smiled or laughed as much with anyone as I have with you, and . . ." She shrugged helplessly. "I'm happy with you. I don't feel anxious, or worried. I don't have to edit what I say or think for fear that you'll think less of me. I can be me and know that's enough."

"It's more than enough," Basil assured her, and bent as if to kiss her, but she stopped him with a hand at his mouth.

Arching one eyebrow, Sherry asked, "Aren't you going to tell me why you love me?"

Straightening, he gave a nod, caught her hand and started across the yard.

"Where are we going?" she asked with surprise.

"Somewhere we can talk," Basil announced, breaking into a jog, and moments later he was hustling her through a set of French doors and into what looked like a cross between an office and a library.

"Whose office is—?" Her question ended on a startled gasp as Basil suddenly tugged her into his arms and kissed her. Sherry hesitated, but then slid her arms around him and kissed him back, her body pressing eagerly against him.

When he broke the kiss and nibbled his way to her ear to say, "Brains," she blinked and pulled back with shock.

"Huh?"

"I love your brain," he explained. "You wanted a list of things I love about you and that's one of them. I love the way you think."

"Oh," she said with relief, "For a minute I thought we'd gone from *Fright Night* to *Zombieland*."

"What?" he asked with bewilderment, apparently not understanding the association.

"Never mind," she said, and smiled. "I like the way you think too."

"Mmm." Basil pulled her closer and bent to kiss her neck. "I love your sense of humor as well. And you also make me laugh more than I ever have before."

"That's nice," Sherry breathed, tipping her head back out of the way as his lips trailed down her throat and along the collar of the scooped necked T-shirt she'd donned that morning.

"And I think you're kind too," he told her, tugging the neckline down so he could run his tongue along the top of her bra. "And forgiving. I like that about you too," he added, catching the lip of the bra cup and tugging it down to free her breast, "And I love your nipples," he mumbled even as he claimed one, sucking it between his teeth.

Sherry groaned, and clutched at his head and one shoulder as he laved and suckled her.

Releasing her breast, he lifted his head and added, "And I love your passion," as he slid a hand between her legs and cupped her through her jeans. He then caught her excited cry with his mouth as he kissed her again.

Sherry sucked violently at his tongue and shifted against his hand as he applied pressure. Then she slid her own hand down to find him through his jeans and pressed firmly.

"God, I love your ambition," Basil muttered, catching her behind the thighs and lifting her onto the end of the desk.

"Basil," Sherry groaned, catching him by the hips and tugging him between her legs and up tight against her.

"I love your hair too." He caught a handful of it and tugged her head back for another kiss, then tugged harder until her face was tipped upward and her neck was bare, and then nipped at her skin before adding, "I love your skin too. So soft, so round."

Round? Sherry blinked her eyes open with confusion, but then he released her hair and his hands were both firmly cupping her breasts through her top. Oh, she thought.

"I feel like I can be myself when I'm with you," he added, kneading her breasts.

"Oh, yes," Sherry gasped, wrapping her legs around him and pulling him tighter against her. "I like it when you're yourself, especially when yourself in me. Maybe we could . . ." Reaching between them, she began to undo his pants, and Basil gave a breathless laugh.

"God, I do love your brain," he muttered, but brushed her hand away and scooped her off the desk and into his arms.

"What—?"

"A bedroom," Basil explained, carrying her to the door. "This is Mortimer's office. He could come back here and . . ."

"Oh," Sherry breathed, and leaned her head in the crook of his neck, then stuck her tongue out to lick him. She followed that up with a nip, and then began to suck lightly, one hand moving over his back and the other over his chest, and Basil growled.

"What?" she asked innocently.

"Tuck your breast back in your top and open the door," he ordered.

"Mmmm," Sherry murmured, even as she did what he asked, first pulling her neckline up to cover her freed breast and then reaching to pull the door open. "I love it when you get all bossy and domineering."

"As do I."

Basil had started to walk, but stopped abruptly at that voice, and Sherry sighed, suspecting there would be no bedroom now as she recognized Lucian's voice. It seemed he and Mortimer were done speaking to her father, she thought as she noted the presence of the fair-haired man behind Lucian.

"Thank you for having the sense not to start something in the office," Lucian said dryly. "I have walked in on quite enough couples in the middle of coitus lately, thank you."

Sherry bit her lip at the word coitus. These brothers were just so darned cute with their antique terminology. Smiling crookedly, she commented, "You make it sound like a daily occurrence."

Lucian gave a put upon sigh. "There are at least a dozen newly mated couples between here and Port Henry—"

"Probably closer to twenty," Basil drawled with amusement.

"Yes, you may be right," Lucian muttered, and then

sighed and said, "The point is, it's like living with a kennel full of dogs when the bitches are in heat. The life mates can't keep their hands off each other. I have come upon them in the kitchen, the office, the living room, the bathroom, the vehicles, the cells, the yard, and even the coat closet."

"The coat closet?" Basil asked with interest.

"Do not even think about it," Lucian said grimly, and then stood aside for them to move past. "You two can use the bedroom Sherry had the last time you stayed here. Your grandfather will take the room Basil used."

"Whose grandfather?" Sherry asked with confusion, glancing to Basil as he started forward.

"Yours, Ms. Carne," Lucian said dryly. "I called Reg Marrone from the cells. Your father spoke to him and he is flying up to see him and meet you. He's bringing your grandmother and I believe one of your aunts."

"To meet me?" Sherry squeaked, turning from Lucian to Basil with alarm.

"They will be here in the morning," Lucian said, his voice trailing them as Basil carried her up the stairs.

"Basil," she began worriedly as he carried her into the bedroom she'd used on the first night she'd spent in this house. "Maybe we shouldn't—"

"Morning is hours away," he said soothingly, letting her feet drop to the floor.

"Yes, but we have to figure out what to say to them. I want my father's family to like me and accept you."

"They are going to love you as much as I do," Basil assured her, pulling her top up and over her head when she automatically raised her arms. Unsnapping and unzipping her jeans next, he added, "And your grandfather and I are already friends. We go way back."

"Yes, but—" Sherry paused to step out of her jeans when he knelt to remove them.

"But what, honey?" he asked, tugging her panties down.

"That was as a friend, not as a grandson-in-law," she pointed out.

Basil straightened abruptly. "You want to marry me?"

She blinked in surprise. "Well, of course. I'm not agreeing to be turned if we don't get married too."

"You're agreeing to the turn?" he asked happily, and when she nodded, slipped his arms around her, lifting her off her feet to swing her around.

"Put me down," Sherry protested on a laugh.

Instead, Basil gave her a hard kiss and then promised, "You won't regret it. I swear, I'll make it my business every day to be sure you are the happiest woman in the world."

"I already am," she assured him gently.

Smiling, he let her slip to her feet, and started to bend to kiss her, but suddenly paused. "Wait a minute, what do you mean that's as a friend not a grandson-in-law? Why wouldn't he want me for a grandson-in-law?"

Sherry wrinkled her nose. "He might be a little put off by the way you've been spreading your seed around all these centuries. I mean a man with fifty kids for his sweet granddaughter? It might be a concern."

"It's not fifty kids, it's—" Basil cut himself off, his eyes narrowing when he noted the twinkle in her eyes. "You're teasing me."

"I am," she agreed, and reached out to begin unbuttoning his shirt. "You did say you liked my sense of humor."

"And I do," he assured her, reaching out to fondle her breasts. He let her remove the shirt, but when she dropped down to work on the snap of his jeans, he added, "But you'll still have to be punished."

"What kind of punishment?" Sherry asked, peering up with a smile as she lowered his zipper.

Basil groaned, his eyes turning pure silver and his semi erection becoming a full one in a heartbeat. Sherry glanced to the tent now poking through the open zipper and smiled, then gave a little gasp of surprise when he suddenly caught her under the arms and pulled her to her feet.

Slipping his arms around her waist, he pulled her close and suggested, "How about a lifetime with me. Will you marry me, Sherry?"

"I thought we'd already agreed to that?" she asked with surprise, pulling back.

"Yeah, but now I'm actually proposing. I wouldn't want our children to think you did it."

Sherry chuckled and hugged him tightly. "God, I do love you, Basil Argeneau."

"Thank God for that, soon-to-be Mrs. Argeneau," he muttered, and pushed her back onto the bed.

Sherry landed with a gasp, and then raised her head

to see that he was finishing what she'd started and removing the rest of his clothes. Watching him strip, she smiled and commented idly, "We should really get married quickly so you don't have to call me that too often."

Basil paused after stepping out of his jeans. "Really? No long engagement and months of planning?"

Sherry grinned and shook her head. "Vegas, baby."

"God I do love your mind," Basil muttered, and crawled onto the bed with her.

Lynsay Sands was born in Canada and is an award-winning author of over thirty books, which have made the Barnes & Noble and *New York Times* bestseller lists. She is best known for her Argeneau series, about a modern-day family of vampires.

Visit her website at: www.lynsaysands.net

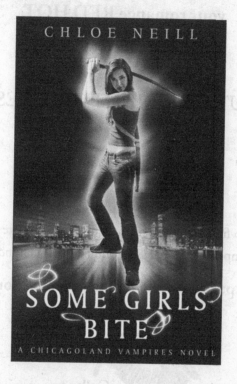